EMERALD GREEN

KERSTIN GIER

EMERALD GREEN

Translated from the German
by Anthea Bell

HENRY HOLT AND COMPANY
NEW YORK

Henry Holt and Company, LLC
Publishers since 1866
175 Fifth Avenue
New York, New York 10010
macteenbooks.com

First published in the United States in 2013 by Henry Holt and Company, LLC.
Originally published in Germany in 2010 by Arena Verlag GmbH
under the title *Smaragdgrün. Liebe geht durch alle Zeiten.*

Library of Congress Cataloging-in-Publication Data
Gier, Kerstin.
[Smaragdgrün. English]
Emerald green / Kerstin Gier ; translated from the German by Anthea
Bell.—First American edition.
pages   cm
"Originally published in Germany in 2010 by Arena Verlag GmbH
under the title Smaragdgrün. Liebe geht durch alle Zeiten."
Sequel to: Sapphire blue.
Summary: Since learning she is the Ruby, the final member of the
time-traveling Circle of Twelve, nothing has gone right for
Gwen and she holds suspicions about both Count Saint-Germain
and Gideon, but as she uncovers the Circle's secrets
she finally learns her own destiny.
ISBN 978-0-8050-9267-7 (hardback)
[1. Time travel—Fiction.   2. Family life—England—London—Fiction.
3. Secret societies—Fiction.   4. Love—Fiction.   5. London (England)—
Fiction.   6. England—Fiction.   7. Great Britain—History—Fiction.]
I. Bell, Anthea.   II. Title.
PZ7.G3523Eme 2013   [Fic]—dc23   2013017885

First American Edition—2013 / Designed by April Ward

Printed in the United States of America

1   3   5   7   9   10   8   6   4   2

For all the girls in the world with marzipan hearts
(and I mean all the girls, because it feels just the
same whether you are fourteen or forty-one.)

Hope is the thing with feathers
That perches in the soul
And sings the tune without the words
And never stops at all.

—EMILY DICKINSON

EMERALD GREEN

PROLOGUE

Belgravia, London,
3 July 1912

"THAT'S GOING to leave a nasty scar," said the doctor, without looking up.

Paul managed a wry smile. "Well, better than the amputation Mrs. Worry-guts here was predicting, anyway."

"Very funny!" Lucy snapped. "I am *not* a worry-guts, and as for *you* . . . Mr. Thoughtless Idiot, don't go joking about it! You know how quickly wounds can get infected, and then you'd be lucky to survive at all at this date. No antibiotics, and all the doctors are ignorant and useless."

"Thank you very much," said the doctor, spreading a brownish paste on the wound he had just stitched up. It burned like hell, and Paul had difficulty in suppressing a grimace. He only hoped he hadn't left bloodstains on Lady Tilney's elegant chaise longue.

"Not that they can help it, of course." Lucy was making an effort to sound friendlier. She even tried a smile.

Rather a grim smile, but it's the thought that counts. "I'm sure you're doing your best," she told the doctor.

"Dr. Harrison *is* the best," Lady Tilney assured her.

"And the only one available," murmured Paul. Suddenly he felt incredibly tired. There must have been a sedative in the sweetish stuff that the doctor had given him to drink.

"The most discreet, anyway," said Dr. Harrison. He put a snow-white bandage on Paul's arm. "And to be honest, I can't imagine that the treatment of cuts and stab wounds will be so very different in eighty years' time."

Lucy took a deep breath, and Paul guessed what was coming. A lock of hair had strayed from the ringlets pinned up on top of her head, and she put it back behind her ear with a look of spirited defiance. "Well, maybe not as a general rule, but if bacteria . . . er, those are single-celled organisms that—"

"Drop it, Luce!" Paul interrupted her. "Dr. Harrison knows perfectly well what bacteria are!" The wound was still burning horribly, and at the same time he felt so exhausted that he wanted to close his eyes and drift away into sleep. But that would only upset Lucy even more. Although her blue eyes were sparkling furiously, he knew her anger only hid her concern for him, and—even worse—her fears. For her sake, he mustn't show either his poor physical state or his own desperation. So he went on talking. "After all, we're not in the Middle Ages; we're in the twentieth century. It's a time of trailblazing medical advances. The first ECG device is already yesterday's news, and for the last few years, they've known the cause of syphilis and how to cure it."

"Someone was paying attention like a good boy in his study of the mysteries!" Lucy looked as if she might explode any minute now. "How nice for you!"

Dr. Harrison made his own contribution. "And last year that Frenchwoman Marie Curie was awarded the Nobel Prize for Chemistry."

"So what did she invent? The nuclear bomb?"

"Sometimes you're shockingly uneducated, Lucy. Marie Curie invented radio—"

"Oh, do *shut up!*" Lucy had crossed her arms and was staring angrily at Paul, ignoring Lady Tilney's reproachful glance. "You can keep your lectures to yourself right now! You! Could! Have! Been! Dead! So will you kindly tell me how I was supposed to avert the disaster ahead of us without you?" At this point, her voice shook. "Or how I could go on living without you at all?"

"I'm sorry, Princess." She had no idea just *how* sorry he was.

"Huh!" said Lucy. "You can leave out that remorseful doggy expression."

"There's no point in thinking about what *might* have happened, my dear child," said Lady Tilney, shaking her head as she helped Dr. Harrison to pack his instruments back in his medical bag. "It all turned out for the best. Paul was unlucky, but lucky as well."

"Well, yes, it could have ended much worse, but that doesn't mean it was all for the best!" cried Lucy. "Nothing turned out for the best, nothing at all!" Her eyes filled with tears, and the sight almost broke Paul's heart. "We've been here for nearly three months, and we haven't done any of the things we planned to do, just the opposite—we've only made matters worse! We finally had those wretched papers in our hands, and then Paul simply gave them away!"

"Maybe I was a little too hasty." He let his head drop back on the pillow. "But at that moment, I felt it was the right thing to do." *Because at that moment, I felt horribly close to death.* Lord Alastair's sword could easily have finished him off. However, he mustn't let Lucy know that. "If we have Gideon on our side, there's still a chance. As soon as he's read those papers, he'll understand what we're doing and why." *Or let's hope so*, he thought.

"But we don't know exactly what's in the papers ourselves. They could all be in code, or . . . oh, you don't even know just what you handed to Gideon," said Lucy. "Lord Alastair could have palmed anything off on you—old bills, love letters, blank sheets of paper. . . ."

This idea had occurred to Paul himself some time ago, but what was done was done. "Sometimes you just have to trust things will be all right," he murmured, wishing that applied to himself. The thought that he might have handed Gideon a bundle of worthless documents was bad enough; even worse was the chance that the boy might take them straight off to Count Saint-Germain. That would mean they'd thrown away their only trump card. But Gideon had said he loved Gwyneth, and the way he said it had been . . . well, convincing.

"He promised me," Paul tried to say, but it came out as an inaudible whisper. It would have been a lie, anyway. He hadn't had time to hear Gideon's answer.

"Trying to work with the Florentine Alliance was a stupid idea," he heard Lucy say. His eyes had closed. Whatever Dr. Harrison had given him, it worked fast.

"And yes, I know, I know," Lucy went on. "We ought to have dealt with the situation ourselves."

"But you're not murderers, my child," said Lady Tilney.

"What's the difference between committing a murder and getting someone else to do it?" Lucy heaved a deep sigh, and although Lady Tilney contradicted her vigorously ("My dear, don't say such things! You didn't ask anyone to commit murder, you only handed over a little information!"), she suddenly sounded inconsolable. "We've got everything wrong that we *could* get wrong, Paul. All we've done in three months is to waste any amount of time and Margaret's money, and we've involved far too many other people."

"It's Lord Tilney's money," Lady Tilney corrected her, "and you'd be astonished to hear what he usually wastes it on. Horse races and dancing girls are the least of it. He won't even notice the small sums I've abstracted for our own purposes. And if he ever does, I trust he'll be enough of a gentleman to say nothing about it."

"Speaking for myself, I can't feel at all sorry to be involved," Dr. Harrison assured them, smiling. "I'd just begun to find life rather boring. But it isn't every day of the week you meet time travelers from the future who know your own job better than you do. And between ourselves, the high-and-mighty manner of the de Villiers and Pinkerton-Smythe gentlemen among the Guardians here is quite enough to make anyone feel a little rebellious in secret."

"How true," said Lady Tilney. "That self-satisfied Jonathan de Villiers threatened to lock his wife in her room if she didn't stop sympathizing with the suffragettes." She imitated a grumpy male voice. *"What will it be next, I wonder? Votes for dogs?"*

"Ah, so that's why you threatened to slap his face," said Dr. Harrison. "Now that was one tea party when I was *not* bored!"

"It wasn't quite like that. I only said I couldn't guarantee what my right hand might not do next if he went on making such remarks."

"'If he went on talking such utter balderdash' . . . those were your precise words," Dr. Harrison set her right. "I remember because they impressed me deeply."

Lady Tilney laughed, and offered the doctor her arm. "I'll show you to the door, Dr. Harrison."

Paul tried to open his eyes and sit up to thank the doctor. He didn't manage to do either of those things. "Mmph . . . nks," he mumbled with the last of his strength.

"What on earth was in that stuff you gave him, doctor?" Lucy called after Dr. Harrison.

He turned in the doorway. "Only a few drops of tincture of morphine. Perfectly harmless!"

But Paul was past hearing Lucy's screech of outrage.

As according to our Secret Service sources, London may expect air raids by German squadrons in the next few days, we have decided to proceed at once to Stage One of the security protocol. The chronograph will be deposited for an unknown period of time in the documents room, from which location Lady Tilney, my brother Jonathan, and I will elapse, thus limiting the time spent elapsing to three hours a day. Traveling to the nineteenth century from the documents room ought not to present any problems; there was seldom anyone there by night, and there is no mention in the Annals of visitors from the future, so it is to be presumed that our presence was never noticed.

As was to be expected, Lady Tilney objected to this departure from her usual routine, and according to herself "could see no kind of logic in our arguments," but in the end, she had to accept the decision of our Grand Master. Times of war call for special measures.

Elapsing this afternoon to the year 1851 went surprisingly smoothly, perhaps because my dear wife had given us some of her wonderful teacakes to take with us and because, remembering heated debates on other occasions, we avoided such subjects as women's suffrage. Lady Tilney greatly regretted being unable to visit the Great Exhibition in Hyde Park, but as we shared her feelings in that respect, the conversation did not degenerate into argument. She did, however, give further evidence of her eccentricity in proposing that from now on we should pass the time by playing poker.

Weather today: fine drizzling rain, temperature a springlike 50° Fahrenheit

FROM *THE ANNALS OF THE GUARDIANS*
30 MARCH 1916

REPORT: TIMOTHY DE VILLIERS, INNER CIRCLE

"Potius sero quam nunquam" (Livy)

ONE

THE END OF THE SWORD was pointing straight at my heart, and my murderer's eyes were like black holes threatening to swallow up everything that came too close to them. I knew I couldn't get away. With difficulty, I stumbled a few steps back.

The man followed me. "I will wipe that which is displeasing to God off the face of the earth!" he boomed. "The ground will soak up your blood!"

I had at least two smart retorts to these sinister words on the tip of my tongue. (Soak up my blood? Oh, come off it, this is a tiled floor.) But I was in such a panic that I couldn't get a word out. The man didn't look as if he'd appreciate my little joke at this moment anyway. In fact, he didn't look as if he had a sense of humor at all.

I took another step back and came up against a wall. The killer laughed out loud. Okay, so maybe he did have a sense of humor, but it wasn't much like mine.

"Die, demon!" he cried, plunging his sword into my breast without any more ado.

I woke up, screaming. I was wet with sweat, and my heart hurt as if a blade really had pierced it. What a horrible dream! But was that really surprising?

My experiences of yesterday (and the day before) weren't exactly likely to make me nestle down comfortably in bed and sleep the sleep of the just. Unwanted thoughts were writhing around in my mind like flesh-eating plants gone crazy. *Gideon was only pretending*, I thought. *He doesn't really love me.*

"He hardly has to do anything to attract girls," I heard Count Saint-Germain saying in his soft, deep voice, again and again. And "Nothing is easier to calculate than the reactions of a woman in love."

Oh, yes? So how does a woman in love react when she finds out that someone's been lying to her and manipulating her? She spends hours on the phone to her best friend, that's how, then she sits about in the dark, unable to get to sleep, asking herself why the hell she ever fell for the guy in the first place, crying her eyes out at the same time because she wants him so much . . . Right, so it doesn't take a genius to calculate that.

The lighted numbers on the alarm clock beside my bed said 3:10, so I must have nodded off after all. I'd even slept for more than two hours. And someone—my mum?— must have come in to cover me up, because all I could remember was huddling on the bed with my arms around my knees, listening to my heart beating much too fast.

Odd that a broken heart can beat at all, come to think of it.

"It feels like it's made of red splinters with sharp edges, and they're slicing me up from inside so that I'll bleed to death," I'd said, trying to describe the state of my heart to Lesley (okay, so it sounds at least as corny as the stuff the character in my dream was saying, but sometimes the truth *is* corny). And Lesley had said sympathetically, "I know just how you feel. When Max dumped me, I thought at first I'd die of grief. Grief and multiple organ failure. Because there's a grain of truth in all those things they say about love: it goes to your kidneys, it punches you in the stomach, it breaks your heart and . . . er . . . it scurries over your liver like a louse. But first, that will all pass off; second, it's not as hopeless as it looks to you; and third, your heart isn't made of glass."

"Stone, not glass," I corrected her, sobbing. "My heart is a gemstone, and Gideon's broken it into thousands of pieces, just like in Aunt Maddy's vision."

"Sounds kind of cool—but no! Hearts are really made of very different stuff, you take my word for it." Lesley cleared her throat, and her tone of voice got positively solemn, as if she were revealing the greatest secret in the history of the world. "Hearts are made of something much tougher. It's unbreakable, and you can reshape it anytime you like. Hearts are made to a secret formula."

More throat-clearing to heighten the suspense. I instinctively held my breath.

"They're made of stuff like *marzipan!*" Lesley announced.

"Marzipan?" For a moment I stopped sobbing and grinned instead.

"That's right, marzipan," Lesley repeated in deadly earnest. "The best sort, with lots of real ground almonds in it."

I almost giggled. But then I remembered that I was the unhappiest girl in the world. I sniffed, and said, "If that's so, then Gideon has *bitten off* a piece of my heart! And he's nibbled away the chocolate coating around it too! You ought to have seen the way he looked when—"

But before I could start crying all over again, Lesley sighed audibly.

"Gwenny, I hate to say so, but all this miserable weeping and wailing does no one any good. You have to stop it!"

"I'm not doing it on purpose," I told her. "It just keeps on breaking out of me. One moment I'm still the happiest girl in the world, and then he tells me he—"

"Okay, so Gideon behaved like a bastard," Lesley interrupted me, "although it's hard to understand why. I mean, *hello?* Why on earth would girls in love be easier to manipulate? I'd have thought it was just the opposite. Girls in love are like ticking time bombs. You never know what they'll do next. Gideon and his male chauvinist friend the count have made a big mistake."

"I really thought Gideon was in love with me. The idea that he was only pretending is so . . ." Mean? Cruel? No word seemed enough to describe my feelings properly.

"Oh, sweetie—look, in other circumstances, you could wallow in grief for weeks on end, but you can't afford to do that right now. You need your energy for other things. Like surviving, for instance." Lesley sounded unusually stern. "So kindly pull yourself together."

"That's what Xemerius said, too. Before he went off and left me all alone."

"Your little invisible monster is right! You have to keep a cool head now and put all the facts together. Ugh, what was that? Hang on, I have to open a window. Bertie just did a disgusting fart. Bad dog! Now, where was I? Yes, that's it, we have to find out what your grandfather hid in your house." Lesley's voice rose slightly. "I must admit Raphael has turned out pretty useful. He's not as stupid as you might think."

"As *you* might think, you mean." Raphael was Gideon's little brother, who had just started going to our school. He'd discovered that the riddle my grandfather had left behind was all about geographical coordinates. And they had led straight to our house. "I'd love to know how much Raphael has found out about the secrets of the Guardians and Gideon's time traveling."

"Could be more than we might assume," said Lesley. "Anyway, he wasn't swallowing my story when I told him the coordinates were only because puzzle games like this were the latest fad in London. But he was clever enough not to ask any more questions." She paused for a moment. "He has rather attractive eyes."

"Yup." They really were attractive, which reminded me that Gideon's eyes were exactly the same. Green and surrounded by thick, dark lashes.

"Not that that impresses me. Only making an observation."

I've fallen in love with you. Gideon had sounded deadly serious when he said that, looking straight at me. And I'd stared back and believed every word of it! My tears started flowing again, and I could hardly hear what Lesley was saying.

". . . but I hope it's a long letter, or a kind of diary, with your grandfather explaining everything the rest of them won't tell you and a bit more. Then we can finally stop groping around in the dark and make a proper plan. . . ."

Eyes like that shouldn't be allowed. Or there ought to be a law saying boys with such gorgeous eyes had to wear sunglasses all the time. Unless they canceled out the eyes by having huge jug ears or something like that.

"Gwenny? You're not crying again, are you?" Now Lesley sounded just like Mrs. Counter, our geography teacher, when people told her they were afraid they'd forgotten to do their homework. "Sweetie, this won't do! You must stop twisting the knife in your own heart with all this drama! We have to—"

"Keep a cool head. Yes, you're right." It cost me an effort, but I tried to put the thought of Gideon's eyes out of my mind and inject a little confidence into my voice. I owed Lesley that. After all, she was the one who'd been propping me up for days. Before she rang off, I had to tell her how glad I was that she was my friend. Even if it made me start to cry again, but this time because it made me so emotional!

"Same here," Lesley assured me. "My life would be dead boring without you!"

When she ended the call, it was just before midnight, and I really had felt a little better for a few minutes. But now, at ten past three, I'd have loved to call her back and go over the whole thing again.

Not that I was naturally inclined to be such a Moaning Minnie. It's just that this was the first time in my life I'd ever suffered from unrequited love. Real unrequited love, I mean. The sort that genuinely hurts. Everything else retreated into the background. Even survival didn't seem to matter. Honestly, the thought of dying didn't seem so bad at that moment. I wouldn't be the first to die of a broken heart, after all—I'd be in good company. There was the Little Mermaid, Juliet, Pocahontas, the Lady of the Camellias, Madame Butterfly—and now me, Gwyneth Shepherd. The good part of it was that I could leave out anything dramatic with a knife, as suggested by Lesley's remark, because the way I felt now, I must have caught TB ages ago, and dying of consumption is much the most picturesque way to go. I'd lie on my bed looking pale and beautiful like Snow White, with my hair spread out on the pillow. Gideon would kneel beside me, feeling bitterly sorry for what he had done when I breathed my last words.

But first I had to go to the toilet, urgently.

Peppermint tea with masses of lemon and sugar was a

cure for all ills in our family, and I must have drunk pints of it. Because when I came in yesterday evening, my mother had noticed right away that I wasn't feeling good. It wasn't difficult to spot that, because crying had made me look like an albino rabbit. And if I'd told her—as Xemerius suggested—that I'd had to chop onions in the limousine on the way home from the Guardians' head-quarters, she'd never have believed my story.

"Have those damn Guardians been doing something to you? What happened?" she had asked, managing to sound sympathetic and furiously angry at the same time. "I'll murder Falk if—"

"No one's done anything to me, Mum," I'd said quickly, to reassure her. "And nothing has happened."

"As if she was going to believe that! Why didn't you try the onion excuse? You never take my good advice." Xemerius had stamped his clawed feet on the floor. He was a small stone gargoyle demon with big ears, bat's wings, a scaly tail like a dragon, and two little horns on a catlike head. Unfortunately he wasn't half as cute as he looked, and no one except me could hear his outrageous remarks and answer him back. There were two odd things about me, by the way, and I just had to live with them. One was that I'd been able to see gargoyle demons and other ghosts and talk to them from early childhood. The other was even odder, and I hadn't known about it until under two weeks ago, when I found out that I was one of a strictly secret bunch of twelve time travelers, which meant going back to somewhere in the past for a couple of hours every day. The curse of time travel—well, okay, so it was supposed to be a gift—ought to have affected my cousin Charlotte, who'd have been much better at it, but it turned out that I'd drawn the short straw. No reason why I should be surprised. I was always left holding the last card when we played Old Maid; if we cast lots in class to see who bought Mrs. Counter's Christmas gift, I always got the piece of paper with her name on it (and how do you decide what to give a geography teacher?); if I had tickets for a concert, you could bet I'd fall sick; and when I particularly wanted to look good, I got a zit on my forehead the size of a third eye. Some people may not understand right away how a zit is like time travel—they may even envy me and think time travel would be fun, but it isn't. It's a nuisance, nerve-racking and dangerous as well. Not forgetting that if I hadn't inherited that stupid gift I'd never have met Gideon and then my heart, whether or not it was made of marzipan, would still be just fine. Because that guy was another of the twelve time travelers. One of the few still alive. You couldn't meet the others except back in the past.

"You've been crying," my mother had said in a matter-of-fact way.

"There, you see?" Xemerius had said. "Now she's going to squeeze you like a lemon until the pips squeak. She won't let you out of her sight for a second, and we can wave good-bye to tonight's treasure hunt."

I'd made a face at him, to let him know that I didn't feel like treasure hunting tonight anymore. Well, you have to make faces at invisible friends if you don't want other people to think you're crazy because you talk to the empty air.

"Tell her you were trying out the pepper spray," the empty air had answered me back, "and it got into your own eyes by mistake."

But I'd been far too tired to tell lies. I just looked at my mum with red-rimmed eyes and tried telling the truth. *Here goes, then*, I'd thought. "It's just . . . no, I don't feel too good. It's . . . kind of a girl thing, you know?"

"Oh, darling."

"If I phone Lesley, I know I'll feel better."

Much to the surprise of Xemerius—me too—Mum had been satisfied with this explanation. She made me peppermint tea, left the teapot and my favorite cup with its pattern of spots on my bedside table, stroked my hair, and otherwise left me in peace. She didn't even keep reminding me of the time, as usual. ("Gwyneth! It's after ten, and you've been on the phone for forty minutes. You'll be seeing each other at school tomorrow.") Sometimes she really was the best mother in the world.

Sighing, I swung my legs over the edge of the bed and stumbled off to the bathroom. I felt a cold breath of air.

"Xemerius? Are you there?" I asked under my breath, and felt for the light switch.

"That depends." Xemerius was dangling head down from the ceiling fixture in the corridor, blinking at the light. "I'm here so long as you don't turn back into a watering can." He raised his voice to a shrill, tearful pitch as he imitated me—rather well, I'm sorry to say. *"And then he said, I have no idea what you're talking about, and then I said, yes or no, and then he said, yes, but do stop crying. . . ."* He sighed theatrically. "Girls get on my nerves worse than any other kind of human being. Along with retired tax-men, saleswomen in hosiery departments, and presidents of community garden societies."

"I can't guarantee anything," I whispered, so as not to wake the rest of my family up. "We'd better not mention You Know Who, or the indoor fountain will come back on again."

"I was sick of the sound of his name anyway. Can we do something sensible for a change? Go treasure hunting, for instance?"

Getting some sleep might have been sensible, but unfortunately I was wide awake now. "Okay, we can start if you like. But first I have to get rid of all that tea."

"What?"

I pointed to the bathroom door.

"Oh, I see," said Xemerius. "I'll just wait here."

I looked better than I expected in the bathroom mirror. Unfortunately there wasn't a sign of galloping consumption. My eyelids were a little swollen—that was all, as if I'd been using pink eye shadow and put on too much.

"Where were you all this time, Xemerius?" I asked when I came out into the corridor again. "Not by any chance with . . . ?"

"With whom?" Xemerius looked indignant. "Are you asking me about the person whose name we don't mention?"

"Well, yes." I would have loved to know what Gideon did yesterday evening. How was the wound in his arm healing up? And had he maybe said something to anyone about me? Like *It's all a terrible misunderstanding. Of course I love Gwyneth. I wasn't pretending at all when I told her so.*

"Oh, no you don't! I'm not falling for that one." Xemerius spread his wings and flew down to the floor. When he was sitting there in front of me, he hardly came above my knee. "But I didn't go out. I was having a good look around this house. If anyone can find that treasure, then I can. If only because none of the rest of you can walk through walls. Or rummage around in your grandmother's chest of drawers without being caught at it."

"Yes, there must be some advantages to being invisible," I said. I didn't point out that Xemerius couldn't rummage around in anything because his ghostly claws couldn't even open a drawer. No ghost I'd ever met could move objects. Most of them, unlike Xemerius, couldn't even manage a breath of cold air. "But you know we're not looking for a treasure, only something left by my grandfather that will help us to find out more."

"This house is full of stuff that might be treasure. Not to mention all the possible hiding places for it," Xemerius went on, taking no notice of me. "Some of the walls on the first floor are double, with passages in between them— passages so narrow you can tell they're not built for people with big bums."

"Really?" I'd never discovered those passages myself. "How do you get into them?"

"The doors are covered up with wallpaper in most of the rooms, but there's still a way in through your great-aunt's wardrobe and another behind that big, solid sideboard in the dining room. And one in the library, hidden behind a swiveling bookcase. Oh, and there's a link between the library and the stairwell leading to Mr. Bernard's rooms, and another going up to the second floor."

"Which would explain why Mr. Bernard always seems to appear out of nowhere," I murmured.

"And that's not all. There's a ladder inside the big chimney shaft on the wall next to number 83 next door. You can climb it all the way up to the roof. You can't get into the shaft from the kitchen anymore, because the old fireplace there has been bricked up, but there's a way in with a flap over it at the back of the built-in cupboard at the end of the first-floor corridor, big enough to let Santa Claus through—or your weirdo of a butler."

"Or the chimney sweep."

"And then there's the cellar!" Xemerius acted as if he hadn't heard my down-to-earth remark. "Do your neighbors know this house has a secret, and there's a second cellar underneath the cellar that everyone knows about? Although if you go looking for anything there, you'd better not be scared of spiders."

"Then we'd better look somewhere else first," I said, quite forgetting to whisper.

"If we knew what we're looking for, of course it would be easier." Xemerius scratched his chin with one of his back paws. "I mean, basically it could be anything: the stuffed crocodile in the recess, the bottle of Scotch behind the books in the library, the bundle of letters in the secret drawer of your great-aunt's desk, the little chest in a hollow place in the brickwork—"

"A chest in the brickwork?" I interrupted him. And what recess was he talking about?

Xemerius nodded. "Oh, dear, I think you've woken your brother up."

I spun round. My twelve-year-old brother, Nick, was standing in the doorway of his room, running both hands through his untidy red hair. "Who are you talking to, Gwenny?"

"It's the middle of the night," I whispered. "Go back to bed, Nick."

Nick looked at me undecidedly, and I could see him waking up more and more every second. "What was all that about a chest in the brickwork?"

"I . . . I was going to look for it, but I think I'd better wait until it's light."

"Nonsense," said Xemerius. "I can see in the dark like a . . . well, let's say an owl. And you can't very well search the house when everyone's awake. Not unless you want even more company."

"I can bring my flashlight," said Nick. "What's in the chest?"

"I don't know exactly." I thought for a moment. "It could be something left there by Grandpa."

"Oh," said Nick, interested. "And whereabouts is this chest hidden?"

I looked inquiringly at Xemerius.

"I saw it to one side of the secret passage behind that fat man with whiskers, the one sitting on his horse," said Xemerius. "But who goes hiding secrets—I mean treasures—in a boring old chest? I think the crocodile is much more promising. Who knows what it's stuffed with? I'm in favor of slitting it open."

I wasn't. I had an idea I'd met that crocodile before. "Let's look in the chest first. A hollow place doesn't sound bad."

"Boring, boring, boring!" repeated Xemerius. "One of your ancestors probably hid his tobacco from his wife in it . . . or . . ." Obviously he had just had an idea he liked, because now he suddenly grinned. "Or the chopped-up body of a maid who stepped off the straight and narrow and went astray!"

"The chest is in the secret passage behind the picture of Great-great-great-great-great-uncle Hugh," I explained to Nick. "But—"

"I'll just get that flashlight!" My brother had already turned back to his room.

I sighed.

"Why are you sighing again?" Xemerius rolled his eyes. "It can't hurt if your brother comes along." He spread his wings. "I'll just do a round of the house and make sure the rest of the family are fast asleep. We don't want that sharp-nosed aunt of yours catching us when we find the diamonds."

"What diamonds?"

"Think positive for once!" Xemerius was already hovering in the air. "Which would you rather, diamonds or the remains of a murdered maidservant? It's all a question of attitude. We'll meet in front of your fat uncle on his horse."

"Are you talking to a ghost?" Nick had reappeared behind me. He switched off the ceiling light in the corridor and put his flashlight on instead.

I nodded. Nick had never doubted that I really could see ghosts—quite the opposite. Even when he was only four and I was eight, he used to stand up for me if people didn't believe it. Aunt Glenda, for instance. We always quarreled when she went to Harrods with us and I talked to the nice uniformed doorman Mr. Grizzle. Mr. Grizzle had been dead for fifty years, so of course people wondered why I stopped and started talking about the Royal Family (Mr. Grizzle was a great admirer of the Queen) and the unseasonably wet June we were having (the weather was Mr. Grizzle's second favorite subject of conversation). A lot of passersby laughed, some said children had such wonderful imaginations (ruffling up my hair to emphasize their point), and many others shook their heads, but no one got as worked up as Aunt Glenda. She used to look terribly embarrassed and haul me on after her, scolding if I braced my feet and stood my ground. She said I ought to follow Charlotte's example (even then, Charlotte was so perfect that she never lost a barrette out of her hair), and worst of all, she threatened me with getting no dessert that evening. But although she carried out her threat (and

I loved all desserts, even stewed plums), I simply couldn't bring myself to walk past Mr. Grizzle without a word. Nick always tried to help by begging Aunt Glenda to let go of me because there was no one else for poor Mr. Grizzle to talk to, and Aunt Glenda cleverly got the better of him by saying, in sugary sweet tones, "Oh, little Nick, when will you understand that your sister is just trying to attract attention? There are no such things as ghosts. Do *you* see a ghost here?"

Nick always had to shake his head sadly and then Aunt Glenda would smile triumphantly. On the day when she decided never to take us to Harrods with her again, Nick had surprised me by changing his tactics. Tiny and plump-cheeked at the time—he was such a cute little boy, with an adorable lisp—he had stopped right in front of Aunt Glenda and asked, "Do you know what Mr. Grizzle said to me, Aunt Glenda? He said you're a nasty frowsty old witch!" Of course Mr. Grizzle would never have said such a thing, he was much too polite, and Aunt Glenda was too good a customer, but my mum *had* said something rather like it the evening before. Aunt Glenda pressed her lips together and stalked on, holding Charlotte's hand. Back home there had been an unpleasant scene with my mother, who was cross because we'd had to find our way home on our own, and Aunt Glenda had said in icy tones that Mum was responsible for the frowsty witch remark, and the up-shot was that we weren't allowed to go shopping with Aunt Glenda ever again. But even now we liked saying "frowsty."

When I got older, I stopped telling people I could see things that they couldn't. That's best if you don't want to be thought crazy. But I never had to pretend to Nick, Caroline, and Lesley, because they believed in my ghosts. I wasn't quite sure about Mum and Great-aunt Maddy, but at least they never laughed at me. Aunt Maddy had strange visions herself at irregular intervals, so she probably knew just how it felt when no one believed you.

"Is he nice?" whispered Nick. The beam of his flashlight danced over the stairs.

"Who?"

"Your ghost, of course."

"It all depends," I said truthfully.

"What does he look like?"

"He's rather cute. But he thinks he's dangerous." As we went down on tiptoe to the second floor, which was occupied by Aunt Glenda and Charlotte, I tried describing Xemerius as well as I could.

"Cool," whispered Nick. "An invisible pet! I wish I had one!"

"Pet! Don't you ever say that when Xemerius is within earshot!" I half hoped to hear my cousin snoring through her bedroom door, but of course Charlotte didn't snore. People who are perfect don't make nasty, frowsty noises in their sleep.

Halfway down to the next floor, my little brother yawned, and I instantly felt guilty. "Listen, Nick, it's three thirty in the morning, and you have to go to school later. Mum will murder me if she finds out I've kept you awake."

"I'm not a bit tired! And it would be mean of you to leave me out now! What did Grandfather hide in the chest?"

"I've no idea. Maybe a book explaining everything to me. Or at least a letter. Grandpa was Grand Master of the Lodge and its Guardians. He knew all about me and this time-travel stuff, and by the time he died, he knew it wasn't Charlotte who inherited the gene. Because I met him in the past, in person, and explained it all to him."

"You're so lucky," whispered Nick, adding almost as if ashamed of himself, "To be honest, I can hardly remember him. But he was always good-tempered and not a bit strict, just the opposite of Lady Arista. And he used to smell of caramel and something herby."

"That was the tobacco he smoked in his pipe— careful!" I stopped Nick just in time. By now we were past the second floor, but there were a few tricky steps on the stairs down to the first floor that creaked badly. Years of sneaking down to the kitchen by night had taught me to avoid them. We carefully walked around the creaking places, and finally reached Great-great-great-great-great-uncle Hugh's portrait.

"Okay. Here we are."

Nick shone his flashlight on our ancestor's face. "It was mean of him to call his horse Fat Annie! She's lovely and slender—he's the one who looks like a fat pig with whiskers."

"I agree with you." I was feeling behind the picture frame for the bolt that started the mechanism to open the secret door. As usual, it stuck a bit.

"All sleeping like babies." Xemerius landed on the stairs beside us, puffing. "That's to say, all but Mr. Bernard. He obviously suffers from insomnia, but don't worry. He's eating a plate of cold chicken in the kitchen and watching a Clint Eastwood film."

"Good." The picture swung out with its usual squealing sound, showing a few steps fitted between the walls. They ended only about six or seven feet away in front of another door. This door led into the first-floor bathroom, and it was hidden on the bathroom side by a floor-length mirror. We often used to come through it for fun—we got our kicks by not knowing if there'd be anyone in there using the bathroom—but we hadn't yet found out what the point of this secret passage was. Maybe one of our ancestors had just thought it would be nice to be able to get away to this quiet place whenever he liked.

"So where's the chest, Xemerius?" I asked.

"On the left. Between the wallsh." I couldn't make him out clearly in the dim light, but it sounded as if he was picking something out of his teeth.

"Xemerius is a bit of a tongue-twister," said Nick. "I'd call him Xemi. Or Merry. Can I go in and get the chest?"

"It's on the left," I said.

"Tongue-twishter yourshelf," said Xemerius. "*Shemi* or *Merry*—no way! I come from a long line of mighty ansheshtral demonsh, and our namesh—"

"Have you got something in your mouth?"

Xemerius spat and smacked his lips. "Not now. I ate the pigeon I found asleep on the roof. Stupid feathers."

"But you can't eat at all!"

"No idea of anything, but always giving us the benefit of her opinion!" said Xemerius, offended. "Won't even let me eat a little pigeon!"

"You can't eat a pigeon," I repeated. "You're a ghost."

"I'm a *demon*! I can eat anything I like! I once ate a whole priest. Vestments and all. Why are you looking at me so incredulously?"

"Why don't you keep your eyes open for anyone coming?"

"Hey, don't you believe me?"

Nick had already climbed down the steps into the bathroom and was shining his flashlight along the wall. "I can't see anything."

"The chest is behind the brickwork, like I said. In a hollow space, bonehead," said Xemerius. "And I'm not lying. If I say I ate a pigeon, then I did eat a pigeon."

"It's in a hollow space behind the brickwork," I told Nick.

"But I can't see a loose brick anywhere." My little brother knelt down on the floor and pressed his hands against the wall, testing it out.

"Hello-o-o, I'm speaking to you!" said Xemerius. "Are you ignoring me, crybaby?" When I didn't reply, he said, "Well, okay, so it was the *ghost* of a pigeon. Comes to the same thing."

"Ghost of a pigeon—are you trying to be funny? Even if pigeons did have ghosts—and I've never seen one—you still couldn't eat them. Ghosts can't kill one another."

"These bricks are all solid as rocks," said Nick.

Xemerius snorted angrily. "First, even pigeons can sometimes decide to stay on the earth and haunt it, don't ask me why. Maybe they have unfinished business with a cat somewhere. Second, kindly tell me how you can tell a ghost pigeon from all the other pigeons. And third, their ghostly life is over if I eat them. Because as I've told you I don't know how often, I'm no ordinary ghost. I'm a *demon*! Maybe I can't do much in your world, but I'm big news in the world of ghosts. When will you finally get the hang of that?"

Nick stood up again and kicked the wall a couple of times. "Nope, nothing we can do about it."

"Ssh! Stop that, it makes too much noise." I put my head into the bathroom and looked at Xemerius reproachfully. "So you're big news. Great. Now what?"

"How do you mean? I never said a word about loose bricks."

"Then how are we to get at the chest?"

"With a hammer and chisel." That was a very helpful answer, only it wasn't Xemerius who gave it, but Mr. Bernard. I froze with horror. There he stood, only a couple of feet above me on the steps. I could see his gold-rimmed glasses sparkling in the dark. And his teeth. Could he be smiling?

"Oh, shit!" Xemerius was so upset that he spat out water on the carpet over the steps. "He must have inhaled the cold chicken to get it inside him so fast. Or else the film was no good. You can't rely on Clint Eastwood these days."

Unfortunately I was unable to say anything but "Wh-what?"

"A hammer and chisel would be the best solution," repeated Mr. Bernard calmly. "But I suggest you put it off until later. If only so as not to disturb the rest of the family when you take the chest out of its hiding place. Ah, I see Master Nick is here too." He looked into the beam of Nick's flashlight without blinking. "Barefoot! You'll both catch your death of cold." He himself was wearing slippers and an elegant dressing gown with an embroidered monogram, WB. (Walter? William? Wilfred?) I'd always thought of Mr. Bernard as a man without any first name.

"How do you know it's a chest we're looking for?" asked Nick. His voice didn't tremble, but I could tell from his wide eyes that he was as startled and baffled as I was.

Mr. Bernard straightened his glasses. "I expect because I walled up that—er—that chest in there myself. It's a kind of wooden box decorated with valuable inlaid intarsia work, an antique from the early eighteenth century that belonged to your grandfather."

"And what's in it?" I asked, finding that I could speak again at last.

Mr. Bernard looked at me with reproof in his eyes. "Naturally it was not for me to ask that question. I simply hid the chest here on behalf of your grandfather."

"He can't try telling me that," said Xemerius grumpily. "Not when he goes around poking his nose into everything else. And slinking along here after lulling a person into a false sense of security with cold chicken. But it's all your fault, you silly watering can! If you had believed me, the senile old sleepwalker could never have taken us by surprise!"

"I will of course be happy to help you to extricate the chest again," Mr. Bernard went on. "But preferably this evening, when your grandmother and aunt will be on their way to the meeting of the ladies of the Rotary Club. So I suggest that we all go back to bed now. After all, you two have to go to school later."

"Yes, and meanwhile he'll hack the thing out of the wall himself," said Xemerius. "Then he can get his hands on the diamonds and leave a few withered old walnuts for us to find. I know his sort."

"Don't be daft," I muttered. If Mr. Bernard had wanted to do anything like that, he could have done it long ago, because no one else knew a thing about that chest. What on earth could be in it for Grandpa to have wanted it bricked up inside his own house?

"Why do you want to help us?" asked Nick bluntly, getting in ahead of me with that question.

"Because I'm good with a hammer and chisel," said Mr. Bernard. And he added, even more quietly, "And because your grandfather, unfortunately, can't be here to help Miss Gwyneth."

Suddenly I felt it hard to breathe again, and I had to fight back tears. "Thanks," I murmured.

"Don't get hopeful too soon. I'm afraid that the key to the chest has . . . has been lost. And I really don't know that I can bring myself to take a sledgehammer to such a beautiful and valuable antique," said Mr. Bernard, sighing.

"Meaning you're not going to tell our mum and Lady Arista anything?" asked Nick.

"Not if you go to bed now." I saw Mr. Bernard's teeth flash in the darkness again before he turned and went back up the steps. "Good night, and try to get some sleep."

"Good night, Mr. Bernard," Nick and I murmured.

"The old villain!" said Xemerius. "He needn't think I'm letting him out of my sight."

The Circle of Blood its perfection will find,
The philosopher's stone shall eternity bind.
New strength will arise in the young at that hour,
Making one man immortal, for he holds the power.

But beware: when the twelfth star shows its own force,
His life here on earth runs its natural course.
And if youth is destroyed, then the oak tree will stand
To the end of all time, rooted fast in the land.

As the star dies, the eagle arises supreme,
Fulfilling his ancient and magical dream.
For a star goes out in the sky above,
If it freely chooses to die for love.

FROM THE SECRET WRITINGS OF COUNT SAINT-GERMAIN

TWO

"WELL?" CYNTHIA DALE, who was in our class at school, had planted herself in front of us with her hands on her hips, elbows pointing out, thus barring our way up to the first floor. Other students, who had to push past to the right or left of us, were complaining of the traffic jam. Cynthia was twisting the ugly tie that was part of the St. Lennox High School uniform in her fingers, and she had a stern expression on her face. "What are your costumes going to be like?" It would be her birthday at the weekend, and she'd asked us to the costume party she gave every year.

She was getting on our nerves. Lesley shook her head. "Did you know you're nuttier all the time these days, Cyn? I mean, you were nuts to begin with, but it's been getting worse and worse. People don't go about asking their guests what they're wearing to a costume party!"

"Exactly. Unless you want to have a party all on your

own," I said, trying to squeeze past Cynthia to one side. But her hand came out, quick as lightning, and grabbed my arm.

"I think up such fascinating themes for my costume parties, but there are always spoilsports who don't stick to the rules," she said. "Remember the Carnival of Animals party, and some people turned up with a feather in their hair and said they were in chicken costume? Yes, you may well look guilty, Gwenny! I know just whose idea that was."

"Not everyone has a mum whose hobby is making papier mâché elephant masks," said Lesley. Feeling cross, I just muttered, "Let us by!" I didn't bother to say how little Cynthia's party mattered to me right now, but I expect anyone could see that from my face anyway.

The grip on my arm only tightened. "And then there was Barbie's Beach Party." An obvious shudder ran down Cynthia's spine at the thought of that one—for very good reasons, by the way. She took a deep breath. "This time I want to make sure. 'Greensleeves Was My Delight' is a wonderful theme, and I'm not having anyone spoil the party this time. Just so as you know, green nail varnish or a green scarf won't do."

"Would you let me pass if I gave you a black eye?" I snapped. "It's sure to be fading to green by the time you throw your party."

Cynthia made out she hadn't heard me. "I'm coming as a flower girl in a green dress with a basket full of green posies. Sarah is coming as a green pepper. She says her costume is brilliant, but I don't know any more about it yet, because she suddenly had to go to the toilet. Gordon is coming as a field of daisies. He'll be in artificial turf all over."

"Cyn . . ." There was just no getting past her.

"And Charlotte is having a costume specially made by a dressmaker, but it's still a secret. Isn't that right, Charlotte?"

My cousin Charlotte, jammed in between a lot of other students, tried to stop, but she had to go with the flow climbing up the stairs. "It's not all that difficult to guess," she told us in passing. "I'll just say tulle in seven different shades of green. And it looks like I'll be coming with King Oberon." She called that last remark back over her shoulder. And she was looking at me with a funny sort of smile, the same as at breakfast, when I'd felt like throwing a tomato at her.

"Good for Charlotte," said Cynthia, pleased. "Coming in green *and* bringing a boy. That's the kind of guest I like."

Surely the boy Charlotte was bringing wouldn't be . . . no, impossible. Gideon would never stick on pointy ears. Or would he? I watched Charlotte moving through the crowd like a queen. She had done her glossy red hair in a kind of braided retro style, and the girls from the younger classes were all looking at her with that mixture of dislike and admiration that comes only from genuine envy. There'd probably be cute braided hairstyles all over the school yard tomorrow.

"So what are you two coming as, and who are you bringing?" asked Cynthia.

"We're coming as little green men from Mars, O best party hostess of all time," said Lesley, with a sigh of resignation. "And you'll have to wait and see who we're bringing. It's a surprise."

"Okay, then." Cynthia let go of my arm. "Little green men from Mars. Not exactly attractive, but original. Don't you dare change your minds." Without saying good-bye, she homed in on her next victim. "Katie! Hi! Stop right there. About my party!"

"Little green men from Mars?" I repeated as I looked automatically at the niche where James, the school ghost, usually stood. This morning it was empty.

"We had to shake her off somehow or other," said Lesley. "Her party! Who wants to bother with that kind of thing?"

"Did I hear something about a party? I'll be there!" Gideon's brother Raphael had emerged behind us, and made his way in between us with a confident look, taking my arm and putting his other arm around Lesley's waist. He'd done his tie up in a very peculiar way. Well, strictly speaking, he'd just tied a double knot in it. "And there was I thinking you Brits don't have much to celebrate! Closing time in the pubs and all that."

Lesley shook free of him. "I'm afraid I'll have to disappoint you. Cynthia's annual costume party isn't the sort of party you'd enjoy. Unless you like the kind where parents keep a beady eye on the buffet to make sure no one mixes anything alcoholic into the drinks or tips over the dessert."

"Yes, Cynthia's mum and dad do that, but they always try playing funny games with us," I defended them. "And they're usually the only ones who dance." I glanced at Raphael sideways, and quickly looked away again because his profile was so like his brother's. "To be honest, I'm surprised Cyn hasn't invited you yet."

"She did." Raphael sighed. "I said I was afraid I had another engagement. I hate themed parties where you have to dress up. But if I'd known you two were going . . ."

I was about to offer to tie his tie properly for him (the school rules were pretty strict about that), when he put his arm around Lesley's waist again and said cheerfully, "Did you tell Gwyneth that we tracked down the location of the treasure in your mystery game? Has she found it yet?"

"Yes," said Lesley briefly. I noticed that she didn't shake herself free this time.

"So how's the game getting along, *mignonne?*"

"It's not really a—" I began, but Lesley interrupted me.

"I'm sorry, Raphael, but you can't play anymore," she said coolly.

"What? Oh, come on, I don't think that's fair!"

I didn't think it was fair, either. After all, we weren't playing a game for poor Raphael to be kept out of, and he'd been a help so far. "Lesley only means that—"

Lesley interrupted me again. "Life isn't fair," she said, if possible even more coolly. "You have your brother to thank for that. As I'm sure you know, we're on different sides in what you call the *game*. And we can't risk you passing on information to Gideon. Who, by the way, is an absolute bas—not a particularly pleasant person."

"Lesley!" Was she out of her mind?

"*What?* This treasure hunt has something to do with my brother and the time-traveling business?" Raphael had let go of Lesley and was standing there as if rooted to the ground. "So what's he supposed to have done to you two?"

"Don't act so surprised!" said Lesley. "I'm sure you and Gideon talk everything over together." She winked at me, but I could only stare back, baffled.

"No, we don't!" cried Raphael. "We spend hardly any time together. Gideon is always off somewhere on secret missions. And if he does happen to be at home, he's brooding over mysterious documents or staring into the depths of space. Or, even worse, Charlotte turns up and gets on my nerves." He looked so unhappy that I'd have liked to put my arms around him, particularly when he added quietly, "I thought we were friends. Yesterday afternoon I felt sure we were going to get on really well together."

Lesley—or perhaps I'd better call her my friend the fridge—just shrugged her shoulders. "Yes, yesterday was nice. But let's be honest. We hardly know each other at all. You can't talk about friendship right away."

"So you were only making use of me to find out those coordinates," said Raphael, looking hard at Lesley, probably hoping she'd contradict him.

"Like I said, life isn't always fair." That was obviously

the end of it so far as Lesley was concerned. She made me walk on. "Gwen, we have to hurry," she said. "Mrs. Counter's handing out the essay subjects today. And I don't want to be landed with research into the extent of the eastern delta of the river Ganges."

I glanced back at Raphael, who was looking rather stunned. He tried to put his hands in his trouser pockets, only to find out that there weren't any in the school uniform.

"Oh, Lesley, do look at him!" I said.

"Or into ethnic groups with names I can't pronounce!"

I grabbed her arm the way Cynthia had grabbed mine just now. "What's the matter?" I whispered. "A proper little ray of sunshine, aren't you? Why do you have to go for Raphael like that? Is this part of some plan that I don't know about?"

"I'm only keeping on the safe side." Lesley looked past me at the bulletin board. "Oh, great! There's a new ad up on it—jewelry design! Speaking of jewelry," she added, fishing inside the neck of her blouse and bringing out a little chain, "look at this! I'm wearing that key you brought back from your travels in time as a pendant. Isn't that cool? I tell everyone it's the key to my heart."

Her diversionary tactics cut no ice with me. "Lesley, Raphael can't help it if his brother is a bastard. And I believe him when he says he doesn't know any of Gideon's secrets. He's new to this country and this school, and he doesn't know anyone yet."

"He's sure to find plenty of people who'll enjoy taking

care of him." Lesley went on staring straight ahead. The freckles on her nose danced in the sunlight. "You wait and see. This time tomorrow, he'll have forgotten all about me, and he'll be calling some other girl *mignonne*."

"Yes, but . . ." Only when I spotted the give-away blush on Lesley's face did light dawn on me. "Oh, now I get it! Giving his brother the cold shoulder has nothing to do with Gideon! You're just shit-scared of falling in love with Raphael!"

"Nonsense. Anyway, he's not my type!"

Aha. That said it all. Well, I was Lesley's best friend, I'd known her forever, and that reply wouldn't have thrown anyone off the right track, even Cynthia.

"Come off it, Lesley. Who's going to believe that?"

Lesley finally looked away from the announcements on the bulletin board and gave me a grin. "So what? We can't both afford to be suffering from hormonal softening of the brain at this particular moment, can we? It's quite enough for one of us not to be responsible for her actions."

"Thanks a lot."

"But it's true! You think of nothing but Gideon, so you simply don't see how serious the situation is. You need someone who can think straight, like me. And I'm not about to be taken in by that Frenchman."

"Oh, Lesley!" I gave her a big hug. No one, *no one* else in the world had such a wonderful, crazy, clever friend as I did. "But it would be terrible if you had to give up your chance of being lucky in love because of me."

"There you go, exaggerating again." Lesley lowered her voice and breathed into my ear, "If he's anything like his brother, he'd have broken my heart after a week at the latest."

"So?" I said, giving her a little tap on the hand. "It's made of marzipan, so you can reshape it anytime you like!"

"Don't laugh at me. All that about marzipan hearts is a metaphor, and I'm really proud of it."

"Of course. One day you'll be quoted all over the world. 'Hearts can't be broken because they're made of marzipan.' From *The Wit and Wisdom of Lesley Hay*."

"Wrong, I'm afraid," said a voice beside us. It belonged to our English teacher, Mr. Whitman, who was much too good-looking for a teacher.

I'd have liked to ask what he thought he knew about female hearts, but it was better not to answer Mr. Whitman back. Like Mrs. Counter, he was apt to hand out extra homework on way-out subjects, and casual as he might seem, he could be very strict.

"Wrong about what?" asked Lesley, throwing caution to the winds.

He looked at us, shaking his head. "I thought we'd gone over the difference between metaphors, similes, symbols, and images quite sufficiently. You can call it a metaphor to speak of broken hearts, but how do you classify marzipan?"

Who on earth was interested? And since when did classes begin out in the corridor? "A symbol . . . er . . . a simile?" I asked hopefully.

Mr. Whitman nodded. "Yes, although not a very good one," he said, laughing. Then he turned serious again. "You look tired, Gwyneth. You've been lying awake all night brooding, at odds with the world, am I right?"

So what business of his was it? And I could do without his sympathetic tone of voice too.

He sighed. "All this is rather too much for you." He was fidgeting with the signet ring that he wore as one of the Guardians. "That was only to be expected. Maybe Dr. White could prescribe you something to help you at least to sleep at night." I cast him an indignant glance, whereupon he gave me an encouraging smile before he turned and went into the classroom ahead of us.

"Did I fail to hear properly, or did Mr. Whitman just suggest giving me sleeping pills?" I asked Lesley. "Right after letting me know I looked terrible, I think."

"Just like him!" snorted Lesley. "He wants you to be a puppet of the Guardians all day and then drugged out of your mind at night so as to keep you from getting any ideas of your own. Well, he's not fooling us." She energetically brushed a lock of hair back from her face. "We're going to show those Guardians that they underestimate you."

"Hm," I said doubtfully, but Lesley was looking at me with grim determination.

"We'll draw up our master plan at first break in the girls' toilets."

★ ★ ★

ANYWAY, MR. WHITMAN was wrong. I didn't look tired (I'd checked in the mirror in the girls' toilets several times), and oddly enough, I didn't feel tired, either. After our nocturnal treasure hunt, I'd soon fallen asleep again, and this time the nightmares stayed away. It could be I'd even had a nice dream, because in those magic seconds between sleeping and waking, I'd felt confident and hopeful. Although it's true that when I was fully awake the gloomy realities came back into my mind, first and foremost: *Gideon was only pretending to love me.*

However, a little of that hopeful mood had lasted into daytime. Maybe that was because I'd finally had a few hours' uninterrupted sleep. Or possibly it had occurred to me, even in my dreams, that galloping consumption could be cured these days. Then again, it could just be that my tear ducts were empty.

"Do you think it's possible that maybe Gideon set out to make me fall in love with him, but then he really did fall in love with me himself, kind of by mistake?" I cautiously asked Lesley when we were packing up our things after classes. I'd avoided the subject all morning, so as to have a clear head when we were drawing up this master plan, but now I just had to talk about the idea or I'd have burst.

"Yes," said Lesley after a moment's hesitation.

"Really?" I asked, surprised.

"Maybe that was what he still had to tell you yesterday evening. I mean, in films we always get so annoyed with those artificial misunderstandings that are meant to heighten suspense before the happy ending, although a few words could clear them up for good."

"Exactly! That's where you always shout at the screen, *Just tell him, you silly cow!*"

Lesley nodded. "But in the film, something always gets in the way. The dog's bitten through the phone cable, the other girl is feeling mean and doesn't pass on the news, the boy's mother says he's gone to California . . . you know the kind of thing?" She gave me her hairbrush and looked at me hard in the mirror. "You know, the more I think about it, the less likely it seems to me that he *could* have failed to fall in love with you."

My eyes felt damp with sheer relief. "In that case, he'd still be a bastard, but . . . but I think I could forgive him."

"So could I," said Lesley, beaming at me. "I have waterproof mascara and lip gloss here. Want to borrow some?"

Well, it couldn't hurt, anyway.

WE WERE LAST to leave the classroom again. I was in such a good mood now that Lesley felt it was her duty to dig her elbow into my ribs. "I really don't want to put a damper on your enthusiasm, but we could be wrong. Because we've seen too many romantic films."

"Yes, I know," I said. "Oh, there's James." Most of the students were already on their way out, so there were only a few left to wonder why I was talking to an empty niche in the wall. "Hello, James!"

"Good day, Miss Gwyneth." As always, he was wearing a flowered tail-coat, knee breeches, and cream stockings. He had brocade shoes with silver buckles on his feet, and his cravat was so elaborately arranged that he couldn't possibly have tied it for himself. The oddest things about him were his curly wig, the powder on his face, and the patches like moles that he had stuck to it. For some reason that I couldn't understand, he called them beauty spots. Without all that, and in sensible clothes, James would probably have been quite good-looking.

"Where were you this morning, James? We had a date to meet at second break, remember?"

James shook his head. "How I hate this fever! And I don't like the dream, either—everything here is so . . . so *ugly!*" He sighed heavily and pointed to the ceiling. "I wonder what philistines painted over the frescos? My father paid a fortune for them. I like the shepherdess in the middle very much, even if my mother says she's too scantily clad." He looked disapprovingly first at me and then at Lesley, his eyes resting for a long time on the pleated skirts of our school uniform and then our knees. "Although if my mother knew the way young persons dress in my fevered dream, she'd be horrified. I'm horrified myself. I would never have thought I could indulge in such a depraved fantasy."

James didn't seem to be having a particularly good day. At least Xemerius had decided to stay at home (James hated Xemerius). To keep an eye on the treasure and Mr. Bernard, or so he said, but I secretly suspected he wanted to look over Aunt Maddy's shoulder again while she was reading. She was halfway through a romantic novel at the moment, and he seemed to be enjoying it.

"Depraved! What a charming compliment, James," I said mildly. I had long ago given up explaining to James that he was not dreaming, but had been dead for about two hundred and thirty years. I suppose no one likes to hear such news.

"Dr. Barrow bled me again just now, and I was even able to drink a few sips of water," he went on. "I had hoped for a different dream this time, but alas, here I am again."

"And I'm very glad to see you," I said warmly. "I'd miss you very much if you went right away."

James managed a smile. "Well, I'd be lying if I were to deny that I've developed a certain affection for you, Miss Gwyneth. And now, shall we go on with our lessons in etiquette?"

"I'm afraid there isn't time, but let's go on tomorrow, okay?" On the stairs I turned back. "Oh, by the way, James, what was the name of your favorite horse in September of the year 1782?"

Two boys pushing a table with an overhead projector on it along the corridor stopped, and Lesley giggled when they both asked, at the same time, "Do you mean me?"

"September last year?" asked James. "Hector, of course. Hector will always be my favorite horse. The most magnificent gray you can imagine."

"And what's your favorite food?"

The boys with the overhead projector looked at me as

if I'd lost my mind. James himself frowned. "What sort of question is that? I have absolutely no appetite just now."

"Never mind. That can wait till tomorrow too. Good-bye, James."

"I'm Finley, you daft cow," said one of the projector pushers, and the other grinned and said, "And my name's Adam, but hey, I don't mind! You're welcome to call me James if you like."

I ignored them both and linked arms with Lesley.

"What was all that about?" she asked on the way downstairs.

"When I meet James at that ball, I want to warn him against catching smallpox," I explained. "He was only twenty-one. Too young to die, don't you agree?"

"I'm not sure that you ought to meddle with that kind of thing," said Lesley. "You know what I mean—fate, pre- destination, and so on."

"But there must be some reason why he's still haunt- ing this building. Maybe I'm predestined to help him."

"Why exactly do you have to go to this ball?" Lesley inquired.

I shrugged my shoulders. "Apparently Count Saint- Germain said I had to in those nutty *Annals*. So he can get to know me better, or something."

Lesley raised her eyebrows. "Or something?"

I sighed. "Whatever. Anyway, the ball is held in September 1782, but James didn't catch smallpox until 1783. If I can manage to warn him, he might be able to go into the country, for instance, when the epidemic breaks out. Or at least keep away from Lord Thingy's house, where he caught it. Why are you grinning like that?"

"You're going to say you come from the future, and you know he's soon going to be infected with smallpox, and by way of proof, you'll tell him the name of his favorite horse?"

"Er . . . well, I haven't quite worked out all the details of the plan yet."

"Vaccination would be better," said Lesley, pushing the door to the school yard open. "But that wouldn't be easy to fix either."

"No. What *is* easy to fix these days?" I said, and groaned. "Oh, damn it!" Charlotte was standing beside the limousine waiting to take me to the Guardians' HQ, where I went every day now. And that could mean only one thing: I was to undergo more torture by minuets, the right way to curtsey, and the date of the Siege of Gibraltar. Useful knowledge for someone going to a ball in 1782, or at least the Guardians thought so.

Oddly enough, that left me cold today, or almost. Maybe because I was too excited by the thought of my next meeting with Gideon.

Lesley narrowed her eyes. "Who's that guy with Charlotte?" She was pointing to red-haired Mr. Marley, an Adept First Degree, whose main distinction along with that resounding title was an ability to blush all over his face and both ears. He was standing beside Charlotte, head hunched down.

I told Lesley who he was. "I think he's scared of Charlotte," I added. "But he still thinks she's great."

Charlotte had spotted us and was waving impatiently.

"At least they go wonderfully well together where their hair color is concerned," said Lesley, hugging me. "Good luck. Remember what we were discussing. And go carefully. Oh, and *please* take a photo of that Mr. Giordano."

"Giordano, just Giordano, if you please," I said, imitating my dancing master's nasal tone of voice. "See you this evening."

"Yes, and Gwenny? Don't make it too easy for Gideon, will you?"

"At last!" Charlotte snapped at me as I went over to the car. "We've been waiting here forever. With everyone staring at us."

"As if that would bother you. Hello, Mr. Marley, how are you?"

"Er. Fine. Er . . . how are you?" And Mr. Marley was already blushing. I felt sorry for him. I blushed easily myself, but with Mr. Marley, the blood didn't go just to his cheeks—his ears and his throat also turned the color of ripe tomatoes. Terrible!

"Very well indeed," I said, although I'd have loved to see his face if I'd said "bloody awful" instead. He held the car door open for us, and Charlotte sat down gracefully on the back seat.

I took the seat opposite her.

The car began moving off. Charlotte looked out of the window, and I stared into space as I wondered whether I ought to be cool and offended when I met Gideon, or perfectly friendly but indifferent. I wished I'd discussed that with Lesley. When we were halfway along the Strand, Charlotte stopped looking at our surroundings and turned her attention to her fingernails instead. Then she suddenly looked up, scrutinized me from head to foot, and asked aggressively, "Who are you going to Cynthia's party with?"

She was obviously spoiling for a fight. What a good thing we'd soon have arrived. The limousine was already turning into the parking area in Crown Office Road. "Hm," I said, "I haven't decided yet. Either Kermit the Frog or Shrek, if he has time. How about you?"

"Gideon said he'd come with me," said Charlotte, looking at me intently. She was only too clearly expecting some reaction.

"Well, that's nice of him," I said in a friendly way, smiling. It wasn't even difficult for me, because by now I was pretty sure how things were with Gideon.

"But I don't know whether I ought to accept his offer." Charlotte sighed, but the lurking, watchful look in her eyes was still the same. "I'm sure he'd hate being with all those childish kids. He's complained to me often enough of the naivety and immaturity of some sixteen-year-olds. . . ."

For a fraction of a second, I considered simply keeping my temper and telling her the truth. But even if I did—well, I wasn't going to give her the satisfaction of having scored a hit. My nod was very understanding. "However, he'll have your mature and enlightened company, Charlotte, and if that's not enough for him, he can always have a serious conversation with Mr. Dale about the terrible consequences of alcohol consumption by the young."

The car braked and went into one of the reserved parking slots outside the house, which for centuries had been the headquarters of the Secret Society of the Guardians. The driver switched off the engine, and at the same moment, Mr. Marley jumped out of the passenger's seat at the front. I managed to open the back door of the car just before he reached it. By now I had a good idea how the Queen must feel, not even allowed to get out of a car by herself.

I picked up my bag, climbed out of the car, ignoring Mr. Marley's hand, and said as cheerfully as I could, "I'd say that green is Gideon's color too."

Aha! Charlotte didn't move a muscle, but that round had definitely gone to me. When I'd taken a few steps and could be sure no one would see it, I allowed myself a tiny little triumphant grin. However, next moment the grin froze on my face. Gideon was sitting in the sun on the steps outside the entrance to the Guardians' HQ. Damn! I'd been much too busy thinking up a good answer to Charlotte to notice my surroundings. My stupid marzipan heart didn't know whether to shrink in discomfort or beat faster for joy.

When Gideon saw us, he stood up and knocked the dust off his jeans. I slowed down, still trying to decide how to behave to him. The "friendly but indifferent" approach probably wouldn't be very convincing if my lower lip was trembling. Unfortunately the "cool but offended for very good reasons" approach couldn't be put into practice either, in view of my overwhelming need just to fling myself into his arms. So I bit my uncooperative lower lip and tried to look as neutral as possible. As I came closer, I saw with a certain satisfaction that Gideon was chewing his own lower lip, and he too seemed rather nervous. Although he needed a shave and his brown hair looked as if he'd been combing it with his fingers, if at all, I was captivated all over again by the way he looked. I stood at the foot of the steps, feeling undecided, and we looked straight into each other's eyes for about two seconds. Then his gaze moved to the front of the house opposite, and he said hello to it. At least, I didn't feel that he was speaking to me. Charlotte pushed past me on her way up the steps. She put one arm around Gideon's neck and kissed him on the cheek.

"Hello, you," she said.

Admittedly that was much more elegant than standing rooted to the spot and goggling stupidly. My behavior must have seemed to Mr. Marley like a little attack of faintness, because he asked, "Would you like me to carry your bag, Miss Shepherd?"

"No, thank you, I'm fine," I said. I pulled myself together, picked up the bag, which had slipped to the ground, and started moving again. Instead of tossing my hair back and sweeping past Gideon and Charlotte with an icy glance, I climbed the steps with all the carefree verve of a snail dying of old age. It could be that Lesley and I had just seen far too many romantic films. But then Gideon moved Charlotte to one side and reached for my arm.

"Can I have a quick word with you, Gwen?" he asked.

I was so relieved that my knees almost gave way. "Of course."

Mr. Marley shifted nervously from foot to foot. "We're a little late already," he murmured, his ears fiery red.

"He's right," chirruped Charlotte. "Gwenny has to practice dancing before she elapses, and you know what Giordano is like if anyone keeps him waiting." I had no idea how she did it, but her peal of silvery laughter really sounded genuine.

"She'll be there in ten minutes' time," said Gideon.

"Can't it wait until later?"

"I said ten minutes." Gideon's tone of voice was on the verge of downright rude, and Mr. Marley looked really alarmed. I expect I did too.

Charlotte shrugged her shoulders. "As you like," she said, tossing her head and sweeping past. She did it very well. Mr. Marley dutifully followed her.

When the pair of them had disappeared into the front hall of the house, Gideon seemed to have forgotten what he wanted to say. He went on staring at the stupid house opposite and rubbed the back of his neck with his hand as if it felt very tense. Finally we both took a deep breath at the same time. "How's your arm?" I asked, and at the same moment Gideon asked, "Are you all right?" and that made us both grin.

"My arm is fine." At last he looked at me. Oh, my God, those eyes! I instantly felt weak at the knees again, and I was glad that Mr. Marley wasn't there with us anymore.

"Gwyneth, I'm terribly sorry about all this. I . . . I behaved very irresponsibly. You really didn't deserve that." He was looking so unhappy that I could hardly bear it. "I tried calling you on your mobile about a hundred times yesterday evening, but I couldn't get through."

I wondered whether to cut this short and fling myself straight into his arms. But Lesley had said I shouldn't make it too easy for him. So I just raised my eyebrows and waited for more.

"I didn't want to hurt you, please believe that," he said, and he obviously meant it, his voice was so husky. "You looked so dreadfully sad and disappointed yesterday evening."

"It wasn't as bad as all that," I said quietly. I thought I could be forgiven for that lie. No need to rub it in about all the tears I'd shed and my fervent wish to die of galloping consumption. "I was just . . . it rather hurt. . . ." (Okay, so that was the understatement of the century!) "It rather hurt to think you'd only been pretending all along, I mean the kisses, saying you loved me. . . ." I was getting embarrassed, so I stopped.

He looked, if possible, even more remorseful. "I promise you nothing like that will ever happen again."

What exactly did he mean? I couldn't quite make it out. "Well, now that I know, of course it wouldn't work another time," I said a bit more firmly. "And between you and me, it was a silly plan anyway. People in love aren't influenced more easily than anyone else—far from it! With all those hormones churning around, you never know what they'll do next." I was living proof of that, after all.

"But people do things out of love that they wouldn't do at all usually." Gideon raised a hand as if to caress my cheek, and then he let it fall again. "If you're in love, the other person suddenly seems more important than yourself." If I hadn't known better, I'd almost have thought he was about to burst into tears. "You make sacrifices . . . that's probably what the count meant."

"I don't think the count has any idea what he's talking about," I said scornfully. "If you ask me, he's not what you might call an expert on love, and as for his knowledge of the female mind, it's . . . it's pathetic!" *Now kiss me; I want to know if stubble feels prickly.*

A smile lit up Gideon's face. "You could be right," he said, taking a deep breath like when someone has had a heavy weight fall from his heart. "I'm glad we've cleared that up, anyway. We'll always stay good friends, won't we?"

What?

"Good friends?" he repeated, and suddenly my mouth felt dry. "Good friends who know they can trust and rely on each other," he added. "It's really important for you to trust me."

It took a couple of seconds, but then it began to dawn

on me that somewhere in this conversation, we'd branched off in different directions. What Gideon had been trying to say wasn't "please forgive me, I love you," but "let's stay good friends." And every idiot knows that those are two totally different things.

It meant that he hadn't fallen in love with me.

It meant that Lesley and I *had* seen too many romantic films.

It meant . . .

"You *bastard*!" I cried. Fury, bright, hot fury was pouring through me so violently that it made my voice hoarse. "What a nerve! How *dare* you? One day you kiss me and say you've fallen in love with me; the next you say you're sorry for telling such horrible lies—and then you want me to *trust* you?"

Now Gideon also realized that we'd been talking at cross purposes. The smile disappeared from his face. "Gwen—"

"Shall I tell you something? I regret every single tear I shed over you!" I was trying to shout at him, but I failed miserably. "And you needn't imagine there were all that many of them!" I just about managed to croak.

"Gwen!" Gideon tried to take my hand. "Oh, God! I'm so sorry. I really didn't want to . . . *please!*"

Please what? I stared angrily at him. Didn't he notice that he was just making everything even worse? And did he think that pleading look in his eyes would change anything? I wanted to turn around, but Gideon had a firm grasp on my wrist.

"Gwen, listen to me. There are dangerous times ahead of us, and it's important for the two of us to stand by each other. I . . . I really do like you very much, I want us to . . ."

He surely wasn't going to say it again. Not that corny old bit about good friends. But he did exactly that.

". . . be good friends. Don't you see? Unless we can trust each other—"

I tore myself away from him. "As if I wanted to be friends with someone like you!" Now my voice was back, and it was so loud that it made the pigeons fly up from the roof. "You don't have the faintest idea what friendship means!"

And suddenly it was dead easy. I tossed my hair back, turned on my heel, and swept away.

You've got to jump off cliffs—
and build your wings on the way down.

Ray Bradbury

THREE

LET'S STAY FRIENDS—I mean, that really was the end!

"What do you bet a fairy dies every time someone says that anywhere in the world?" I asked. I'd locked myself into the ladies to call Lesley on my mobile, and I was doing my best not to scream, although only half an hour after my conversation with Gideon, that's what I still felt like doing.

"He said he wants you to *be* friends," Lesley corrected me. As usual, she'd noticed every word.

"It's exactly the same," I said.

"No. I mean yes, maybe." Lesley sighed. "I don't understand. Are you sure you definitely let him finish what he was saying? Remember how in *Ten Things I Hate About You*—"

"I did let him finish what he was saying. Unfortunately, I'd add." I looked at the time. "Oh, shit. I told Mr.

George I'd be back in a minute." I glanced at myself in the mirror above the old-fashioned washbasin. "Oh, *shit!*" I said again. There were two circular red patches on my cheeks. "I think I have some kind of allergic reaction."

"Only caused by rage," was Lesley's diagnosis when I told her what I saw. "How about your eyes? Are they flashing dangerously?"

I stared at my reflection. "Yes, sort of. I look a bit like Helena Bonham Carter as Bellatrix Lestrange in *Harry Potter*. Rather threatening."

"That sounds okay. Listen, you go out now and flash them at everyone for all you're worth, right?"

I nodded obediently and promised to do just that.

After that phone call, I felt a bit better, even if cold water couldn't wash away my fury or the two red spots on my cheeks.

If Mr. George had been wondering where I'd been for so long, he didn't show it.

"Everything all right?" he asked in kindly tones. He'd been waiting for me outside the Old Refectory.

"Everything's fine!" I glanced through the open doorway, but there was no sign of Giordano and Charlotte after all, even though I was far too late for my lesson by now. "I just had to . . . er, put some new rouge on."

Mr. George smiled. Apart from the laughter lines around his eyes and at the corners of his mouth, nothing in his round, friendly face showed that he was well over seventy. The light was reflected on his bald patch, so that his whole head reminded me of a bowl polished until it shone.

I couldn't help it, I had to smile back. The sight of Mr. George always had a soothing effect on me. "Honestly. You rub it into your face there," I said, pointing to my two furious red spots.

Mr. George gave me his arm. "Come along, my brave girl," he said. "I've let them know that we're going downstairs for you to elapse."

I looked at him in surprise. "But what about Giordano and colonial policy in the eighteenth century?"

Mr. George smiled slightly. "Let's put it this way: I used the short wait while you were in the bathroom to tell Giordano we were afraid you wouldn't have time for his lessons today."

Dear, good Mr. George! He was the only one of the Guardians who seemed to bother about me as a real person at all. Although maybe a little minuet dancing might have calmed me down a bit. Like the way some people work off their aggression on a punching bag. Or by going to the gym. On the other hand, I could really do without Charlotte's supercilious smile right now.

"The chronograph is waiting," he added.

I was happy to take Mr. George's arm. For once, I was even looking forward to elapsing—my daily few hours of controlled travel back to the past—and not just to get away from the horrible present day that meant Gideon. Because today's journey back in time was the key point to the master plan that Lesley had thought up with me. If it worked as we hoped.

On the way down to the depths of the huge, vaulted cellars, Mr. George and I went right through the Guardians' headquarters. It was hard to get a clear idea of the place, which occupied several buildings. There was so much to see, even in the winding corridors, that you might easily think you were in a museum. Countless framed paintings, ancient maps, handmade tapestries, and whole collections of swords hung on the walls. China that looked valuable, leather-bound books, and old musical instruments were on display in glass-fronted cupboards, and there were any number of chests and carved wooden boxes. In other circumstances, I'd have loved to find out what was inside them.

"I don't know much about cosmetics, but if you want to let off steam to someone about Gideon—well, I'm a good listener," said Mr. George.

"About Gideon?" I said slowly, as if I had to stop and work out who Gideon was. "Oh, everything's fine between Gideon and me." So there! I punched the wall in passing. "We're *friends*, nothing more. Just *friends*." Unfortunately the word didn't really come out very easily. I was kind of grinding my teeth as I said it.

"I was sixteen once myself, Gwyneth." Mr. George's little eyes twinkled kindly at me. "And I promise I won't say I warned you. Even though I did—"

"I'm sure you were a really nice boy when you were sixteen." Hard to imagine Mr. George ever cunningly deceiving someone by kissing her and saying nice things without meaning them. *You only have to be in the same room and I need to touch you and kiss you.* I tried to shake off the memory of the way Gideon had looked at me by treading extra firmly as I walked along. The china in the glass-fronted cupboards shook slightly, clinking.

Right. Who needs to dance a minuet to work off aggression? This would do just fine. Although smashing one of those expensive-looking vases might have had an even better effect.

Mr. George looked sideways at me for some time, but finally he just pressed my arm and sighed. We were passing suits of armor at irregular intervals, and as usual, I had an uncomfortable feeling that I was under observation.

"There's someone inside that armor, isn't there?" I whispered to Mr. George. "Some poor novice who can't go to the toilet all day, right? I can tell he's staring at us."

"No," said Mr. George, laughing quietly. "But there are security cameras installed behind the visors of the helmets. That's probably why you feel you're being watched."

Oh. Security cameras. At least I didn't have to feel sorry for security cameras.

When we had reached the first flight of stairs down to the vaults, it struck me that Mr. George had forgotten something. "Don't you want to blindfold me?"

"I think we can dispense with that today," said Mr. George. "There's no one here to say otherwise, is there?"

I looked at him in surprise. Normally I had to go the whole way with a black scarf tied around my eyes, because the Guardians didn't want me to be able to find my own way to the place where they kept the chronograph that made controlled time travel possible. For some reason, they thought that if I knew the way, I'd steal it, which of course was utter nonsense. I didn't just think the thing uncanny—I mean, it was fueled by blood! I ask you!—I hadn't the faintest idea how you set the countless little cogwheels, levers, and flaps to get it to work. But all the Guardians were absolutely paranoid about the possibility of theft.

That was probably because there had once been two chronographs. And almost seventeen years ago, my cousin Lucy and her boyfriend, Paul, Numbers Nine and Ten in the Circle of Twelve, the time travelers, had gone off with one of them. So far I hadn't found out just why they stole it. But I was groping around blindly in the dark about this whole business, anyway.

"Oh, and by the way, Madame Rossini asked me to tell you that she's decided on a different color for your ball dress. I'm afraid I've forgotten what color, but I'm sure you'll look bewitching in it." Mr. George chuckled. "Even if Giordano has been telling me, yet again, about all the many terrible faux pas you're bound to make in the eighteenth century."

My heart jumped. I'd have to go to that ball with Gideon, and I couldn't imagine being in any fit state to dance a minuet with him tomorrow without *really* breaking something. His foot, for instance.

"Why the hurry?" I asked. "I mean, from our point of

view, why does the ball absolutely have to be tomorrow evening? Why can't we simply wait a few weeks? After all, surely the ball is held on that one day in 1782 anyway, whatever the date here when we go to it?" Quite apart from Gideon, this was a question that had been on my mind for some time.

"Count Saint-Germain has worked out precisely how much time in the present should be allowed to pass between your visits to him," said Mr. George, letting me go down the spiral staircase first.

The farther and deeper down we went through the labyrinth of cellars, the stronger the musty smell. Down here there were no pictures on the walls, and although movement detectors saw to it that a bright light came on wherever we went, the corridors branching off to our left and right were lost in eerie darkness after a few yards. Apparently people had been lost down here several times. Some hadn't come up until several days later, in parts of the city far away from the Temple. But that was just hearsay.

"But *why* did the count say it had to be tomorrow? And why do the Guardians follow his instructions so slavishly?"

Mr. George didn't answer that. He only sighed heavily.

"I was only thinking that if we gave ourselves a couple of weeks' more time, well, the count wouldn't even notice, would he?" I said. "He's sitting there in 1782, and time isn't going any more slowly for him. But then I could learn all that minuet stuff at my leisure, and I might even know

who was besieging whom in Gibraltar and why." I pre-
ferred to leave Gideon out of it. "Then no one would have
to go on and on at me, and be afraid of all the dreadful
mistakes I'd make at the ball, just in case the way I behave
shows that I come from the future. So why does the count
say it absolutely has to be tomorrow, in our time, when I
go to the ball?"

"Yes, why?" murmured Mr. George. "It's almost as if he
were afraid of you. And of what you might find out if you
had more time."

It wasn't far now to the old alchemical laboratory.
Unless I was mistaken, it must be just around the next corner. So I slowed down. "Afraid of me? He throttled me
without even touching me, and since he can read thoughts,
he knows perfectly well that *I* am terrified of *him*, not the
other way around."

"He throttled you? Without touching you?" Mr.
George had stopped and was staring at me. He looked
shocked. "Dear heavens. Gwyneth, why didn't you tell us
about this before?"

"Would you have believed me?"

Mr. George passed the back of his hand over his bald
patch and was just opening his mouth to say something
when we heard footsteps coming and a heavy door slammed
shut. Mr. George looked alarmed—more alarmed than I'd
have expected—led me around the corner in the direction
from which the sound of the door had come, and took a
black scarf out of his jacket pocket.

It was Falk de Villiers. Gideon's uncle and Grand

Master of the Lodge, walking energetically along the corridor. But he smiled when he saw us.

"Ah, there you are. Poor Marley has just been ringing up to the house to ask what had become of you, so I thought I'd take a look."

I blinked and rubbed my eyes, as if Mr. George had only just taken the blindfold off, but that was obviously an unnecessary bit of playacting, because Falk de Villiers didn't even notice. He opened the door to the chronograph room, once the old alchemical laboratory.

Falk was maybe a year or so older than my mum and very good-looking, like all the members of the de Villiers family I'd met so far. I always thought of him as the lead wolf of the pack. His thick hair had gone gray early and made an intriguing contrast with his amber eyes.

"There, you see, Marley? No one's gone missing," he said in a jovial tone to Mr. Marley, who had been sitting on a chair in the chronograph room and now jumped up, nervously kneading his fingers.

"I only . . . I thought that, to be on the safe side . . ." He stammered. "I do apologize, sir. . . ."

"No, no, we're glad to know that you take your duties so seriously," said Mr. George, and Falk asked, "Where's Mr. Whitman? He and I had a date to see Dean Smythe over a cup of tea, and I was going to collect him."

"He's just left," said Mr. Marley. "They said they really did have to meet him."

"Right, then I'll be off. I may catch up with him on the way. Coming, Thomas?"

After a brief sidelong glance at me, Mr. George shook his head.

"And we'll see each other again tomorrow, Gwyneth. When you're off to the great ball." But halfway out the door, Falk turned again and said, as if casually, "Oh, and give your mother my regards, Gwyneth. Is she all right?"

"My mum? Yes, she's fine."

"Glad to hear it." I must have been looking rather bewildered, because he cleared his throat and added, "Mothers who are on their own and working full-time don't always have an easy life these days, so I'm pleased for her."

Now I was intentionally looking bewildered.

"Or—or maybe she isn't on her own? An attractive woman like Grace is bound to meet a lot of men, so perhaps there's someone in particular. . . ."

Falk was looking at me expectantly, but when I frowned, puzzled, he looked at his watch and cried, "Oh, so late already. I really must be on my way."

"Was that a question he asked?" I said when Falk had closed the door behind him.

"Yes," said Mr. George and Mr. Marley at the same time, and Mr. Marley went scarlet. "Er," he added, "at least, it sounded to me as if he wanted to know whether your mother has a steady boyfriend," he muttered.

Mr. George laughed. "Falk's right, it really is late. If Gwyneth is to get any homework done this evening, we have to send her back into the past now. What year shall we pick, Gwyneth?"

As I'd agreed with Lesley, I said as indifferently as

possible, "I don't mind. It was 1956 the other day—am I right, was it 1956? There were no rats in the cellar then. It was even quite comfortable." Of course I didn't breathe a word about meeting my grandfather in secret in the comfort of the rat-free cellar. "I managed to learn my French vocabulary there without trembling with fright the whole time."

"No problem," said Mr. George. He opened a thick journal, while Mr. Marley pushed aside the wall hanging that hid the safe containing the chronograph.

I tried to peer over Mr. George's shoulder as he leafed through the journal, but his broad back got in the way.

"Let's see. That was 24 July 1956," said Mr. George. "You spent all afternoon there and came back at six thirty in the evening."

"Six thirty would be a good time," I said, crossing my fingers that our plan would work out. If I could go back to the exact time when I had left the room on that visit, my grandfather would still be down there, and I wouldn't have to waste any time looking for him.

"I think we'd better make it six thirty-one," said Mr. George. "We don't want you colliding with yourself."

Mr. Marley, who had put the chest containing the chronograph on the table and was now taking the device, which was about the size of a mantelpiece clock, out of its velvet wrappings, murmured, "But strictly speaking, it's not night there yet. Mr. Whitman said—"

"Yes, we know that Mr. Whitman is a stickler for the rules," said Mr. George, as he fiddled with the little cogwheels. In between delicate colored drawings of patterns, planets, animals, and plants, there were gemstones set into the surface of the strange machine, so big and bright that you felt they must be imitations—like the interlinking beads that my little sister liked to play with. All the time travelers in the Circle of Twelve had different jewels allotted to them. Mine was the ruby, and the diamond, so big that it was probably worth the price of a whole apartment block in the West End of London, "belonged" to Gideon. "However, I think we are gentlemen enough not to leave a young lady sitting on her own in a vaulted cellar at night, don't you agree, Leo?"

Mr. Marley nodded uncertainly.

"Leo?" I said. "That's a nice name."

"Short for Leopold," said Mr. Marley, his ears shining like the rear lights of a car. He sat down at the table, put the journal in front of him, and took the top off a fountain pen. The small, neat handwriting in which a long series of dates, times, and names had been recorded there was obviously his. "My mother thinks it's a terrible name, but it's traditional to call every eldest son in our family Leopold."

"Leo is a direct descendant of Baron Miroslav Alexander Leopold Rakoczy," explained Mr. George, turning around for a moment and looking me in the eye. "You know—Count Saint-Germain's legendary traveling companion, known in the *Annals* as the Black Leopard."

I was baffled. "Oh, really?"

In my mind, I was comparing Mr. Marley with the thin, pale figure of Rakoczy, whose black eyes had terrified me so badly. But I didn't really know whether I ought to tell him he was lucky not to look like his shady ancestor, or whether maybe it was even worse to be red-haired, freckled, and moonfaced.

"You see, my paternal grandfather—" Mr. Marley was beginning, but Mr. George quickly interrupted him. "I am sure your grandfather would be very proud of you," he said firmly. "Particularly if he knew how well you have passed your exams."

"Except in the Use of Traditional Weapons," said Mr. Marley. "I was marked only satisfactory there."

"Oh, well, no one needs that these days. Use of traditional weapons is an outmoded subject." Mr. George put his hand out to me. "Here we are, Gwyneth. Off to 1956 you go. I have set the chronograph to exactly three and a half hours. Keep a tight hold on your bag and be sure not to leave anything lying around in the cellar when you travel back, remember? Mr. Marley will be waiting for you here."

I clutched my schoolbag with one arm and gave Mr. George my free hand. He put my forefinger into one of the tiny compartments behind flaps in the chronograph. A needle went into it, and the magnificent ruby lit up and filled the whole room with red light. I closed my eyes while I let the usual dizzy feeling carry me away. When I opened them a second later, Mr. Marley and Mr. George had disappeared, and so had the table.

It was darker, the room was lit by only a single electric bulb, and my grandfather Lucas was standing in the light of it looking at me, puzzled.

"You . . . you—didn't it work, then?" he cried, alarmed. In 1956, he was thirty-two years old, and he didn't look much like the old man of eighty I'd known when I was a little girl. "You disappeared over there, and now here you are again."

"Yes," I said proudly, suppressing my instinct to hug him. It was the same as at our other meetings: the sight of him brought a lump to my throat. My grandfather had died when I was ten years old, and it was both wonderful and sad to see him again six years after his funeral. Sad not because when we met in the past he wasn't the grandfather I had known, but a kind of unfinished version of him, but because I was a complete stranger to him. He hadn't the faintest idea how often I had sat on his lap or that, when my father died, he was the person who comforted me by telling me stories, and we always used to say good night in a secret language of our own invention that no one else understood. He didn't know how much I had loved him, and I couldn't tell him. No one likes to hear that kind of thing from someone after spending only a few hours with her. I ignored the lump in my throat as well as I could. "For you, only about a minute has probably passed, so I'll forgive you for not shaving that mustache off yet. But for me it's been a few days, and all kinds of things have happened."

Lucas stroked his mustache and grinned. "So you simply . . . Well, that was very clever of you, granddaughter."

"Yes, wasn't it? But to be honest, it was my friend Lesley's idea. So that we could be sure I'd meet you and then we wouldn't have to waste any time."

"And I haven't had a moment to wonder what to do next. I was just beginning to get over your visit and thinking about it all." He examined me with his head to one side. "Yes, you do look different. You didn't have that barrette in your hair earlier, and somehow you seem thinner."

"Thanks," I said.

"It wasn't a compliment. You look as if you were in rather a bad way." He came a little closer and scrutinized me critically. "Is everything all right?" he asked gently.

"Everything's fine," I meant to say cheerfully, but to my horror, I burst into tears. "Everything's fine," I sobbed.

"Oh, dear," said Lucas, patting me clumsily on the back. "As bad as all that?"

For several minutes, I couldn't do anything but let the tears flow. And I'd thought I was back in control of myself! Fury at the way Gideon had behaved seemed the right reaction—very brave and adult. And it would look much better in a film than all this crying. I'm afraid Xemerius was only too right to compare me to an indoor fountain.

"Friends!" I finally sniffed, because my grandfather had a right to an explanation. "He wants us to be friends. And for me to trust him."

Lucas hunched his head down and frowned, looking baffled. "And that makes you cry because . . . ?"

"Because yesterday he said he loved me!"

If possible Lucas looked even more puzzled than before. "Well, that doesn't necessarily seem a bad way to start a friendship."

My tears dried up as if someone had turned off the electricity powering the indoor fountain. "Grandpa! Don't be so dim!" I cried. "First he kisses me, then I find out that it was all just tactics and manipulation, and then he comes out with that let's-be-friends stuff!"

"Oh. I see. What a . . . what a scoundrel!" Lucas still didn't look entirely convinced. "Forgive me for asking silly questions, but I hope we're not talking about that de Villiers boy, are we? Number Eleven, the Diamond?"

"Yes, we are," I said. "That's exactly who we're talking about."

My grandfather groaned. "Oh, really! Teenagers! As if all this weren't complicated enough already!" He threw me a fabric handkerchief, took my schoolbag out of my hand, and said firmly, "That's enough crying. How much time do we have?"

"The chronograph's set for me to travel back at ten P.M. your time." Funnily enough, crying had been good for me, much better than the adult, being-furious variant. "Do you have anything to eat? I'm feeling a bit peckish."

That made Lucas laugh. "In that case we'd better go upstairs, little chicken, and find you something to peck at. It's claustrophobic down here. And I'll have to call home and say I'll be late back." He opened the door. "Come along, and you can tell me all about it on the way. And if anyone sees you, don't forget that you're my cousin Hazel from the country."

ALMOST AN HOUR LATER, we were sitting in Lucas's office, thinking so hard that the steam was practically coming out of our ears. In front of us we had piles of paper with scribbled notes, mostly consisting of dates, circles, arrows, and question marks, as well as thick leather-bound folio volumes (the *Annals of the Guardians* for several decades back) and the usual plate of biscuits. All through the ages, the Guardians seemed to have ample stocks of those.

"Too little information to go on, too little time," Lucas kept saying. He was prowling restlessly up and down the room, ruffling his hair. In spite of the stuff he put on it to keep it smooth, it was beginning to stick out in all directions. "What do you think I can have hidden in that chest?"

"Maybe a book containing all the information I need," I said. We had passed the young man on guard by the stairs without any difficulty. He had been asleep, the same as on my last visit, and the fumes of alcohol he gave off were enough to make any passerby feel drowsy too. In fact the Guardians seemed to be much less strict than I'd have expected in 1956. No one thought it odd for Lucas to be working late or for his cousin Hazel from the country to be keeping him company. Not that there were many people left in the building at this time of the evening.

Young Mr. George had obviously gone home, which was a pity. I'd have liked to see him again.

"A book—well, maybe," said Lucas, thoughtfully munching a biscuit. He had been about to light a cigarette three times, but I'd taken it out of his hand. I didn't want to be smelling of cigarette smoke again when I traveled back. "The code and the coordinates make sense, I like that bit, and it sounds like me. I've always had a weakness for codes. Only how did Lucy and Paul know it was in the thingy . . . in the *Yellow Horse* book?"

"*Green Rider*, Grandpa," I said patiently. "The book was in your library, and the piece of paper with the code was between its pages. Maybe Lucy and Paul left it there."

"But that's not logical. If they disappear into the past in 1994, then why do I leave a chest walled up in my own house so many years later?" He stopped prowling and bent over the books. "This is driving me crazy! Do you know what it's like to feel the solution is within reach? I wish travel into the future by chronograph were possible. Then you could interview me in person."

Suddenly I had an idea, and it was such a good one that I was tempted to pat myself spontaneously on the back. I thought of what Grandpa had told me last time we met. According to him, Lucy and Paul, getting bored with the time they spent elapsing here, had traveled farther back in the past and seen exciting things, like a performance of *Hamlet* in 1602, in Shakespeare's own lifetime.

"I know!" I cried, doing a little dance for joy.

My grandfather frowned. "You know what exactly?" he asked, intrigued.

"Suppose you send me farther back into the past with *your* chronograph?" I said excitedly. "Then I could meet Lucy and Paul and simply ask them."

Lucas raised his head. "And *when* would you meet them? We don't know what time they're hiding in."

"But we do know when they visited you here. If I joined them then, we could all discuss it together—"

My grandfather interrupted me. "But at the time of their visits here in 1948 and 1949, when they arrived from the years 1992 and 1993"—at the mention of each date, he tapped our notes and ran his forefinger along several lines with arrows pointing to them—"at those times, Lucy and Paul didn't know enough either, and they told me everything that they did know then. No, if you meet them at all it would have to be after they ran away with the chronograph." Once again he tapped our notes. "That would make sense. Anything else would just add to the confusion."

"Then . . . then I'll travel to the year 1912, when I met them once before, at Lady Tilney's house in Eaton Place."

"That would be a possibility, but it doesn't work out in terms of time." Lucas looked gloomily at the clock on the wall. "You weren't even sure of the exact date, let alone the time of day. Not forgetting that we'd have to read your blood into the chronograph first, otherwise you couldn't use it for time travel." He ruffled his hair up again. "And finally you'd have to get from here to Belgravia on your

KERSTIN GIER

own, and that's probably not so simple in 1912 . . . oh, and we'd need a costume . . . no, with the best will in the world, it can't be done in such a short time span. We'll have to think of something else. The solution's on the tip of my tongue. I just need more time to think it over, and maybe a cigarette. . . ."

I shook my head. I wasn't giving up so easily. I knew it was a good idea. "We could take the chronograph to just outside Lady Tilney's house in *this* time, and then I'd travel straight back to 1912—that would save a lot of time, wouldn't it? And as for the costume . . . why are you staring at me like that?"

All of a sudden, Lucas's eyes were wide open. "Oh, my God!" he whispered. *"That's* it!"

"What?"

"The chronograph! Granddaughter, you're a genius!" Lucas came around the table and hugged me.

"I'm a genius?" I repeated. It was my grandfather's turn to do a kind of dance of joy this time.

"Yes! And I'm another! Geniuses, the pair of us, because now we know what's hidden in the chest!"

Well, I didn't. "So what is it?"

"The chronograph!" cried Lucas.

"The chronograph?" I echoed him.

"It's only logical. Whatever period Lucy and Paul took it to, somehow or other it must have made its way back to me, and I hid it. For you! In my own house. Not particularly original, but very logical!"

"You think so?" I stared at him uncertainly. It seemed

to me very far-fetched, but then logic had never been my strong point.

"Trust me, granddaughter, I just know I'm right!" The enthusiasm in Lucas's face gave way to a frown. "Of course that opens up all sorts of new possibilities. Now we must think hard." He cast another glance at the clock on the wall. "Damn it, we need more time."

"I can try to get them to send me back to 1956 again next time I elapse," I said. "Only it won't be tomorrow afternoon, because that's when I have to go to that ball and see the count again." The mere idea immediately made me feel queasy once more, and not just because of Gideon.

"No, no, no!" cried Lucas. "That won't do. We must be one step ahead before you face the count again." He rubbed his forehead. "Think, think, think!"

"Can't you see the steam coming out of my ears? I've done nothing but think for the last hour," I assured him, but he'd obviously been talking to himself.

"First we must read your blood into the chronograph. You won't be able to do that without help in the year 2011; it's much too complicated. And then I must explain how to set the chronograph itself." Another anxious look at the clock. "If I call our doctor now, he could be here in half an hour, that is if we're lucky enough to find him at home. . . . The only trouble is, how do I explain why I want him to take some of my cousin Hazel's blood? Back when Lucy and Paul were here, we took their blood officially, for scientific purposes, but you're here incognito, and it must stay that way, or—"

"Hang on," I interrupted him. "Can't we take some of my blood ourselves?"

Lucas looked at me, intrigued. "Well, I'm trained in a good many skills, but I'm no use with medical needles. To be honest, I can't even stand the sight of blood. It turns my stomach—"

"I can take the blood from myself," I said.

"Really?" He looked astonished. "They teach you how to use medical needles in school in your time?"

"No, Grandpa, they don't," I said impatiently, "but we do learn that if you cut yourself with a knife, blood flows. Do you have a knife?"

Lucas hesitated. "Well, I don't know if that's a good idea."

"Okay, I have one of my own." I opened my schoolbag and took out the glasses case in which Lesley had hidden the Japanese vegetable knife, in case I was attacked while traveling in time and needed a weapon. My grandfather looked very surprised when I opened the case.

"Before you ask, no, this isn't part of the usual students' school equipment in 2011," I said.

Lucas swallowed, then he straightened his back and said, "All right. Then let's go to the Dragon Hall, stopping off on the way to collect a pipette from the doctor's laboratory." He glanced at the volumes of the *Annals* on the table and stuck one under his arm. "We'll take this with us. And the biscuits. For my nerves! Don't forget your bag."

"But why are we going to the Dragon Hall?" I put the glasses case back in my bag and stood up.

"That's where the chronograph is." Lucas closed the door behind me and listened for sounds in the corridor, but all was quiet. "If we meet anyone, we'll say I'm giving you a guided tour of the building, right, Cousin Hazel?"

I nodded. "You mean the chronograph is just left standing around? In our time, it's locked in a safe down in the cellar for fear of thieves."

"Its shrine in the Dragon Hall is locked too, of course," said Lucas, urging me on down the stairs. "But we're not really afraid of theft. There aren't even any time travelers among us who could use it. The only real excitement was when Lucy and Paul elapsed to spend time with us, but that's years ago now. At the moment, the chronograph isn't the focus of the Guardians' attention. Which is lucky for you and me, I'd say."

The building did indeed seem to be empty, although Lucas told me in a whisper that it was never entirely deserted. I looked longingly out of the windows at the mild summer evening. What a pity I couldn't go out again and explore the year 1956 more closely. Lucas noticed my glance and said, smiling, "Believe me, I'd far rather be sitting somewhere comfortable with you, smoking a cigarette, but we have work to do."

"You really should lay off the cigarettes, Grandpa. Smoking is so bad for your health. And please, do shave that mustache off. It doesn't suit you a bit."

"Sssh," whispered Lucas. "If anyone hears you calling me Grandpa, that really will take some explaining."

But we didn't meet anyone, and when we entered the

Dragon Hall a few minutes later, we could see the evening sun still sparkling on the Thames beyond the gardens and walls. The Dragon Hall was as overwhelmingly beautiful a sight in 1956 as in 2011, with its majestic proportions, deep windows, and elaborate painted carvings on the walls, and as always, I put my head back to admire the huge carved dragon winding its way over the ceiling past the huge chandeliers, looking as if it was just about to take off into the air.

Lucas bolted the door. He seemed much more nervous than I was, and his hands were shaking when he took the chronograph out of its shrine—a small cupboard—and put it on the table in the middle of the Hall.

"When I was sending Lucy and Paul back with it, it was a tremendous adventure. We had such fun," he said.

I thought of Lucy and Paul, and nodded. Yes, I'd met them only once, at Lady Tilney's house, but I could imagine what my grandfather meant. Stupidly, at the same moment, I thought of Gideon. Had his enjoyment of our adventures together been just pretense as well? Or only the bit where he pretended to love me?

I swiftly brought the Japanese vegetable knife and what I was about to do with it to the front of my mind instead. And guess what, it worked. At least, I didn't burst into tears.

My grandfather wiped the palms of his hands on his trousers. "I'm beginning to feel too old for these adventures," he said.

My eyes went to the chronograph. To me, it looked

exactly like the one that had sent me here, a complicated device full of flaps, levers, little drawers, cogwheels, and knobs, covered all over with miniature drawings.

"I don't object if you contradict me," said Lucas, sounding slightly injured. "Something along the lines of *but you're much too young to feel old!*"

"Oh. Yes, of course you are. Although that mustache makes you look decades older."

"Arista says it makes me look serious and statesman-like."

I merely raised my eyebrows in a meaningful way, and my young grandfather, muttering to himself, bent over the chronograph. "Now, watch carefully: you set the year with these ten little wheels. And before you ask why so many, we feed in the date in Roman numerals—I hope you know those."

"I think so." I took a spiral notebook and a pen out of my bag. I was never going to remember all this unless I wrote it down.

"And you set this one," said Lucas, pointing to another cogwheel, "to the month you want. But watch out—with this one, for some reason, and only this one, we work to an old Celtic calendar system in which month one is November, so October is number twelve."

I rolled my eyes. That was so typical of the Guardians! I'd suspected for a long time that they coded simple things to make them as complicated as possible, just to emphasize their own importance. But I gritted my teeth, and after about twenty minutes, I realized that the whole thing wasn't witchcraft after all, once you understood the system.

"I can do it now." I interrupted my grandfather as he was about to begin again from the beginning, and I closed my notebook. "Now we must read my blood in. And then . . . how late is it?"

"It's important that you don't make any mistakes at all setting the chronograph. . . ." Lucas was staring unhappily at the Japanese vegetable knife now that I'd taken it out of the glasses case again. "Otherwise you'll land somewhere . . . well, sometime else. And even worse, you won't have any control over when you go back to. Oh, my God, that knife looks terrible. Are you really going to do it?"

"Of course I am." I rolled up my sleeve. "I just don't know the best place to cut myself. A cut on the hand would attract attention when I travel back. And we wouldn't get more than a few drops out of a finger."

"Not if you nearly saw off your fingertip," said Lucas, with a shudder. "You bleed like a stuck pig then. I did it myself once—"

"I think I'll go for my forearm. Ready?" It was kind of funny that Lucas was more scared than I was.

He swallowed with difficulty and clutched the flowered teacup that was supposed to catch my blood. "Isn't there a main artery running along just there? Oh, my God, I feel weak at the knees. You'll end up bleeding to death here in 1956 because of your own grandfather's carelessness."

"Yes, it's a good big artery, but you'd have to slit it

lengthwise to bleed to death. Or so I've read. That's where many would-be suicides go wrong, and then they're found and survive, but next time, they know how to do it properly."

"For God's sake!" cried Lucas.

I did feel a little queasy myself, but there was no alternative. Desperate times call for desperate measures, as Lesley would say. I ignored Lucas's shocked expression and put the blade to the inside of my forearm about four inches above my wrist. Without pressing very hard, I ran it over the pale skin. It was meant to be only a trial cut, but it went deeper than I'd expected, and the thin red line quickly grew broader. Blood dripped from it. The pain, an uncomfortable burning sensation, began a second later. A thin but steady rivulet of blood ran into the teacup trembling in Lucas's hand. Perfect.

"Cuts through skin as if it were butter," I said, impressed. "Lesley said so. It really is a murderously sharp knife."

"Put it away," Lucas insisted. He looked as if he might throw up any moment. "Good heavens, you're a brave girl, a real Montrose. True to the family motto—"

I giggled. "Yes, I must inherit it from you."

Lucas's grin was rather wry. "Doesn't it hurt?"

"Of course it does," I said. "Is that enough?"

"Yes, it ought to be enough." Lucas retched a little.

"Want me to open a window?"

"All right." He put the cup down beside the chronograph and took a deep breath. "The rest is easy." He picked up the pipette. "I just have to put three drops of your blood into each of these two openings—see, under the tiny raven here and under the yin and yang sign? Then I turn the wheel and press this lever down. There we go. Hear that?"

Inside the chronograph, several little cogwheels began turning. There was a grinding, crunching, humming sound, and the air seemed to be warming up. The ruby flickered briefly, and then the sound of the little wheels died away and all was still again. "Uncanny, isn't it?"

I nodded, and tried to ignore the goose bumps all over me. "So now the blood of all the time travelers except Gideon is in the original chronograph, right? What would happen if his blood was read in as well?" I had folded Lucas's handkerchief and was pressing it to the cut.

"Apart from the fact that no one knows for sure, the information is strictly secret," said Lucas. Some color was coming back into his face. "Every Guardian has to kneel down and swear an oath never to mention the secret to anyone outside the Lodge. He swears on his life."

"Oh."

Lucas sighed. "But I tell you what . . . I have rather a weakness for breaking oaths." He pointed to a little compartment on the chronograph, decorated with a twelve-pointed star. "One thing's certain: when the blood of all the Twelve is read in, it will complete a process inside the chronograph, and something will land in this compartment. The prophesies speak of the 'essence' under the twelve-pointed star or, alternatively, of the philosopher's stone. *The precious stones shall all unite, the scent of time shall fill the night, once time links the fraternity, one man lives for eternity."*

"Is that all there is to the secret?" I said, disappointed. "Just vague, confused stuff again."

"Well, if you put all the hints together, it's fairly concrete. *Under the sign of the twelvefold star, all sickness and ills will flee afar.* Sounds as if, used properly, the substance produced in the chronograph will be able to cure all human diseases."

That sounded a good deal better.

"Well, in that case, I suppose going to all this trouble would pay off," I murmured, thinking of the Guardians' mania for secrecy and their complicated rules and rituals. If a cure for all diseases was the outcome, you could almost understand why they thought so well of themselves. Yes, it would be worth waiting a few hundred years for such a miraculous medicine. And Count Saint-Germain would definitely deserve respect for finding out about it and making the discovery possible. If only he weren't such a repellent character. . . .

"But Lucy and Paul doubt whether we really ought to believe the philosopher's stone theory," said Lucas, as if he had guessed my thoughts. "They say that someone who doesn't shrink from murdering his own great-great-great-grandfather won't necessarily have the good of all mankind at heart." He cleared his throat. "Has it stopped bleeding?"

"Not yet, but it's slowing down." I held my hand in the air to speed up the process. "And now what do we do? Shall I just try the thing out?"

"For heaven's sake, it's not a car to be taken for a test drive," said Lucas, wringing his hands.

"Why not?" I asked. "Wasn't that the whole idea?"

"Well, yes," he said, squinting at the thick folio volume he had brought. "I suppose you're right. At least that way we can make sure it works, even if we don't have much time left." Suddenly he was all eager again. Leaning forward, he opened the volume of the *Annals*. "We have to take care not to pick a date when you'd burst into the middle of a Lodge meeting here. Or run into one of the de Villiers brothers. They spent hours and hours of their lives elapsing in the Dragon Hall."

"Could I maybe meet Lady Tilney? Alone?" I'd had another good idea. "Preferably sometime after 1912."

"I wonder if that would be wise." Lucas was leafing through the volume. "We don't want to make things more complicated than they already are."

"But we can't afford to waste our few chances," I cried, thinking of what Lesley kept on telling me. I was to exploit every opportunity, she said, and above all, ask as many questions as I could think of. "Who knows when the next chance may come?" I asked. "There could be something else in the chest, and it might not get me any farther. When did you and I first meet?"

"On 12 August 1948, at twelve noon," said Lucas, deep in the Annals. "I'll never forget it."

"Exactly, and to make sure you never forget it, I'm going to write it down for you," I said. Yes, I really was a

bit of a genius, I thought. I scribbled on a page in my notebook:

For Lord Lucas Montrose—important!!!
12 August 1948, 12 noon, the alchemical laboratory.
Please come alone.
Gwyneth Shepherd

I tore the page out with a flourish and folded it.

My grandfather glanced up from the folio for a moment. "I could send you to the year 1852, 16 February, at
midnight. That's where Lady Tilney elapses after leaving
her own time on 25 December 1929, at nine A.M.," he murmured. "Poor thing, she couldn't even spend Christmas
Day in comfort at home. At least they gave her a kerosene
lamp. Listen, this is what it says here: *12:30 P.M.: Lady Tilney
comes back from the year 1852 seeming very cheerful. By the light
of the kerosene lamp she took, she finished making two crochet-
work piglets for the charity bazaar on Twelfth Night, to be held
this year on the theme of Country Life.*" He turned to look at
me. "Crochet-work pigs! Can you imagine it? Of course,
she may get the shock of her life if you suddenly appear
out of nowhere. Do we really want to risk it?"

"She's armed only with a crochet hook, and they have
blunt ends as far as I remember." I bent over the chronograph. "Right, first the year. 1852, that begins with M, right?
MDCCCLII. And the month of February is number three
in the Celtic calendar you were talking about—no, four—"

"What are you doing? We have to bandage that cut and do some thinking first."

"No time," I said. "The day . . . this lever sets it, right?"

Lucas was looking anxiously over my shoulder. "Not so fast! It has to be exactly right, or else . . . or else . . ." He was looking likely to throw up again. "And you must never be holding the chronograph, or you'll take it into the past with you. And then you couldn't get back."

"Like Lucy and Paul," I whispered.

"Let's choose a brief three-minute window of time, to be on the safe side. Make it twelve thirty to twelve thirty-three A.M. Then at least she'll be sitting comfortably making crochet-work piglets. If she happens to be asleep, don't wake her, or she might have a heart attack—"

"But then wouldn't it say so in the *Annals*?" I interrupted him. "When I met Lady Tilney I got the impression that she was a pretty tough character, not the sort to fall down in a faint."

Lucas moved the chronograph over to the window and put it down behind the curtain. "We can be sure there won't be any furniture standing here. No need to roll your eyes. Timothy de Villiers once made a crash landing on a table and broke his leg."

"So suppose Lady Tilney is standing right here looking dreamily out at the night? Oh, don't look at me like that! Only joking, Grandpa." I pushed him gently aside, knelt on the floor in front of the chronograph, and opened the little flap just under the ruby. It was exactly the right size for my finger.

"Wait a moment! Your cut!"

"We can see to that in three minutes' time. See you then," I said, taking a deep breath and pressing my fingertip down firmly on the needle.

The familiar dizzy roller-coaster sensation came over me, and as the red light began to glow and Lucas was saying, "But I still have to . . . ," everything blurred before my eyes.

While rumor has it that the Jacobite army has reached Derby and is now advancing on London, we have moved into our new headquarters. We sincerely hope that reports of 10,000 French soldiers joining the forces of Prince Charles Edward Stuart, the Young Pretender to the throne (known to the populace as Bonnie Prince Charlie), will prove mistaken, so that we can celebrate a peaceful Christmas in the city. It is impossible to imagine more suitable accommodation for the Guardians than the venerable buildings here in the Temple. The Knights Templar themselves were, after all, guardians of great mysteries. Not only is Temple Church within sight of our premises, its catacombs are connected to ours. Officially we will be going about our everyday professions from the Temple, but there will also be accommodation for adepts, novices, and guests, and of course for our servants, as well as several laboratories designed for alchemical purposes. We are glad to say that the slanders spread by Lord Alastair (see report of 2 December) have not succeeded in disrupting the good relations of Count Saint-Germain with the Prince of Wales and that, thanks to the patronage of His Highness, we have been able to acquire this complex of buildings. The solemn ceremony in which the secret documents of the Lodge are transferred from the hands of Count Saint-Germain to the members of the Inner Circle is to take place in the Dragon Hall today.

From *The Annals of the Guardians*

18 December 1745

Report: Sir Oliver Newton, Inner Circle

fOUR

IT TOOK ME a few seconds to get used to the different lighting conditions. The hall was lit only by an oil lamp on the table. The picture I saw by its warm but meager light was a comfortable still life: a basket, several balls of pink wool, a teapot with a felt tea cozy, and a cup decorated with roses. Also Lady Tilney, who was sitting on a chair doing crochet, and at the sight of me let her hands sink to her lap. She was obviously older than when we last met, with silver strands in her red hair, which had been neatly permed. All the same, she still had the same majestic, unapproachable look as my grandmother. And she didn't look in the least likely to scream or go for me brandishing her crochet hook.

"Happy Christmas," she said.

"Happy Christmas," I replied, slightly bewildered. For a moment I didn't know what to say next, but then I pulled myself together. "Don't worry, I'm not after some of your blood or anything like that." I stepped out of the shadow of the curtain.

"Oh, we settled all that business about the blood long ago, Gwyneth," said Lady Tilney, with a touch of reproof in her voice, as if I ought to know exactly what she was talking about. "I've been wondering when you'd turn up again. Tea?"

"No, thank you. Look, I'm afraid I only have a few minutes." I went a step closer and handed her the note. "My grandfather has to get this so that . . . well, so that everything will happen the way it did happen. It's very important."

"I understand." Lady Tilney took the note and unfolded it at her leisure. She didn't seem in the least annoyed.

"Why were you expecting me?" I asked.

"Because you told me not to be scared when you visited me. Unfortunately you didn't say when that would be, so I've been waiting years and years for you to try scaring me." She laughed quietly. "But making crochet pigs has a very soothing effect. To be honest, it easily sends you to sleep out of sheer boredom."

I had a polite "It's for a good cause, though," on the tip of my tongue, but when I glanced at the basket, I exclaimed instead, "Oh, aren't they cute!" And they really were. Much larger than I'd have expected, like real soft toys, and true to life.

"Take one," said Lady Tilney.

"Do you mean it?" I thought of Caroline and put my hand into the basket. The pigs felt all soft and fluffy.

"Angora and cashmere wool," said Lady Tilney with a touch of pride in her voice. "I never use any other. Most people crochet with sheep's wool, but it's so scratchy."

"Er, yes. Thank you." Clutching the little pink pig to my breast, I spent a moment pulling my thoughts together. Where had we been? I cleared my throat. "When do we meet next time? In the past, I mean?"

"That was 1912. Although it's not next time from my point of view." She sighed. "What exciting days those were—"

"Oh, hell!" My stomach was doing its roller-coaster ride again. Why on earth hadn't we chosen a larger window of time? "Then anyway, you know more than I do," I said hastily. "There's no time to go into detail, but . . . maybe you can give me some good advice to help me?" I had taken a couple of steps back in the direction of the window, out of the circle of lamplight.

"Advice?"

"Yes. Well, something like: beware of . . . ?" I looked at her expectantly.

"Beware of what?" Lady Tilney looked back at me just as expectantly.

"That's just what I don't know! What *ought* I to beware of?"

"Pastrami sandwiches, for one thing, and too much sunlight. It's bad for the complexion," said Lady Tilney firmly—and then she blurred in front of my eyes and I was back in the year 1956.

Pastrami sandwiches, for heaven's sake! I ought to

have asked *who* I ought to beware of, not *what*. But it was too late now. I'd lost the opportunity.

"What on earth is that?" cried Lucas, when he saw the piglet.

Yes, and instead of making use of every precious second to get information out of Lady Tilney, I'd been idiot enough to spend time on a pink soft toy. "It's a crochet pig, Grandfather, you can see it is," I said wearily. I was really disappointed in myself! "Angora and cashmere. Other people use scratchy sheep's wool."

"Our test seems to have worked, anyway," said Lucas, shaking his head. "You can use the chronograph, and we can make a date to meet. In my house."

"It was over much too quickly," I wailed. "I didn't find anything out."

"At least you have a . . . er, a pig, and Lady Tilney didn't have a heart attack. Or did she?"

I shook my head helplessly. "Of course not."

Lucas put the chronograph back in its velvet wrappings and took it over to the shrine. "Don't worry. This way we have enough time to smuggle you back down to the cellar and go on making plans while we wait for you to travel back. Although if that useless Cantrell has slept off his hangover, I don't know how we'll talk our way out of it this time."

I FELT positively euphoric when I finally landed back in the chronograph room in my own time. So maybe the trip to acquire the pink piglet (I'd stuffed it into my schoolbag) hadn't brought much in the way of results, but Lucas and I had worked out a cunning plan. If the original chronograph really was in that chest, we wouldn't have to depend on chance anymore.

"Any special incidents?" Mr. Marley asked.

Well, let's think: I've spent all afternoon conspiring with my grandfather, breaking all the rules. We read my blood into the chronograph, then we sent me back to the year 1852 to conspire with Lady Tilney. Okay, I hadn't actually been conspiring with her, but it was a forbidden meeting all the same.

"The lightbulb in the cellar flickered now and then," I said, "and I learned French vocabulary by heart."

Mr. Marley bent over the journal, and in his neat, small handwriting, he actually did enter *1943 hours, the Ruby back from 1956, did her homework there, lightbulb flickered.* I suppressed a giggle. He had to keep such meticulous records of everything! I'd bet his star sign was Virgo. But it was later than I liked. I hoped Mum wouldn't send Lesley home before I was back.

However, Mr. Marley didn't seem to be in any hurry. He screwed the top back on his fountain pen infuriatingly slowly.

"I can find my own way out," I said.

"No, you mustn't," he said in alarm. "Of course I'll escort you to the limousine." Mr. Marley closed the journal and stood up. "And I have to blindfold you—you know I do."

Sighing, I let him tie the black scarf around my head. "I still don't understand why I'm not supposed to know the way to this room." Quite apart from the fact that I knew it perfectly well by now.

"Because that's what it says in the *Annals*," said Mr. Marley, sounding surprised.

"What?" I exclaimed. "My name's in the *Annals*, and they say I mustn't know the way here and back? Why not?"

Now Mr. Marley's voice was distinctly uncomfortable. "Naturally your name isn't there, or all these years the other Ruby, I mean Miss Charlotte, of course, wouldn't have—" He cleared his throat, then fell silent, and I heard him opening the door. "Allow me," he said, taking my arm. He led me out into the corridor. I couldn't see him, but I felt sure he was blushing furiously again. I felt as if I were walking along beside a radiant heater.

"What exactly does it say about me there?" I asked.

"I'm sorry, but I really can't . . . I've said too much already." You could almost hear him wringing his hands, or at least the hand that wasn't holding me. And this character claimed to be a descendant of the dangerous Rakoczy! What a joke!

"Please, *Leo*," I said, sounding as friendly as I could.

"I'm sorry, but you won't learn any more from me." The heavy door latched behind us. Mr. Marley let go of my arm to lock it, which seemed to take a good ten minutes, while I tried to save a bit of time by taking a firm step forward, not too easy with my eyes blindfolded. Mr. Marley had grabbed my arm again, and a good thing, because without a pilot, I could have run straight into a wall down here. I decided to try flattering him. It couldn't hurt.

Maybe he'd be prepared to come out with more information later.

"Did you know that I've met your ancestor in person?" In fact I'd even taken a photograph of him, but unfortunately I couldn't show it to Mr. Marley. He'd have told tales of me for bringing forbidden objects back from the past.

"Really? I envy you. The baron must have been an impressive personality."

"Er, yes, very impressive." You bet he was! That creepy old junkie! "He asked me about Transylvania, but unfortunately there wasn't much I could tell him about it."

"Yes, living in exile must have been hard for him," said Mr. Marley. Next moment, he let out a shrill "eek!"

A rat, I thought, and in panic I snatched the blindfold off. But it wasn't a rat that had made Mr. Marley squeal. It was Gideon. Still as unshaven as this afternoon, in fact more so, but with his eyes extremely bright and watchful. And looking so incredibly, outrageously, impossibly good.

"Only me," he said, smiling.

"I can see that," groused Mr. Marley. "You scared me stiff."

Me too. My lower lip began trembling again, and I dug my teeth into it to keep the stupid thing still.

"You can go home now. I'll escort Gwyneth to the car," said Gideon, holding out his hand to me as if I was sure to take it.

I looked as haughty as you can with your front teeth

digging into your lower lip—probably I just looked like a beaver, if a haughty beaver—and ignored his hand.

"You can't," said Mr. Marley. "It's my job to escort Miss Gwyneth to the—aargh!" He was staring at me in horror. "Oh, Miss Gwyneth, why did you take the scarf off? That's against the rules."

"I thought it was a rat you'd seen," I said, casting a dark glance at Gideon. "And I wasn't all that wrong, either."

"Now look what you've done!" said Mr. Marley accusingly to Gideon. "I don't know what I can . . . the rules say that . . . and if we—"

"Don't be so uptight, Marley. Come on, Gwen, let's go."

"But you can't. . . . I must insist that . . . ," stammered Mr. Marley. "And . . . and . . . and you have no right to tell me what to do—"

"Then go tell tales of me." Gideon took my arm and simply hauled me on. I thought of resisting, but then I realized that would only lose me even more time. We'd probably still be standing here arguing tomorrow morning. So I let him lead me away, glancing back apologetically at Mr. Marley. "See you, Leo."

"Yes, exactly. See you, Leo," said Gideon.

"You . . . you haven't heard the last of this," stammered Mr. Marley, behind us. His face was shining like a beacon in the dark corridor.

"No, sure, we're trembling with fright already." Gideon didn't seem to mind that Mr. Marley could still hear him as he added, "Stupid show-off."

I waited until we had turned the next corner and then

shook myself free of his hand and quickened my pace until I was almost running.

"Ambitious to compete in the Olympic Games?" inquired Gideon.

I spun around to face him. "What do you want?" Lesley would have been proud of the way I spat that at him. "I'm in a hurry."

"I only wanted to make sure you understood my apology this afternoon." All the mockery had gone out of his voice now.

But not out of mine. "Yup, I did," I snorted. "Which doesn't mean I accepted it."

"Gwen—"

"Okay, you don't have to say you really like me again. Guess what, I liked you too. In fact, I liked you a lot. But that's all over now." I was running up the spiral staircase as fast as I could go, with the result that by the time I reached the top, I was right out of breath. I felt like hanging over the banisters gasping for air. But I wasn't going to expose my weakness like that. Particularly as Gideon didn't seem to have been exerting himself at all to keep up. So I hurried on, until he grabbed my wrist and made me stand still. I winced as his fingers pressed on my cut. It started bleeding again.

"It's okay for you to hate me, really, I don't have any problem with that," said Gideon, looking seriously into my eyes. "But I've discovered things that make it necessary for you and me to work together. So that you . . . so that we'll get out of all this alive."

I tried to free myself, but he only held my wrist more firmly. "What sort of things?" I asked, although I would rather have shrieked, "Ouch!"

"I don't know exactly, not yet. But it could turn out that I was wrong about Lucy and Paul and their intentions. So it's important for you to—" He stopped, let go of me, and looked at the palm of his hand. "Is that *blood*?"

Damn. I mustn't look guilty. "Nothing to speak of. I cut myself on the edge of a piece of paper at school this morning. So to stick to the subject. Until you can be more specific"—I felt really proud of coming out with that phrase!—"I'm definitely not working with you on anything."

Gideon tried to take my arm again. "Here, that cut looks nasty. Let me look. . . . We'd better go to see Dr. White. He may still be in the building."

"You probably mean you don't want to say anything more precise about what you claim to have discovered." I had my arm stretched right out, to keep him away and so that he couldn't examine my wound.

"Because I'm not quite sure myself what to make of it yet," said Gideon. And like Lucas just now, he added in a rather desperate tone of voice, "I need more time!"

"Who doesn't?" I started off again. We had already reached Madame Rossini's studio, and it wasn't far from there to the front door. "Good-bye, Gideon. See you tomorrow—unfortunately."

I was secretly waiting for him to grab me and hold me

back again, but he didn't. He didn't follow me, either. I'd have loved to see the expression on his face, but I didn't turn back to look at him. Anyway, that would have been a silly thing to do, because then he'd have seen the tears pouring down my cheeks once more.

NICK WAS WAITING at the front door of our house for me. "At last!" he said. "I wanted us to start without you, but Mr. Bernard said we ought to wait. He's made sure the flush of the toilet in the blue bathroom is out of order, so no one can use it, and he says he'll have to take out the tiles there to dismantle the cistern. We've bolted the secret door on the inside. Clever, eh?"

"Very clever."

"But Lady Arista and Aunt Glenda will be home in an hour's time, and they're sure to say he'd better put off the repair work until tomorrow."

"Then we'll have to hurry." I gave him a quick hug and dropped a kiss on his untidy red hair. There had to be time for that! "You didn't tell anyone, did you?"

Nick looked a little guilty. "Only Caroline. She was so . . . oh, well, you know how she always knows when there's something in the air, and she asked lots of questions. But she'll keep quiet and help us to throw Mum, Aunt Maddy, and Charlotte off the scent."

"Particularly Charlotte," I said, talking more to myself than Nick.

"They're all still upstairs in the dining room. Mum invited Lesley to stay to supper."

In the dining room, they were just leaving the table. Which meant that Aunt Maddy moved to her armchair by the fireplace and put her feet up while Mr. Bernard and Mum cleared the supper things away. They were all pleased to see me, all but Charlotte, that is. Oh, well, maybe she was just very good at hiding her delight.

Xemerius came down from the chandelier and cried, "There you are at last! I was nearly dying of boredom."

Although there was still a delicious smell of supper and Mum said she was keeping something hot for me, I heroically claimed that I wasn't hungry because I'd already had supper at the Temple. My stomach cramped indignantly at this shocking lie, but I couldn't possibly waste time satisfying its demands.

Lesley grinned at me. "It was a wonderful curry. I could hardly stop eating. My mum is in one of her terrible experimental phases right now. Even our dog won't eat the macrobiotic stuff she cooks these days."

"All the same, you look quite . . . well, let's say well nourished," said Charlotte sharply. She'd braided her hair and pinned it up again, but a few little locks had come loose and were framing her face very prettily. How could anyone look so beautiful and be so mean?

"You're lucky. I wish I had a dog, too," said Caroline. "Or any kind of pet."

"Never mind. We have Nick," said Charlotte. "That's almost like having a monkey."

"Not forgetting you, you nasty, poisonous spider!" said Nick.

"Well said, young man!" crowed Xemerius, back up on the chandelier. He clapped his paws.

Mum was helping Mr. Bernard to stack the dirty dishes in the dumbwaiter. "You know you can't have a pet because Aunt Glenda's allergic to animals, Caroline."

"We could get a naked mole rat," said Caroline. "That would be better than nothing."

Charlotte opened her mouth and then shut it again, obviously because she couldn't think of anything nasty to say about naked mole rats.

Aunt Maddy had made herself comfortable in her chair. She pointed sleepily to her round, rosy cheek. "Give your old great-aunt a kiss, Gwyneth. It's a shame we see so little of you these days. Last night I had another dream about you, and I have to say it wasn't a nice dream. . . ."

"Could you tell me about it later?" As I kissed her, I whispered in her ear, "And could you please help to keep Charlotte away from the blue bathroom?"

Aunt Maddy's dimples deepened, and she winked at me. All of a sudden, she looked wide awake again.

Mum, who had a date to meet a friend of hers, was in a much better mood today than for the last few days. No worried expression, no exaggerated sighing when she looked at me. To my surprise, she even said Lesley could stay a bit longer and spared us the usual lecture on the dangers of traveling by bus at night. Even better, she said Nick could help Mr. Bernard to repair the lavatory cistern that was supposed to have gone wrong, however long it took. Caroline was the only one out of luck. She was sent to bed. "But I want to be there when they discover the tr—when they dismantle the cistern," she begged, holding back a tear when she couldn't soften Mum's heart.

"I'm going to bed now too," Charlotte told Caroline. "With a good book."

"*In the Shadow of Vampire Mountain*," said Xemerius. "She's reached page 413, where the young, although also undead, Christopher St. Ives finally gets beautiful Mary Lou into bed."

I looked at him with amusement, and to my surprise, he suddenly seemed slightly embarrassed. "I only peeked at it, honest," he said, jumping off the chandelier and down to the windowsill.

Aunt Maddy quickly moved in on Charlotte's announcement. "Oh, my dear, I thought you might keep me company in the music room for a while," she said. "I'd love a game of Scrabble."

Charlotte rolled her eyes. "Last time we had to throw you out of the game because you insisted that there was such a word as *earcat*."

"And so there is. It's a cat with ears." Aunt Maddy got up and took Charlotte's arm. "But I don't mind if you say it doesn't count today."

"Nor do *springbird* and *cowjuice*," said Charlotte.

"Oh, but there's definitely a springbird, darling," said Aunt Maddy, winking at me again.

I hugged my mum before going up to my room with

Lesley. "And by the way, I'm to give you regards from Falk de Villiers. He wanted to know if you have a steady boyfriend."

I'd have done better to keep this message until Charlotte and Aunt Maddy had left the room, because they both stopped dead, rooted to the spot, and looked at Mum with great interest.

"What?" Mum blushed slightly. "And what did you tell him?"

"Well, I said it was ages since you'd been out with a man, and the last guy you did see regularly was always scratching himself when he thought no one was looking."

"You never said that!"

I laughed. "No, I didn't."

"Oh, are you two talking about that good-looking banker Arista wanted to marry you off to, Grace? Mr. Itchman," said Aunt Maddy. "Bet you he had lice or something."

Lesley giggled.

"His name was Hitchman, Aunt Maddy." My mother rubbed her arms, shivering. "A good thing I never got to find out for sure about the lice or whatever he had. What did you really tell him, then? Falk, I mean."

"Nothing," I said. "Want me to ask him next time I get the chance whether *he* has a steady girlfriend?"

"Don't you dare," said Mum. Then she grinned and added, "He doesn't. I happen to know that from a friend. She has a friend who knows him quite well . . . not that I'd be interested in any of that."

"No, of course not!" said Xemerius. He flew off the windowsill and settled in the middle of the dining table. "Can we finally get a move on?"

HALF AN HOUR later, Lesley was up to date with the latest developments, and Caroline was the owner of a genuine vintage pink crochet piglet from the year 1929. When I told her where it came from, she was very impressed and said she was going to call her pig Margaret in honor of Lady Tilney. She dropped happily off to sleep cuddling the piglet when everything was quiet again.

Except for Mr. Bernard's hammering and chiseling, of course. That could be heard all over the house. We'd never have managed to get any bricks out of the wall in secret. And Mr. Bernard and Nick didn't get the little chest up to my room in secret either. Aunt Maddy came in right behind them.

"She caught us on the stairs," said Nick apologetically.

"And she recognized that little chest at once," said Aunt Maddy. She sounded excited. "Oh, it belonged to my brother Lucas! It stood in the library for years, and then—just before his death—it suddenly disappeared. So I think I have a right to know what you're planning to do with it."

Mr. Bernard sighed. "I'm afraid we had no choice," he told me. "Lady Arista and Miss Glenda were coming home at that very moment."

"Yes, so I was the lesser of two evils, right?" Aunt Maddy smiled with self-satisfaction.

"Just so long as Charlotte doesn't know what was going on," said Lesley.

"Don't worry, she went to her room in a fury just because I put down the word *cardscissors*."

"Which as everyone knows are scissors for cutting card," said Xemerius. "Essential in every household."

Aunt Maddy knelt beside the chest on the floor and stroked its dusty lid. "Wherever did you find it?"

Mr. Bernard looked inquiringly at me, and I shrugged my shoulders. Since she was here anyway, we might as well let her in on the whole story.

"I walled it up on your brother's instructions," said Mr. Bernard, with dignity. "That was on the evening before his death."

"Only the evening before his death?" I echoed him. It was news to me too.

"And what's in it?" Aunt Maddy wanted to know. She was standing up again, looking for somewhere to sit. Since she couldn't see anywhere else, she sat down beside Lesley on the edge of my bed.

"Yes, that's the vital question," said Nick.

"The vital question," said Mr. Bernard, "is how we're going to open the chest. Because the key to it disappeared, along with Lord Montrose's diaries, at the time of that burglary."

"What burglary?" asked Lesley and Nick in chorus.

"Thieves broke in on the day of your grandfather's funeral," Aunt Maddy explained. "While we were all saying our last good-byes to him at the graveyard. Such a sad day, wasn't it, dear Mr. Bernard?" she added, looking up at him. He was listening with no sign of emotion.

The story did seem vaguely familiar. As far as I remembered, the burglars had been disturbed and ran away before they could take anything. But when I told Nick and Lesley that, Aunt Maddy contradicted me.

"No, no, my little angel. The police only assumed that nothing had been stolen because all the ready cash, the deeds to this house, and valuable jewelry were still in the safe."

"And that made sense only if it was the diaries, and nothing else, that the burglars were after," said Mr. Bernard. "I allowed myself to put that hypothesis to the police at the time, but no one believed me. What's more, there was no sign that anyone had tried breaking into the safe. They'd have had to know the combination. So it was thought that Lord Montrose must have put his diaries somewhere else."

"I believed you, dear Mr. Bernard," said Aunt Maddy. "But I'm sorry to say that no one thought my opinion was worth much at the time. Or at any other time, really," she added wistfully. "Anyway, three days before Lucas died, I had a vision, and I was convinced that he hadn't died a natural death. But as usual, people thought I was crazy. Yet it was such a clear vision: a huge panther leaped at Lucas's chest and tore his throat to pieces."

"Oh, *very* clear," muttered Lesley, and I asked, "What about the diaries?"

"They never turned up," said Mr. Bernard. "Nor did

the key to this chest, which was with them, because Lord Montrose always kept it stuck inside his current diary, as I know because I saw it with my own eyes."

Xemerius was flapping his wings impatiently. "Why don't you stop all this nattering and fetch a crowbar?"

"But . . . but Grandpa had a heart attack," said Nick.

"Well, that's what it looked like after the event, anyway." Aunt Maddy sighed deeply. "After all, he was eighty years old. He collapsed at his desk in his office at the Temple. My vision obviously wasn't a good enough reason for them to have an autopsy done. Arista was very cross with me when I wanted her to insist."

"This is giving me goose bumps," whispered Nick, moving a little closer and snuggling up to me. For a while, no one said anything. Xemerius kept circling around the ceiling light saying, "Oh, get a move on!" But of course I was the only one who could hear him.

"That adds up to a lot of coincidences," said Lesley at last.

"Yes," I agreed. "Lucas has the chest walled up, and purely by chance, he dies next day."

"Right, and purely by chance, I have a vision three days before his death," said Aunt Maddy.

"And purely by chance, his diaries vanish without trace," added Nick.

"And purely by chance," said Mr. Bernard almost apologetically, "the key that Miss Lesley here is wearing on a chain around her neck is the very image of the key to this chest. I couldn't help staring at it all through supper."

Lesley put her hand to her chain, looking baffled. "What, this one? The key to my heart?"

"But that can't be it," I said. "I pinched it from a desk drawer in the Temple sometime in the eighteenth century. That would be rather too much of a coincidence, don't you think?"

"Chance is the only legitimate ruler of the universe, as Einstein said. And he ought to know." Aunt Maddy leaned forward to look at the key with interest.

"It wasn't Einstein, it was Napoleon," Xemerius called down from the ceiling. "And Napoleon didn't have all his marbles at the time."

"I could be wrong, of course. Old keys look very like one another," said Mr. Bernard.

Lesley fiddled with the clasp of the chain and handed me the key. "It's worth a try, anyway."

I passed the key on to Mr. Bernard. The rest of us were holding our collective breath as he knelt by the chest and put the key into the delicate little lock. It turned easily.

"That's amazing!" whispered Lesley.

Aunt Maddy nodded, satisfied. "You see, it's not just chance and coincidence! It's fate. And now, Mr. Bernard, don't keep us in suspense any longer. Lift the lid."

"Just a moment!" I took a deep breath. "It's important for all of us here in this room to keep absolutely quiet about what's inside the chest!"

Look how fast I'd caught the habit! Only a couple of days ago, I'd been grumbling about the Guardians and all their secrecy, and here I was, practically founding a secret society of my own. All we needed was for me to say everyone must be blindfolded before leaving my room.

"Sounds like you already know what's in it," remarked Xemerius. He had already tried putting his head through the wood to see inside the chest several times, but he had withdrawn it again each time, coughing.

"Of course we won't breathe a word," said Nick, sounding slightly insulted, and Lesley and Aunt Maddy also looked quite indignant. There was even one eyebrow raised on Mr. Bernard's impassive face.

"Swear it," I demanded, and to make sure they realized how seriously I meant it, I added, "Swear by your lives!"

Aunt Maddy was the only one to jump up and put her hand enthusiastically on her heart. The others were still hesitating. "Can't we swear by anything else?" grumbled Lesley. "I'd have thought our left hands would do."

I shook my head. "Go on, swear it!"

"I swear by my life!" cried Aunt Maddy happily.

"I swear," murmured the others, rather embarrassed. Nick began giggling nervously, because Aunt Maddy had begun humming the national anthem to show what a solemn occasion it was.

When Mr. Bernard—glancing at me first, to make sure that I agreed—lifted the lid of the chest, it creaked slightly. He carefully unfolded several old velvet wrappings, and when he had finally revealed what was inside them, everyone but me went *ooh!* and *ah!* in surprise. Even Xemerius cried, "Wow, the cunning old devil!"

"Is that by any chance what I think it is?" asked Aunt Maddy after a while. Her eyes were still as round as saucers.

"Yes," I said, pushing the hair back from my face. "It's a chronograph."

NICK AND AUNT MADDY had left reluctantly, Mr. Bernard inconspicuously, and Lesley only under protest. However, her mother had already rung her mobile twice to ask whether she had (a) by any chance been murdered, or was (b) lying hacked to pieces somewhere in Hyde Park, so really she had no choice.

First, however, she made *me* swear that I would stick strictly to our master plan. "By your life," she demanded, and I went along with her. Although unlike Aunt Maddy, I spared her the national anthem.

At last my room was quiet again, and two hours later, after my mum had put her head around the door to look in on me, so was the whole house. I had struggled hard with myself, deciding whether to try the chronograph out right away or not. It wouldn't make any difference to Lucas whether I traveled back to 1956 today, or tomorrow, or not for another four weeks. And a good night's sleep for a change would probably work wonders for me. On the other hand, tomorrow I had to go to that ball and face Count Saint-Germain again, and I still didn't know just what he was planning.

I went downstairs with the chronograph wrapped in

my dressing gown. "Why are you dragging that thing all around the house?" asked Xemerius. "You could simply travel back in time from your own room."

"Yes, but how do I know who was sleeping there in 1956? And then I'd have to go all over the house, and I might be taken for a burglar again. No, I want to travel straight to the secret passage. Then I won't risk being seen by someone when I land. Lucas will be waiting for me in front of Great-great-great-great-uncle Hugh's portrait."

"You get the number of greats different every time," Xemerius pointed out. "If I were you, I'd just say *my fat forefather.*"

I ignored him and concentrated on the creaking steps on the stairs. A little later, I was pushing the portrait soundlessly aside—Mr. Bernard had oiled the mechanism, so it didn't squeal. He had also fitted bolts to both the bathroom door and the door out to the stairs. I hesitated to bolt them both at first, because if for some reason I arrived outside the secret passage when I traveled back, I'd have shut myself out of the passage and the chronograph in to it.

"Cross your fingers and hope it works," I told Xemerius when I finally knelt on the floor, pushed my forefinger into the little flap underneath the ruby, and pressed it firmly down on the needle. (By the way, you don't get used to the pain. It hurts like hell every time.)

"I would if I had any," Xemerius was saying—then he had disappeared, and the chronograph with him.

I took a deep breath, but the musty air in the corridor didn't really help me to get over the roller-coaster feeling. I stood up rather unsteadily, grasped Nick's flashlight more firmly, and opened the door out into the stairway. It was creaking and squealing again like something in a classic horror movie as the painting swung aside.

"Ah, there you are," whispered Lucas. He'd been waiting on the other side of it, and he was also armed with a flashlight. "For a split second I was afraid it might be a ghost appearing on the stroke of midnight—"

"In Peter Rabbit pajamas?"

"I had a drink or so earlier because . . . but I'm glad that I was right about the contents of the chest."

"Yes, and luckily the chronograph still works. We have an hour, as agreed."

"Then come along, quick, before he starts bawling again and wakes the whole house up."

"Before who starts bawling?" I whispered back in alarm.

"Little Harry, of course. He's getting teeth or something. Keeps on howling like a siren, anyway."

"*Uncle* Harry?"

"Arista says we have to leave him to cry for educational reasons or he'll grow up to be a wimp. But it's more than anyone can stand. Sometimes I go in to see him on the sly, wimp or no wimp. If you sing him 'The Fox Went Out on a Chilly Night,' he stops yelling."

"Poor Uncle Harry. Sounds like a classic case of early childhood imprinting, if you ask me." No wonder he was so keen on shooting everything he could turn his sporting gun on these days—wild duck, stags, grouse, pheasants, and in particular, foxes. He was chairman of a society campaigning for it to be legal to hunt foxes with hounds again in Gloucestershire. "Maybe you ought to try singing him something else. And buy him a cuddly fox toy."

We reached the library unnoticed, and when Lucas had closed the door and locked it behind us, he breathed a sigh of relief. "We made it!" The room itself was much the same as in my own time, except that the two armchairs by the fireplace had different covers, a Scottish plaid pattern in green and blue instead of the present cream roses on a moss-green background. There was a teapot on a warming plate on the little table between the chairs, plus two cups and—I closed my eyes, and when I opened them again it was true, it wasn't a hallucination—there was a plate of sandwiches! Not dry biscuits, but real, nourishing sandwiches! I couldn't believe it. Lucas dropped into one of the armchairs and pointed to the other one.

"Do sit down, and if you're hungry, help yours—" But I already *had* helped myself. I was digging my teeth into the first sandwich.

"You've saved my life," I said with my mouth full. Then something occurred to me. "They're not pastrami sandwiches, I hope?"

"No, ham and cucumber," said Lucas. "You look tired."

"So do you."

"I still haven't quite recovered from all the excitement yesterday evening. Just now, like I told you, I had to have a whisky. Well, two whiskies. But now two things are clear to me . . . yes, help yourself to another sandwich, and take the time to chew it properly. It's quite alarming to see you bolt them down like that."

"Carry on," I said. Oh, how good the food tasted! I felt I'd never in my life eaten such delicious sandwiches. "What two things are clear to you?"

"Well, first, good as it is to see you, our meetings must take place much farther in the future if they're to produce results. We should meet as close as possible to your date of birth. By then, perhaps I'll have understood what Lucy and Paul are planning and why, and I'll certainly know more than I do now. That means next time we meet should be in 1993. Then I'll also be able to help you over this business with the ball."

Yes, that sounded logical.

"And second, none of it will work unless I make my way much farther into the Guardians' center of power, right into the Inner Circle."

I nodded vigorously. I couldn't say anything because my mouth was too full.

"So far I haven't felt very keen on that kind of thing." Lucas glanced at the Montrose family's coat of arms hanging above the fireplace. A sword surrounded by roses, and under it the words HIC RHODOS, HIC SALTA, meaning something like "Show what you can really do."

"I certainly started out from a good position in the Lodge—after all, representatives of the Montrose family were among the founder members in 1745, and I'm also married to a potential gene carrier from the Jade line. However, I didn't really intend to commit myself to the Lodge any more than necessary. . . . Well, that's all changed now. For you and Lucy and Paul, I'll go so far as to butter up Kenneth de Villiers. I don't know whether I'll succeed, but—"

"Oh, yes, you will! You'll even get to be Grand Master," I said, brushing crumbs off my pajamas. I only just managed to suppress a satisfied belch. It felt wonderful to have a full stomach again. "Let's think; in the year 1993, you'll be—"

"Ssh!" Lucas leaned forward and put a finger on my lips. "I don't want to hear it. Maybe it's not very sensible of me, but I don't want to know what the future has in store for me unless it will help where you're concerned. I have thirty-seven years to live before we meet again, and I'd like to spend them as . . . well, as free of anxiety as possible. Can you understand that?"

"Yes." I looked at him sadly. "Yes, I can understand it very well." In the circumstances, it probably wasn't a good idea to tell him that Aunt Maddy and Mr. Bernard suspected he hadn't died a natural death. I could always warn him about that when we met in 1993.

I leaned back in my chair and tried to smile. "Then let's talk about the magic of the raven, Grandpa. Because there's something you don't yet know about me."

London is still under attack. Yesterday and the day before, German squadrons were flying overhead all day, dropping bombs which severely damaged the entire London area. The London County Council has now made vaults under parts of the City and the Royal Courts of Justice accessible for use as public air raid shelters. So we have begun walling up some of our passages, we have tripled the number of guards on duty in the cellars, and we have armed them with contemporary as well as traditional weapons.

The three of us elapsed from the documents room to the year 1851 again today, after going through the security process. We all brought books, and if only Lady Tilney had shown a little more sense of humor regarding my jocular remarks on her reading matter, instead of starting a quarrel again, everything would have gone smoothly. I stand by my opinion that the works of this modern German poet Rilke are sheer nonsense, one cannot understand a word of them, and furthermore it is unpatriotic to read German literature when we are in the middle of a war. I hate it when anyone tries to make me change my mind, which Lady Tilney is intent upon doing. She was just trying to explain a particularly confused passage about withered hands hopping about, damp and heavy like toads after rain, when there was a knock at the door. Of course . . . and so mystery why

Lady

blood   a yard

eighty-five   green   year

FROM *The Annals of the Guardians*

2 April 1916

"Duo quum faciunt idem, non est idem" (Terence)

Marginal note: 17/5/1986
Page obviously rendered illegible by spilt coffee. Pages 34 to 36
missing entirely. I would like to see a rule introduced to the effect
that novices may read the Annals only under supervision.

D. Clarkson, archivist (sorely tried!)

f I V E

"OH, NO, you've been crying again!" said Xemerius, who was waiting for me in the secret passage.

I simply said yes. Saying good-bye to Lucas had been very hard, and I wasn't the only one who had had to suppress a few tears. We wouldn't see each other again for thirty-seven years, at least from his point of view, and that seemed an unimaginably long time to both of us. I felt like traveling to the year 1993 right away, but Lucas had made me promise to get a good night's rest. If you could call it that—it was two in the morning, and I'd have to get up again at quarter to seven. Mum would probably have to use a crane to haul me out of bed.

As Xemerius didn't answer back, I shone the flashlight on his face. I was probably just imagining it, but I thought he looked a little sad, and I realized that I'd neglected him all day.

"Nice of you to wait for me, Xemi . . . Xemerius," I

said, suddenly feeling a wave of affection. I'd have liked to stroke him, but you can't stroke or pet ghosts.

"I wasn't waiting, I just happen to be here. I've been looking around for a good place to hide that thing." He pointed to the chronograph. I wrapped it in my bathrobe again and got it first balanced on my hip, then tucked under my arm.

Xemerius flew upstairs beside me. "If you break through the back of your wardrobe—it's only plasterboard, you can do it easily—you could crawl into the space behind it. There are all sorts of possible hiding places there."

"I think I'll just put it under my bed for tonight." I felt so tired that my legs were heavy as lead. I had switched off the flashlight; I could find the way to my bedroom in the dark. I could probably even do it in my sleep. I was half-asleep anyway by the time I was passing Charlotte's room, so I almost dropped the chronograph when her door suddenly opened and I was caught in the light from inside.

"Oh, shit," muttered Xemerius. "Everyone was fast asleep just now, honest!"

"Aren't you a bit too old for Peter Rabbit pajamas?" asked Charlotte. She was leaning in the doorway, looking very pretty in a nightie with spaghetti straps, and her hair fell in glossy waves over her shoulders. (That's the good thing about braided hairstyles—the braids act as built-in curlers, so you look like a Christmas tree fairy when you undo them.)

"Are you crazy, scaring me like that?" I whispered so that Aunt Glenda wouldn't wake up as well.

"Why are you slinking along my corridor in the middle of the night? And what's that you're carrying?"

"What do you mean, your corridor? Do you expect me to climb up the outside of the house to reach my room?"

Charlotte moved away from the door frame and came a step closer. "What's that under your arm?" she repeated, threateningly this time. It sounded even worse because she was whispering. And she looked so . . . well, dangerous that I didn't dare to pass her.

"Uh-oh," said Xemerius. "Someone has a bad attack of PMS. I wouldn't want to tangle with her today."

I had no intention of doing any such thing. "You mean my bathrobe?"

"Show me what's inside it!" she demanded.

I stepped back. "You *are* crazy! Why on earth do you want me to show you my bathrobe in the middle of the night? Now let me by, please. I want to go to bed."

"And I want to see what you're carrying," hissed Charlotte. "Do you really think I'm as naive as you? Do you think I didn't notice those conspiratorial looks and all that whispering? If you want to keep something secret from me, you'll have to be more subtle about it. What about the little chest that your brother and Mr. Bernard took up to you? Was what you're carrying under your arm inside it?"

"She's not stupid," said Xemerius, scratching his nose with one wing.

At any other time of day, and if I'd been less sleepy, I'm sure I'd have thought up some story on the spur of the moment, but right now, my nerves just weren't up to it. "None of your business!" I snapped.

"Oh, yes, it is," snapped Charlotte back. "I may not be the Ruby and a member of the Circle of Twelve, but unlike you, at least I *think* like one! I couldn't hear everything you lot were saying up in your room, the doors in this house are too thick, but what I did hear was quite enough!" She took another step toward me and pointed to my bathrobe. "So show me *that* this minute, if you don't want me to take it."

"You were eavesdropping on us?" I suddenly felt sick to my stomach. How much had she found out? Did she know that *that* was the chronograph? And it seemed to have doubled its weight within the last minute. I gripped it firmly in both hands for safety's sake, dropping Nick's flashlight on the floor with a clatter. By now I wasn't so sure that I wanted Aunt Glenda to go on sleeping.

"Did you know that Gideon and I were trained in Krav Maga?" Charlotte took another step closer to me, and I automatically took one back.

"No, but did *you* know that at this moment you look like that crazy rodent in *Ice Age*?"

"Maybe we're in luck and Krav Maga is just some kind of harmless smut," said Xemerius. "Like Kama Sutra. Ha, ha, ha!" He giggled. "'Scuse me, I always think up my best jokes in desperate situations."

"Krav Maga is an Israeli martial arts technique, and very effective," Charlotte informed me. "I could flatten you with a kick to the solar plexus. Or I could break your neck with a single blow!"

"And I could call for help!" So far our conversation had all taken place in whispers, and it must have sounded like two snakes talking: *hiss, hiss, hiss.*

What would happen if I brought everyone else in this house on the scene? It would probably keep Charlotte from breaking my neck, but then everyone would know what I was carrying wrapped in my bathrobe.

Charlotte seemed to guess my thoughts. She laughed scornfully as she came closer, dancing about on tiptoe. "Go on, then, scream!"

"I would if I were you," said Xemerius.

But I didn't have to after all, because Mr. Bernard appeared behind Charlotte. As usual, he seemed to materialize out of nothing. "Can I help you young ladies in any way?" he asked, and Charlotte spun around like a scalded cat. For a fraction of a second, I thought she was going to kick Mr. Bernard in the solar plexus, purely as a reflex action, but luckily she didn't, although her toes were twitching.

"I sometimes feel hungry in the night myself. I'd be happy to make you a little snack, since that's what I'm off to do anyway," said Mr. Bernard, impassively.

I was so relieved to see him that I burst into hysterical giggles. "I've just been doing that very thing," I said, jerking my chin at the bundle I was clutching to my breast. "But the Karate Kid here is suffering from low blood sugar. I bet she urgently needs a snack."

Charlotte strolled very slowly back to her room. "I'll be keeping my eye on you," she said, pointing her forefinger accusingly at me. She looked as theatrical as if she were about to declaim something dramatic. However, all she said was, "And on you too, Mr. Bernard."

"We'll have to be careful," I whispered when she had closed the door of her room and the corridor was dark again. "She's trained in Taj Mahal."

"That's not a bad one either," said Xemerius appreciatively.

I held my bathrobe firmly. "And she suspects something! She may even know exactly what we found. She's sure to tell the Guardians tales of us, and when they hear that we—"

"There must be better times and places to discuss these matters," Mr. Bernard interrupted me in an unusually severe tone. He picked Nick's flashlight up from the floor, switched it on, and let the beam travel up the door of Charlotte's room to the semicircular fanlight at the top. It was tilted open.

I nodded, showing that I understood. Charlotte could hear every word. "Yes, you're right. Good night, Mr. Bernard."

"Sleep well, Miss Gwyneth."

MY MUM didn't need a crane to get me out of bed in the morning. Her tactics were even meaner. She used the horrible plastic Santa Claus that Caroline had won at the Brownies party last year. Once he was wound up, he kept going, "Ho, ho, ho, merry Christmas, all!" in a hideous plastic croak.

At first I tried to block out the noise with my quilt. But after sixteen repetitions of "ho, ho, ho," I gave up and threw the quilt back. At once, I was sorry I'd done that, because now I remembered what was going to happen today. The ball.

If no miracle happened this afternoon, letting me travel back to my grandfather in 1993, I'd have to face the count without whatever information Lucas could give me.

I bit my tongue. I ought to have traveled back in time again last night after all. On the other hand, then presumably Charlotte would have been on my trail, so all things considered, I'd been right in deciding not to.

I staggered out of bed and into the bathroom. I'd had only three hours' sleep. After Charlotte's performance last night, I'd played it safe and, under Xemerius's orders, I really had broken through the back of the wardrobe and found a space behind it full of old junk—including a crocodile just like the one in the space under the musicians' gallery in the ballroom. Twin crocodiles, maybe. I slit the crocodile's belly open and hid the chronograph inside it.

After that, totally exhausted, I had fallen asleep, which at least meant I didn't have bad dreams. In fact I didn't dream at all. Unlike Aunt Maddy. When I tottered down to the first floor for breakfast—late, because I'd had to spend ages searching for Mum's concealer to disguise the shadows around my eyes—she intercepted me in the corridor and took me into her room.

"Anything wrong?" I asked, but I knew I could have spared myself the question. If Aunt Maddy was up by seven thirty, something was definitely very wrong. Her hair was tousled, and one of the two curlers that were meant to keep her blond locks off her forehead had come loose and was hanging down almost over her ear.

"Oh, Gwyneth, darling, you may well ask!" Aunt Maddy sat down on her unmade bed and stared at the flower pattern on the lavender wallpaper. "I had a vision!"

Oh, not again!

"Let me guess—someone crushed a ruby heart under the heel of his boot," I suggested. "Or maybe there was a raven flying into a shop window display of . . . er . . . clocks?"

Aunt Maddy shook her head so hard that the second curler was also in danger. "No, Gwyneth, you mustn't joke about these things. I may not always know what my visions mean, but later on they're sure to make sense." She reached for my hand and drew me closer. "And this time it was so clear. I saw you in a blue dress with a full skirt, and there was candlelight everywhere and people playing stringed instruments."

I couldn't help getting goose bumps. Not only did I have misgivings about that ball, Aunt Maddy had to go and have another vision. And I hadn't mentioned the ball to her, or told her the color of my ball dress.

Aunt Maddy was glad to see that she finally had my full attention. "At first it all seemed very peaceful, with everyone dancing, including you, but then I saw that the ballroom had no ceiling. Terrible black clouds were gathering in the sky above you, and a huge bird came out of them ready to swoop down on you," she went on. "Then, when you tried to escape, you ran straight into . . . oh, it was horrible! Blood everywhere, everything was red with blood, even the sky turned red, and the raindrops were drops of blood—"

"Aunt Maddy . . . ?"

She was wringing her hands. "Yes, I know, my love, it's so dreadful, and I do hope it doesn't mean what may be the most obvious thing to—"

"You've skipped a bit, I think," I said, interrupting her again. "*What* did I . . . I mean, what did the Gwyneth in your dream run into?"

"It wasn't a dream, it was a vision." Aunt Maddy opened her eyes even wider, if that was possible. "A sword. You ran straight into it."

"A sword? Where did it come from?"

"It was . . . I think it was simply hanging in the air," said Aunt Maddy, flapping her hand about vaguely. "But that's not the important part," she went on, sounding slightly annoyed. "The important part is all the blood."

"Hm." I sat down on the bed beside her. "And what exactly do you want me to do with that information?"

Aunt Maddy looked around, fished the jar of sherbet lemons off her bedside table, and put one in her mouth.

"Oh, darling, I don't know myself. I just thought maybe it would come in useful to you . . . as a warning. . . ."

"Right. I promise I'll do my best not to run into any swords hanging in the air." I gave Aunt Maddy a kiss and got up. "And maybe you ought to get a little more sleep. This isn't your good time of day."

"You're right, that's what I ought to do." She stretched out and put the quilt over her. "But don't make light of it," she said. "Please look after yourself."

"I will." At the door I turned back again. "Er . . . ," I said, clearing my throat. "There wasn't by any chance a lion in your dream, was there? Or a diamond? Or . . . or maybe the sun?"

"No," said Aunt Maddy, her eyes already closed.

"That's what I thought," I muttered, closing the door quietly behind me.

WHEN I ARRIVED at the breakfast table, I noticed at once that Charlotte was missing.

"The poor girl is sick," said Aunt Glenda. "A slight temperature and a bad headache. I should think it's the flu that's going around. Can you make our apologies for your cousin at school, please, Gwyneth?"

I nodded grimly. Flu—that was a real laugh! Charlotte wanted to stay here so that she could search my room in peace.

The same idea had obviously occurred to Xemerius, who was crouching in the fruit bowl on the breakfast table. "I told you she isn't stupid."

And Mr. Bernard, coming in with a plate of scrambled eggs, gave me a warning glance.

"These last few weeks have been too upsetting for the poor girl," said Aunt Glenda. Nick snorted rudely, but our aunt ignored him. "No wonder her body is crying out for time off now."

"Don't talk nonsense, Glenda," said Lady Arista sternly, sipping her tea. "We Montroses have the stamina to stand up to much worse. Personally," she added, straightening her thin back, "I have never had a single day's sickness in my life."

"To be honest, I don't feel too good myself," I said. I didn't, particularly when I remembered that there was no way to lock my bedroom door from the outside. Like almost all the doors in our house, it had only an old-fashioned bolt to lock it on the inside.

My mother immediately jumped up and put her hand on my forehead.

Aunt Glenda rolled her eyes. "Isn't that just typical! Gwyneth simply can't bear not to be the center of attention."

"It feels cool." Mum actually took hold of the tip of my nose as if I were five years old. "And this is dry and warm, just as it should be." She stroked my hair. "I can spoil you at the weekend if you like. We could have breakfast in bed—"

"Ooh, yes, and you can read us the Peter Rabbit stories like you used to," said Caroline, who had the pink crochet pig on her lap. "Then we'll feed Gwenny chopped-up apple and make her cold compresses."

Lady Arista placed a slice of cucumber on her toast, where she had already neatly stacked sliced cheese, ham, tomato, and scrambled egg. "Gwyneth, you don't look in the least unwell. You look the picture of health."

Would you believe it? I was so tired that I could hardly prop my eyes open, I looked like something a vampire had bitten—and now this!

"I shall be in the house all day," said Mr. Bernard. "I can make Miss Charlotte chicken soup and look after her." Although he was speaking to Aunt Glenda it was meant for me, and I understood him only too well.

Unfortunately, Aunt Glenda had other plans for him. "I can look after my own daughter, Mr. Bernard. I want you to go to Walden-Jones to collect my orders and Charlotte's costume for the party."

"That's in Islington," said Mr. Bernard, looking at me anxiously. "It will mean that I'm out of the house for some time."

"Yes, so it will." Aunt Glenda frowned, slightly annoyed.

"On the way back, you could get some flowers, please, Mr. Bernard," said Lady Arista. "A few springlike arrangements for the entrance hall, the dining table, and the music room. Nothing garish, not like those bright parrot tulips you got the other day. I suggest shades of white, pale yellow, and lilac."

Mum kissed us all good-bye before setting off to go to work. "If you see any pots of forget-me-not, you could get me a couple, Mr. Bernard. Or lily of the valley if the florist has any."

"Certainly," said Mr. Bernard.

"And while you're about it, we might as well have a few lilies too," I groused. "They can be planted on my grave when I'm dead and gone because I was sent to school when I was sick." But my mother was already out of the doorway.

"Don't worry, " Xemerius tried to console me. "If that red-headed battle-ax stays at home, Charlotte can't simply march into your room. Even if she does, she'd have to think of opening up the back of your wardrobe and crawling into the space behind it. And even if she did think of it, she'd never pluck up the courage to investigate the insides of the crocodile. Now are you glad I made you slit it open last night?"

I nodded, although inwardly I shuddered at the thought of crawling into that dark corner full of cobwebs, and of course I was still worried. If Charlotte really guessed or actually knew what she ought to be looking for, she wasn't going to give up in a hurry. And I would be home even later than usual if I couldn't manage to put off going to that ball. I'd be home too late, possibly. What would happen if the Guardians discovered that the stolen chronograph was here in our house? A chronograph needing only Gideon's blood to close the Circle! I suddenly had goose bumps all over. They'd probably freak out when they suddenly realized how close they were to completing the mission of their lives. And who was I to keep something hidden from them, something that might turn out to be a cure for all the diseases in the world?

"*And* there's always a chance that the poor girl really is sick," said Xemerius.

"Yes, right, and the earth is flat," I replied. Stupidly, I said it out loud. Everyone else at the table looked at me, taken aback.

"No, Gwenny, the earth is a globe," Caroline kindly told me. "I couldn't believe it at first, either. But apparently it flies through the universe at lightning speed." She broke off a piece of her toast and held it in front of the crochet pig's pink nose. "Still, that's the way it is. Isn't it, Margaret? Have another bit of toast and ham?"

Nick quietly went, "Oink!" and Lady Arista's mouth twisted in disapproval. "Don't we have a rule? No soft toys or dolls here at mealtimes, and no friends, real or imaginary."

"But Margaret is being very good," said Caroline. All the same, she obediently put the pig on the floor under the table.

Aunt Glenda sneezed reproachfully. These days she was obviously allergic to soft toys too.

ALTHOUGH XEMERIUS had promised to guard the chronograph with his life (at this point I laughed, if not very heartily) and tell me at once if Charlotte was trying to get into my room, I couldn't stop wondering what would happen if the Guardians got their hands on the chronograph. But brooding was no use. I had to get through the day somehow and hope for the best. First on my to-do list: I got off the bus one stop early to find a cure for my weariness in Starbucks.

"Can you add three espressos to a caramel macchiato?" I asked the guy behind the counter.

"If you give me your mobile number," he said, grinning.

I took a rather closer look at him and grinned back, feeling flattered. With his dark hair and long fringe, he reminded me of one of those good-looking guys from a French feature film. Of course he was good-looking only until I compared him with Gideon in my mind, which stupidly I did at once.

"She already has a boyfriend," someone said behind me. It was Raphael; his green eyes were twinkling at me when I turned around, frowning. "Anyway she's too young for you, as you can easily tell from her school uniform. A caffè latte and a cranberry muffin, please."

I rolled my eyes and took my specially strong brew with an apologetic smile. "I don't have a boyfriend, as it happens, but right now I do have . . . well, kind of a time problem. Ask me again in another two years."

"I will," said the guy.

"He won't, you know," said Raphael. "Bet you he asks every pretty girl for her phone number."

I simply walked off, but Raphael caught up with me. "Hey, hang on! Sorry I disturbed your flirtation." He looked suspiciously at his coffee. "Do you think he spat in this?"

I took a large sip from my paper cup and promptly burnt my lips, tongue, and the front of my palate. When I could think again, I wondered whether an intravenous coffee injection might not have been a better idea.

"I went to the cinema with that girl Celia from our class yesterday," Raphael went on. "Terrific girl. Amazingly pretty and funny, don't you think?"

"Uh?" I said with my nose in the milk foam. (The company of Xemerius was beginning to infect me.)

"We had a lot of fun together," he went on. "Only don't tell Lesley. She might feel jealous."

I had to laugh. How sweet—he was trying to manipulate me. "Okay. I'll be silent as the grave."

"So you really do think she might be jealous?" asked Raphael eagerly.

"Oh, sure, green with jealousy. Seeing that there's no one called Celia in our class."

Raphael rubbed his nose, looking awkward. "That blonde? The one throwing the party?"

"Cynthia."

"I really did go to the cinema with her, though," said Raphael, unhappily. The school uniform, with its unfortunate combination of dismal yellow and navy blue, looked even worse on him than on us. And the way he ran his hand through his hair reminded me of Nick and appealed to my maternal feelings. I thought he'd earned a reward for not being as arrogant and high-handed as his big brother.

"I'll break it to Lesley gently, okay?" I offered.

He smiled hesitantly. "But don't tell her I got the names mixed up. . . . Oh, better not tell her anything . . . or maybe—"

"You just leave it to me." As we parted, I gave his tie a little tug. "Hey, congratulations! You tied it properly today."

"Cindy did it for me," said Raphael with a wry grin. "Or whatever her name is."

OUR FIRST CLASS that day was English with Mr. Whitman. He acknowledged my apologies on behalf of Charlotte with a nod, although I couldn't resist drawing quotation marks in the air with my fingers around the word *sick*.

"You should have brought it with you," Lesley whispered, as Mr. Whitman handed out our marked homework from last week.

"What, the chronograph? To school? Are you crazy? Suppose Mr. Whitman discovered it! Poor Mr. Squirrel, he'd have a heart attack. Quite apart from the fact that he'd tell his friends the other Guardians right away, and then they would hang, draw, and quarter me, or break me on the wheel, or do whatever else their stupid Golden Rules say is the penalty for a case like mine." I handed Lesley the key to the chest. "Here you are, the key to your heart. I really wanted to give it to Raphael, but I suppose you wouldn't like that."

Lesley rolled her eyes and peered at the front row, where Raphael was sitting and being very careful not even to glance at her.

"Put it back on again at once," I said. "And don't let Charlotte take it away from you."

"Krav Maga," murmured Lesley. "Wasn't there a film

where Jennifer Lopez could do that? The one where she beat up her violent ex-husband at the end? I'd like to learn Krav Maga too."

"Do you think Charlotte might just kick the wardrobe open? Come to think of it, I wouldn't be surprised if she and Gideon had been taught how to open locks without a key. They probably had a workshop with an MI6 agent: *No need for a sledgehammer—just try the elegant hairpin method.*" I heaved a sigh.

"If Charlotte really knew what we'd found, she'd have told the Guardians by now. She thinks she's going to discover something that will make her look important and you look bad."

"Yes, and if she does find it—"

"I very much hope you two are talking about sonnet number 130." Mr. Whitman was suddenly towering over us.

"We've talked of nothing else for days," said Lesley.

Mr. Whitman raised an eyebrow. "I can't help getting the impression that you girls have recently had your minds on things that are no help to your schoolwork. Maybe a letter to your parents would be a good idea. Considering the fees they pay for the privilege of having you educated here, I think they can expect a certain amount of commitment on your part in return." He put our homework down on the table in front of us. "A little more attention to Shakespeare would have improved your essays. Only average marks, I'm afraid."

"And why does he think that is?" I muttered crossly. The nerve of it! First I had to devote all my spare time to time travel, trying on costumes, and having dancing lessons, and now Mr. Whitman told me I was neglecting my schoolwork!

"Charlotte has shown you that it's perfectly possible to combine the two, Gwyneth," said Mr. Whitman, as if he had guessed my thoughts. "*Her* marks are excellent. And she never complained. You'd do well to follow her example and exercise a little self-discipline."

I stared angrily after him as he walked away.

Lesley dug a friendly elbow in my ribs. "One of these days, we'll tell horrible Mr. Squirrel what we think of him. When we're about to leave school at the latest. But it would be a sheer waste of energy today."

"Yes, you're right. I need all my energy just to stay awake." I promptly yawned. "I wish those three espressos I drank would hurry up and find their way into my bloodstream."

Lesley nodded. "Okay, and once they have, we urgently need to think how you can get out of going to that ball."

"BUT YOU CAN'T be sick!" said Mr. Marley, wringing his hands in desperation. "All the preparations have been made. I don't know how I'm going to tell the others."

"It's not your fault that I'm sick," I said in a weary voice, hauling myself out of the limousine with difficulty. "Or mine either. It's an act of God, and there's nothing to be done about those."

"Oh, yes, there is! There must be!" Mr. Marley looked at me indignantly. "You don't look as sick as all that," he added, which was rather unfair, because I'd overcome my vanity and wiped Mum's concealer off my face again. At first Lesley had thought of helping me out a little with some gray and lilac eye shadow, but after one look at my face, she put her makeup bag away again. The rings under my eyes could have featured in any vampire film just the way they were, and I was pale as a corpse into the bargain.

"Maybe, but it's not how sick I look that matters—it's how sick I really am," I said, handing Mr. Marley my schoolbag. Seeing that I was so weak and feeble, he was welcome to carry it this time. "And I do think that, under these circumstances, the visit to the ball can be postponed."

"Impossible!" cried Mr. Marley, only to clap his hand to his mouth next moment and look around in alarm in case he'd been heard. "Do you know how much time and trouble has gone into those preparations?" he went on in a whisper as we made for the headquarters of the Lodge. I was trailing along in such a limp way that we made only slow progress. "It wasn't easy to get your school principal to let that amateur dramatics society use the art room in the cellar for their rehearsal. *Today!* And Count Saint-Germain expressly said that—"

Mr. Marley was getting on my nerves. (Amateur dramatics society? Mr. Gilles, the principal? I didn't understand any of this.) "Listen, I'm sick! Sick! I took three aspirins, but they didn't help. In fact it's getting worse and worse. I'm running a high temperature as well. And I'm short of breath." To emphasize what I said, I clung to the rail of the flight of steps leading up to the house and did some heavy breathing.

"*Tomorrow!* You can be sick tomorrow," bleated Mr. Marley. "Mr. George! Tell her she can't be sick until tomorrow, or the whole timetable will be *ruined!*"

"Aren't you feeling well, Gwyneth?" Mr. George, who had appeared in the doorway, considerately put an arm around me and led me into the house. This was better.

I nodded as if I were suffering. "I probably caught Charlotte's flu bug." Ha, ha! Exactly! We both had the same imaginary flu. Might as well go the whole hog. "My head is splitting."

"Oh, dear, it's really very unfortunate just now," said Mr. George.

"That's what I've been trying to get her to understand," said Mr. Marley, trotting busily along after us. For a change, his face wasn't red as a lobster but white with red spots, as if it couldn't make up its mind which was the right color for this situation. "Surely Dr. White can give her an injection of something, can't he? She only has to get through a few hours."

"Yes, that's a possibility," said Mr. George.

Shaken, I gave him a sidelong glance. I'd have expected a little more sympathy and support from Mr. George. I was beginning to feel genuinely sick, but with fear. I somehow had a feeling that if the Guardians realized I was simply pretending, they wouldn't handle me with kid gloves. But it was too late now. There was no going back.

Instead of making for Madame Rossini's studio, where I was supposed to be getting dressed in my eighteenth-century clothes, Mr. George took me to the Dragon Hall, and Mr. Marley followed us, still carrying my bag and talking to himself indignantly.

Dr. White, Falk de Villiers, Mr. Whitman, and a man I didn't know (maybe the minister of health?) were sitting around the table. When Mr. George gently pushed me into the room, they all turned their heads to the doorway and stared. I was feeling more and more uncomfortable.

"She says she's sick!" exclaimed Mr. Marley, as he marched into the room after us.

Falk de Villiers stood up. "Close the door first, please, Marley. Now, let's start again. Who's sick?"

"*She* is!" Mr. Marley pointed his forefinger accusingly in my direction, and I only just resisted the temptation to roll my eyes.

Mr. George let go of me, sat down with a groan on an empty chair, and mopped the sweat off his bald patch with his handkerchief. "That's right. Gwyneth isn't feeling well."

"I'm really sorry," I said, taking care to look down and to my right. I'd read, somewhere, that people always look up and to their left when they're telling lies. "But I don't feel up to going to that ball today. I can hardly keep on my feet, and it's getting worse all the time." I emphasized my point by leaning on the back of Mr. George's chair for support.

Only now did I notice that Gideon was present, too, and my heart missed a couple of beats.

It was so unfair that the mere sight of him was enough to upset me, while he stood casually by the window, hands deep in the pockets of his jeans, just smiling at me. Well, okay, it wasn't an outright, broad, beaming smile, only a tiny lift of the corners of his mouth, but his eyes were smiling at the same time, and for some reason, I had a lump in my throat again.

I quickly looked in another direction, and saw little Robert, Dr. White's son who had drowned in a swimming pool when he was seven, over by the fireplace. The little ghost boy had been shy at first, but by now he trusted me. He gave me a big wave, but I could only nod briefly to him.

"What kind of sudden, unexpected sickness do you have, if I may ask?" Mr. Whitman looked at me with mockery in his eyes. "You were sound as a bell in school just now." He folded his arms before obviously thinking better of it and changing his tactics. At this point, he switched to his soft, nice-guy voice, gentle and sympathetic. "If you are by any chance nervous about the ball, Gwyneth, we can understand that. Maybe Dr. White can give you something to help with your stage fright."

Falk nodded. "We really can't put off today's appointment," he said.

Now Mr. George was stabbing me in the back as well. "Mr. Whitman is right, and a little stage fright is perfectly normal. Anyone would feel nervous in your place. So there's no need to be ashamed of it."

"And you won't be on your own," added Falk. "Gideon will be with you the whole time."

I didn't mean to do it, but I glanced quickly at Gideon and looked away again just as quickly when his eyes seemed to fasten on mine.

"Before you know it," Falk went on, "you'll be back again, and it will all be over."

"And just think of that lovely dress," said the man I took to be the minister of health, trying to tempt me. Hello? Did he think I was a ten-year-old still playing with Barbie dolls?

The others murmured their agreement, and they all smiled at me encouragingly, except for Dr. White, whose eyebrows were drawn together in his usual frown. His hostile expression would have terrified anyone. Little Robert put his head apologetically on one side.

"My throat hurts, I have a headache, and my joints all ache," I said as firmly as I could. "I don't think that's how stage fright feels. My cousin stayed at home with flu today, and now I've caught her bug. It's as simple as that!"

"Someone ought to explain to her again that this is an event of historical importance," squeaked Mr. Marley in the background, but Mr. Whitman interrupted him.

"Gwyneth, do you remember our conversation this morning?" he asked, and his tone of voice became, if anything, a tad slimier.

Which one did he mean? Surely he wasn't seriously describing his grousing about the trouble with my schoolwork as a conversation? Yes, he obviously was.

"It may be because of our training, but I feel fairly sure that in your place, Charlotte would have been aware of her duty. She would never rate her own physical state above her mission in our cause."

Well, it wasn't my fault if they'd gone and trained the wrong girl, was it? I clung even harder to the back of the chair. "Honestly, if Charlotte felt as sick as I do, she wouldn't be able to go to that ball either."

Mr. Whitman looked as if he was about to lose his temper any moment now. "I don't think you understand what I'm talking about."

"This is getting us nowhere!" That was Dr. White, speaking in his usual brusque way. "We're only losing valuable time. If the girl really is sick, we can hardly talk her back into good health. And if she's only pretending—" He pushed his chair back, got to his feet, and came around the table toward me so quickly that little Robert found it hard to keep up with him. "Mouth open!"

This was really going too far! I stared at him indignantly, but he had taken my head in both hands, and his fingers ran down from my ears to my throat. Then he put a hand on my forehead. My heart sank.

"Hm," he said, and now his expression was even darker, if possible. "Swollen lymph nodes, high temperature—this really doesn't look good. Open your mouth, please, Gwyneth."

Astonished, I did as he said. Swollen lymph nodes? High temperature? Was I genuinely sick with sheer fright now?

"Just as I thought." Dr. White had taken a wooden spatula out of his breast pocket and pressed my tongue down with it. "Pharynx inflamed, tonsils swollen . . . no wonder you have a sore throat. It must hurt like hell when you swallow."

"You poor thing," said Robert sympathetically. "Now I expect you'll have to take horrible cough syrup." He made a face.

"Are you cold?" his father asked me.

I nodded uncertainly. Why on earth was he doing this? Why was he helping me? Dr. White, of all people, who always acted as if I'd take the first opportunity I got of running off with the chronograph?

"I thought so. Your temperature will go on rising for a while." Dr. White turned to the others. "Seems like a viral infection."

The Guardians present looked upset. I forced myself not to look at Gideon, although I'd have loved to see his face.

"Can you give her anything for it, Jake?" asked Falk de Villiers.

"Something to lower her temperature, that's all. But there's no way she can be fit for the ball this evening in a hurry. She ought to be in bed." Dr. White looked grimly at me. "If she's lucky, it'll be the one-day infection that's going around at present. But it could well take several days for her to—"

"All the same, surely we could—" Mr. Whitman began.

"No, we couldn't," Dr. White rudely interrupted him. I was doing my best not to stare at him as if he were the seventh wonder of the world. "Apart from the fact that Gideon can hardly push her to the ball in a wheelchair, it would be irresponsible and an offense against the Golden Rules to send her into the eighteenth century with an acute viral infection."

"That's true," said the unknown man whom I took for the minister of health. "We don't know how the immune system of people in the late eighteenth century would react to a modern virus. It could have devastating effects."

"As with the Maya Indians in the past," murmured Mr. George.

Falk sighed deeply. "Well, the decision seems to have been made for us. Gideon and Gwyneth won't go to the ball this evening. Maybe we can bring Operation Opal forward instead. Marley, would you please let the others know about our change of plan?"

"Yes, sir." Mr. Marley made for the door, visibly upset. The glance he cast me was full of reproach. I couldn't have cared less. The main thing was that I'd put off the visit to the ball. I still couldn't grasp my luck.

Now I did risk a cautious look at Gideon. Unlike the others, he didn't seem to be bothered by the postponement of our excursion, because he was smiling at me. Did he guess that I was faking my infection? Or was he just glad to be spared the nuisance of dressing in those clothes today? One way or another, I resisted the temptation to smile back and let my eyes go to Dr. White, who was standing there talking to the minister of health.

I'd have loved a private word with him. But the doctor seemed to have forgotten me entirely, he was so deep in his conversation.

"Come along, Gwyneth," I heard a sympathetic voice saying. Mr. George. "We'll take you straight off to elapse, and after that, you can go home."

I nodded.

That sounded like the idea of the day.

A journey back in time with the aid of the chronograph can last for between 120 seconds and 240 minutes. With the Aquamarine, Citrine, Jade, Sapphire, and Ruby, the minimum setting is 121 seconds, the maximum setting 239 minutes. To avoid uncontrolled time travel, the gene carriers have to elapse for 180 minutes every day. If they elapse for less than that time, there can be uncontrolled time travel within the next twenty-four hours (see Records of Time Travel, *6 January 1902, 17 February 1902— Timothy de Villiers).*

According to the empirical investigations of Count Saint-Germain in the years 1720 to 1738, a gene carrier can elapse, with the aid of the chronograph, for up to five and a half hours a day, i.e., 330 minutes. If that time is exceeded, gene carriers will suffer headache and sensations of vertigo and weakness, and their faculties of perception and coordination will be severely affected. The de Villiers brothers were able to establish these facts in three parallel experiments on themselves in the year 1902.

FROM THE CHRONICLES OF THE GUARDIANS, VOLUME 3,
CHAPTER 1: "THE MYSTERIES OF THE CHRONOGRAPH"

SIX

I'D NEVER BEFORE elapsed in such comfort as I did that afternoon. I'd been given a hamper to take along with me, containing rugs, a thermos flask of hot tea, biscuits (of course), and fruit cut up small in a lunch box. I almost had a guilty conscience as I settled down on the green sofa. I thought briefly of taking the key out of its secret hiding place and setting off upstairs, but that would only mean additional complications and the risk of being caught. I was somewhere in the year 1953. I hadn't asked the precise date, because I'd had to act the part of a poor feeble invalid with flu.

Once Falk had decided on a change of plan, hectic activity had broken out among the Guardians. In the end, I'd been sent off to the chronograph room with the reluctant Mr. Marley. It was obvious that he didn't want to be lumbered with me, and would much rather have stayed to join the discussion. So I dared not ask him any questions about

Operation Opal; I just looked as grumpy as he did. Our relationship had definitely deteriorated over the last two days, but Mr. Marley was the last person I was bothered about right now.

So in the year 1953, I ate first the fruit, then the biscuits, and finally I nestled down under the rugs and stretched out on the sofa. In spite of the uncomfortable light cast by the naked bulb in the ceiling, it wasn't five minutes before I was fast asleep. Not even the thought of the headless ghost who was supposed to haunt these cellars could keep me awake. I woke up feeling refreshed, just in time to travel back, which was a good thing, because otherwise I'd have crash-landed at Mr. Marley's feet flat on my back.

While Mr. Marley, after greeting me with a single nod, was making his entry in the journal (probably something along the lines of *Instead of doing her duty, that spoilsport Ruby lounged around in the year 1953, feeding her face with fruit*), I asked him whether Dr. White was still in the building. I really did want to know why he hadn't given me away by telling the others I was only pretending.

"He doesn't have the time to bother about your little aches and pains . . . I mean about your flu," replied Mr. Marley. "At the moment, the others are all setting off to the Ministry of Defense for Operation Opal." The words *And I can't be there, all because of you* hung in the air as clearly as if he had said them out loud.

Ministry of Defense? Why on earth . . . ? I knew it was no use asking Mr. Huffy there just what *that* was about. In his present mood, he wasn't about to tell me anything. In fact he seemed to have decided it would be better not to talk to me at all anymore. He blindfolded me, fastidiously using his fingertips, and led me through the labyrinth of corridors in the cellars with one hand on my elbow and the other on my waist. I found this physical contact more unpleasant with every step we took, particularly as his hands were hot and sweaty. I could hardly wait to shake them off when we had finally gone up the spiral staircase to the ground floor. Sighing, I took off the blindfold and said I'd find my own way from there to the limousine.

"I haven't given you permission yet," protested Mr. Marley. "Anyway, it's my duty to escort you to the front door of your house."

"Oh, stop that!" I hit out at him in annoyance when he tried to put the scarf around my head again. "I know the rest of the way, and if you insist on going to my front door, then you're definitely not doing it with your hand on my waist." And I set off again.

Mr. Marley followed me, snorting indignantly. "You're acting as if I'd touched you improperly!"

"Yes, so I am," I said, to annoy him.

"That is really—" cried Mr. Marley, but whatever he was going to say was drowned out by excitable shouting in a strong French accent.

"Don't you dare leave 'ere without zis ruff, young man!" The door to the sewing room flew open, and out came Gideon, closely followed by a furious Madame Rossini. She was waving her hands about in the air, along with the intricately pleated piece of white fabric they were holding.

"You stay 'ere! Do you zink I 'ave made you zis ruff just for fun?"

Gideon had already stopped when he saw us. I had stopped too, but unfortunately not in the same casual way—more like someone turned into a pillar of salt. Not because I was surprised by his peculiar padded jacket, with shoulders that made him look like a wrestler on anabolic steroids, but because whenever we met, I obviously couldn't do a thing but goggle at him. With my heart thudding.

"As if I would touch you at all *of my own free will!* I'm doing it only because I have to," groused Mr. Marley behind me. Gideon raised an eyebrow and gave me a sardonic smile.

I quickly smiled back just as sardonically, letting my glance wander as slowly as possible from the weird jacket down over the comical padded trunk-hose and his stockinged calves, all the way to the buckled shoes he was wearing.

"Auzenticity, young man!" Madame Rossini was still waving the stiff, pleated collar about. "'Ow often do I 'ave to tell you? Ah, 'ere is my leetle swan-necked beauty." A broad smile spread over her round face. *"Bonsoir, ma petite.* Tell zat idiot not to make me so angry."

"Okay, hand the thing over." Gideon let Madame Rossini put the ruff around his neck. "Although I'm not likely to come face-to-face with anyone—and even if I did, I can't imagine that people went about day and night wearing starched pie-frills like this."

"Oh, yes, zey did—at least ze gentlemen at court."

"I don't know what's bothering you. It really suits you," I said with a mean grin. "Makes your head look like an enormous chocolate in its little paper case."

"Yes, I know." Gideon was grinning too. "Good enough to eat. But at least it takes people's eyes off these trunk-hose. Or so I hope."

"Zey are very, very sexy," claimed Madame Rossini. I couldn't help giggling.

"Glad to see I've cheered you up a bit," said Gideon. "My cloak, please, Madame Rossini."

I bit my lower lip to keep the giggles back. All I needed now was to be fooling around with this bastard as if nothing had happened! As if we were really friends. But it was too late.

In passing, he caressed my cheek, and it was so quick that I was incapable of any reaction. "Get well soon, Gwen."

"Ah, zere 'e goes! At least 'e looks right for 'is adventure in ze time of Queen Elizabeth ze First, zat little rebel." Madame Rossini was grinning. "But I am sure 'e will take ze ruff off on ze way, zat bad boy."

I was staring after the bad boy myself. Hm . . . maybe the trunk-hose were just a tiny bit sexy after all.

"Come on, we have to go as well," said Mr. Marley, taking my elbow and then letting go of it at once, as if it had burnt him. He kept several feet away from me on the way to the car. All the same, I heard him mutter, "Outrageous. She is *definitely* not my type."

* * *

MY FEARS that Charlotte might have found the chrono-graph by now were unfounded. I'd underestimated my family's ingenuity. When I arrived home, Nick was play-ing with a yo-yo outside my door.

"Only members allowed into HQ," he said. "Pass-word?"

"I'm the boss, remember?" I ruffled his red curls. "Yuck, is that chewing gum again?" Nick began to protest indignantly, but I took my chance to slip into my room.

I hardly recognized it. Aunt Maddy, called in by Mr. Bernard, who was probably still chasing from flower shop to flower shop, had spent all day in here, and she had given the room a little of her own special Aunt Maddy touch. I wasn't exactly untidy, but all the same, my things, for some unknown reason, had a tendency to lie around cov-ering all parts of the floor. Today, for the first time in a long while, you could see the rug again, and the bed was neatly made. Aunt Maddy had conjured up a pretty white bedspread from somewhere. My clothes lay neatly folded on a chair, loose sheets of paper, exercise books, and text-books had been sorted and stacked on my desk, and even the pot with the dead fern on the windowsill had gone. Instead there was a beautiful flower arrangement there, smelling deliciously of freesias. Even Xemerius wasn't dangling untidily from the ceiling light, but sitting decora-tively on the chest of drawers with his dragon tail coiled around him, right beside a huge dish of candy.

"Gives the room a totally different feeling, doesn't it?"

he said. "I must say, your auntie knows something about feng shui."

"Don't worry, I haven't thrown anything away," said Aunt Maddy, who was sitting on the bed with a book. "I just cleared up a bit and did some dusting, so that I could make myself comfortable."

I couldn't help it, I had to give her a big kiss. "And I was worrying dreadfully all day."

Xemerius nodded energetically. "You were right to worry. We'd hardly read ten pages—er, I mean, Aunt Maddy had hardly read ten pages, before Charlotte came slinking in," he said. "She looked really surprised to see your auntie. But she made a quick recovery, claimed she wanted to borrow an eraser."

Aunt Maddy told the same story. "Since I'd just tidied your desk, I was able to help her. Oh, and I sharpened your crayons and sorted them by color. Later she came back, saying it was to return the eraser. Then Nick and I took turns all afternoon. I had to go to the loo now and then, after all."

"Five times, to be precise," said Nick, who had followed me in.

"All that tea I drank," she said apologetically.

"Oh, thank you, Aunt Maddy. You've both been wonderful." I tousled Nick's hair again.

Aunt Maddy laughed. "I like to make myself useful. And I told Violet that we'd have to meet in your room tomorrow."

"Aunt Maddy! You haven't gone and told Violet anything about the chronograph, have you?" cried Nick.

Aunt Maddy's friend Violet Purpleplum was much what Lesley was to me.

"Of course not!" She looked at him indignantly. "I swore by my life not to breathe a word! I told her the light is better for needlework up here, and Arista can't disturb us. Although one of your window frames needs repairing, Gwyneth dear. There's a draft coming from somewhere. I could feel a breath of cold air all the time."

Xemerius looked guilty. "I don't do it on purpose," he said. "But the book was so exciting."

My thoughts were already busy with the coming night. "Aunt Maddy, who was sleeping in my room in November 1993?"

My great-aunt frowned thoughtfully. "Let me think— 1993? Was Margaret Thatcher still prime minister? If so, then . . . oh, what was her name?"

"Oh, dear! Your old auntie is getting it all confused," said Xemerius. "You'd do better to ask me! That was the year *Groundhog Day* hit cinema screens—I've seen it fourteen times—and the affair between Prince Charles and Camilla Parker-Bowles went public, and the name of the prime minister was—"

"It doesn't really matter," I interrupted him. "I only want to know if I can travel back from here safely to 1993." I suspected that Charlotte might have dug out a black combat suit and was now lurking in the corridor all around the clock. "Was anyone sleeping in this room at the time or not, Aunt Maddy?"

"Lanfairpwllgwyngyllgogerychwyrndrobwll-llantysiliogogogoch," cried Aunt Maddy. Xemerius, Nick, and I stared at her, baffled.

"Now she's gone right off her rocker," said Xemerius. "I thought as much this afternoon, when she kept laughing at the wrong places in her book."

"Lanfairpwllgwyngyllgogerychwyrndrobwlllllanty-siliogogogoch," repeated Aunt Maddy, beaming happily and popping a sherbet lemon into her mouth. "That's the name of our housekeeper's hometown in Wales. No one can say I don't have a good memory."

"Aunt Maddy, I only want to know whether—"

"Yes, yes, yes. Our housekeeper at the time was called Gladiola Langdon, and at the beginning of the nineties, she slept in what is now your mother's room," Aunt Maddy interrupted me. "Surprised, are you? Contrary to general opinion, your great-aunt has a fully functioning brain. At the time, the other rooms up here were used only occasionally, as guestrooms; the rest of the time they were empty. Gladiola was rather hard of hearing, so you can get into your time machine and climb out of it again in 1993. There's nothing to worry about." She giggled. "Gladiola Langdon—I don't think we'll ever forget her apple pie. Poor soul, it never occurred to her to core the apples and throw the cores and pips away."

★　★　★

MUM HAD A RATHER guilty conscience about the flu I'd claimed to have. Falk de Villiers himself had called her in the afternoon and passed on Dr. White's prescription of bed rest and plenty of hot drinks. She told me about a hundred times how sorry she was she hadn't listened to me, and she squeezed me three lemons with her own hands. Then she sat beside my bed for half an hour to make sure I finished the hot lemon drink. I must have made my teeth chatter rather too convincingly, because she wrapped me in two extra blankets and put a hot-water bottle down at my feet.

"I'm a terrible mother," she said, stroking my head. "And you're having such a difficult time at the moment anyway!"

She was right about that, and not just because I felt like I was in a sauna. You could probably have fried eggs on my tummy. For a few seconds, I allowed myself to wallow in self-pity. But then I said, "You're not a terrible mother at all, Mum."

Mum looked, if anything, even more upset. "I do hope those old men won't make you do anything dangerous. They're so obsessed with all their mysteries."

I quickly drank four mouthfuls of my hot lemon straight off. As usual, I was torn both ways: should I tell Mum everything or not? It wasn't a good feeling to be telling her lies, or at least concealing such important things from her. But then again, I didn't want her worrying about me or picking a fight with the Guardians. And she probably wouldn't be very happy to know I was hiding the stolen chronograph here and traveling back in time with it unsupervised.

"Falk assured me that all you do in the past is sit in a cellar getting your homework done," she said. "He said I had nothing to worry about except making sure that you saw enough daylight."

I hesitated for a second again, and then I smiled wryly. "He's right. It's dark and dead boring down there."

"Good. I'd hate it if anything like what happened to Lucy back in the past also happened to you."

"Mum, what exactly *did* happen back then?" It wasn't the first time I had asked that question in the last two weeks, and she still hadn't given me a satisfactory answer.

"You know what happened." Mum stroked my forehead again. "Oh, my poor little mousie! You're burning with fever."

I gently pushed her hand away. I was burning all right, but not with fever.

"Mum, I really do want to know just what happened to Lucy," I said.

She hesitated for a moment, and then she told me all over again what I already knew: Lucy and Paul thought the Circle of Blood ought not to be closed, so they had stolen the chronograph and gone into hiding with it, because the Guardians didn't see things the same way.

"And since it was totally impossible to escape the Guardians and their network—you can bet they had eyes and ears everywhere, people planted in Scotland Yard and the Secret Service—in the end, all Lucy and Paul could do was travel into the past with the chronograph," I said, unobtrusively loosening the bedclothes over my feet to get a bit of cool air. "You just don't know what year they went to."

"That's right. Believe me, it wasn't easy for them to go away, leaving everything here behind them." Mum looked as if she were fighting back tears.

"Yes, but *why* did they think the Circle of Blood ought not to be closed?" Heavens above, I was boiling hot! Why had I ever claimed to be having shivering fits?

Mum stared past me into space. "All I know is that they didn't trust Count Saint-Germain's motives, and they were convinced that the secret of the Guardians was built on a foundation of lies. I'm sorry now that I didn't ask more questions at the time . . . but I think Lucy was glad of that. She didn't want to put me in danger too."

"The Guardians think the secret of the Circle of Blood is some kind of miracle-working medicine. A cure for all the diseases of mankind," I said, and I could tell from Mum's expression that this information wasn't news to her. "Why would Lucy and Paul want to keep this miraculous cure from being found? Why would they be against it?"

"Because . . . because they thought the price to be paid was too high." Mum whispered those words. A tear ran out of the corner of her eye and down her cheek. She quickly wiped it away with the back of her hand and stood up. "Try to get some sleep, darling," she said in her normal voice. "I'm sure you'll soon feel warmer. Sleep is always the best medicine."

"Good night, Mum." In other circumstances, I'd certainly have bombarded her with more questions, but I could hardly wait for her to close my bedroom door. I flung the blankets off with great relief and opened the window so suddenly that I scared two pigeons (or were they the ghosts of pigeons?) off the sill where they had settled down for the night. By the time Xemerius came back from his flight around the house, checking up on everything, I had changed my sweat-drenched pajamas for a clean, dry pair.

"Everyone in bed, including Charlotte," reported Xemerius. "Although she's staring at the ceiling with her eyes wide open and doing stretching exercises for her calves. You look like a lobster."

"I feel like a lobster." Sighing, I bolted the door. I didn't want anyone, least of all Charlotte, coming into this room while I was gone. Whatever she planned to do with her well-stretched calves, she wasn't getting in to do it here.

I opened the wardrobe and took a deep breath. It was difficult clambering through the hole and crawling over to the crocodile with the chronograph hidden inside it. My clean pajamas were soon dirty gray all down the front, and any number of cobwebs were clinging to me. Disgusting.

"You have a . . . a little something there," said Xemerius as I crawled out again with the chronograph under my arm. The little something turned out to be a spider the size of Caroline's hand. (Well, almost, anyway.) It cost me enormous self-control to hold back a scream that would have woken up not only everyone in the house but the whole of this part of town. Once I'd shaken it off, the spider scuttled under my bed. (It's amazing how fast something with eight legs can run.)

I stood there gasping for about a minute. Then I shook myself again with disgust as I set the chronograph.

"Don't carry on like that," said Xemerius. "Some spiders are easily twenty times that big."

"Where? On Planet Zog? There, that should be okay." I lifted the chronograph up on its little chest in the wardrobe and put my finger into the compartment under the ruby. "I'll be back in an hour and a half. And keep an eye on Tarantula there, will you?" Holding Nick's flashlight, I waved to Xemerius and took a deep breath.

With a dramatic flourish, he put a hand to his breast. *"Wilt thou be gone? It is not yet near day. . . ."*

"Oh, shut up, Juliet," I said, pressing my finger firmly down on the needle.

When I took my next breath, my mouth was full of flannel. I hastily spat it out and switched on the flashlight. It was a bathrobe, right in front of my face. The wardrobe was crammed full of clothes hanging in two rows, and it took me some time to scramble to my feet in there among them.

"Did you hear that?" asked a woman's voice outside the wardrobe.

Oh, no. Please not!

"What is it, darling?" That was a man's voice. It sounded very, very hesitant.

I was transfixed with fright.

"There's a light in the wardrobe," said the woman's voice. It sounded the opposite of hesitant. In fact, to be precise, it sounded very much like my aunt Glenda.

Hell! I switched off the flashlight and cautiously retreated behind the second row of clothes until I could feel the wall at my back.

"Perhaps you—"

"No, Charles!" The voice was more imperious than ever. "I am not imagining things, if that's what you were going to say."

"But I—"

"There was a light in the wardrobe, and you will now kindly get up and investigate it. Or else you can spend the night in the sewing room." Charlotte had obviously inherited her mother's way of hissing. "Or no—wait! You'd better not—if Mrs. Langdon sees you there in the morning, Mother will ask me whether our marriage is going through a bad patch, which is the last thing I want, because our marriage is not going through a bad patch, or not *my* marriage anyway, even if you only married me because your father wanted to be related to the aristocracy."

"But, Glenda—"

"Don't you try pretending to me! Only the other day, Lady Presdemere told me that . . ." And Aunt Glenda went on calling her unfortunate husband names, which made her forget all about the light in the wardrobe. She also forgot that it was the middle of the night, and she went on nagging him for what felt like two hours. All I heard from Charles was a terrified squeak now and then. No wonder those two got divorced. You couldn't help wondering how on earth they had ever managed to bring dear little Charlotte into the world first.

At long last, Glenda told her husband that he was trying to spoil her well-earned sleep, and then the bedsprings creaked. Only moments later, I heard her snoring. Hot milk and honey helps some people to sleep. With Aunt Glenda it seemed to be different.

Cursing Aunt Maddy and her phenomenal memory, I waited another half an hour to be on the safe side and then cautiously pushed the wardrobe door open. After all, I couldn't spend the whole of my time in 1993 there. Grandpa must be sick with anxiety by now. It was a little lighter in the room than in the wardrobe. At least, there was enough light for me to see the outlines of the furniture and not bump into anything.

I stole over to the door as quietly as possible and pressed the handle down. At exactly that moment, Aunt Glenda sat up in bed. "There's an intruder here! *Charles!*"

I didn't wait for poor Charles to wake up or for the light to go on, I flung the door open and sprinted as fast as I could along the corridor and downstairs, then all along the corridor on the second floor and on down the next flight of stairs, without looking out for creaking steps. I didn't know myself just where I was running, but I had an odd sense of *déjà vu*—hadn't I done all this once before?

On the first floor, I crashed into a figure which, after my first moment's fright, turned out to be my grandfather. He took hold of me and steered me into the library.

"What's all this racket about?" he whispered when he had closed the door. "And why are you so late? I've been cooling my heels in front of Great-great-great-uncle Hugh's portrait, thinking something must have happened to you."

"It did. Thanks to Aunt Maddy, I landed right in Aunt Glenda's bedroom," I said breathlessly. "And I'm afraid she saw me. She's probably phoning the police at this very moment."

The sight of Lucas was a bit of a shock. In 1993 he looked like the grandpa I'd known when I was a little girl. There was only a slight resemblance to the young Lucas who kept his hair down with some kind of gel or cream. It was silly, but that brought tears to my eyes.

Grandpa didn't notice. He was listening at the door. "Wait here while I take a look around." He turned briefly to me and smiled. "There are sandwiches over there, just in case. And if anyone happens to come in—"

"I'm your cousin Hazel," I said, finishing his sentence.

"No, if anyone comes in, you'd better hide! At the far side of the room, under the desk."

But there was no need to hide. Lucas soon returned. I'd used the time to get my breath back, eat a sandwich, and work out how many minutes I had left before I traveled back.

"Don't worry," he said. "She's just telling Charles he's responsible for the nightmares she's had ever since the wedding." He shook his head. "Who'd have thought the sole heir to a chain of hotels would put up with that sort of thing? Never mind, we can forget Glenda. Let's have a look at you, granddaughter. Exactly as I remember you, maybe even a little prettier. What happened to your pajamas? You look like a chimney sweep."

I waved that question away. "It wasn't too easy getting here. In 2011 I can't just carry the chronograph around the house, because Charlotte suspects something, and she's watching me like a lynx. Maybe she's breaking open the lock of my door at this very second. It wouldn't surprise me. And now I don't have much time left, because I had to wait about upstairs in the wardrobe forever." I clicked my tongue, annoyed. "And if I don't travel back to my own room, I've locked myself out of it—oh, wonderful!" I dropped into an armchair with a groan. "What a mess! We'll have to meet some other time, and before that wretched ball. I suggest we meet up on the roof. I think it's the only place where we won't be disturbed. How about tomorrow at midnight, from your point of view? Or is it too difficult for you to climb up to the roof unnoticed? There's a way up the chimney, Xemerius says, but I don't know whether—"

"Hang on a minute," said Grandpa, grinning. "I've had a few years to think this over, after all, and I have something ready for you in advance." He pointed to the table. There was a book lying on it beside the plate of sandwiches, a really fat volume.

"*Anna Karenina?*"

Grandpa nodded. "Open it!"

"You've hidden a code in it?" I suggested. "Like in *The Green Rider*?"

I didn't believe this! Lucas had spent thirty-seven years setting me another puzzle? I'd probably have to spend days counting letters. "You know, I'd really rather you just told me what it says. We still have a few minutes left."

"Don't jump to conclusions. Read the first lines," Grandpa told me.

I opened the book at the first chapter. *"Happy families are all alike; every unhappy family is unhappy in its own way.* Er—yes. Very nicely put. And so wise. But all the same—"

"Looks normal, doesn't it?" Lucas was beaming. "But it's a specially prepared edition! The first three hundred and last three hundred pages are genuine Tolstoy, as well as two hundred pages in the middle. But the rest of it is from me to you—set in exactly the same typeface. A perfect disguise! In here you'll find all the information that I've been able to gather in thirty-seven years—although I don't yet know exactly what was the particular reason for Lucy and Paul to run away with the chronograph." He took the book from me and riffled through the pages. "We have proof that the count withheld certain important documents from the Guardians right from the year of the Lodge's foundation onward, prophesies suggesting that the philosopher's stone isn't what he wanted to make everyone think."

"Then what is it?"

"We aren't quite sure yet. We're working on getting those documents." Grandpa scratched his head. "Listen,

I've done a lot of thinking—and I realize that I won't still be alive in the year 2011. I'll probably have died before you're old enough for me to tell you everything I manage to discover before my death."

I didn't know what to say, but I nodded.

My grandpa smiled his wonderful Grandpa smile, the one that creased up his whole face in wrinkles. "It's not so bad, Gwen. I assure you, even if I had to die today, I wouldn't be sad about it. I've had a wonderful life." The laughter lines deepened. "It's just a shame that I won't be able to help you in your own time."

I nodded again, fighting back tears.

"Oh, come along, little Raven. You should know better than anyone that death is part of life." Lucas patted my arm. "I might at least be expected to have the decency to haunt this house as a ghost when I'm dead. You really could do with some support."

"Yes, that would be nice," I whispered, "but not so nice too." The ghosts I knew were not particularly happy. I was sure they would rather have been somewhere else. Not one of them enjoyed being a ghost. In fact, most of them didn't even think they were dead. No, it was a good thing that Grandpa wouldn't be among them.

"When do you have to travel back?" he asked.

I looked at the clock. My God, to think time could pass so fast! "In nine minutes. And I have to elapse in Aunt Glenda's bedroom, because in my own time, I've bolted the door of the room on the inside."

"We could try simply pushing you into the room a few

seconds in advance," said Lucas. "You'd disappear before she really grasped the fact that—"

At that moment, there was a knock on the library door. "Lucas, are you in there?"

"Hide!" whispered Lucas, but I'd already reacted, diving under the desk just before the door opened and Lady Arista came in. I could only see her feet and the hem of her bathrobe, but her voice was unmistakable.

"What are you doing down here in the middle of the night? And are those by any chance tuna sandwiches? You know what Dr. White said." She dropped, sighing, into the chair I had warmed for her. Now she was in view up to the shoulders, which were ramrod straight as usual. I wondered if she'd see part of me, too, if she turned her head.

She clicked her tongue, sounding annoyed. "Charles just came to see me. He says Glenda's been threatening to hit him."

"Oh, dear," said Lucas. He sounded remarkably relaxed about it. "Poor lad. What did you do?"

"Gave him a whisky," replied my grandmother, and she giggled.

I held my breath. My grandmother, giggling? I'd never heard her do such a thing. We were always surprised when she even laughed, and giggling was in an entirely different league. Rather as if you were hearing an opera by Wagner played on the descant recorder. "And then he started crying!" said my grandmother scornfully. That sounded more like Lady Arista. "So after that I needed a whisky."

"That's my girl!" I could tell from his voice that my

grandfather was smiling, and suddenly I had a warm sensation around my heart. The two of them looked really happy together. (Well, from the neck down, anyway.) Only now did I realize that I'd had no real idea what their marriage was like.

"High time for Glenda and Charles to move out of this house at long last," said Lady Arista. "I don't think our children are especially good at choosing partners, do you? Harry's Jane is such a bore, Charles is a weakling, and Grace's Nicholas is as poor as a church mouse."

"But he makes her happy, and that's what matters."

Lady Arista stood up. "Yes, I like Nicholas best of them all. It would be much worse if Grace had stayed fixated on that impossible de Villiers boy, the ambitious one." I could see her giving herself a little shake. "The de Villiers men are all shockingly arrogant. I hope Lucy will soon see reason."

"I think Paul is rather different from the rest of them." Grandpa was grinning. "He's a nice boy."

"I doubt it—there's little to choose between them in that family. Coming upstairs with me?"

"I was going to read for a little longer—"

Yes, and you're also going to talk to your granddaughter from the future, please. Because my time was running out. I couldn't see the clock from here, but I could hear it ticking. And I was beginning to get that damn roller-coaster sensation in the pit of my stomach.

"*Anna Karenina.* Rather a melancholy book, don't you think, my dear?" I saw my grandmother's slender hands pick up the book and open it at random. Presumably Lucas was holding his breath—I know I was holding mine. *"Can one ever explain to someone else exactly how one feels?* Maybe I ought to reread it sometime. But I'd need my glasses."

"I'm rereading it first," said Lucas firmly.

"Yes, but no more reading tonight." She put the book back on the table and bent down to Lucas. I couldn't see for sure, but it looked as if the two of them were kissing.

"I'll come straight up in a couple of minutes, honey-bunch," said Lucas, which was a mistake on his part, because at the word *honeybunch*—Good heavens! He meant *Lady Arista!*—I jumped so violently that my head banged against the desktop.

"What was that?" asked my grandmother sternly.

"What do you mean?" I saw Lucas's hand sweeping *Anna Karenina* off the table.

"That noise!"

"I didn't hear anything," said Lucas, but he couldn't prevent Lady Arista from turning my way. I could almost feel her eyes sparkling suspiciously above her Roman nose.

Now what?

Lucas cleared his throat and gave the book a good kick. It slid over the parquet floorboards in my direction and came to rest eighteen inches from the desk. My stomach cramped as Lady Arista took a step toward me.

"But that's . . . ," she was murmuring to herself.

"Now or never," said Lucas, and I assumed that he meant it for me. With a sudden gesture I put out my arm, snatched the book, and clutched it to my breast. My grandmother let out a little scream of surprise. But before she could bend down to look under the desk, her embroidered slippers blurred before my eyes.

Back in 2011, I crawled out from under the desk with my heart thudding and thanked my stars that no one had moved it an inch since 1993. Poor Lady Arista—after seeing the desk grow an arm and gobble up a book, she'd probably needed another whisky.

As for me, all I needed was my bed. When Charlotte barred my way up on the second floor, I wasn't even startled anymore, as if my heart had had quite enough excitement for one day.

"I heard you were very sick and had to stay in bed." She switched on a flashlight, dazzling me with its bright LED beam. That reminded me that I'd left Nick's flashlight behind somewhere in 1993. Presumably in the wardrobe.

"That's right. Obviously I caught your bug," I said. "Seems to be a bug that keeps us from sleeping at night. I went to find something to read. And what are you doing? A little fitness training?"

"Why not?" Charlotte came a step closer and directed the beam of the flashlight on my book. *Anna Karenina*. Isn't that rather heavy going for you?"

"You think so? Well then, maybe we'd better swap. I'll give you *Anna Karenina*, and you can lend me your copy of *In the Shadow of Vampire Mountain*."

Charlotte was so taken aback that she said nothing for a full three seconds. Then she dazzled me with the bright flashlight again. "Show me what's in that chest . . . and then maybe I can help you, Gwenny. Help you to avert the worst . . ." She could sound all gentle and persuasive when she liked, almost concerned on my behalf.

Tensing my stomach muscles, I pushed past her. "Forget it, Charlotte. And stay away from my room, will you?"

"If I'm on the right track, then you really are even stupider than I thought." Her voice was back to normal. But although I expected her to go on standing in my way, and probably to smash my shinbone at the very least, she let me pass. Only the beam of the flashlight followed me a little distance.

We can't stop time, but it will sometimes stand still for love.

PEARL S. BUCK

SEVEN

AT ALMOST ten o'clock, there was a knock at the door of my room. I woke from deep sleep abruptly, although it was the third time I'd been woken that morning. The first time had been at seven, when Mum came in to see how I was ("Your temperature's gone right down—it just shows what a tough constitution you have. You can go back to school tomorrow!") The second time was Lesley waking me three-quarters of an hour later. She'd come in on her way to school on purpose, because I'd sent her a text message in the middle of the night.

I was surprised that the message had made any sense at all, because when I wrote it, I was almost out of my mind with fear, and my hands had trembled so much that I could hardly press the letter keys. The only way into my locked room had been from outside, over the windowsill, which was about forty feet above the road. Xemerius had come up with the idea that if I climbed out the window of

Nick's room, I could keep close to the wall of the house and work my way along it to the sill of my own window. Xemerius himself had contributed nothing to the success of the operation except to say, "Don't look down!" and add, "My word, it's a long way to the road!"

Lesley and I had only a few minutes before she had to go on to school, while I went back to catching up with my sleep. Until I heard loud voices outside the door. It opened, and Mr. Marley's red head appeared.

"Good morning," he said stiffly.

Xemerius, who had been dozing at the foot of my bed, sat up with a start. "What's that gingernob doing here?"

I pulled the covers up to my chin. "House on fire or something?" I asked Mr. Marley, not very imaginatively. According to my mother, I wasn't expected to elapse until this afternoon. And then not, I sincerely hoped, straight from my bed!

"This is going too far, young man!" cried a voice behind him. It was Aunt Maddy. She nudged Mr. Marley to make him move aside and pushed her way past him into my room. "Obviously you have no manners at all, or you wouldn't just burst into a young lady's room like that!"

"Yes, and I'm not fit to be seen in public yet myself," said Xemerius, licking his forepaw.

"I . . . I . . . ," stammered Mr. Marley, red as beetroot in the face.

"It's really no way to behave!"

"You keep out of this, Aunt Maddy!" A third person appeared: Charlotte in jeans and a bright green sweater that made her hair shine like fire. "Mr. Marley and Mr. Brewer have just come to fetch something." Mr. Brewer was obviously the young man in the black suit who now appeared. That made four of them. My bedroom was beginning to feel like Victoria Station at rush hour, only with nowhere near enough space in it.

Charlotte made her way to the front, using her elbows. "Where's the chest?" she asked.

"Telltale tit, your tongue shall be split!" sang Xemerius.

"What chest?" I was still huddled under my quilt as if rooted to the spot. And I didn't want to get out of bed, because I was still wearing the grubby pajamas, and I had no intention of giving Mr. Marley a look at them. It was bad enough for him to see my untidy hair.

"You know perfectly well what chest!" Charlotte was looming over me. "So where is it?"

Aunt Maddy's curls shook with her indignation. "No one is to touch that chest!" she said in surprisingly imperious tones.

But they were nothing compared with the cutting edge of Lady Arista's voice. "Madeleine! I told you to stay downstairs." Now my grandmother also entered the room, straight as a ramrod, chin in the air. "This is none of your business."

Meanwhile Charlotte had fought her way through the crowd over to the wardrobe. She flung the door open and pointed to the chest. "There it is!"

"It certainly is my business. It's *my* chest," cried Aunt

Maddy again, this time with desperation in her voice. "I only lent it to Gwyneth!"

"Nonsense," said Lady Arista. "That chest belonged to Lucas. All these years I've wondered where it was." Her icy blue eyes examined me. "Young lady, if Charlotte is right in what she says, I wouldn't care to be in your shoes."

I pulled the quilt a little farther up and considered disappearing under it entirely.

"It's locked," Charlotte announced, leaning over the chest.

Lady Arista put out her hand. "The key, Gwyneth."

"I don't have it." My voice was muffled by the quilt. "And I don't see what—"

"Don't be so stubborn," Lady Arista interrupted me. But as the key was back on its chain around Lesley's neck, there was nothing I could do but keep on being stubborn.

Charlotte began searching the drawers of my desk, and Aunt Maddy slapped her fingers. "You should be ashamed of yourself!"

Mr. Marley cleared his throat. "With respect, Lady Montrose, at the Temple we have ways and means of opening locks without a key. . . ."

"*Ways and means,*" said Xemerius, imitating his mysterious tone of voice. "As if there is anything magical about a crowbar!"

"Very well, you had better take the chest away with you," said Lady Arista. She turned to the door. "Mr. Bernard," I heard her call, "please show these gentlemen downstairs."

"You'd have thought the Guardians had enough antiques already," said Xemerius. "A greedy bunch, if you ask me."

"I want to make a formal protest again," said Aunt Maddy, while Mr. Marley and the other man carried the chest out of my room without so much as a civil goodbye. "This is . . . is trespassing. When Grace hears that people have been simply marching into her apartment, she'll be furious."

"This is still *my* house," said Lady Arista coolly. She was already turning to go. "And *my* rules apply here. One may perhaps ascribe the fact that Gwyneth is unaware of her duties and unfortunately shows that she is unworthy of the Montrose family to her youth and lack of training, but you, Madeleine, ought to know what your brother was working for all his life! I would have expected more of a sense of the honor of the Montroses from you. I am severely disappointed. By you both."

"And I'm disappointed too!" Aunt Maddy put her hands on her hips and stared angrily at the retreating figure of Lady Arista. "By *you* both. After all, we're a family!" And as Lady Arista couldn't hear her anymore, she turned to Charlotte. "Little bunny! Oh, how could you?"

Charlotte went red. For a moment she looked like the unspeakable Mr. Marley, and I wondered where my mobile was. I'd have loved to take a photo for posterity. Or maybe for purposes of blackmail later.

"I couldn't allow Gwyneth to sabotage something that she doesn't even *understand*," said Charlotte. Her voice shook slightly. "Simply because she always wants to be the center of attention. She . . . she has no respect for the mysteries! She doesn't deserve to be linked to them." She gave me a nasty look, which seemed to help her to recover her self-control. "You brought it on yourself!" she spat, with new venom. "And I even offered to help you! But no, you just have to go around breaking rules the whole time." With those words, she was her old self again, doing what she did best: tossing her head and marching out.

"Oh dear, oh dear, oh dear," said Aunt Maddy, sitting down on the edge of my bed. Xemerius was only just in time to roll out of her way. "What are we going to do now? I'm sure they'll come for you when they've opened the chest, and they won't be gentle." She fished her bag of sherbet lemons out of her pocket and put five in her mouth at once. "I can't bear it."

"Take it easy, Aunt Maddy!" I ran the fingers of both hands through my hair and grinned at her. "When they get inside the chest, they'll find my school atlas and the *Collected Works of Jane Austen* that you gave me for Christmas."

"Oh." Aunt Maddy rubbed her nose and heaved a sigh of relief. "I *thought* it would be something like that, of course," she said, sucking sherbet lemons vigorously. "Then where . . . ?"

"In a safe place, I hope." Sighing deeply myself, I swung my legs over the edge of the bed. "But in case they do happen to come back again—with a warrant to search the house or something—maybe I'd better go and shower.

By the way, thanks very much for your advice yesterday. So all the rooms up here were empty in 1993, were they? I landed right in Aunt Glenda and ex-Uncle Charlie's bedroom!"

"Oops," said Aunt Maddy, almost choking on a sherbet lemon in alarm.

I DIDN'T SEE Charlotte and my grandmother anymore that morning. The phone rang on the lower floors a couple of times, and once it rang up on our floor, but it was only Mum wanting to know how I was.

Later in the day, Aunt Maddy's friend Mrs. Purpleplum came to see her, and I heard the pair of them giggling like two little girls. Otherwise all was quiet. Before I was collected and driven to the Temple at midday, Xemerius and I had been able to read some of *Anna Karenina*, or rather the part of it that Tolstoy hadn't written. Pages 300 to 500 were mostly full of texts copied from the *Chronicles* and *Annals of the Guardians*. Lucas had written *These are only the interesting parts, dear granddaughter*, but to be honest, I didn't think any of it very interesting at first. "The General Laws of Time Travel," written by Count Saint-Germain himself, was too much of a strain on my brain from the first sentence. *Although, in the present, the past has already happened, one must take the greatest care not to allow the past to endanger the present by making it the present.*

"Do you understand that?" I asked Xemerius. "On the one hand, everything has already happened anyway, so it's going to happen the way it did happen; on the other hand, you mustn't risk infecting anyone with a flu virus. Or what *does* it mean?"

Xemerius shook his head. "Let's just skip that bit, okay?"

But even the essay by a certain Dr. M. Giordano (surely that couldn't be a coincidence?) entitled "Count Saint-Germain—Time Traveler and Visionary—Analysis of the Sources from Records of the Inquisition and Letters," published in a journal of historical research in 1992, began with a sentence that took up eight lines and looked like going on forever, which didn't exactly make you want to read more.

Xemerius seemed to feel the same. "Boring, boring, boring!" he complained, and I skipped to the place where Lucas had collected all the rhymes and verses. I knew some of them already, but those new to me were confused and full of symbolism, and you could interpret them as meaning all sorts of things, depending how you looked at them, just like Aunt Maddy's visions. The words *blood* and *ever* kept coming up, often rhyming with *flood* and *never*.

"Well, they're not by Shakespeare, anyway," Xemerius agreed with me. "Sounds like a couple of drunks got together to think up some rhymes to sound as cryptic as possible. Hey, folks, let's think what rhymes with *fox of jade*. *Marmalade, wade, made*? No, let's try *masquerade*, sounds—hic!—much more mysterious."

I couldn't help laughing. Those verses really were the

end! But I knew Lesley would fall on them gleefully. She loved anything cryptic, and she was firmly convinced that reading *Anna Karenina* would get us a whole lot farther.

"Today is the beginning of a new era!" she had announced dramatically early that morning, waving the book in the air. "Knowledge is power!" She stopped short for a moment. "I heard that in some film, but I can't remember straight off which it was. Never mind, now we can finally get to the bottom of the mystery."

Maybe she was right. But later, when I was sitting on the green sofa in the year 1953, I didn't feel in the least powerful or knowledgeable, I just felt terribly alone. How I wished Lesley could be with me. Or at least Xemerius.

Leafing aimlessly through Lucas's special edition of the book, I stumbled on the passage that Mr. Marley had mentioned. In October 1782, there was indeed an entry in the *Annals* which ran as follows: *Before leaving, the count impressed it upon us again that, in future, points of contact between the power of the mysteries and the female time travelers, in particular the last-born, the Ruby, must be kept as slight as possible and also that we must never underestimate the destructive force of feminine curiosity.* Hm, yes. I could well believe the count had said that. In fact, I could almost hear his tone of voice. "Destructive force of feminine curiosity"—huh!

However, that didn't help me much over the ball, which unfortunately was only postponed, not canceled, quite apart from the fact that all this garbage from the Guardians didn't make me exactly keen to face the count again.

With a certain uneasiness, I turned to the study of the Golden Rules. There was a lot about honor and conscience here, and the duty of not doing anything in the past that could change the future. I'd probably broken Rule Four—no objects must be transported from one period to another—on every single one of my journeys through time. And the same with Rule Five, about never influencing the fate of people in the past. I put the book on my lap and thoughtfully chewed my lower lip. Maybe Charlotte was right, and I was hopelessly addicted to breaking rules on principle. Were the Guardians searching my room at this very moment? Or even the whole house—with tracker dogs and metal detectors? A little while ago, anyway, it hadn't seemed as if our little deception had been enough to shake Charlotte's credibility.

Although when Mr. Marley came to collect me from the house, he *did* seem slightly shaken. He could hardly look me in the eye, even though he was trying to act as if nothing had happened.

"Probably ashamed of himself," suggested Xemerius. "I'd love to have seen his silly face when he opened the chest. I hope he got such a fright that he dropped the crowbar on his foot."

It certainly must have been an embarrassing moment for Mr. Marley when he found my books in the chest. And for Charlotte, of course. But she certainly wasn't about to give up in a hurry.

Mr. Marley was now apparently trying to make light conversation, probably to hide his guilt feelings as he held a black umbrella over me on the way from the car to the headquarters of the Lodge. "Very cool today, don't you think?" he said briskly.

That was really too much for me, so I answered him back just as briskly. "Yes, and when do I get my chest back?"

He couldn't think of any answer to that; he just went red as a lobster again.

"Can I at least have my books back, or are they still being searched for fingerprints?" No, I wasn't feeling sorry for him today.

"We . . . regrettably . . . maybe . . . a mistake," he stammered, and Xemerius and I went "Uh?" in unison.

Mr. Marley was visibly relieved to meet Mr. Whitman at the entrance to the building. Once again, he looked like a film star on the red carpet. He had obviously just arrived, like us, because he was taking off his coat with great elegance and shaking raindrops out of his thick hair. He smiled at us with his perfect white teeth. All we needed was a storm of camera flashes. If I'd been Cynthia, I'm sure I'd have been slobbering over him, but I was totally immune to his good looks and charm, not that he often switched on the charm for me, anyway. Also Xemerius was fooling around behind his back, making faces.

"Gwyneth, so I hear you're feeling better?" asked Mr. Whitman.

Who'd told him that?

"A bit." To take his mind off my nonexistent flu and because I was in full swing anyway, I quickly went right on. "I was just asking Mr. Marley about my chest. Maybe you can tell me when I'm getting it back and why you had it taken away in the first place."

"That's the spirit! Attack is the best form of defense," Xemerius encouraged me. "I can see you're going to manage here just fine without me, so I'll fly off home to read some—er, to see everything's okay. See you later, alligator! Teehee!"

"I . . . we . . . misinformed," Mr. Marley went on stammering.

Mr. Whitman clicked his tongue in annoyance. Beside him, Mr. Marley looked even more awkward. "Marley, you can take a break for lunch now."

"Yes, sir. Take a break for lunch, sir." Mr. Marley almost clicked his heels in military style.

"Gwyneth, your cousin suspects that you are in possession of an item that doesn't belong to you," said Mr. Whitman when Mr. Marley had hurried off. He was looking at me hard. Lesley had nicknamed him Squirrel because of his lovely brown eyes, but with the best will in the world, I couldn't see anything cute about them now, and none of the warmth you're always supposed to sense in brown eyes. Under that gaze, my spirit of contradiction slipped away to the farthest corner of my mind. Suddenly I wished Mr. Marley had stayed. I had much more fun arguing with him than with Mr. Whitman. It was difficult lying to Mr. Whitman, maybe because of his experience as a teacher, but all the same, I tried.

"Charlotte probably feels a bit left out," I murmured,

looking down. "She's not having an easy time right now, so it could be that she invents things to . . . er . . . get herself a little attention again."

"Yes, the others think so too," said Mr. Whitman thoughtfully. "But I consider Charlotte a well-balanced character, who doesn't need that kind of thing." He bent his head so close to my face that I could smell his aftershave. "If her suspicion should, after all, be confirmed . . . well, I'm not sure whether you are really aware of the consequences of your actions."

That made two of us. It cost me a great effort to look into his eyes again. "May I at least ask what item you're talking about?" I tentatively inquired.

Mr. Whitman raised one eyebrow and then, surprisingly, smiled. "It is quite possible that I have underestimated you, Gwyneth. But that's no reason for you to overestimate yourself."

For a few seconds, we stared into each other's eyes, and I suddenly felt exhausted. What was the point of all this playacting? Suppose I simply handed the chronograph over to the Guardians and let things take their course? Somewhere at the back of my mind, I heard Lesley saying *Pull yourself together, for goodness' sake!* But why bother? I was groping about in the dark and getting no further anyway. Mr. Whitman was right. I could be massively overestimating myself and just making everything even worse. I didn't even know exactly why I landed myself with such nerve-racking situations. Wouldn't it feel good to hand over responsibility, leaving it to other people to make the decisions?

"Well?" asked Mr. Whitman in a soft voice, and now there really was a warm light in his eyes. "Is there something you want to tell me, Gwyneth?"

Who knows—maybe I'd even have done just that if Mr. George hadn't joined us at that moment. He had put an end to my moment of weakness with the words "So there you are, Gwyneth." Mr. Whitman had clicked his tongue with annoyance again, but he didn't return to the subject in front of Mr. George.

And now here I was, sitting all alone on the green sofa in the year 1953, still struggling to get my composure back. And a bit of confidence.

"Knowledge is power," I said through gritted teeth, trying to motivate myself, and I opened the book again. The entries from the *Annals* that Lucas had copied were mainly from the years 1782 and 1912, *because those, dear granddaughter, are the years that matter most to you. In September 1782, the so-called Florentine Alliance was smashed, and the traitor in the Inner Circle of Guardians unmasked. Although it does not say so explicitly in the* Annals, *we can assume that you and Gideon will be involved in those events in some way.*

I looked up. Was that the clue that I'd been looking for, wondering why the ball mattered so much? If so, then I was no wiser than before. *Thanks a lot, Grandpa*, I sighed. That was about as useful as *beware of pastrami sandwiches*. I turned the page.

"Don't be scared," said a voice behind me.

Those must certainly fall into the category of Famous Last Words, the sort that are the last thing you hear before your death. (Along with "it isn't loaded" and "he only wants to play.") Of course I was terribly scared.

"Only me." Gideon was standing behind the sofa smiling down at me. The sight of him instantly switched my body into emergency mode again, with all kinds of contradictory feelings swirling about inside me, unable to decide which way to go.

"Mr. Whitman thought you could do with a little company," said Gideon casually. "And I remembered that the lightbulb down here really must need changing." He threw a bulb up in the air like a juggling ball, caught it, and at the same time dropped on the sofa beside me in one graceful movement. "Hey, you're very comfortable down here. Cashmere blankets! And grapes. I think Mrs. Jenkins must have a soft spot for you."

As I stared at his handsome, pale face and tried to get my chaotic feelings under control, at least I had the presence of mind to close *Anna Karenina*.

Gideon was looking at me attentively, his gaze wandering from my forehead over my eyes and down to my mouth. I wanted to turn away and move farther along the sofa, but at the same time, I couldn't get enough of the sight of him, so I went on staring at him like a rabbit hypnotized by a snake.

"A little hello, maybe?" he said, looking me in the eye again. "Even if you're cross with me at the moment."

The amused way the corners of his mouth lifted brought me back to myself. "Thanks for reminding me." I put the hair away from my forehead, straightened my back, and opened my book, quite close to the beginning this time. I'd simply ignore him—he needn't think everything was okay between us.

But it wasn't so easy to put Gideon off his stroke. He looked up at the ceiling. "I'd have to switch the light out for a while to change the bulb. That would make it rather dark in here."

I said nothing.

"Do you have a flashlight with you?"

I didn't reply.

"On the other hand, the light doesn't seem to be giving much trouble today. Maybe we'll just wait until it does."

I sensed the sidelong look he was giving me as clearly as if he were touching me, but I went on staring at my book.

"Can I have some of your grapes?"

At this I lost my patience. "Oh, have the whole bunch—but leave me in peace to read!" I snapped at him. "And just keep your mouth shut, will you? I don't feel like making silly small talk with you."

He said nothing for the time it took him to eat the grapes. I turned a page, although I hadn't read a single word.

"I hear you had visitors this morning." He began juggling two grapes. "Charlotte said something about a mysterious chest."

Oh, so that's the way the wind was blowing! I let the

book sink to my lap. "Which part of *keep your mouth shut* don't you understand?"

Gideon grinned broadly. "Hey, I'm not making small talk. I'd like to know what gave Charlotte the idea that you may have something in your hands that was passed on to you by Lucy and Paul."

He was here to interrogate me, obviously. Probably on behalf of Falk and the others. *Be nice to her, then she's sure to tell you whether she's keeping something hidden, and if so, where.* After all, thinking women stupid was the de Villiers family hobby.

I drew my legs up on the sofa and sat cross-legged. When I was angry, it was easier to look him in the eye without letting my lower lip quiver. "Ask Charlotte yourself what gave her the idea," I said coldly.

"I did." Gideon sat cross-legged too, so that we were sitting opposite each other like two Native Americans in a tepee. Was there an opposite of smoking the pipe of peace? "She thinks that somehow or other you've come by the stolen chronograph, and your brother and sister, your great-aunt, and even your butler are helping you to hide it."

I shook my head. "I must say, I'd never have suspected Charlotte of having too much imagination. Seems that all we have to do is carry an old chest through the house, and she goes right off her head."

"What was in the chest?" he asked, in a rather uninterested tone. My goodness, how transparent!

"Nothing! We use it as a card table when we play poker."

I thought this was such a good idea that I only just managed to suppress a grin.

"Arizona hold 'em?" inquired Gideon, paying more attention now.

Ha, ha. "Texas hold 'em," I said. As if he could unsettle me with such a feeble ruse. Lesley's father had taught us to play poker when we were twelve. He thought that all girls should learn—why, he never told us. Thanks to him, anyway, we knew all the tricks and were world champions at bluffing. To this day, Lesley rubbed her nose when she had a good hand, but I was the only person who knew. "Also Omaha, but not so often. You know," I said, leaning confidingly forward, "we're forbidden to play games of chance at home—my grandmother has some very strict rules. We began playing poker just out of protest and sheer defiance, Aunt Maddy, Mr. Bernard, Nick, and me. But then we started really enjoying it."

Gideon had raised one eyebrow. He looked kind of impressed. I couldn't blame him.

"Although maybe Lady Arista is right, and gambling is the root of all evil," I went on. I was in my element now. "At first we played for sherbet lemons, but now the stakes are higher. My brother lost all his pocket money last week. My word, if Lady Arista got to hear about that . . ." I leaned even farther forward and looked deep into Gideon's eyes. "But don't let Charlotte know, or she'd tell tales of us. I'd sooner she invented stories about stolen chronographs!" I sat up straight again, feeling extremely pleased with myself.

Gideon was still looking impressed. He gazed at me for a while in silence, and then he suddenly put out his hand and stroked my hair, which wrecked my self-control right away.

"Stop that!" He really was trying every trick in the book! Bastard. "What do you want here anyway? I don't need company." Unfortunately it didn't sound as venomous as I'd intended, more like rather pathetic. "Shouldn't you be traveling around on secret missions, getting blood out of people?"

"You mean Operation Trunk-hose yesterday evening?" He had stopped the stroking, but now he took a strand of my hair in his fingers and played with it. "Mission accomplished. Elaine Burghley's blood is in the chronograph." For a couple of seconds, he stared past me into space, looking sad. Then he had control of himself again. "So all we need is blood from the obstinate Lady Tilney, Lucy, and Paul. But now that we know what time Paul and Lucy are living in, and under what names, that's only a formality. In fact, I'm going to see Lady Tilney tomorrow morning."

"I thought you'd had some doubts about the aims we're all supposed to be pursuing," I said, freeing my hair from his hand. "Suppose Lucy and Paul are right, and the Circle of Blood should never be closed? You did say that was a possibility."

"Correct. But I'm not about to say so to the Guardians. You're the only person I've told."

Oh, what a cunning psychological move! *You're the only one I trust.*

But I could be cunning as well if I wanted. (I only had to remember the poker story.) "Lucy and Paul said the count can't be trusted. Do you think so too?"

Gideon shook his head. Suddenly his face was serious, and he looked tensed up. "No. I don't think he's evil. I just think . . ." He hesitated. "I think he considers the welfare of an individual less important than the common good."

"Including his own welfare?"

He didn't reply to that, but put out his hand again. This time he wound my strand of hair around his finger as if around a curler. Finally he said, "Suppose you could develop something sensational, for example—well, let's say a cure for cancer and AIDS and all the other diseases in the world. But to get hold of it, you had to let someone die. Would you do that?"

Let someone die? Was that why Lucy and Paul had stolen the chronograph? *Because they thought the price to be paid was too high*, I heard my mother's voice saying. Was the price a human life? I instantly had vivid scenes from films before my eyes, with crosses hanging upside down, human sacrifices on an altar, hooded men murmuring Babylonian incantations. Although that didn't seem quite right for the Guardians—maybe with one or two exceptions.

Gideon was looking at me expectantly.

"Sacrifice one human life to save many others?" I murmured. "I don't think the price for curing all those dreadful things would be too high, if you look at it from a practical viewpoint, I mean. How about you?"

Gideon said nothing for quite a long time. He just let

his eyes wander over my face and went on playing with my strand of hair. "Yes, I do think it would be too high," he finally said. "The end doesn't always justify the means."

"Does that mean you're not going to carry on doing what the count tells you to do?" I burst out with that—admittedly not very subtly. "Like playing with my feelings, for instance? Or with my hair?"

Gideon took his hand out of my hair and looked at it in surprise, as if it didn't belong to him. "I didn't . . . the count didn't tell me to play with your feelings."

"Oh, no?" All of a sudden, I was furiously angry with him. "Well, he more or less told me he did. Oh, come on! He was impressed, he said, to see how well you'd played your part, when you'd had so little time to manipulate my feelings—and when, stupidly, you'd put so much energy into working on the wrong victim, meaning Charlotte."

Gideon sighed and rubbed his forehead with the back of his hand. "The count and I did have a few conversations about . . . well, the things men do talk about. His view is—and please remember, the man lived over two hundred years ago, so we might take that into account—his view was that women are ruled solely by their emotions, whereas men let reason guide them. So it would be better for me if my female partner in time travel were in love with me, and then I could control what she did if there was any difficulty. I thought—"

"You thought!" I interrupted him angrily. "You thought: right, so I'll see about getting that to work as well!"

Gideon unwound his long legs, stood up, and began pacing up and down the room. For some reason or other, he suddenly looked upset. "Gwyneth, I didn't make you do anything, did I? In fact, I've often been pretty lousy to you."

I stared at him, speechless for a moment. "And I'm supposed to be grateful to you for that, am I?"

"Of course not," he said. "Or rather, yes."

"What does that mean?"

His eyes flashed at me. "Why do girls fancy guys who treat them badly? Obviously nice types aren't half so interesting. That sometimes makes it difficult to preserve your respect for girls." He was still prowling up and down the room, with long, almost angry strides. "Especially as boys with jug ears and spots don't take liberties nearly so often."

"You're just so cynical and superficial." I was totally baffled by the turn this conversation had suddenly taken.

Gideon shrugged his shoulders. "Who's being superficial here, I wonder? Or would you have let Marley kiss you?"

For a moment, I was genuinely put off my stroke. Maybe there was a tiny, *very* tiny grain of truth in what he said. . . . But then I shook my head. "You've forgotten something in your impressive chain of reasoning. In spite of your spot-free appearance—oh, and congratulations on your healthy sense of self-confidence—I wouldn't have let you kiss me if you hadn't lied to me and pretended to have real feelings for me." All of a sudden, tears shot into my eyes. But I went on, even though my voice was unsteady. "I wouldn't . . . wouldn't have fallen in love with you." Or even if I had, I wouldn't have let it show.

Gideon turned away from me. For a moment, he stood there motionless, then he suddenly kicked the wall with all his might. "Damn it, Gwyneth, have you been so scrupulous about the truth with *me*? You lied to me whenever you could, isn't that more like it?"

As I was looking for an answer—he really was an expert at turning the tables—the familiar old dizzy sensation came over me, and this time it made me sick to my stomach. Horrified, I clutched *Anna Karenina* to my breast. It was probably too late to pack up the basket.

I just had time to hear Gideon say, "Okay, so you let me kiss you, but you never trusted me." I didn't catch the rest, because next moment I landed in the present, and I had to concentrate on not throwing up in front of Mr. Marley's feet.

When I finally had my stomach under control again, Gideon had traveled back too. He was leaning against the wall. All the anger had left his face, and it wore a melancholy smile. "I'd really like to join in one of your poker games someday," he said. "I'm rather good at bluffing." Then he left the room without once looking back.

25 June 1542. *Still at the convent of S., investigating the case of young Elisabetta, who, according to her own father, is with child by a demon. In my report to the head of the Congregation, I did not conceal my suspicion that M. is inclined to entertain religious ideas of transfiguration—to put it kindly—and feels that he is called by the Lord God to root out evil from the world. He would clearly rather accuse his daughter of witchcraft than accept the fact that she does not comply with his concept of morality. I have mentioned above his good relations with R.M., and his influence in this region is considerable, so we cannot yet consider the case closed. The interrogation of the witnesses was grotesque. Two of Elisabetta's young fellow pupils confirmed what the conte said about the appearance of a demon in the convent garden. Little Sofia—who had no credible story to explain why, purely by chance, she happened to be hiding behind a bush in the garden at midnight—described a giant with horns, burning eyes, and cloven hooves, who, curiously enough, played Elisabetta a serenade on a violin before committing the sin of unchastity with her. The other girl witness, a close friend of Elisabetta, made an impression of being far more sensible. She spoke of a well-dressed and very tall young man, who beguiled Elisabetta with fair words. He would appear from nowhere and could then dissolve into thin air again, although she herself had not seen him do it. For her own part, Elisabetta told me that the*

young man who so cleverly made his way into the convent walls had neither horns nor cloven hooves, but was descended from a well-respected family and that she even knew his name. I was already feeling glad that I could bring the matter to a satisfactory conclusion when she added that, unfortunately, she could not tell me of any way to get in touch with him, since he had flown through the air to her from the future, to be precise, from the year of Our Lord 1723. You may imagine my desperation with regard to the state of mind of the persons surrounding me. I hope very much that the head of the Congregation will soon recall me to Florence, where genuine cases worthy of investigation await me.

FROM THE RECORDS OF THE INQUISITION,
AS DRAWN UP BY FATHER GIAN PETRO BARIBI
OF THE DOMINICAN ORDER
ARCHIVES OF THE UNIVERSITY LIBRARY, PADUA
(DECIPHERED, TRANSLATED, AND EDITED
BY DR. M. GIORDANO)

EIGHT

SHIMMERING BIRDS of paradise, leaves, and flowers in shades of blue and silver twined their way over the brocade bodice, and the sleeves and skirt were made of heavy, midnight blue silk that rustled at every step, swishing with a sound like the sea on a stormy day. I realized that anyone would have looked like a princess in that dress, but all the same, I was amazed by the sight of my own reflection in the mirror.

"It's . . . it's incredibly lovely!" I whispered in awe.

Xemerius snorted. He was sitting beside the sewing machine on a leftover scrap of brocade, picking his nose. "Girls!" he said. "First they do all they can to get out of going to a ball, and as soon as they have some silly old outfit like this to wear, they practically wet themselves with excitement."

I ignored him and turned to the creator of this

masterpiece. "But the other dress was perfect too, Madame Rossini."

"Yes, I know." She was smiling broadly. "You can 'ave it on another time."

"Madame Rossini, you're an artist!" I assured her fervently.

"*Oui, n'est-ce pas?*" She winked at me. "And as an artist, you 'ave to look at zings a leetle bit differently. Ze other dress was too pale for ze white wig—you 'ave a complexion zat cries out for strong . . . *comment on dit?* Contrasts!"

"Oh, my goodness, yes, the wig." I sighed. "It's going to ruin the whole effect. Could you take a quick picture of me first, please?"

"*Bien sur.*" Madame Rossini moved me to a stool at the dressing table and took my mobile when I held it out to her.

Xemerius unfolded his wings, flew over to me, and made a rather clumsy landing right in front of the china head with the wig on it.

"I suppose you know what usually lives in a wig like this, do you?" He put his head back and looked up at the towering white-powdered heap of imitation hair. "Crab lice, certainly. Probably moths as well. Maybe even worse." He raised his paws in a theatrical gesture. "All I'll say is TARANTULA."

I bit back a sharp reply—I'd been about to tell him that urban legends were old hat these days—and yawned ostentatiously.

Xemerius put his claws on his sides. "It's true," he

said. "And there's more than just spiders for you to beware of. There are certain counts to watch out for too. In
case you'd forgotten that fact in your enthusiasm for this
costume."

Unfortunately he was right. But today, well again and
declared fit to go to the ball even by the Guardians, all I
wanted was to think positively. And where could that be
done more easily than in Madame Rossini's studio?

I looked sternly at Xemerius and then let my eyes wander over all the dresses hanging side by side on clothes
rails. Each was more beautiful than the last.

"I don't suppose you happen to have anything green?"
I asked wistfully. I had remembered Cynthia's party and
Lesley's idea for us to go as little green men from Mars.
"We'll only need green garbage bags, a few pipe cleaners,
some empty cans, and a few polystyrene foam balls," she
had said. "With a stapler and a hot-melt glue gun, we can
turn ourselves into really cool Martians in no time. Kind
of live works of modern art, and it won't cost us a penny."

"Green? *Mais oui*, said Madame Rossini. "When everyone still thought zat red-'eaded clothes 'anger would travel
to ze past, I used many shades of green. It 'armonized perfectly with red 'air, and of course with zat bad boy's green
eyes."

"Uh-oh!" said Xemerius, threatening her with one paw.
"Keep off, lady. This is dangerous ground!"

He was right there. Zat bad boy—the bastard!—was
definitely not on the list of positive things that I wanted to
think about. (But if Gideon really was going to turn up at

the party with Charlotte, I would most certainly not be wearing a garbage bag, whatever Lesley said about cool modern art.)

Madame Rossini brushed my long hair and fixed it on top of my head with a scrunchie. "By ze way, 'e will be wearing green zis evening, a dark sea green. I 'ave spent hours choosing ze fabric so zat your colors will not clash. In ze end, I looked at it all by candlelight. *Absolument onirique.* Togezzer you will look like ze sea king and ze sea queen."

"*Abso-loo-mont!*" crowed Xemerius. "And if you don't both end up dead, you'll have lots of little sea princes and princesses together!"

I sighed. He'd have done better to stay at home keeping an eye on Charlotte. But he'd insisted on coming to the Temple with me, and that was rather sweet of him too. Xemerius knew how scared I was of the ball.

As Madame Rossini divided my hair into three strands and plaited them in a braid, which she then gathered into a bun, fixing it in place with hairpins, she was frowning with concentration. "Green, you said? Let me zink. We 'ad a riding 'abit of ze late eighteenth century, green velvet, and zere was—ah, yes, just ze thing!—an evening ensemble of 1922, eau-de-nil silk with a 'at to match and a coat and a 'andbag, *très chic.* And I 'ave copied several dresses by Balenciaga zat Grace Kelly wore in ze sixties. But ze best of all is a ball dress ze color of rose leaves. It would really suit you."

She carefully picked up the wig. Snow white and

decorated with blue ribbons and brocade flowers, it reminded me slightly of a wedding cake with several tiers. It even gave off a fragrance of vanilla and orange. Madame Rossini skillfully put the wedding cake over the bird's nest of hair on top of my head, and when I next looked in the mirror, I hardly knew myself.

"Hey, I look like a cross between Marie Antoinette and my grandmother," I said. And because of my black eyebrows, I also looked a little bit like Groucho Marx, if he'd dressed up as a woman.

"Nonsense," said Madame Rossini, fixing the wig with large hairpins. They looked like little daggers, with glittering artificial jewels at the ends that stuck out of the structure of white curls like blue stars. "It is ze contrasts zat matter, my leetle swan-necked beauty. Ze contrasts are important." She pointed to the makeup box lying open on the dressing table. "And ze makeup—smoky eyes were in vogue by candlelight in ze eighteenth century. Now, a little powder, *et c'est parfait*! You will be ze loveliest lady at ze ball!"

Not that she would ever know, because of course she wouldn't be there. I smiled at her. "You're so sweet to me! You're the nicest of them all. And you deserve an Oscar for your costumes."

"I know," said Madame Rossini modestly.

"IT IS IMPORTANT zat ze 'ead go into ze car first and out of it first when you get out. Always ze 'ead first, sweet'eart!" Madame Rossini had accompanied me to the

limousine and was helping me to get in. I felt rather like
Marge Simpson, except that my towering pile of hair was
white and not blue, and luckily there was room for it in
the car.

"Who'd have thought such a slender girl could take up
so much space!" said Mr. George, laughing, as I finally got
my skirts neatly spread out on the seat.

"Too true. I really need a postcode all to myself in these
clothes."

Madame Rossini blew me a cheerful good-bye kiss.
She was such a darling! When I was with her, I always entirely forgot how horrible my life was at the moment.

The car started moving off. At that moment, the front
door of the Guardians' headquarters flew open, and out
came Giordano in a hurry. His plucked eyebrows were
raised, and I was sure he was deathly pale under his fake
tan. His mouth with its puffy lips was opening and closing, making him look like a deep-sea fish on the verge of
extinction. Luckily I couldn't make out what he was saying to Madame Rossini, but I could well imagine it. *Stupid
thing. No idea of history and dancing the minuet. She'll put us
all to shame with her ignorance. A disgrace to the human race.*

Madame Rossini gave him a sugary sweet smile and
said something that made his fishy mouth close abruptly.
But then I lost sight of them both as the driver turned into
the street leading to the Strand.

I leaned back, grinning, but my good mood quickly
went away again during the drive, giving way to alarm

and anxiety. I was afraid of just about everything: the uncertainty of it all, the people, the looks, the questions, the dancing, and most of all, of course, I was afraid of another meeting with the count. My fears had followed me into my dreams yesterday, although I was glad I had at least slept through the night. Just before waking up, I had a particularly confused dream in which I stumbled over my own skirts and then fell down a huge staircase to land in front of Count Saint-Germain, who helped me to my feet, hauling me upright by my throat without touching me. As he did so, he snapped, oddly enough in Charlotte's voice, "You are a disgrace to the whole family." And Mr. Marley stood beside him, holding up Lesley's backpack and saying reproachfully, "There's only one pound twenty left on the Oyster card."

"How unfair! When I'd only just topped it up!" Lesley had laughed herself silly over my dream this morning. Although it hadn't really been so far-fetched: her backpack had been stolen after school yesterday just as she was about to get into the bus, roughly snatched off her back by a young man who, according to Lesley, could run faster than Dwain Chambers.

By now we were fairly well used to the Guardians and what they might do. And we wouldn't have expected anything else of Charlotte, who must have been behind the theft (indirectly, anyway). All the same, we thought those methods a little, well, crude. If we'd needed further evidence, it was the fact that the woman next to Lesley had been carrying a Hermès bag. I mean, honestly! What thief worth his salt would steal a shabby old rucksack instead of that?

According to Xemerius, as soon as I'd left the house yesterday, Charlotte had combed my room for the chronograph, searching every nook and cranny. She'd even looked under my pillow—what an original idea for a hiding place! After her meticulous exploration of my wardrobe, she had finally discovered the place where I had loosened the plasterboard and then crawled through into the lumber room beyond with a triumphant grin on her face (so Xemerius said). Not even the sister of my little spider friend had been able to scare her. She didn't hesitate to reach right inside the crocodile, either.

Of course, if she'd done that a day earlier . . . but the early bird catches the worm, as Lady Arista was always saying, and only the early bird. After Charlotte had crawled out of the lumber room and the wardrobe, frustrated, she had set her sights on Lesley, and that cost my friend her rucksack. So now the Guardians were in possession of a recently topped-up Oyster card, a pencil case, and a lip gloss (cherry tint), as well as a couple of books from the school library about the extent of the eastern delta of the river Ganges—but that was all.

Not even Charlotte could hide this setback behind the usual arrogant expression on her face when she appeared at the breakfast table this morning. Lady Arista, on the other hand, had the decency to admit that she had been wrong.

"The chest is on its way back to us," she said coolly. "Charlotte's nerves are obviously rather on edge, and I must admit that I was mistaken in believing what she said. Let us now consider the matter closed and turn to other subjects."

That was a genuine apology, at least by Lady Arista's standards. While Charlotte, on hearing these words, stared intently at her plate, the rest of us exchanged glances of astonishment and then obediently turned to the only other subject that occurred to us in a hurry, the weather.

Only Aunt Glenda, who had red blotches on her throat, wasn't taking anything that reflected badly on her daughter. She couldn't help saying, "I'd have thought we ought to be grateful to Charlotte for retaining a sense of responsibility and keeping her eyes open, instead of saying she was wrong. But there we are, ingratitude is only too widespread. I am sure that—"

However, we never found out what Aunt Glenda was sure of, because Lady Arista said, in icy tones, "If you don't want to change the subject, Glenda, you are of course at liberty to leave the table." Which Aunt Glenda did, along with Charlotte, who said she wasn't hungry anymore.

"Everything all right?" Mr. George, who was sitting opposite me—or diagonally opposite me, because my skirts were so huge that they filled half the car—and so far had left me to my thoughts, was smiling at me. "Did Dr. White give you something to help with your stage fright?"

I shook my head. "No," I said. "I was too scared of seeing double in the eighteenth century." Or worse, but I wasn't going to say so to Mr. George. At the soirée last Sunday, I had needed Lady Brompton's special punch to help me keep calm—and it was the same punch that had made me perform "Memory" from *Cats* to the astonished guests, about two hundred years before Andrew Lloyd Webber composed it. I'd also had a conversation out loud with a ghost in front of everyone, which I certainly wouldn't have done entirely sober.

I'd hoped I could have at least a few minutes alone with Dr. White, so that I could ask why he had helped me out, but he had examined me in front of Falk de Villiers and pronounced me better, to everyone's delight. When I gave him a conspiratorial wink as we parted, Dr. White only frowned and asked whether I had something in my eye. Remembering that, I sighed.

"Don't worry," said Mr. George sympathetically. "It won't last long, and you'll soon be back. You'll be through with the whole occasion before supper."

"But I can do all sorts of things wrong in that time. I might even cause an international crisis. Just ask Giordano. The wrong sort of smile, the wrong sort of curtsey, saying the wrong thing—and wow! The whole eighteenth century goes up in flames."

Mr. George laughed. "Oh, Giordano is just envious. He'd commit murder for a chance to travel in time."

I stroked the soft silk of my skirts, running my fingers over the embroidered outlines of the pattern. "Seriously, I still don't understand why the ball is so important. And what I have to do there."

"You mean as well as dancing and amusing yourself and enjoying the privilege of meeting the famous Duchess of Devonshire in person?" When I didn't smile back, Mr. George suddenly turned serious, took a handkerchief out of his breast pocket, and dabbed his forehead with it. "My dear girl, the day is of the utmost importance, because at that ball it will be discovered which of the Guardians of the time is the traitor who has been passing on information to the Florentine Alliance. Through your presence, the count hopes to induce both Lord Alastair and the traitor to give themselves away."

Ah. Well, at least that was more specific than the mysterious stuff in the middle of *Anna Karenina*.

"So strictly speaking, we're decoys?" I frowned. "But . . . er . . . wouldn't you have found out ages ago whether the plan worked? And who the traitor was? I mean, it all happened two hundred and thirty years ago."

"Yes and no," replied Mr. George. "For some reason, the reports on those days and weeks in the *Annals* are extremely vague. In addition, a whole section is missing. There are several references to the traitor who has been dismissed from his high office, but his name is never given. Four weeks later, there is a brief mention, almost by the way, saying that no one honored the traitor by attending his last rites, because he had earned no honor."

I had goose bumps again. "You mean the traitor was dead four weeks after being thrown out of the Lodge? How . . . practical."

Mr. George wasn't listening to me anymore. He

tapped on the window between us and the driver. "I'm afraid the gateway will be too narrow for the limousine. You'd better drive into the school yard through the side entrance." He smiled at me. "Here we are! And you look lovely—I've been wanting to say so all this time. As if you'd stepped straight out of an old painting."

The car stopped in front of the steps up to the school building.

"Only much, much more beautiful," said Mr. George.

"Thank you." I felt so embarrassed that I quite forgot what Madame Rossini had said—*Always ze 'ead first, sweet'eart!*—and I made the mistake of trying to get out of the car in the same way as usual, with the result that I got hopelessly entangled in my skirts and felt like an angry little bee caught in a spider's web. As I cursed and Mr. George had a fit of helpless giggles, two hands were reached out to me, and since I had no other option, I took them both and let them pull me out and set me on my feet.

One hand belonged to Gideon; the other to Mr. Whitman. I dropped them as if I'd burnt myself.

"Oh . . . thanks," I murmured, hastily smoothing down my dress and trying to calm my racing pulse. Then I took a closer look at Gideon—and grinned. I just couldn't help it. Although Madame Rossini was right about the beautiful sea-green fabric, and the magnificent coat fitted Gideon's broad shoulders perfectly, and he was a truly dazzling sight down to his buckled shoes, the white wig destroyed the whole effect.

"And I thought I was the only one who had to look like an idiot in a wig," I said.

His eyes sparkled with amusement. "At least I convinced Giordano that he could leave out the face powder and beauty spots."

Well, he was pale enough anyway. For a second or so, I reveled in the sight of the finely traced lines of his chin and lips, then I pulled myself together and looked at him as darkly as I could.

"The others are waiting downstairs. We'd better hurry before there are too many people around," said Mr. Whitman, glancing at the pavement, where two ladies walking their dogs had stopped and were looking curiously our way. If they didn't want to attract attention, I thought, the Guardians oughtn't to drive such flashy cars. Or drive people in peculiar historical costumes about London. Gideon put out his hand, but at that moment I heard a dull thud behind me and looked around. Xemerius had landed on the car roof and lay there on the metal for a moment, flat as a flounder.

"Ouf!" he gasped. "Couldn't you have waited for me?" He'd missed the moment when we left the Temple because of a cat, if I understood him correctly. "I had to fly the whole way! But I did want to say good-bye to you." He scrambled up and hopped onto my shoulder, and I felt something like a cold, wet hug.

"Right, Grand Mistress of the Order of the Crochet Pigs," he said. "When you're dancing with Him Whose

Name We Don't Mention," he added, giving Gideon a nasty look, "don't forget to give him a good kick. And watch out for that count." There was genuine concern in his voice. I swallowed, but next moment he added, "If you mess things up, you'll have to see how you get by without me in future. I'll be looking for a new human." He gave me a cheeky grin and flew toward the dogs, who tore free of their leashes a moment later and ran in panic, with their tails between their legs.

"Asleep and dreaming, Gwyneth?" Gideon gave me his arm. "Sorry, of course I mean Miss Gray! Would you be kind enough to follow me to the year 1782?"

"Oh, forget it—you can leave out the playacting until we arrive," I said in an undertone, so that Mr. George and Mr. Whitman, going ahead of us, couldn't hear it. "And for now, I'd like to keep physical contact with you to an absolute minimum, if you don't mind. What's more, I know my way around here. After all, this building is my school."

It was as good as deserted that early Friday evening. In the foyer we met Mr. Gilles the principal, pulling a golf bag along behind him. He'd already changed his suit for a pair of check trousers and a polo shirt. However, he politely welcomed "our esteemed Mr. Whitman's amateur dramatics society." Then he shook hands with us all. "I'm very keen on art. It's a pleasure to make the school available for rehearsals while you can't use your usual rehearsal room. What delightful costumes!" When he got to shaking hands with me, he stopped in surprise. "Well, well, I know that face. You're one of those naughty frog girls, aren't you?"

I forced a smile. "Yes, Mr. Gilles," I said.

"I'm glad you've found such a nice hobby. I'm sure it will keep you from thinking up any more stupid ideas like that frog." He beamed jovially at everyone. "Good luck to you all, then—or what is it you say in the theater, 'break a leg'?" He waved cheerfully to us again, and then disappeared through the doorway with his golf clubs, off to enjoy the weekend. I watched him go, feeling a little envious. For once I'd happily have changed places with him, even if it meant turning into a middle-aged baldie in check trousers.

"Naughty frog girl?" inquired Gideon on the way down to the art room in the cellars, and looking curiously at me sideways.

I was concentrating on holding my rustling skirts far enough up not to trip over them. "A couple of years ago, my friend Lesley and I had to put a squashed frog into another girl's soup—Mr. Gilles still holds it against us."

"You *had* to put a frog in another girl's soup?"

"Yes," I said, giving him a haughty look. "For educational reasons, one sometimes has to do things that may seem odd to outsiders."

Down in the cellar, right under the quote from Edgar Degas painted on the wall—*A picture should be painted with the same care that a criminal puts into carrying out his crime*—the usual suspects were already gathered around the chronograph: Falk de Villiers, Mr. Marley, and Dr. White, who was setting out surgical instruments and bandages on one of the tables. I was glad that at least we'd left Giordano behind at the Temple. He was probably still standing at the top of the steps up to the entrance, wringing his hands.

Mr. George winked at me. "I've just had a bright idea," he whispered. "If you find yourself at a loss, you can simply faint—ladies were always fainting in those days. No one knows for sure whether it was because their corsets were laced so tightly, or because of the bad air, or because fainting came in useful."

"I'll keep that at the back of my mind," I said. In fact, I was tempted to try out Mr. George's idea right away. Unfortunately Gideon seemed to have seen through me, because he took my arm with a slight smile.

And then Falk unwrapped the chronograph, and when he beckoned me over, I resigned myself to my fate, not without putting up a fervent prayer to heaven that Lady Brompton had passed on the recipe for her special punch to her good friend Lady Pympoole-Bothame.

MY IDEAS of a ball were vague. My ideas of a ball in past history were zero. So it was probably not surprising that, after Aunt Maddy's vision and my dreams that morning, I expected something between *Gone with the Wind* and the glittering parties in *Marie Antoinette*. The good part of my dream had been that I'd looked amazingly like Kirsten Dunst.

But before I could check my ideas against the real thing, we had to come up from the cellar. (Again! I only hoped that my calves wouldn't suffer long-term damage from all that climbing up and down stairs.)

Though I might moan about it, however, I had to admit that this time the Guardians had fixed things very neatly. Falk had set the chronograph so that we arrived when the ball in the house up above us had been in progress for hours.

I was enormously relieved not to have to file past our hosts. Secretly I'd been terrified that there'd be a master of the ceremonies banging his stick on the floor and announcing our false names in a loud voice. Or even worse, announcing the truth: "Ladies and gentlemen!" *Knock, knock.* "Gideon de Villiers and Gwyneth Shepherd, confidence tricksters from the twenty-first century. Kindly notice that the young woman's corset, as well as the hoops of her skirt, are made not of whalebone but of high-tech carbon fiber! Furthermore, the pair entered the house surreptitiously by way of the cellar!"

And this was a particularly dark cellar, so that unfortunately there was no alternative to taking Gideon's hand, or my dress and I would never have made it to the top of the stairs intact. Only at the front of the cellar were there torches in holders, casting a flickering light on the walls where you turned off into the media rooms in the time when this building was my school. It looked as if now there were larders and pantries for provisions down here, probably a good idea, because the place was freezing cold. Out of sheer curiosity, I glanced into one of the rooms, and was rooted to the spot with amazement. I'd never seen so much food all at once! There was obviously going to be some kind of banquet after the ball, because countless platters, dishes, and large basins lavishly piled high with things to eat were sitting around on tables and the floor. Much of it was artistically arranged and surrounded by wobbly transparent aspic. I saw large quantities of meat—it smelled much too strong for my liking—and there was a breathtaking amount of confectionery in all shapes and sizes, plus an amazingly lifelike gilded figure of a swan.

"Hey, look, they even have to chill their table decorations," I whispered.

Gideon made me go on. "It's not a table decoration; it's a real swan. What they call a centerpiece," he whispered back, but at almost the same moment, he jumped, and I'm afraid I have to admit that I let out a screech.

Because a figure was emerging from the shadows, right behind a cake with about nineteen layers and two dead nightingales on top of it, and was coming toward us in silence with a drawn sword.

It was Rakoczy, the count's right-hand man, and he could have walked straight into a job in a haunted house with his dramatic appearances. He welcomed us in a husky voice and then whispered, "Follow me."

As I tried to get over my fright, Gideon asked him impatiently, "Shouldn't you have been here to meet us?"

Rakoczy didn't seem to want to answer that. I wasn't surprised. He was exactly the sort who can never admit to a mistake. Without a word, he took a torch from its holder, beckoned us to follow, and stole along a corridor that branched off and led to another flight of stairs.

I could hear stringed instruments playing music above

us now, and a babble of voices getting louder and louder. Just before we reached the top of the stairs, Rakoczy left us, with the words, "I'll be keeping watch over you from the shadows, along with my men." Then he disappeared, as silent as a leopard.

"I guess he didn't get an invitation," I said, trying to make a joke of it. "He's gate-crashing." In fact the idea that one of Rakoczy's men was lurking in every dark corner, watching us in secret, gave me the creeps.

"Of course he was invited, but I expect he doesn't want to part with his sword, and swords aren't allowed in a ball-room." Gideon looked me up and down. "Any cobwebs left on your dress?"

I gave him an indignant glance. "No, they've all mi-grated to your brain," I said, pushing past him. I cautiously opened the door.

I'd been worrying over how we'd get into the foyer unnoticed, but when we plunged into the noise of the milling throng of guests at the ball, I wondered why we'd gone to all that trouble with the cellar. Presumably just out of habit. We could easily have traveled straight to the ballroom, and no one would have noticed our sudden appearance.

Lord and Lady Pympoole-Bothame's house was magnificent—my friend James hadn't exaggerated. What with damask wallpaper, stucco decoration, paintings, fres-cos on the ceilings, and crystal chandeliers, I hardly recog-nized my own school. The floors were covered with mosaic tiles and thick rugs, and on the way to the first floor, it

seemed to me that there were more passages and stair-
cases than in my own day.

And the place was full. Full and very noisy. In the
twenty-first century, this party would have been closed
down by the police because of the risk of overcrowding,
or maybe the neighbors would have complained of the
Pympoole-Bothames for disturbing their night's rest. And
that was only in the foyer and the corridors.

The ballroom was in a different league. It took up half
the first floor and was teeming with people. They stood
around in little groups or formed long lines in order to
dance. The room was buzzing like a beehive with their
voices and laughter, although the beehive comparison
wasn't quite right, because the decibel count must have
been as high as the sound of a jumbo jet taking off from
Heathrow. After all, there were up to four hundred people
here, all shouting at each other, and the twenty-man orchestra in the gallery was trying to rise above their voices.
The whole scene was lit by such vast numbers of candles
that I automatically looked around for a fire extinguisher.

In fact, after that soirée we'd been to at the Bromptons'
house, this ball was like a nightclub by comparison with
one of Aunt Maddy's tea parties, and I could see why people
would call it a glittering occasion.

Our appearance didn't attract any special attention,
particularly as there was coming and going in the ballroom
the whole time. All the same, several of the white-wigged
guests were staring curiously at us, and Gideon took my
arm more firmly. I sensed that I was being inspected from

head to foot and felt an urgent wish to look at myself in a mirror, just in case I'd made a mistake and there was a cobweb on my dress after all.

"It's all fine," said Gideon. "You look perfect."

I cleared my throat, embarrassed.

Gideon grinned down at me. "Ready?" he whispered.

"Ready when you are," I replied automatically. It just slipped out, and for a moment I thought of the fun we'd had before he let me down so treacherously. Although, come to think of it, even then, it hadn't been as much fun as all that.

A couple of girls began whispering as we passed them. I wasn't sure if it was because of my dress or because they thought Gideon looked so cool. I stood up as straight as possible. The wig was surprisingly well balanced and followed every movement I made, although its weight must have been like those jugs of water that African women carry on their heads. As we crossed the ballroom, I kept my eyes open for James. After all, his parents were giving the ball. Surely he'd be somewhere here. Gideon, who towered over most of the people in the ballroom, had quickly spotted Count Saint-Germain. He was standing, elegant as ever, on a small balcony, talking to a small man in brightly colored clothes who struck me as vaguely familiar.

Without thinking much of it, I lost myself in daydreams and regretted it a moment later when I remembered how, last time we met, Count Saint-Germain had broken my heart into ten thousand tiny pieces with his gentle voice.

"My dear children, you are wonderfully punctual," said the count, beckoning us over. He nodded graciously to me (I supposed that was an honor, considering that, as a woman, I had an intelligence quotient reaching about as far as from the balcony door to the nearest candle). Gideon, on the other hand, got a warm embrace. "Well, what do you say, Alcott? Do you see any of my inheritance in this fine young man's features?"

The man dressed as brightly as a parrot shook his head, smiling. His thin, long face was not just powdered, he had also rubbed red rouge on his cheeks, so that he looked like a clown.

"Ah, how can anyone compare such a youthful face with my old one?" The count gave a wry, self-mocking smile. "The years have wreaked havoc with my features. Sometimes I hardly know myself in the mirror." He fanned himself with a handkerchief. "May I introduce you? Sir Alfred Alcott, First Secretary of the Lodge at this period."

"We have already met on my various visits to the Temple," said Gideon, with a slight bow.

"So you have." The count laughed.

Now I knew why the parrot looked familiar. He was the man who had welcomed us to the Temple on our first meeting with the count, and he had ordered the coach to drive us to Lord Brompton's house.

"I'm afraid you have missed the appearance of the duke and duchess," Alcott said. "Her Grace's hairstyle was greatly admired. I fear the wigmakers of London will hardly be able to move for customers tomorrow."

"A truly beautiful woman, the duchess! What a shame she feels that she has to meddle with politics and men's affairs in general. Alcott, could you find these new arrivals something to drink?" As so often, the count spoke in a soft, gentle voice, but in spite of the noise surrounding us, he could be heard very distinctly. I shivered at the sound, and definitely not just because of the cold night air blowing in through the open doorway of the balcony.

"Of course." The First Secretary's eagerness to oblige reminded me of Mr. Marley. "White wine? I will be back in a moment."

Just my luck. No punch this time.

The count waited for Alcott to disappear into the ballroom, then put his hand in his coat pocket and brought out a sealed letter, which he handed to Gideon. "This is for your Grand Master. It contains details concerning our next meeting."

Gideon pocketed the letter and handed the count another sealed envelope in return. "And this is a full report on the events of the last few days. You'll be glad to hear that the blood of Elaine Burghley and Lady Tilney has been read into the chronograph."

I jumped in surprise. Lady Tilney? How had he fixed that? Last time we met, it hadn't seemed at all likely that she'd give her blood voluntarily. I cast Gideon a suspicious sidelong glance. Surely he hadn't taken blood from her by force? I imagined her desperately defending herself by pelting him with crochet pigs.

The count clapped him on the shoulder. "Then now

we have only to track down Sapphire and Black Tourma-line." He was leaning on his cane, but there was nothing frail about his posture. Indeed, he looked very powerful. "Ah, if *he* only knew how close we are to changing the world!" He jerked his head in the direction of the ballroom, where I saw Lord Alastair of the Florentine Alliance on the other side of the room, loaded with any amount of jewelry, just like last time I saw him. The large gems in his many rings sparkled right across the ballroom. So did his eyes, icy and full of hatred, even at this distance. A menac-ing, black-clad figure towered up behind him, but this time I didn't make the mistake of thinking he was a guest at the ball. The black figure was a ghost who went around everywhere with Lord Alastair, just as little Robert went around with Dr. White. When the ghost saw me, his mouth moved, and I was glad it was so noisy that I couldn't hear the nasty remarks he was making. It was bad enough to have him haunting my dreams.

"There he stands, dreaming of running us through with his sword," said the count, sounding almost pleased about it. "In fact he's thought of nothing else for days. He has even managed to smuggle his sword into this ball-room." He stroked his chin. "Which is why he is neither dancing nor sitting down, merely standing around stiffly, like a tin soldier, waiting for his opportunity."

"And I wasn't allowed to bring my own sword," said Gideon reproachfully.

"Have no fear, dear boy. Rakoczy and his men will not

take their eyes off Alastair. We can leave any bloodshed to the bold Kurucs this evening."

I glanced again at Lord Alastair and the black-clad ghost, who was now waving his sword at me in a blood-thirsty way. "But would he really . . . in front of all these people . . . I mean, even in the eighteenth century, surely you couldn't commit murder and simply get away with it?" I swallowed. "Lord Alastair wouldn't risk ending up on the gallows because of us, would he?"

The count's heavy lids hid his dark eyes for a few seconds, as if he were concentrating on the way his enemy's mind worked.

"No, he's too clever for that," he said slowly. "But he also knows how few chances he will ever get of having you two within reach of his sword again. He won't miss this one. As I have passed information to the man whom I believe to be the traitor in our ranks—and only to him!—about the time when you two will have to return to the cellar, unarmed and alone, in order to travel back, we shall see what happens—"

"Oh," I said. "But—"

The count raised his hand. "Don't be anxious, child. The traitor has no idea that Rakoczy and his men are keeping watch on everything you do. Alastair sees himself committing the perfect murder: the corpses will dissolve into thin air the next moment. Very useful." He laughed. "With me, of course, that would not work, so he destines me for a different kind of death."

Well, great.

Before I could digest the news that we were fair game to be thrown to the wolves, which changed my attitude to balls in general and this one in particular, the garishly dressed First Secretary—I'd forgotten his name again—returned with two glasses of white wine. In his wake came another old acquaintance, fat Lord Brompton. He was delighted to see us and kissed my hand more often than I thought quite proper.

"The evening is saved!" he cried. "I'm so glad you are here. Lady Brompton and Lady Lavinia saw you as well, but they were held up on the dance floor." He laughed so much that his fat paunch wobbled. "I'm told to take you both over to join the dancing."

"A good idea," said the count. "Young people should dance! I never missed an opportunity to do so in my own youth."

So here we went. Now everyone was going to see that I had two left feet and wasn't very good at turning right, a problem that Giordano had described as "a striking lack of any sense of direction." I was about to drain my glass of white wine, but Gideon took it away from me and handed it to the First Secretary.

On the dance floor, they were getting into position for the next minuet. Lady Brompton waved to us enthusiastically, Lord Brompton disappeared into the crowd, and just before the music began, Gideon stationed me in the row of ladies. To be precise, I was in between a pale gold dress and a green embroidered one. The green dress, a sideways glance told me, belonged to Lady Lavinia. She was just as beautiful as I remembered her, and even for the fashions of this period, her décolletage was generous, giving anyone who wanted a good look. In her place, I wouldn't have ventured to bend over. But Lady Lavinia didn't seem bothered.

"How wonderful to see you again!" She cast a radiant smile all around, but directed it mainly at Gideon, and then sank into the opening curtsey. I imitated her. In sudden panic, I found that I couldn't feel my feet.

A number of instructions were buzzing around in my head, and I almost muttered out loud, "Left is the side where your thumb is on the right!" but then Gideon stepped past me, performing the *tour de main*, and oddly enough, my legs seemed to find the right rhythm of their own accord.

The cheerful sound of the orchestra filled every corner of the ballroom, and the conversations around us died down.

Gideon put his left hand on his hip and gave me his right hand. "Wonderful music, these Haydn minuets," he said in a conversational tone. "Did you know that the composer almost joined the Guardians? In about ten years from now, on one of his visits to England. He was thinking of settling permanently here in London at the time."

"You don't say." I danced past him, tilting my head slightly to one side so as not to lose sight of him. "All I knew about Haydn until now was that he liked torturing children." At least, he'd tortured me as a child when Charlotte used to practice her piano sonatas with the same grim determination that she was now putting into searching for the chronograph.

But I couldn't explain that to Gideon further, because by now we had danced out of a figure of four into a large circle, and I had to concentrate on going around to the right.

Just how it happened I didn't know, but all of a sudden, I was really enjoying myself. The candles cast a beautiful light on the magnificent ball dresses, the music no longer sounded boring and dry as dust but exactly right, and the dancers in front of me, behind me, and beside me were laughing happily. Even the wigs didn't look quite so silly, and for a moment, I felt light as air and free. When the circle broke up, I danced toward Gideon as if I'd never done anything else in my life, and he was looking at me as if we were suddenly alone in the ballroom.

In my curious mood of elation I couldn't help smiling at him radiantly, never mind Giordano's stern warning never to show my teeth in the eighteenth century. For some reason or other, my smile seemed to be making Gideon struggle to stay calm and composed. He took my outstretched hand, but instead of just placing his fingers lightly under mine, he took them and held them hard.

"Gwyneth, I'm not going to let anyone—"

But I never found out what he wasn't going to let anyone do, because at that moment Lady Lavinia reached for his hand, placing mine in the hand of her own dancing partner, and saying with a smile, "Let's change partners for a little while, all right?"

No, it was not all right from my point of view, and Gideon, too, hesitated briefly. But then he bowed to Lady Lavinia and abandoned me like the unimportant little sister I was supposed to be. My cheerful mood disappeared as quickly as it had come.

"I have been admiring you from afar," said my new partner, as I came up out of my curtsey and offered him my hand. I'd have liked to wrench it right away again, because his fingers were damp and sticky. "My friend Mr. Merchant has already had the pleasure of meeting you at Lady Brompton's soirée. He wanted to introduce us, but now I can introduce myself. I am Lord Fleet. *The* Lord Fleet."

I smiled politely. A friend of Mr. Merchant the bosom groper, was he? As the next sequence of dance steps took us away from each other, and I was hoping that *the* Lord Fleet would take the chance to wipe his damp hands on his evening breeches, I glanced at Gideon for help. But he seemed to be deep in contemplation of Lady Lavinia. The man beside him, too, seemed to have eyes for nothing but her, or rather her plunging neckline, while he studiously ignored the lady he was supposed to be dancing with. And the man beside *him*—oh, my God! It was James! *My* James. I'd found him at last! He was dancing with a girl in a dress the color of plum jam, and he looked as alive as anyone can if he's wearing a white wig and has white powder on his face.

Instead of giving my hand back to Lord Fleet, I danced past Lady Lavinia and Gideon in the direction of James, saying as nicely as I could, "Please would you all move one place up?" and taking no notice of the protests. Two more changeover steps, and I was facing James.

"Excuse me, please move one place up." I gave the plum-jam girl a little nudge that sent her straight into the arms of the man opposite her, and then I offered the astonished James my hand and tried, breathlessly, to fall back into the rhythm of the dance. A glance to the left showed me that the other dancers were also rearranging their positions, and then dancing on as if nothing had happened. I didn't look at Gideon, for safety's sake, but stared at James. It was hard to believe that I could hold his hand and the hand felt warm and alive!

"You have upset the whole set," he said reproachfully, examining me from head to toe. "And you pushed Miss Amelia away from me in an extremely uncivil manner."

Oh, yes, this was James! The same supercilious tone of voice that I knew so well. I beamed at him. "I'm really sorry, James, but I just have to talk to you about something very important."

"As far as I am aware, we have not been introduced," said James, nose in the air, while he stepped gracefully from foot to foot.

"I'm Penelope Gray from . . . from the country. But that doesn't matter. I have some information that will be very, very important for you, so you must meet me somewhere—it's urgent. If you value your life," I added for extra dramatic effect.

"What in the world are you thinking of?" James looked at me, baffled. "Whether you are from the country or not, your behavior is most improper."

"Yes, I know." Out of the corner of my eye, I saw that the line of dancers was being disturbed again, this time on the men's side. Something sea green was approaching, keeping in time with the dance steps. "But all the same, it's important for you to listen to me. This is a matter of life and . . . I mean, it's about . . . about your horse. Hector, the gray. You absolutely must meet me in Hyde Park tomorrow morning at eleven. On the bridge over the lake." I could only hope that the lake and the bridge were both there in the eighteenth century.

"You want me to meet you? In Hyde Park? Because of *Hector*?" James's raised eyebrows almost touched his hairline.

I nodded.

"Excuse me," said Gideon, with a little bow, and he pushed James gently aside. "I think there's some mistake here."

"You may well say so!" Shaking his head, James turned back to Miss Plum Jam, while Gideon took my hand and led me, not at all gently, into the next figure of the dance.

"Are you crazy?" he asked. "What was all that about?"

"I met an old friend, that's all." I turned once more to

look at James. Had he taken me seriously? Probably not. He was still shaking his head.

"You really are hell-bent on attracting attention, aren't you?" said Gideon in a furious whisper. "Why can't you do as you're told for three hours, just for a change?"

"What a stupid question! Because I'm a woman and totally unacquainted with reason, of course. Anyway, you were the first to step out of line in the dance with Lady Oops My Bosom Is Falling Right Out of My Dress."

"Yes, but only because she—oh, stop it!"

"Stop it, yourself!" We glared angrily at each other as the final note on the violins died away. At last! That must have been the longest minuet in the world ever. I sank into my curtsy, relieved, and turned to walk away before Gideon could offer me his hand again (or rather, grab my own roughly). I was annoyed with myself for not thinking over what to say to James better—it seemed rather unlikely that he would turn up to meet me in the park. I'd have to talk to him again, and this time I'd tell him the whole truth.

But where was he? Those silly white wigs made all the men look alike. The lines of dancers had wound their zigzag way right through the huge ballroom, and now we had reached the other side of it. I craned my neck to see above the crowd, trying to get a sense of direction. Just as I thought I'd caught a glimpse of James's red velvet coat, Gideon took me by the elbow.

"This way," he said briefly.

I'd had about enough of his tone of command! But

there was no need for me to shake him off this time. Lady Lavinia did it for me, coming between us in a cloud of lily-of-the-valley perfume.

"You promised me another dance!" she said, pouting, and at the same time, her smile conjured up cute little dimples in her cheeks.

Behind her, Lord Brompton was making his way toward us, breathing heavily. "There, that's enough dancing for this season," he announced. "I'm getting too fa—too old for that pleasure. Speaking of pleasure, did anyone else see my wife with that dashing rear admiral, the one said to have lost an arm in battle recently? Not a word of truth in it! I clearly saw him taking her in *two* arms." He laughed, and his many chins wobbled alarmingly.

The orchestra began playing again, and rows of dancers were forming. "Oh, please! Surely you won't refuse me," said Lady Lavinia, clinging to the lapels of Gideon's coat and looking appealingly up at him. "Just this one dance."

"I have already promised to find my sister something to drink," said Gideon, casting me a dark look. Well, of course he was cross to be kept from flirting with Lady Lavinia. "And the count is expecting our company over there." The count had now left his place on the balcony, but not to sit down and rest. His eagle eyes were bent on us, and he looked as if he could hear every word we said.

"It would be an honor for me to find your lovely sister a drink," said Lord Brompton, winking at me. "You'd be leaving her in the very best of hands."

"There, you see!" Lady Lavinia drew Gideon away, laughing, and moved onto the dance floor.

"I'll be right back," he assured me, over his shoulder.

"Don't hurry," I muttered.

Lord Brompton and his rolls of fat started moving. "I know a good place to sit," he said, beckoning me on. "They call it the old maids' corner, but we won't let that bother us. We'll shock the old maids into going away by telling improper stories!" He led me up a few steps to a small gallery where there was a sofa. From up there, you had a good view of the whole ballroom, and sure enough, the sofa was already occupied by two ladies who were not as young as they had been, and probably not as pretty. But they happily adjusted their skirts to make room for me.

Lord Brompton rubbed his hands. "Comfortable, don't you think? I'll be back in a minute with the count and something to drink. I'll make haste!" And he really did, pushing his huge body through the sea of velvet, silk, and brocade like a galumphing hippopotamus. I took advantage of being above the crowd to look out for James, but I couldn't see him anywhere. However, I did spot Lady Lavinia and Gideon dancing, quite close, and I felt a pang to see how well they harmonized. Even the color of their clothes matched, as if Madame Rossini had chosen them herself. And whenever their hands touched, electric sparks seemed to fly between them. I felt as if I could hear Lady Lavinia's musical chime of laughter all the way from where I was sitting.

The two old maids beside me sighed wistfully. I

abruptly got to my feet. I really didn't have to put up with this. Wasn't that James's red coat just disappearing through one of the doorways? I decided to follow him. After all, this was his home and also my school, so I'd soon find him. And then I would try to straighten out the Hector business.

As I left the ballroom, I glanced at Lord Alastair, who was still standing in the same place and never took his eyes off the count. His ghostly friend was shaking his sword with a murderous light in his eyes, and he would certainly be croaking words full of hatred. None of them noticed me. But my disappearance did seem to register with Gideon. There was another disturbance in the line of dancers.

Damn! I turned and made my escape. The corridors outside were more dimly lit, but there were still any number of guests milling around in them. I had the impression that several of the couples were looking for a quiet, private corner somewhere, and right opposite the ballroom, there was a kind of gambling salon to which a few gentlemen had withdrawn. Cigar smoke wafted through the half-open door. I thought I saw James's red coat at the end of the passage, just turning the corner, and I ran after him as fast as my dress would let me. When I reached the next passage, however, there was no sign of him, which meant that he must have gone into one of the rooms opening off it. I opened the nearest door and closed it again at once when the glimmer of light caught a chaise longue in front of which a man (not James) was kneeling, busy taking off a lady's garter. Well, if you could call her a *lady* in those circumstances. Smiling slightly, I made for the next door. These party guests behaved very much like people partying in my own time.

I heard raised voices in the corridor behind me. "Why are you in such a hurry? Can't your sister be left on her own for five minutes?" Unmistakably the voice of Lady Lavinia!

Like lightning, I slipped into the nearest room and leaned against the door from the inside to get my breath back.

Cowards die many times before their deaths;
The valiant never taste of death but once.
Of all the wonders that I yet have heard,
It seems to me most strange that men should fear;
Seeing that death, a necessary end,
Will come when it will come.

WILLIAM SHAKESPEARE, *JULIUS CAESAR*

NINE

IT WASN'T DARK as I had expected. The room was lit by a few candles, casting their light on a bookcase and a desk. Obviously I was in some kind of study.

And I wasn't alone.

On the chair behind the desk sat Rakoczy, with a glass and two bottles in front of him. One bottle contained something liquid with a red glow—it looked like red wine— while the contents of the other, a delicate and gracefully curving flask, were a suspiciously grubby gray. The baron's sword lay right across the desk.

"That was quick," said Rakoczy. His voice, with its harsh east European accent, sounded slightly blurred. "I was just wishing for the presence of an angel, and lo and behold, the pearly gates open and send me the most charming angel that heaven can offer. This wonderful medicine is better than any I have ever tried."

"Er . . . weren't you supposed to be watching over us

from the shadows, or something?" I asked, wondering whether it mightn't be a better idea to clear out of this room right away, even if I risked running straight into Gideon's clutches. I didn't much like Rakoczy, even when he was stone-cold sober.

However, my remarks did seem to bring him some way back to himself. He frowned. "Oh, so it's you!" he said, still in a blurred voice but sounding considerably less ecstatic. "Not an angel, only a stupid little girl." And with a single, supple movement, almost faster than I could blink, he had picked the delicate little flask up from the desk and was advancing on me with it. Heaven knows what kind of substance he'd been taking, but it didn't seem to affect his ability to move fast. "Although a very beautiful stupid little girl." He was so close now that his breath hit my face. It smelled of wine and something else, a sharper, strange odor. He stroked my cheek with his free hand and ran a rough thumb over my lower lip. I was transfixed with terror.

"I'll wager these lips have never done anything forbidden, am I right? A little of Alcott's miraculous potion here will change all that."

"No, thanks." I ducked under his arm and stumbled out into the room. *No, thanks*—oh, great! Next thing I knew I'd be bobbing him a curtsey! "Keep that stuff away from me, will you?" I said rather more firmly. Before I could take another step, with the vague idea of jumping out of the window, Rakoczy was beside me, forcing me over to the desk again. He was so much stronger than me that he didn't even notice my resistance. "Ssh, ssh, never fear, little one, I promise you'll like this." There was a little plop as he took the cork out of the little flask, and then he tipped my head back by force. "Drink this!"

I pressed my lips together and tried to push Rakoczy away with my free hand. I might just as well have had a shot at shifting a mountain. Desperately, I thought of what little I knew about self-defense—Charlotte's knowledge of Krav Maga would have come in very useful at this point. When the flask was already touching my lips and the sharp smell of the liquid inside it rose to my nostrils, I finally had a good idea. I snatched a hairpin out of my towering wig and dug it as hard as I could into the hand holding the flask. At the same time, the door flew open and I heard Gideon call, "Let go of her at once, Rakoczy!"

Too late, I realized that it would have been better to run the hairpin into Rakoczy's eye, or at least his throat. It stuck there in his flesh, but he didn't even drop the flask. However, his iron grip on me did slacken, and he turned around. Gideon, who was standing in the doorway with Lady Lavinia, looked at him in horror.

"What the hell are you doing?"

"Nothing at all! I only wanted to help this little girl to . . . to gain a little more enlightenment!" Rakoczy threw back his head with a raucous laugh. "Will *you* venture to try a sip? I assure you, it will give you sensations such as you have never known before!"

I took my chance to break free.

"Are you all right?" Gideon was looking at me with

concern, while Lady Lavinia clung anxiously to his arm. Would you believe it? The pair of them had probably been looking for a room where they could smooch in peace, while Rakoczy was trying to get heaven knew what kind of drug inside me and then do heaven knew what else. And now I was expected to be grateful to Gideon and Lady Big-Tits for picking this, of all rooms!

"I'm just fine!" I growled, crossing my arms so that no one could see how my hands were shaking.

Rakoczy, still laughing, took a gulp from the flask himself and then put the cork firmly back in.

"Does the count know you're experimenting with drugs in this quiet little study, instead of devoting yourself to your duties?" asked Gideon in icy tones. "Surely you had other things to do this evening?"

Rakoczy was swaying slightly. He looked in surprise at the hairpin still sticking in the back of his hand, then pulled it out with a jerk and licked the blood away like a big cat. "The Black Leopard is capable of anything—at any time!" he said. Then he put his hands to his head, staggered around the desk, and fell heavily into the chair. "Although there really does seem to be something about this potion that . . . ," he murmured, whereupon his head dropped forward and hit the top of the desk with a crash.

Shuddering, Lady Lavinia leaned against Gideon's shoulder. "Is he . . . ?"

"Probably not, I'm afraid." Gideon went over to the desk, took the little flask, and held it up to the light. Then he uncorked it, and sniffed. "I've no idea what it is, but if even Rakoczy is poleaxed so quickly . . ." He put down the flask again. "Opium is my guess. Didn't mix with alcohol and his usual drugs."

Well, that was obvious. Rakoczy lay there as if he were dead. You couldn't hear him breathing.

"Maybe someone gave it to him—someone who didn't want him to have all his senses about him this evening," I said. My arms were still crossed. "Can you find his pulse?" I'd have felt for it, but I couldn't bring myself to go any closer to Rakoczy. Shaking all over as I was, it was hard enough even to keep on my feet.

"Gwen? Are you really sure you're all right?" Gideon looked at me with a frown. I hate to admit it, but at that moment I'd have loved to fling myself into his arms and have a good cry. But he didn't look at all keen to give me a comforting hug, rather the opposite. When I nodded, he said angrily, "What the hell were you doing here, any-way?" He pointed to the motionless Rakoczy. "It could easily have been you down and out on the floor!"

By now my teeth were chattering so much that I could hardly speak. "I . . . I had no idea that—" I stammered, but Lavinia, still sticking to Gideon like a very large, very green burr, interrupted me. She was obviously one of those women who hate anyone else to attract attention.

"Death!" she whispered dramatically, looking at Gideon with her eyes very wide. "I felt the breath of Death when it entered this room. Oh, please . . ." Her eyelids fluttered. "Hold me tight—"

I wouldn't have believed it—she simply fainted away!

For no reason at all, and of course falling very elegantly into Gideon's arms. I don't know why, but I was infuriated to see him catch her, so infuriated that I forgot about my trembling and my chattering teeth. But at the same time—as if I hadn't run the gamut of enough feelings already—I sensed tears coming into my eyes. Oh, damn it, falling down in a faint was definitely the best option. Except that of course there'd have been no one to catch me.

At that moment, the dead Rakoczy said, in a voice so hoarse and deep that it could have come from the world beyond the grave, *"Dosis sola facit venenum.* Have no fear. Only the quantity makes the poison. It would take more than that to finish me off."

Lavinia (I'd decided that she was no lady, so far as I was concerned), let out a little shriek of alarm and opened her eyes to stare at Rakoczy. Then she must have remembered that she was supposed to be in a deep swoon, and with a dramatic groan for effect, she sank limply back into Gideon's arms.

"I shall be better in a moment. No need for any fuss." Rakoczy had raised his head and was looking at us with bloodshot eyes. "My fault! It should be taken only a few drops at a time, he says."

"Who says?" asked Gideon, holding Lavinia in his arms like a store display mannequin.

With some difficulty, Rakoczy got himself into a sitting position, let his head drop back, and looked up at the ceiling with a peal of laughter. "Do you see the stars all dancing?"

Gideon sighed. "I'll have to find the count," he said. "Gwen, if you could just lend me a hand . . . ?"

I stared at him blankly. "Lend you a hand with *her*? You must be joking!" With a couple of steps, I was in the doorway and then out in the corridor, so that he wouldn't see the silly tears flowing down my face in torrents. I didn't know either why I was crying or where I was going as I ran away. It must have been posttraumatic reaction, the kind you're always reading about. People do the weirdest things when they're in shock, like that baker up in Yorkshire who crushed his arm in the dough press. He finished baking seven more trays of cinnamon croissants before he called the emergency services. Those cinnamon croissants were the nastiest sight the paramedics had ever seen.

I hesitated when I reached the stairs. I didn't want to go down, in case Lord Alastair was already waiting there to commit his perfect murder, so I ran on up. I hadn't gone far before I heard Gideon behind me, calling, "Gwenny! Please stop! Please!"

For a moment, it occurred to me that he might simply have dropped Lavinia on the floor so that he could run after me, but it was no good: I was still feeling furious, or sad, or scared, or all of them together. I stumbled on up the stairs, blinded by tears, and into the next corridor.

"Where do you think you're going?" Now Gideon was beside me, trying to take my hand.

"Anywhere! Away from you, that's all," I sobbed, running into the nearest room. Gideon followed me. Of course. I nearly passed my sleeve over my face to wipe away the tears, but I remembered Madame Rossini's makeup at the last minute. I probably looked battered enough already. I glanced around the room, so as not to have to look at Gideon. Light from candles in brackets on the walls fell on the pretty furnishings, all in shades of gold. There was a sofa, a delicate little desk, a few chairs, a painting of a dead pheasant and some pears, a collection of exotic-looking sabers above the mantelpiece, and magnificent golden yellow curtains at the windows. For some reason, I had a sudden feeling that I'd been here before.

Gideon was standing in front of me, waiting.

"Leave me alone," I said, rather feebly.

"I *can't* leave you alone. Whenever I leave you alone, you do something rash without thinking first."

"Go away!" I felt like throwing myself on the sofa, staying there for a while, and drumming on the cushions with my fists. Was that too much to ask?

"No, I won't," said Gideon. "Listen, I'm sorry that happened. I ought not to have allowed it."

My God, wasn't that downright typical? A classic case of overresponsibility syndrome. It was nothing to do with Gideon that I'd happened to meet Rakoczy, was it? Or that right now Rakoczy didn't have all his marbles, as Xemerius would say. On the other hand, a few guilt feelings wouldn't hurt him.

So I said, "But you did!" And I added, "Because you had eyes only for *her!*"

"You're jealous!" Gideon had the nerve to burst out laughing. He sounded kind of relieved.

"You'd like that, wouldn't you?" My tears had stopped, and I surreptitiously wiped my nose.

"The count will wonder where we are," said Gideon, after a slight pause.

"Then he can just send his Transylvanian friend looking for us, that's what your count can do." I finally managed to look him in the eye again. "He's not even really a count. His title's as much of a fake as the rosy cheeks of that . . . what was her name again?"

Gideon laughed quietly. "I've forgotten her name already."

"Liar!" I said, but stupidly I couldn't help grinning a bit myself.

Next moment Gideon was serious again. "The count's not responsible for Rakoczy's behavior. He'll certainly be reprimanded for that. You don't have to like the count, you only have to respect him."

I snorted angrily. "I don't *have* to do anything," I said, abruptly turning toward the window. And there I saw . . . *myself*! In my school uniform, peering out from behind the curtain with a rather foolish expression on my face. Good heavens! That was why the room had looked familiar to me! It was Mrs. Counter's classroom, and the Gwyneth behind the curtain had just traveled to the past for the third time. I made a sign with my hand for her to hide again.

"What was that?" asked Gideon.

"Nothing!" I said, sounding as stupid as possible.

"At the window." He put his hand out into thin air—a reflex action as he felt for the sword he wasn't wearing.

"Nothing, I said." What I did next has to be put down to posttraumatic shock again—like that baker and the blood in his cinnamon croissants. In the normal way, I'd never have done such a thing. But I also thought I'd seen something green scurry past the doorway, and . . . and well, fundamentally I did it only because I already knew I was going to do it. You might say there was nothing else that I *could* do.

"There could be someone standing behind the curtain listening to—" Gideon was still saying as I flung my arms around his neck and planted my lips on his. And while I was about it, I also pressed the rest of me close to him. Lady Lavinia herself couldn't have done it better.

For a few seconds, I was afraid Gideon would push me away, but then he gave a quiet groan, put his arms around my waist, and drew me even closer. He returned the kiss so warmly that I forgot everything else and closed my eyes. It was the same as when we'd been dancing just now; suddenly it didn't matter what was happening around us or what was going to happen next. It didn't even matter that he was really an utter bastard—all I knew was that I loved him, and I always would, and I wanted him to go on kissing me forever.

A small inner voice was whispering to me, saying I'd better come to my senses, but Gideon's lips and hands were telling me the opposite. So I can't say how long it was before we moved apart and stared at each other, stunned.

"Why . . . why did you do that?" asked Gideon, breathing heavily. He seemed totally bewildered. He took a few steps back, almost swaying, as if to put as much distance between us as possible.

"What do you mean, why?" My heart was thudding so fast and so noisily that he could surely hear it. I glanced at the door. I'd probably only imagined the glimpse of a green dress that I thought I'd seen out of the corner of my eye, and the dress was still lying on the rug one floor lower down with Lady Lavinia inside it, waiting to be kissed awake.

Gideon had narrowed his eyes suspiciously. "But you . . ." With a couple of strides, he was at the window, pulling the curtains aside. There he went again—typical! No sooner did he do something . . . er, nice, than he had to do his best to spoil it as fast as possible.

"Looking for anything in particular?" I asked sarcastically. Of course there was no one behind the curtains now. My younger self had traveled back some time ago and would be just wondering where on earth she'd learnt to kiss so improbably well.

Gideon turned around again. The bewilderment had disappeared from his face, giving way to his usual arrogant expression. He leaned back against the windowsill with his arms folded. "What was all that in aid of, Gwyneth? A few seconds earlier, you were still looking at me as if you hated my guts."

"I wanted—" I began, but then I thought better of it. "Why ask in that silly way? You've never told me why you kissed me either, have you?" A little defiantly, I added, "I just felt like it. And you didn't have to go along with me."

Although then I'd probably have sunk right into the earth with shame.

Gideon's eyes flashed. "You just felt like it?" he repeated, coming toward me again. "Damn it, Gwyneth! There are very good reasons why . . . For days now, I've been trying to . . . I mean, all this time . . ." He frowned, obviously annoyed by his own stammering. "Do you think I'm made of *stone*?" He said that in quite a loud voice.

I didn't know what to say. And it was probably more of a rhetorical question. No, of course I didn't think he was made of stone, but what in the world was that supposed to mean? The unfinished sentences before he asked it didn't exactly make it any clearer, either. We looked at each other for a little while, and then he turned away and said, in a perfectly normal voice, "We must go. If we don't get down to the cellar punctually, the whole plan will fail."

Oh, yes, too true. The plan. The plan seeing us as potential murder victims who would conveniently disappear into thin air.

"Wild horses aren't dragging me down there, not while Rakoczy's lying over that desk, stoned out of his mind," I said firmly.

"Look, first, he'll be back on his feet again by now, and second, at least five of his men are waiting down there." He put out his hand to me. "Come on, we must hurry. And there's nothing to be afraid of; Alastair wouldn't stand a chance against those Kurucs, even if he brought reinforcements with him. They can see in the dark like cats, and I've seen them do things with knives and swords that verge on magic." He waited until I had put my hand in his, then smiled slightly, and added, "And I'm still here as well."

But before we'd even started, Lavinia appeared in the doorway, and with her—as breathless as she was—the First Secretary in his bright parrot plumage.

"Ah, here they are. Both of them," said Lavinia. She looked remarkably fit for someone who had been fainting away just now, if not quite as beautiful as before. Streaks of reddened skin showed through the layer of pale powder on her face. All that running up and down stairs must have made her break out in a sweat. There were spots of red on her plunging neckline too.

I was glad to see that Gideon didn't even glance at her. "I know we're late, Sir Alfred," he said. "We were just on our way down."

"That . . . won't be necessary," replied Alcott, gasping for air. "There's been a little change of plan."

He didn't have to explain any further, because Lord Alastair came into the room after him, not in the least out of breath, but smiling unpleasantly.

"So we meet again," he said. He was followed like a shadow by his ghostly black-clad ancestor, who instantly started uttering murderous threats. "May the unworthy die an unworthy death!" and so on. I'd nicknamed him Darth Vader when we last met, because of his hoarse voice, and I envied everyone else present, who could neither see him nor hear him. His dead beetle-black eyes fixed on us with sheer hatred in them.

Gideon bowed his head. "Lord Alastair, what a surprise."

"Just as I intended," said Lord Alastair, smiling smugly. "A surprise is what I wanted to give you."

Almost imperceptibly, Gideon steered me farther into the corner, so that the desk was between us and the visitors, which didn't make me feel much better, because it was a very fragile lady's desk in the Rococo style. I'd rather it had been a good stout oak table.

"I understand you," said Gideon politely.

I understood him too. The murder scene had obviously been simply shifted from the cellar to this pretty room, because the First Secretary was the traitor in the ranks of the Guardians and Lavinia was a snake in the grass. Simple, really. Instead of shaking with fear, I suddenly felt more like giggling. This was just too much for one day!

"But I thought you'd have been a little more discriminating in your murder plans, after getting the lines of descent of the time travelers into your hands," said Gideon.

Lord Alastair made a dismissive gesture. "The family trees that the demon from the future brought us showed only that it is impossible to wipe out your lines of descent entirely," he said. "I prefer the direct method."

"Madame d'Urfé alone, the lady who lived at the court of the king of France, had so many descendants that it would take more than one human life to track them all down," added the First Secretary. "Putting an end to you here and now seems to me an absolute necessity. If you hadn't defended yourself so ably in Hyde Park the other day, it would all be over and done with now."

"What are you getting in return for this, Alcott?"

asked Gideon, sounding as if he were really interested. "What can Lord Alastair offer you to make you break the Guardians' oath and betray the Lodge?"

"Well, I—" Alcott obligingly began to tell us, but Lord Alastair cut him short.

"A clear conscience! That's what he gets in return. The certainty that the angels in heaven will praise his deeds is worth far more than gold. We must rid the earth of demonic monstrosities like you two, and God will thank us for shedding your blood."

Sure, sure. Briefly I felt a spurt of hope that Lord Alastair just needed someone to listen to him. Maybe he only wanted an appreciative audience to hear him talk about his religious delusions. But then Darth Vader hissed, "Your lives are forfeit, demons' brood!" and I abandoned that idea again.

"So you think God would approve of the murder of an innocent girl? Interesting." Gideon's hand went to the inside pocket of his coat, and then he imperceptibly jumped.

"Is this what you were looking for?" asked the First Secretary maliciously. He reached into the pocket of his own lemon-yellow coat and brought out a small black pistol, holding it up in his fingertips. "Undoubtedly some diabolical weapon from the future, am I right?" He looked at Lord Alastair for approval. "I asked our seductive friend Lady Lavinia to search you thoroughly for such weapons, time traveler."

Lavinia cast Gideon a guilty smile, and for a moment,

he looked as if he could have kicked himself. Understandably, because the pistol would have saved us. Men with swords stood no chance against a Smith & Wesson automatic. I wished the treacherous Alcott would accidentally pull the trigger and shoot himself in the foot. The noise of the shot might also be heard in the ballroom—or then again, it might not.

However, Alcott put the pistol back into his pocket, and my heart sank.

"Surprised, are you? I thought of everything. I knew that dear Lady Lavinia had gambling debts," said Alcott in a conversational tone. Like most villains, he evidently longed to have his cunning admired. I thought his long face was rather ratlike. "Debts for large sums of money that she could no longer, as usual, pay off by showing . . . er, *generosity* to her creditors." Here he laughed in a slimy way. "You must forgive me, my lady, for not being especially interested in those services of yours. But this wipes out your debts."

Lavinia didn't look particularly pleased. "I'm so sorry— I had no other choice," she said to Gideon, but he didn't appear to be listening to her at all. I thought it more likely that he was wondering how fast he could get to the fireplace and snatch one of the sabers off the wall above it before Lord Alastair ran him through with his sword. Following his eyes, I came to the conclusion that he didn't have much chance of success, unless he'd forgotten to let me know that he was really Superman. The fireplace was too far away, and moreover, Lord Alastair, who never took his eyes off Gideon, was standing much closer to it.

"This is all very well," I said slowly, playing for time, "but you've reckoned without the count."

Alcott laughed. "I suppose you mean without Rakoczy?" He rubbed his hands. "Well, his special . . . let's call them preferences will make him unable to do his duty tonight, don't you agree?" He was all puffed up with pride. "His liking for intoxicating substances made him easy prey, if you know what I mean."

"But Rakoczy isn't alone," I said. "His Kurucs are keeping watch on every move we make."

Slightly unsettled, Alcott looked briefly at Lord Alastair and then laughed again. "Oh, yes, and where are those Kurucs of yours now?"

Down in the cellar, presumably.

"Waiting in the shadows," I murmured in as menacing a tone as I could manage. "Ready to strike at any time. And they can do things with their swords and knives that verge on magic."

But unfortunately Alcott wasn't to be intimidated. He made a few nasty remarks about Rakoczy and his Kurucs, praising himself all over again for his brilliant planning and his even more brilliant change of plan. "I'm afraid our clever friend the count will wait for you and his Black Leopard in vain today," he said, turning to Gideon. "Why not ask me what plans I have for *him*?"

But Gideon had obviously lost any interest in Alcott's boasting. He said nothing. Lord Alastair seemed to have had enough of the First Secretary's time-wasting babbling as well. He wanted to get down to business. "You had better go away," he impatiently told Lady Lavinia, drawing his sword and pointing it at her.

So now came the crunch.

"And I always thought you were a man of honor and wouldn't fight a duel with an unarmed opponent," said Gideon.

"I am indeed a man of honor—but you are a demon. I am not going to fight a duel with you, I'm going to slaughter you," said Lord Alastair coldly.

Lady Lavinia let out a stifled sound of horror. "I didn't want this," she whispered, looking in Gideon's direction.

No, sure. *Now* she had scruples! You silly cow, fall down in another faint, why don't you?

"Get her out of here, I said!" For once, Lord Alastair took the words out of my mouth. He let his sword whistle through the air, trying out the blade.

"Of course—this is no sight for a lady." Alcott bundled Lavinia out into the corridor. "Close the door, and make sure no one tries to get in."

"But—"

"I haven't given you back your IOUs yet," hissed Alcott. "If I say so, the bailiffs will come to your house tomorrow, and then it won't be your house anymore for quite some time."

That shut Lavinia up. Alcott bolted the door, turned to us, and took a dagger out of his coat pocket, rather a delicate model. I ought to have been feeling terrified, but somehow the fear wouldn't really set in. Probably because the whole thing seemed to me downright absurd. Unreal. Like a clip from a film.

And surely we'd be traveling back any moment now?

"How much time is there still to go?" I whispered to Gideon.

"Too much," he said, through gritted teeth.

Alcott's rat face wore a look of cheerful excitement. "I'll deal with the girl," he said, positively bubbling over with his thirst for action. "You deal with the boy. But be careful—he's cunning, and he's quick."

Lord Alastair just snorted scornfully.

Since Gideon still seemed to be eyeing up the sabers so tantalizingly out of reach and his whole body was tense with concentration, I looked around for an alternative weapon. On the spur of the moment, I picked up one of the upholstered chairs and pointed its fragile legs at Alcott.

For some reason, he thought that amusing. He just grinned even more murderously than before and slowly advanced on me. Well, one thing was for sure: whatever his motives, he wasn't about to have a clear conscience ever again in this life.

Lord Alastair was also coming closer.

And then everything happened at once.

"Stay right there," Gideon called to me, as he overturned the delicate little desk and, with a kick, sent it slithering over the polished wooden floorboards toward Lord Alastair. At almost the same time, he tore one of the heavy candleholder brackets off the wall and flung it with all his might at the First Secretary. It hit Sir Alfred on the head with a nasty sound, and he dropped to the floor like a stone. Gideon didn't wait to see if his throw had been on target. While the bracket was still in the air, he had dived for the collection of sabers on the wall. In his own turn, Lord Alastair had stepped aside to avoid the desk skidding his way, but instead of preventing Gideon from snatching a saber off the wall, he took a few quick steps toward me. All this had happened in the time it takes to blink an eye, and I hardly had time to raise the chair I was holding, with the firm intention of smashing it down over Lord Alastair's head, before he was lunging at me with his sword.

The blade passed through my dress and ran far into me under the left side of my rib cage. Before I could really grasp what had happened, Lord Alastair withdrew his sword again, uttered a cry of triumph, and spun around to meet Gideon, pointing the sword at him. The end of the blade was red with my blood.

The pain got to me a second later. Like a puppet with its strings cut, I fell forward on my knees and instinctively put my hand to my breast. I heard Gideon shout my name; I saw him wrench two sabers at once off the wall, swinging them above his head like a samurai warrior. Meanwhile I finally dropped to the ground, and the back of my head didn't even hit the floorboards too hard (a wig like the one I was wearing came in useful). Then, as if by magic, the pain went away. For a moment, I stared at nothing, astonished. Then I was hovering in the air, weightless, bodiless, rising higher and higher in space, up to the stucco decoration on the ceiling. Little golden motes of dust danced around me in the candlelight. It was almost as if I had turned into one of them.

I saw myself lying far below, eyes wide open, struggling for air. A bloodstain was slowly spreading over the dark blue silk of my dress. The color quickly drained out of my face until my skin was as white as my wig. I watched in surprise as my eyelids quivered and then closed.

But the part of me hovering in the air could still see everything that was going on:

I saw the First Secretary lying motionless beside the candleholder bracket. He was bleeding from a large wound in his temple.

I saw Gideon, white with anger, rushing toward Alastair. His lordship retreated to the doorway, parrying Gideon's saber thrusts with his own sword, but after only a few seconds, Gideon had driven him into a corner of the room.

I saw the two of them fighting a fierce duel, although from up where I was floating, the clash of their blades was muted.

His lordship feinted and then tried to lunge under Gideon's left arm, but Gideon saw through his intention, and at almost the same moment, his blade pierced Lord Alastair's unguarded right upper arm. Alastair looked at his adversary incredulously and then his expression distorted into a silent scream. His fingers opened, and his sword fell to the floor with a clatter: Gideon had pinned his arm to the wall. Stuck like that, he began hissing furious curses, in spite of the pain he must have been feeling.

Gideon turned away without giving him another glance and flung himself down on the floor beside me. That's to say, beside my body—I myself was still hovering around in the air, feeling useless.

"Gwyneth! Oh, my God! Gwenny! Please don't!" He pressed his hand to the spot below my breast where the sword had made a tiny hole in my dress.

"Too late!" cried Darth Vader in ringing tones. "Do you not see the lifeblood draining out of her?"

"She'll die—there's nothing you can do to change that!" said Lord Alastair, from where he was pinned to the wall, taking care not to move his immobilized arm. Blood was dripping from it, forming a little puddle beside his feet. "I ran her right through her demonic heart!"

"Keep your mouth shut," Gideon snapped furiously. He had both hands on my wound now and was pressing down on it with his full weight. "I'm not letting her bleed to death. If we can only get back in time. . . ." He sobbed desperately. "You mustn't die, Gwenny, do you hear me?"

My breast was still rising and falling, and my skin was covered with tiny beads of sweat, but you couldn't rule out the possibility that Darth Vader and Lord Alastair were right. I mean, I was already flying through the air as a glittering mote of dust, and there wasn't a trace of color left in my face down below. Even my lips had gone gray.

Gideon had tears pouring down his face. He was still

pressing his hands down on my wound as hard as he could. "Stay with me, Gwenny, stay with me," he whispered, and suddenly I couldn't see anything, but I did feel the hard floor under me again and the dull pain inside me and the full weight of my body. I drew a last rattling breath, and knew I wouldn't have the strength for another.

I wanted to open my eyes to look at Gideon for the last time, but I couldn't do it.

"I love you, Gwenny. Please don't leave me," said Gideon. That was the last thing I heard before a great void swallowed me up.

All kinds of inanimate items and materials can be transported through space in both directions without any problems. However, at the moment when an item is transported, it must not be in contact with anything or anyone, apart from the time traveler who is carrying it.

The largest object so far moved through time was a refectory table twelve feet long, taken from the year 1805 by the de Villiers twins in 1900 and back again (see Volume 4, Chapter 3, "Experiments and Empirical Investigations," pp. 188 ff.). No plants or parts of plants, and no living creatures of any kind, can be transported, since time travel would destroy or entirely dissolve their cell structure, as many experiments on algae, various seedlings, slipper animalcules, woodlice, and mice have shown (again, see Volume 4, Chapter 3, "Experiments and Empirical Investigations," pp. 194 ff.).

The transportation of any items, other than under supervision or for experimental purposes, is strictly forbidden.

FROM *THE CHRONICLES OF THE GUARDIANS*,
VOLUME 2: *GENERAL LAWS OF TIME TRAVEL*

TEN

"SHE LOOKS to me strangely familiar," I heard someone say. There was no mistaking James's plummy tone of voice.

"Of course she does, bonehead," replied another voice that could only belong to Xemerius. "It's Gwyneth, but wearing a wig and minus her school uniform."

And now other sounds and agitated voices began getting through to me. It was like a radio with the volume slowly being turned up. I was still lying on my back, or maybe I was lying on my back again. The terrible weight on my breast had gone away, and so had the dull pain deep inside me. Was I a ghost like James now?

Someone cut my bodice open and ripped it apart, with an ugly tearing noise.

"He got her aorta," I heard Gideon saying desperately. "I tried to stop the flow of blood, but . . . but it went on too long."

Cool hands were feeling my upper body and touched a painful spot under my rib cage. Then Dr. White said, sounding relieved, "It's only a superficial cut! Good heavens, what a fright you gave me!"

"What? But that can't be so. She—"

"The sword only scratched her skin. See that? Madame Rossini's corset has obviously done good service. *Aorta abdominalis*—good God, Gideon, what on earth do they teach you in medical school? For a moment, I really believed you." Dr. White's fingers were pressing against my throat. "And her pulse is strong."

"Is she all right?"

"What exactly happened?"

"How could Lord Alastair do such a thing to her?"

Mr. George, Falk de Villiers, and Mr. Whitman all spoke at once. There wasn't another squeak out of Gideon. I tried to open my eyes, and this time it was easy. I could even sit up without difficulty. I was surrounded by the familiar, brightly painted walls of our school art room in the cellar, and the heads of the assembled Guardians were bending over me. They were all smiling at me, even Mr. Marley.

Only Gideon was staring at me as if he couldn't believe his eyes. His face was white as a sheet, and I could still see the traces of tears on his cheeks.

Farther away stood James, holding his lace handkerchief to his eyes. "Tell me when it's safe to look again."

"Not yet, anyway, or you'll be struck blind on the spot," said Xemerius, who was sitting cross-legged at my feet. "Half her bosom is falling out of her bodice."

Oops. He was right. Feeling embarrassed, I tried to cover myself up with the torn remnants of Madame Rossini's wonderful dress. Dr. White gently pressed me back on the table where they must have laid me down.

"I'll have to clean this scratch and put a dressing on it," he said. "Then I'll give you a thorough examination. Do you feel pain anywhere?"

I shook my head, only to groan "ouch!" next moment. I had a splitting headache.

Mr. George put his hand on my shoulder from behind me. "Oh, my God, Gwyneth, you gave us quite a fright." He laughed softly. "That's what I call a really good faint! When Gideon came back with you in his arms, I seriously thought you could be —"

"Dead," said Xemerius, finishing the sentence that Mr. George had left tactfully hanging in the air. "To be honest, you certainly looked dead. And that boy was beside himself. Yelling for vein clamps and stammering all sorts of other confused stuff. And shedding buckets of tears. What are *you* staring at?"

This last remark was for little Robert, who was gazing at Xemerius, fascinated. "He's so cute. May I stroke him?"

"Not if you want to keep your hand, kid," said Xemerius. "It's bad enough having that perfumed coxcomb there thinking I'm a cat all the time."

"Oh, really. Cats don't have wings. I know that perfectly well," cried James, with his eyes still shut tight. "You're a cat out of my fevered dreams. A degenerate cat."

"One more word, and I'll eat you," said Xemerius.

Gideon had taken a couple of steps away and dropped into a chair. He took off his wig, ran all his fingers through his dark hair, and buried his face in his hands. "I don't understand it," he said indistinctly through his fingers.

I felt just the same. How could this be possible? I mean, I'd just died, and now here I was feeling alive and well again! Can you imagine a thing like that? I looked down at the injury that Dr. White was treating. He was right—it really was just a scratch. The cut I'd given myself with the vegetable knife had been far longer and hurt much more.

Gideon's face surfaced from his hands again. How green his eyes were in his pale face! I remembered the last thing I'd heard him say, and once again I tried to sit up, but Dr. White wouldn't let me.

"Can someone please take this unspeakable wig off her?" he said brusquely. Several hands at once began taking the hairpins out, and it was a wonderful feeling to be free of the wig again.

"Careful, Marley," warned Falk de Villiers. "Remember Madame Rossini!"

"Yes, sir," stammered Mr. Marley, almost dropping the wig in alarm. "Madame Rossini, sir."

Mr. George took the hairpins out of my hair, and gently undid the braid. "Better like that?" he asked. Yes, it was much better.

"Curlylocks, Curlylocks, wilt thou be mine? Thou shalt not wash dishes nor yet feed the swine," sang Xemerius in a silly voice. "Your hair's a mess—pity you don't have a hat, that's the answer to a bad hair day. Oh, I'm so glad you're still alive and I don't have to look for a new human. It's making me talk nonsense! Curlylocks, indeed."

Little Robert giggled.

"Can I look now?" asked James, but he didn't wait for an answer. After one glance at me, he closed his eyes again. "Upon my word! It really is Miss Gwyneth. Forgive me for not recognizing you when that young dandy carried you past my niche just now." He sighed. "That in itself was odd enough. You never see people properly dressed in this house now."

Mr. Whitman put an arm around Gideon's shoulders. "What exactly happened, my boy? Were you able to give the count our message? And did he give you instructions for the next meeting?"

"Oh, get him a whisky and leave him in peace for a few minutes," growled Dr. White, sticking two small strips of plaster over my wound. "He's in shock."

"No. No, I'm fine," murmured Gideon. He cast another quick glance at me, then took the sealed letter from his coat pocket and handed it to Falk.

"Come along," said Mr. Whitman. He helped Gideon to his feet and led him to the door. "There's a bottle of whisky up in the principal's office. And a sofa in case you want to lie down for a while." He looked around. "Coming with us, Falk?"

"Certainly," said Falk. "I hope old Gilles has enough whisky for us all up there." He turned to the others. "And don't take Gwyneth home in that bedraggled state, is that clear?"

"Perfectly clear, sir," Mr. Marley assured him. "Clear as day, if I may say so."

Falk cast his eyes upward. "No one's stopping you," he said, and then he, Mr. Whitman, and Gideon disappeared through the doorway.

IT WAS MR. BERNARD'S evening off, so Caroline opened the door to let me in. She was talking nineteen to the dozen. "Charlotte's been trying on her elf costume for the party, it's ever so beautiful, and she was going to let me pin the wings on, but then Aunt Glenda said I must go and wash my hands first because she was sure I'd been petting dirty animals again—"

She got no farther, because I grabbed her and hugged her so tightly that she could hardly breathe.

"'That's right, go on, squash her!" said Xemerius, flying into the house after me. "Your mum can always get another little girl if you hug this one to death."

"My darling, sweet, dearest, cute little sister," I was murmuring into Caroline's hair, laughing and crying at the same time. "Oh, I love you so much!"

"Okay, I love you too, but you're blowing into my ear," said Caroline, cautiously wriggling free. "Come on, we're in the middle of supper. There's going to be chocolate cake from the Hummingbird Bakery for dessert."

"Oh, I love, love, *love* chocolate devil's food cake!" I cried. "And I love life that gives us such wonderful things!"

"Aren't you overdoing it a bit? Anyone would think you'd just been having electric shock treatment." Xemerius sneezed grouchily.

I meant to give him a reproachful look, but I could only smile lovingly at him. My darling, cute, grouchy little gargoyle demon! "I love you too," I told him.

"Oh, wow!" he groaned. "If you were a TV program, I'd switch channels."

Caroline was looking at me rather anxiously. On the way up to the first floor, she took my hand. "What's the matter with you, Gwenny?"

I wiped the tears off my cheek and laughed. "I'm absolutely fine," I assured her. "I'm just so happy. Because I'm alive. And because I have such a wonderful family. And because these banisters feel so wonderfully smooth and familiar. And because life is just so, so, so good." When the tears came back into my eyes again, I wondered whether it was really just aspirin that Dr. White had dissolved in a glass of water for me. But my euphoria could be simply because of the overwhelming fact that I'd survived, and now I wouldn't have to spend the rest of my days as a tiny mote of dust.

So outside the dining room door I picked Caroline up in the air again and whirled her around in a circle. I was the happiest person in the world because I was alive, and Gideon had said "I love you." Of course the last bit could have been a near-death hallucination. I mustn't rule that possibility out entirely.

My sister squealed happily while Xemerius mimed holding a remote control and trying in vain to work it.

When I put her down again, Caroline asked, "Is what Charlotte said true? You're going to Cynthia's party as a green garbage sack?"

That brought me down to earth from my euphoria trip for a moment.

"Ha, ha, ha!" laughed Xemerius. "I can just see it: a happy green garbage sack who wants to hug and kiss everyone because life is so, so, so wonderful."

"Er—no, not if I can help it." Good heavens, I hoped I could convince Lesley that it would be better to keep her modern art Martians for another party later. If the rumor was already going the rounds, she must be really keen on the idea, and when Lesley was really keen on something, it was very difficult to get her to change her mind. I knew that from past experience.

My whole family was sitting around the dining table, and I had to exert great self-control to keep myself from hugging them all with the same enthusiasm—I could even have hugged Aunt Glenda and Charlotte. (Which just shows what a peculiar state of mind I was in.) But Xemerius gave me a warning glance, so I contented myself with a beaming smile and only ruffled Nick's hair in passing. However, when I was sitting in front of my plate—my mother had already put the starter on it—I immediately forgot all about self-control again.

"Asparagus quiche!" I cried. "Oh, isn't life just

wonderful? There's so, so, so much to be happy about, isn't there?"

"If you say *wonderful* once again, I'm going to throw up over your silly asparagus quiche," growled Xemerius.

I smiled at him, put a piece of quiche in my mouth, beamed happily around the table, and asked, "How was your day, all of you?"

Aunt Maddy beamed back. "Well, yours seems to have been pretty good, anyway."

Charlotte's fork scraped over her plate with a harsh, grating noise.

Yes, in the end, my day really had been pretty good. Even though Gideon, Falk, and Mr. Whitman hadn't shown up again before I left, so I'd had no chance of checking up on whether "I love you, Gwenny. Please don't leave me" was all my imagination or whether Gideon had really said it. The other Guardians had done their best to improve what Falk de Villiers had called my "bedraggled" appearance. Mr. Marley had even wanted to brush my hair with his own hands, but I said I'd rather do it myself. Now I was wearing my school uniform, and my hair was neatly combed and hanging down my back again.

Mum patted my hand. "I'm glad you're better again, darling."

Aunt Glenda muttered something featuring the words "constitution of an ox." Then she asked, with an artificial smile, "So what's all this I hear about a green garbage sack? I can't believe that you and your friend Lassie will go to the party the Dales are giving for their daughter like that! Tobias Dale would take it as a political insult, I'm sure. He's a really big noise among the Tories."

"Uh?" I went.

"What did you say?" Xemerius corrected me.

"Glenda, I am surprised at you!" Lady Arista clicked her tongue. "None of my granddaughters would ever dream of such a thing. Going to a party in a garbage sack! What nonsense!"

"Well, it's better than nothing for someone who doesn't have a green costume to wear," said Charlotte nastily. "At least, for Gwen it will be."

"Oh, dear." Aunt Maddy looked sympathetic. "Let's think. I have a fluffy green toweling bathrobe I could lend you."

Charlotte, Nick, Caroline, and Xemerius giggled, and I grinned at Aunt Maddy. "That's really nice of you, but I don't think Lesley would like it. Little green men from Mars don't wear bathrobes."

"There you are! They mean it seriously," snapped Aunt Glenda. "My word, that girl Lassie is a bad influence on Gwyneth." She wrinkled up her nose. "Not that you'd expect anything else from the child of such lower-class parents. It's bad enough having her sort allowed to go to St. Lennox High School at all. I for one certainly would not allow my daughter to mingle with—"

"That will do, Glenda!" Mum's eyes flashed angrily at her sister. "Lesley is a clever, well-brought-up girl, and her parents are not lower class! Her father is . . . is . . ."

"A civil engineer," I prompted her.

"A civil engineer, and her mother works as . . ."

"As a dietician," I said.

"And the dog studied at Goldsmiths' College," said Xemerius. "Very respectable family."

"Our costumes don't make any political statement," I assured Aunt Glenda and Lady Arista, who were looking at me with raised eyebrows. "It's just supposed to be modern art." On the other hand, it would be typical Lesley if she also gave the whole thing a political meaning, just to put the crowning touch on it. As if it weren't bad enough that we were going to look terrible. "And it's Cynthia who's giving the party, not her parents—or the theme might not have been so green after all."

"That's not funny," said Aunt Glenda. "And I call it very impolite not to take any trouble with your costumes, when the other guests and the hosts of the party are sparing no expense. Charlotte's costume, for instance, cost—"

"A fortune, and suits her perfectly. You've said so thirty-four times already today," Mum interrupted.

"You're just envious. You always were. But at least I'm concerned for my daughter's welfare, unlike you," snapped Aunt Glenda. "The fact that you take so little interest in the company Gwyneth keeps and won't even get her a good costume, speaks for—"

"The company Gwyneth keeps?" Mum rolled her eyes. "How unrealistic can you get, Glenda? This is a school friend's birthday party, that's all! It's bad enough for the poor kids anyway, having to dress up."

Lady Arista put her knife and fork down with a clatter. "My goodness, you two are over forty and still acting like teenagers! Of course Gwyneth is not going to any party in a garbage sack. And now we will change the subject, if you please."

"Yes, let's talk about despotic old dragons," suggested Xemerius. "And women of over forty who still live with their mothers."

"You can't tell Gwyneth what to—" Mum began, but I kicked her shin under the table and grinned at her.

She sighed, but then she grinned back.

"I'm afraid I can't sit by and watch Gwyneth tarnishing the reputation of our—" Aunt Glenda began, but Lady Arista didn't let her finish what she was saying.

"Glenda, if you don't keep your mouth shut, you can go to bed without any supper," she snapped, and that made us all laugh, except Lady Arista herself and Aunt Glenda—even Charlotte laughed.

At that moment, the front doorbell rang.

No one reacted for a few seconds. We just went on eating until we remembered that it was Mr. Bernard's day off. Lady Arista sighed. "Would you be good enough to answer it again, Caroline? If it's Mr. Turner about this year's floral decorations for the lampposts in the street, tell him I'm not at home." She waited until Caroline had disappeared and then shook her head. "That man is a *plague*! I will say only this: orange begonias! I very much hope there is a special hell for people who like orange begonias!"

"So do I," agreed Aunt Maddy loyally.

A minute later, Caroline was back. "It's Gollum!" she said. "And he wants to see Gwyneth."

"Gollum?" repeated Mum, Nick, and I in chorus. It so happened that *Lord of the Rings* was our favorite film of all time. Caroline was the only one who hadn't been allowed to see it yet, because she was too young.

Nick laughed. "Wow, that's great, my preciousssss! I must take a look at Gollum."

"Me too," said Xemerius, but he went on dangling lazily from the chandelier, scratching his tummy.

"You must mean *Gordon*," said Charlotte, standing up. "And he wants to see me. He's too early, that's all. I said eight thirty."

"Oh, a boyfriend, little bunny?" inquired Aunt Maddy. "How nice! That will give you something new to think about."

Charlotte looked annoyed. "No, Aunt Maddy. Gordon is just a boy in my class, and I'm helping him with an essay."

"But he said Gwyneth," insisted Caroline. However, Charlotte had already pushed her aside and hurried out of the room. Caroline went after her.

"He can eat with us," Aunt Glenda called after them. "Charlotte is always ready to help others," she added, turning to us. "By the way, Gordon Gelderman is the son of Kyle Arthur Gelderman."

"Hear, hear," said Xemerius.

"Whoever he may be," said Mum.

"*Kyle Arthur Gelderman*," repeated Aunt Glenda, stressing every syllable this time. "The department store tycoon! Doesn't that mean anything to you? Typical—you have no idea about the people your daughter mixes with. Your commitment as a mother leaves much to be desired. Well, the boy isn't interested in Gwyneth, anyway."

Mum groaned. "Glen, you really ought to take some more of those tablets for the change of life."

Lady Arista was frowning so sternly that her eyebrows almost met in the middle, and she was already taking a deep breath, probably to send Mum and Aunt Glenda to bed without any dessert, when Caroline came back, saying triumphantly, "And Gollum *did* want to see Gwyneth!"

I'd just put a large piece of quiche in my mouth. I almost spat it out again when I saw Gideon come into the room, followed by Charlotte, whose face had suddenly turned to stone.

"Good evening," said Gideon politely. He was wearing jeans and a washed-out green shirt. He'd obviously showered since we got back, because his hair was still damp and curling wildly around his face. "I'm sorry, I really didn't mean to disturb you in the middle of your evening meal. I just wanted to see Gwyneth."

For a moment, there was silence. That is, if you don't count Xemerius, who was killing himself with laughter as he swung from the chandelier. I couldn't say a word, because I was busy getting that piece of quiche down. Nick giggled, my mum looked from Gideon to me and back again several times, Aunt Glenda got red marks on her throat, and the way Lady Arista looked at Gideon you might have thought he was an orange begonia.

Only Aunt Maddy remembered her manners. "You're not disturbing us at all," she said in friendly tones. "Here, sit down beside me. Charlotte, lay another place, would you?"

"Yup, a plate for Gollum," Nick whispered to me, grinning.

Charlotte ignored Aunt Maddy and went back to her own place at the table, still with that stony expression.

"That's very kind of you, but no thanks. I've already eaten this evening," said Gideon.

I'd finally managed to get the bit of quiche down, and I quickly got to my feet. "And I've had enough," I said. "Is it all right if I leave the table?" I looked first at Mum and then at my grandmother.

The two of them exchanged a strange look, as if they understood something that we didn't. Then they sighed deeply in unison.

"Of course," said Mum.

"But there's chocolate cake for dessert," Caroline reminded me.

"We'll save a piece for Gwyneth." Lady Arista nodded to me. Rather awkwardly, I went toward Gideon.

"And there was deathly silence in the room," Xemerius whispered from the chandelier. "All eyes rested on the girl in the piss-yellow blouse. . . ."

Eek, he was right. I was cross with myself for not showering and changing quickly when I came in—the stupid school uniform was about the least attractive outfit I had. But who could have guessed I'd have a visitor this evening? And one I wanted to look good for?

"Hi," said Gideon, smiling for the first time since he'd come into the room.

I smiled shyly back. "Hi, Gollum."

Gideon's smile widened.

"Even the shadows on the walls were silent, while the two of them looked at each other as if they'd just sat on a whoopee cushion," said Xemerius, coming down from the chandelier and flying after us. "Romantic violin music began to play as the girl in the piss-yellow blouse and the boy who badly needed a haircut walked out of the room side by side." He was still flying along behind us, but when we reached the stairs, he turned left. "The clever and handsome demon Xemerius would have followed them to play gooseberry, if he hadn't had to satisfy his appetite after seeing so many emotions on display. Today he was finally going to eat the ghost of the fat clarinet player who haunted number 23 and murdered the music of Glen Miller all day." He waved, and then disappeared through the window of the corridor.

WHEN WE REACHED my room, I saw with relief that, luckily, I'd had no time to wreck the wonderfully tidy state in which Aunt Maddy had left it on Wednesday. Okay, so the bed was unmade, but it was the work of a moment to pick up the few clothes lying around and put them on the chair with the others. Then I turned to Gideon, who hadn't said a word all the way upstairs. Well, he'd had no choice, because I was still feeling so shy that, after Xemerius left us, I'd started talking nineteen to the dozen. I'd chattered and chattered as if I were under some compulsion, telling him about all the pictures we passed, about eleven thousand of them. "Those are my great-grandparents—I've no idea why they had themselves painted in oils, there were photographers in their day. The fat child on the stool is Great-great-great-great-great-uncle Hugh as a little boy, with his sister Petronella and three rabbits. This is a duchess whose name I can't remember—no relation, but in the picture she's wearing a necklace that belonged to the Montrose family, so she's allowed to hang here. And now we're on the second floor, so you can admire Charlotte in all the pictures in this corridor. Every three months, Aunt Glenda takes her to a photographer who apparently also takes pictures of the royal family. This one's my favorite: Charlotte aged ten with a pug who had bad breath. Somehow you can see it from the way Charlotte looks, don't you think?" And so on and so forth. It was terrible. I didn't manage to stop until we reached my room, and then only because there were no pictures there.

I straightened the bedspread, unobtrusively hiding my Hello Kitty nightshirt under the pillow, and then turned to look at Gideon. I waited. It would be fine for him to say something now.

But he didn't. He just kept smiling at me as if he couldn't really believe in what he saw. My heart leaped and then missed a beat. Oh, great! It could cope with a sword thrust, no problem, but Gideon was too much for it. Especially when he was looking the way he did now.

"I tried to call you before I came, but you weren't answering your mobile," he said at last.

"The battery needs recharging." It had given out in the middle of my conversation with Lesley in the limousine taking me home. Gideon didn't reply to that, so I took the mobile out of my skirt pocket and began looking for the charger. Aunt Maddy had coiled its cable up neatly and put it away in a drawer in my desk.

Gideon was leaning back against the door. "That was quite a day, wasn't it?"

I nodded. The mobile was plugged in again now. Since I didn't know what else to do, I propped myself on the edge of the desk.

"I think it was the worst day in my entire life," said Gideon. "When you were lying there on the floor . . ." His voice faltered slightly. He moved away from the door and came toward me.

I suddenly felt an overpowering need to comfort him. "I'm sorry I . . . I gave you such a fright. But I really did think I was going to die."

"So did I." He swallowed and took another step toward me.

Even though Xemerius had gone off for his date with the clarinet player long ago, part of my mind was still adding his running commentary. "His flashing green eyes kindled the flame of her heart under the piss-yellow blouse. Clinging close to his manly breast, she let her tears flow freely."

Oh, for heaven's sake, Gwyneth! How hysterical can you get?

I clutched the edge of the desk harder.

"You really ought to have known better—I mean, about what had happened to me," I said. "After all, you're studying medicine."

"Yes, and that's exactly why I knew for certain that you—" He stopped in front of me, and for a change, he was the one biting his lower lip, which somehow went to my heart. He slowly raised his hand. "The point of the sword had gone *that* far into you." He spread his thumb and forefinger quite a long way apart. "A little scratch wouldn't have made you collapse. And then all the color went out of your face at once, and you broke out in a cold sweat. So I knew that Alastair must have hit a major artery. You were suffering from internal bleeding."

I stared at his hand in front of my face.

"But you've seen the wound yourself now. It really is nothing," I said, clearing my throat. Something about being so close to him was affecting my vocal cords. "It . . . it must have been . . . Maybe it was simply the shock. You know, I imagined I was seriously wounded, so it looked as if I was really—"

"No, Gwenny, you didn't imagine it."

"But then how did I get off so lightly, with just that little injury?" I whispered.

He lowered his hand and began pacing up and down the room. "That's what I didn't understand myself at first," he said almost fiercely. "I was so . . . so relieved that you were alive, I convinced myself that there'd be some logical explanation for the wound. But under the shower just now, light suddenly dawned on me."

"Ah, that must be it," I said. "I haven't showered yet." I loosened my convulsive grip on the edge of the desk and sat down on the rug. Okay, that was better. At least my knees had stopped shaking.

With my back against the side of my bed, I looked up at him. "Do you have to prowl around like that? It's making me nervous. I mean, even more nervous than I am already."

Gideon knelt down on the rug right in front of me and put his hand on my shoulder, without stopping to think that from now on, I was in no position to listen properly to what he was saying, since my mind was busy with less important ideas such as "I hope at least I smell good" and "I mustn't forget to breathe."

"You know the feeling when you're solving Sudoku and you find the *one* number that makes it easy to fill in all the other spaces at once?"

I tentatively nodded.

Lost in thought, Gideon was caressing me. "I've been thinking over so many things for days, but only this evening did I find that one magic number. Do you see what I mean? I read those papers over and over again, so often that I almost knew them by heart—"

"What papers?" I interrupted him.

He let go of me. "The papers that Paul got from Lord Alastair in return for our family trees. Paul gave them to me on the day you had your conversation with the count." When he saw all the question marks in my face, he gave me a wry smile. "I'd have told you then, only you were too busy asking me weird questions and then running away, acting all insulted. I couldn't go after you because Dr. White insisted on cleaning my wound, remember?"

"That was only on Monday, Gideon."

"Yes, you're right. Seems like an eternity ago, doesn't it? So when he finally let me go home, I was calling you every ten minutes, to tell you that I . . ." He cleared his throat, and then took my hand again. "To explain it all to you, but your mobile was always busy."

"Maybe because I was telling Lesley what a bastard you are," I said. "We do have a landline, you know."

He took no notice of that. "In the intervals between calling you, I started reading the papers. They're prophesies and notes from the count's private papers. Documents that the Guardians don't know about. Documents that he intentionally kept from his own people."

I groaned. "Let me guess. More silly verses, and you didn't understand a word of what they said."

Gideon leaned forward. "No," he said slowly. "Far from it. They were perfectly clear. They say that if the philosopher's stone is to take full effect, someone must die." He was looking straight into my eyes. "And that someone is you."

"Oh. I see." I wasn't as impressed as I probably should have been. "Then I'm the price that has to be paid."

"I was shocked when I read that." A strand of hair fell over Gideon's face, but he didn't notice it. "At first I couldn't believe it, but the prophesies all agreed. The ruby-red life is extinguished, the raven's death reveals the end, the twelfth star fades, and so on and so forth. It went on like that forever." He paused for a moment. "And the notes that the count had written in the margins were even clearer. As soon as the circle is closed and the elixir has reached its true destination, you're to die. He says so almost word for word."

I swallowed after all. "How am I supposed to die?" Instinctively, I thought of the bloodstained blade of Lord Alastair's sword again. "Did the papers say that as well?"

Gideon smiled slightly. "Well, as usual, the prophesies are vague on that point, but they make one thing very clear. It's obvious that I—I mean the Diamond, the Lion, Number Eleven—will have something to do with it." The smile disappeared from his face, and there was a note in his voice that I'd never heard before. "The papers say that you're going to die *because of me*. For love."

"Oh. Um. Er," I said, not very imaginatively. "But they're only a set of old rhymes."

Gideon shook his head. "Don't you understand? I couldn't let that happen, Gwenny. It's the only reason I went along with your silly game and made out that I'd been lying and playing with your feelings."

Light finally dawned. "So in case I got some silly idea

of dying for love of you, next day you made sure I'd hate you? That was very . . . how can I put it? . . . very chivalrous of you." I leaned forward and put the unruly strand of hair back from his face. "Really, very chivalrous."

Gideon grinned faintly. "Most difficult thing I've ever done, believe me."

Once I'd started, I couldn't keep my hands off him. My fingers wandered slowly over his face. He obviously hadn't gotten around to shaving, but the stubble felt kind of sexy.

"*Let's stay friends*—that was a really brilliant move," I murmured. "The moment you said that, I hated your guts."

Gideon groaned. "But that's not what I wanted. I *really* wanted us to be friends," he said. He took my hand and held it tight for a moment. "The idea that saying so would infuriate you so much . . ." He left the rest of his sentence hanging in the air.

I leaned even closer and took his face in both my hands. "Well, maybe you'd better remember it for future reference," I whispered. "You never, never, *never* say that to anyone you've kissed."

"Wait, Gwen, that's not all. There's something else I have to—" he began, but I didn't intend to delay this any longer. I cautiously placed my lips on his and began kissing him.

Gideon responded, gently and carefully at first, but when I put my arms around his neck and nestled against him, he kissed me harder. His left hand was buried in my hair and his right hand began stroking my throat, slowly wandering on down. Just as it reached the top button of my blouse, my mobile rang. Reluctantly, I moved away from him.

"It's Lesley," I said, looking at the display. "I'll have to answer—just a quick reply, anyway, or she'll be worrying."

Gideon grinned. "That's okay. I've no intention of dissolving into thin air."

"Lesley? Can I call you back?"

But Lesley wasn't listening to me. "Gwen, listen, I've been right through *Anna Karenina*," she said excitedly. "And I think I know what the count really plans to do with the philosopher's stone."

I couldn't have cared less about the philosopher's stone. At this moment, anyway.

"That's great," I said, glancing at Gideon. "You must tell me all about it later—"

"Don't worry," said Lesley. "I'm on my way."

"Really? But I—"

"Well, to be precise, I'm here already."

"Where?"

"Here. I'm standing at the end of the corridor leading to your room, and your mum and your brother and sister are just coming upstairs after me. With your great-aunt puffing along in their wake. Oh, they've overtaken me now. I'm afraid they'll be knocking on your door any moment—"

But Caroline didn't go to the trouble of knocking. She just flung the door open and cried, beaming happily, "Chocolate cake for everyone!" Then she turned to the others. "Told you so," she said. "They're not necking at all."

THE CIRCLE OF TWELVE

NAME	GEMSTONE	ALCHEMICAL QUALITY	ANIMAL	TREE
Lancelot de Villiers 1560–1607	Amber	*Calcinatio*	Frog	Beech
Elaine Burghley 1562–1580	Opal	*Putrefactio et mortificio*	Owl	Walnut
William de Villiers 1626–1689	Agate	*Sublimatio*	Bear	Pine
Cecilia Woodville 1628–1684	Aquamarine	*Solutio*	Horse	Maple
Robert Leopold, Count Saint-Germain 1703–1784	Emerald	*Distillatio*	Eagle	Oak
Jeanne de Pointcarré, Madame d'Urfé (1705–1775)	Citrine	*Coagulatio*	Snake	Ginkgo
Jonathan and Timothy de Villiers 1875–1944 1875–1930	Carnelian	*Extractio*	Falcon	Apple
Margaret Tilney 1877–1944	Jade	*Digestio*	Fox	Linden
Paul de Villiers b. 1974	Black Tourmaline	*Ceratio*	Wolf	Mountain Ash
Lucy Montrose b. 1976	Sapphire	*Fermentatio*	Lynx	Willow
Gideon de Villiers b. 1992	Diamond	*Multiplicatio*	Lion	Yew
Gwyneth Shepherd b. 1994	Ruby	*Projectio*	Raven	Birch

FROM *THE CHRONICLES OF THE GUARDIANS*, VOLUME 4,
THE CIRCLE OF TWELVE

ELEVEN

THE DAY REALLY had been full of all kinds of strange revelations, and the most important was that Gideon really did love me after all! Oh, and then of course there was the bit about Lord Alastair's sword and dying. But in a way, the family picnic in my room this evening seemed the strangest of today's events. Here was almost everyone who meant most to me in the world, sitting on the rug, laughing, all of them talking at once: Mum, Aunt Maddy, Nick, Caroline, Lesley—and Gideon! And they all had chocolate on their faces. (As Aunt Glenda and Charlotte had lost their appetite and Lady Arista had no sweet tooth at all, we had the whole chocolate cake to ourselves.) Maybe it was because of the cake that Gideon and my family immediately seemed to be on very good terms, or maybe it was because he was more relaxed than I'd ever seen him before. Even though Mum and Aunt Maddy kept asking him any number of questions, ranging from genuinely curious to embarrassing, and Nick still insisted on calling him Gollum.

When we'd finished the last crumbs, Aunt Maddy got up, groaning. "I think I'd better go down and give Arista some moral backing—Mr. Turner managed to slip into the house when that boyfriend of Charlotte's arrived, and I'm sure they're still quarreling about begonias." She gave Gideon one of her dimpled, rosy smiles. "You know, you're unusually nice for one of the de Villiers family, Gideon."

Gideon got to his feet as well. "Thank you very much," he said cheerfully, shaking hands with Aunt Maddy. "I'm delighted to have met you properly."

"See that?" Lesley whispered, nudging me in the ribs. "Good manners. Gets his bum off the floor when a lady stands up. Cute little bum too. Pity he's such a bastard."

I rolled my eyes.

Mum brushed crumbs off her dress and hauled Caroline and Nick up. "Come along, you two—time for bed."

"Mum!" said Nick, sounding deeply injured. "It's a Friday, and I'm twelve."

"And I want to stay here, please." Caroline looked innocently up at Gideon. "I like you," she said. "You're ever so nice and ever so good-looking."

"Yes, *ever so*," Lesley whispered to me. "Is he by any chance blushing?"

Seemed like it. How sweet.

Lesley's elbow landed in my ribs. "You're gawping like a sheep," she hissed. At that moment, Xemerius flew through the closed window and came down on my desk, with a satisfied belch.

"When the clever and extraordinarily handsome demon returned from his outing, full of hope, he was disappointed to see that in his absence the girl had lost neither the piss-yellow blouse nor her innocence," he quoted from his unwritten novel.

I mouthed a silent "shut up!" in his direction.

"All I mean," he said, sounding hurt, "is that it was a good opportunity. You're not as young as you were, and who knows, you may be hating the guy's guts again tomorrow."

When Aunt Maddy had left and Mum had shooed my brother and sister out of the room ahead of her, Gideon closed the door behind them and looked at us, grinning.

Lesley raised both hands. "No, forget it! *I'm* not going. I have important things to discuss with Gwen. Strictly secret things."

"Then I'm not going, either," said Xemerius, hopping on my bed and curling up on the pillow.

"Lesley, I don't think we need to keep things secret from Gideon anymore," I said. "It wouldn't be a bad idea if, for the common good, we pooled all our knowledge to date." I thought I'd put that rather well.

"Especially as I doubt whether Google will be much help in the circumstances," said Gideon with a touch of sarcasm. "Sorry, Lesley, but I hear that Mr. Whitman was showing people a folder in which you'd . . . er, collected up all sorts of information."

"Oh, yes?" Lesley put her hands on her hips. "And there was I just now, thinking maybe after all you weren't such an arrogant asshole as Gwen always said, but quite cute! Cute, that's a joke! It was . . ." She wrinkled up her nose, looking rather embarrassed. "How mean of Mr. Squirrel to show my folder around! Those Internet researches were all we had to go on at first, and I was quite proud of them."

"But now we've found out far more," I said. "In the first place, Lesley is a genius, and in the second place, I've had several conversations with my grandf—"

"Of course we are not about to give away our sources!" Lesley's eyes flashed at me. "He's still one of the arrogant sort, Gwen. Even if he's cast some kind of spell over you, remember, it's only hormonal."

Gideon gave us a broad grin as he sat down cross-legged on the rug. "Okay. Then I'll be the first to tell you two what I know," he said. And without waiting to get the go-ahead from Lesley, he began talking about the papers that Paul had given him again. Unlike me, Lesley was more than horrified to hear that I was supposed to die as soon as the Circle of Blood was closed. She went really pale under her freckles.

"Can I have a look at those papers?" she asked.

"Sure." Gideon took several folded sheets out of his jeans pocket and a few more from the breast pocket of his shirt. The papers were rather yellowed, and as far as I could see, they looked flimsy along the folds.

Lesley stared at him blankly. "You just walk about

with stuff like this in your pockets? Those documents are valuable originals, not . . . not snot-rags." She put out her hand for them. "They're practically falling apart. Isn't that just typical of a man?" Carefully, she unfolded the papers. "And you're sure they're not forgeries?"

Gideon shrugged his shoulders. "I'm not a graphologist or a historian. But they look exactly like the other originals, the papers in the keeping of the Guardians."

"Yes, and I bet those are kept under glass and at the right temperature," said Lesley, still accusingly. "The way such things ought to be stored."

"But how did the Florentine Alliance people get their hands on the papers?" I asked.

Gideon shrugged again. "Theft, I assume. I haven't had time to sift right through the *Annals* for a clue. Or to check up on all of what they say. But I've been going around with *these* papers for days. I know them by heart, although I can't make much of most of the contents. Apart from that one crucial point."

"At least you didn't go straight off to Falk and show them to him," I said appreciatively.

"Although I did think of doing just that. But then . . ." Gideon sighed. "Right now I simply don't know who can be trusted."

"Trust no one," I whispered, rolling my eyes dramatically. "Or that's what my mother told me."

"Your mother," murmured Gideon. "I'd be interested to know how much *she* knows about everything."

"And it means that when the Circle is closed, and the count has this elixir he's after, Gwyneth will . . ." Lesley couldn't bring herself to finish the sentence.

"Die, yes," I said.

"Pop her clogs, pass over to the other side, kick the bucket, go west, shuffle off this mortal coil, breathe her last, start pushing up the daisies." Xemerius made his own drowsy contribution.

"Will be murdered!" Lesley reached for my hand with a dramatic gesture. "Because you're not about to fall down dead of your own accord!" She ran her fingers through her hair, which was sticking out untidily in all directions already. Gideon cleared his throat, but Lesley wasn't letting him get a word in edgeways. "To be honest, I've had a bad feeling about it all along," she said. "Those other rhymes are terribly . . . terribly ominous, too. All about the raven, the ruby, and the number twelve, and the outlook is kind of grim for them. And it does fit with what I've found out myself." She let go of my hand and reached for her backpack—a brand-new one!—to fish out *Anna Karenina*. "Well, really I suppose Lucy and Paul and your grandfather found it out—and Giordano."

"Giordano?" I repeated, bewildered.

"Yes, haven't you read his essays?" Lesley leafed through the book. "The Guardians *had* to take him into the Lodge, to keep him from broadcasting his theories to the world at large."

I shook my head, feeling a bit ashamed of myself. I'd lost all interest in Giordano's writings after the first long-winded sentence. (Even apart from the fact that they were by *Giordano*—well, I mean to say!)

"Wake me up if this gets interesting," said Xemerius, closing his eyes. "I need a nap to help me digest my supper."

"No one has ever taken Giordano really seriously, not even the Guardians," Gideon said. "He's published confused theories in dubious journals about the supernatural. The readers of such things regard the count as One Transformed and an Ascended Master, whatever that's supposed to mean."

"I can tell you all about it!" Lesley held *Anna Karenina* under his nose as if she were producing Exhibit A in court as evidence. "As a historian, Giordano stumbled on letters and records of the Inquisition from the sixteenth century. The sources show that when the count was a very young man and on one of his journeys in time, he met a girl who was living in a convent—Elisabetta di Madrone, daughter of the Conte di Madrone—seduced her, and made her pregnant. And on that occasion . . ." She hesitated for a moment. "Or, well, presumably either before or after it, he told her all kinds of things about himself—maybe because he was still young and rash, or simply because he'd lulled himself into a false sense of security."

"*What* kinds of things?" I asked.

"He was very free with information, beginning with his origins and his real name, going on to the fact that he could travel in time, and finally claiming that he was in possession of priceless secrets. Secrets that would enable him to create the philosopher's stone."

Gideon nodded, as if he knew the story, but he didn't fool Lesley.

"Unfortunately, that didn't go down too well in the sixteenth century," she went on. "At that time, people thought the count was a dangerous demon, and this girl Elisabetta's father was so furious about what had happened to his daughter that he founded the Florentine Alliance and devoted the rest of his life to looking for the count and others like him. So have many generations after him—" She stopped. "Where was I? My goodness, my head's so full of information that I feel it might explode any moment now."

"What on earth does any of this have to do with Tolstoy?" asked Gideon, looking impatiently at Lucas's special edition of the novel. "Don't snap my nose off, but so far you haven't told me anything really new."

Lesley cast him a dark glance.

"Well, you've told me a lot I didn't know," I was quick to say. "But you were going to explain what the count really intends to do with the philosopher's stone, Lesley!"

"Right." Lesley frowned. "But I had to go farther back, because of course it was some time before the descendants of the Conte di Madrone got on the track of the first time traveler, Lancelot de Villiers, in—"

"You can cut it short if you like," Gideon interrupted her. "We don't have all the time in the world. The day after tomorrow we're meeting the count again, and meanwhile, on his instructions, I'm supposed to be getting some blood from Lucy and Paul. I'm afraid that if I don't succeed, he'll come up with an alternative plan." He sighed. "Well?"

"But we can't neglect the details." Lesley also sighed and buried her face in her hands for a moment. "Oh, all right. The Guardians think the philosopher's stone is something that will work wonders for mankind, because it will be a cure for all sickness and disease, right?"

"Right," Gideon and I said in unison.

"But Lucy and Paul and Gwenny's grandfather and, yes, strictly speaking, the Alliance people as well, all thought that was a lie."

I nodded.

"Hang on." Gideon's eyebrows were drawn together. "Gwenny's grandfather? Our Grand Master before Uncle Falk took over?"

I nodded, this time a little guiltily. He was staring at me, and suddenly he looked as if light had dawned on him. "Go on, Lesley," he said. "What exactly did you find out?"

"Lucy and Paul thought the count just wants the philosopher's stone for himself." Lesley stopped for a moment, to make sure that we really were hanging on her lips. "Because he intends the stone to make him, and only him, *immortal.*"

Gideon and I said nothing. I was suitably impressed, speaking for myself. I wasn't so sure about Gideon. His face didn't even begin to tell me what he was thinking.

"Of course the count had to invent all that about the benefit to mankind, blah-blah-blah, so that he could convince people it would be a good idea to work for him,"

Lesley went on. "He could hardly have built up such a massive secret organization if he'd said what he was really planning to do."

"You mean that's all? It's simply because that old buffer the count is scared of dying?" I said. I was almost disappointed. Was that really supposed to be the secret behind the secret? All the fuss and expense, just for this?

As I was shaking my head skeptically and trying to think what to say next, something beginning with "but," Gideon's eyebrows moved even closer together.

"It would fit," he murmured. "Damn it, Lesley's right! It does fit."

"What fits?" I asked.

He jumped up and began prowling around my room. "I can't believe that my family's been blindly falling for his tricks for centuries," he said. "That *I've* been blindly falling for his tricks!" He stopped in front of me and took a deep breath. "*The precious stones shall all unite, the scent of time shall fill the night, once time links the fraternity, one man lives for eternity.* Read that the right way, and you see what it's all about. *Under the sign of the twelvefold star, all sickness and ills will flee afar.* Of course! If it's going to give someone eternal life, that substance must be able to cure anything." He rubbed his forehead and pointed to the papers lying on the rug. They looked the worse for wear. "And the prophesies that the count never let the Guardians see say so even more clearly. *The philosopher's stone shall eternity bind. New strength will arise in the young at that hour, making one man immortal, for he holds the power.* It's so simple! Why didn't I catch on long ago? I was so stunned by the idea that Gwyneth was going to die and it could be my fault, I just didn't see the truth. Although it was staring me right in the face!"

"Oh, well," said Lesley, allowing herself a small, triumphant smile. "I guess your strengths lie in other areas. Right, Gwenny?" She added, kindly, "And you had plenty of other problems on your hands."

I reached for Gideon's papers. *"But beware: when the twelfth star shows its own force, his life here on earth runs its natural course. And if youth is destroyed, then the oak tree will stand, to the end of all time, rooted fast in the land,"* I read hesitantly, trying to ignore the fact that the little hairs on my arms stood up when I took in those words. "Okay, so I'm the twelfth, I get that, but the rest of it might as well be in Chinese, for all the sense it makes to me."

"Here, see what's written in the margin? *As soon as I have the elixir, she must die!"* murmured Lesley, her head beside mine as we looked at the papers. "You get that bit, don't you?" She hugged me hard. "You must never, never go near that murderer again, understand? That grisly Circle of Blood simply mustn't be closed, not at any price." She held me a little way away from her. "Lucy and Paul were acting for the best when they ran off with the chronograph. It's a shame there was a second one lying about." Letting go of me, she looked accusingly at Gideon. "And to think that someone in this room had nothing better to do than go around busily getting blood from all the time travelers to fuel it! Promise me, here and now, that the count will never get a chance to throttle Gwyneth, or stab her—"

Xemerius woke from deep sleep with a start. "Poison her, shoot her, hang her, behead her, trample her to death, drown her, throw her off a tower block," he cried enthusiastically. "What are you talking about?"

"*As the star dies, the eagle arises supreme, fulfilling his ancient and magical dream*," said Gideon quietly. "Except that she *can't* die!"

"*Mustn't* die, you mean," Lesley corrected him.

"Must, can, should, would," droned Xemerius, and he dropped his head on his paws again.

Gideon got down on the floor in front of us. His expression was very serious again. "That was what I was going to tell you just now, before we started—" He cleared his throat. "Did you tell Lesley how Lord Alastair ran you through with his sword?"

I nodded, and Lesley said, "She was really amazingly lucky that he didn't wound her seriously."

"Lord Alastair is one of the best swordsmen I know," said Gideon. "And he did wound Gwyneth seriously. It was a very dangerous wound indeed." He touched my hand with his fingertips. "As a matter of fact, it was a fatal wound."

Lesley was gasping for air.

"But I only imagi—" I murmured, and then I thought of the way I'd floated up to the ceiling and the spectacular view I had from up there of what was going on down below.

"No." Gideon shook his head. "You didn't only imagine it! I don't know if anyone *could* imagine a thing like that. And I was there at the time!" For a moment, he seemed unable to go on, then he got himself under control. "When we traveled back, you hadn't been breathing for at least half a minute, and when I arrived in the cellar with you, you still had no pulse, I'm certain of that. Then a minute later, you sat up as if nothing had happened."

"Does that mean . . . ," asked Lesley, and this time she was the one gawping like a sheep.

"It means Gwenny is the one who's immortal," said Gideon, giving me a flickering smile. I could only stare back, baffled.

Xemerius had sat up and was scratching his tummy uncertainly. His mouth opened and then closed, but instead of making any comment, he just spat a little gush of water over my pillow.

"Immortal?" Lesley's eyes were wide open. "Like . . . like the Highlander?"

Gideon nodded. "Except that she won't die even if she's beheaded." He stood up again, and his face set hard. "Gwyneth can't die, unless she takes her own life." And he recited, in a low voice, *"For a star goes out in the sky above, if it freely chooses to die for love."*

WHEN I OPENED my eyes, the light of the rising sun was flooding into my room, and little dust motes were dancing in the air, bathed in bright, rosy light. I was wide awake at once—it wasn't at all like the last few mornings.

Cautiously, I felt beneath my nightdress for the wound under my breast and ran my finger along the scab over it.

Immortal.

I'd refused to believe what Gideon said at first, because it was so absurd, and my life seemed about to collapse under the sheer weight of all these complications anyway. My mind just wouldn't face facts.

But deep inside, I'd known that Gideon was right as soon as he said it: Lord Alastair's sword had killed me. I had felt the pain and watched what little life was left in me simply drain away. I had drawn my last breath—and here I was, alive and well.

The subject of immortality had kept us talking all the rest of the evening. After the first shock, there was no stopping Lesley and Xemerius, in particular.

"Does that mean she'll never get any wrinkles?"

"Suppose an eight-ton concrete block falls on you, would you have to live forever squashed as flat as a postage stamp?"

"Maybe you're not really immortal, you just have nine lives, like a cat."

"If someone put out one of her eyes, would it grow back?"

Gideon didn't know the answers to any of these questions, but that didn't bother anyone much. We'd probably have gone on all night if Mum hadn't come in and sent Lesley and Gideon home. She was firm about it. "Don't forget, you were still sick only yesterday, Gwyneth," she told me. "I want you to get a good night's sleep."

A good night's sleep—as if I could think of sleeping after a day like this! And there was still so much to discuss!

I went downstairs with Gideon and Lesley to say good night at the front door. Lesley, like the good friend she is, took the hint at once and went a little way ahead, looking as if she was making an urgent phone call. (I heard her telling her dog, "Hi, Bertie, I'm on my way home.") Xemerius wasn't so considerate. He dangled upside down from the roof of the porch, chanting, "Necking in the porch, fit to make it scorch. If things get too hot, I shall laugh a lot."

Finally, and reluctantly, I'd said good night to Gideon and gone back to my room, firmly intending to spend all night thinking, phoning, and making plans. But I thought I'd just lie down on my bed for a few minutes first, and then I fell fast asleep. It must have been the same with the others. When I woke in the morning, I didn't see a single missed call on the display of my mobile.

I looked accusingly at Xemerius, who had curled up at the end of my bed and was now stretching and yawning. "You might have woken me!"

"Am I your alarm clock, O immortal mistress?"

"I thought ghosts—I mean demons—didn't need any sleep."

"Maybe we don't *need* it," said Xemerius, "but after such a hearty supper, I felt I could do with a little nap." He wrinkled up his nose. "Like you could do with a shower right now."

He was right. All the others were asleep (it was

Saturday, after all), so I could spend ages in the bathroom, using vast amounts of shampoo, shower gel, toothpaste, body lotion, and Mum's antiwrinkle cream.

"Let me guess," said Xemerius dryly later, when I came out and beamed at my own reflection in the mirror as I got dressed. "Life is wonderful, wonderful, wonderful, and you feel reborn—ha, ha, ha!"

"That's right. You know, all of a sudden, I seem to be seeing life through entirely new eyes—"

Xemerius snorted. "Maybe you think you've seen a great light, but it's really just hormones. One day up in the clouds, the next day down in the dumps," he said. "*Girls!* And this will go on for the next twenty or thirty years. Then, next thing we know, it'll be all that change-of-life stuff. Or come to think of it, maybe not with you. An immortal with a midlife crisis somehow doesn't sound right."

I gave him a forgiving smile. "You know, my little grouch, you're really—" But the ring tone of my mobile interrupted me. It was Lesley, wanting to know when we were going to meet to stick the Martian costumes for Cynthia's party together.

Party! How could she think of a thing like that now? "Listen, Lesley, I've been thinking I may not go at all. So much has happened, and—"

"You *must* come. And you will." Lesley obviously wasn't taking no for an answer. "Because I organized company for us yesterday, and it would be very embarrassing if I had to call that off."

I groaned. "Not your silly cousin again, and his friend

who's always farting, Lesley?" For a frightful moment, I imagined a green garbage sack slowly inflating itself. "You promised, after last time, that you'd never do that again. I hope I don't have to remind you of those chocolate marshmallows that—"

"How stupid do you think I am? I never make the same mistake twice, you know I don't!" Lesley paused for a moment, and then went on, apparently unruffled. "On the way to the bus stop yesterday, I told Gideon about the party. He positively insisted on coming with us." Another little pause. "And his little brother too. So you can't wriggle out of it now."

"Lesley!" I could imagine exactly how that conversation had gone. Lesley was a brilliant manipulator. Gideon probably didn't even know what had hit him.

"You can thank me later," said Lesley, giggling. "Now we just have to think how to fix our costumes. I've already stuck feelers into a green kitchen sieve—that'll look good as a hat for a Martian. You can have it if you like."

I groaned. "Oh, my God! Are you really asking me to go on my first official date with Gideon in a garbage sack with a kitchen sieve on my head?"

Lesley hesitated, but only for a moment. "It's art! And witty. And it won't cost us anything," she explained. "Anyway, he's so crazy about you, he won't mind at all."

I could see I'd have to try a little more subtlety here. "Okay," I said, pretending to be resigned to my plastic fate. "If you absolutely insist, we'll go as Martian garbage men. You're so cool! And I'm a little envious of you, because you couldn't care less whether Raphael thinks girls with feelers and sieves on their heads are sexy. And you don't mind whether you crackle while you're dancing and you'll feel like . . . well, like a garbage sack. Or give off a faintly chemical smell . . . while Charlotte sweeps past us in her elf costume making snide remarks."

Lesley didn't reply for all of three seconds. Then she said slowly, "No, I don't care in the least about any of that—"

"I know. Otherwise I'd have suggested letting Madame Rossini dress us. She said she'd lend us anything she has that's green. The kind of dresses that Grace Kelly and Audrey Hepburn wear in films. Charleston dance dresses from the golden twenties. Or ball gowns from—"

"Okay, okay," Lesley interrupted me impatiently. "You hooked me when you said 'Grace Kelly.' So let's forget the stupid garbage sacks. Do you think your Madame Rossini is awake yet?"

"HOW DO I LOOK?" Mum pirouetted on her own axis. Since Mrs. Jenkins, the secretary at the Guardians' Lodge, had phoned this morning asking her to come with me when I went to the Temple to elapse, she'd changed three times already.

"Great," I said, without really looking. The limousine would be coming around the corner at any moment. Would Gideon be in it to collect me? Or would he be waiting for me at the Guardians' headquarters? Yesterday evening had ended far too suddenly. There was still so much we had to say to each other.

"If I may say so, I thought the blue outfit was better," remarked Mr. Bernard, who was dusting the picture frames in the hall with a huge feather duster.

Mum ran straight upstairs again, calling back, "You're right, Mr. Bernard! This one looks much too formal. Too elegant for a Saturday afternoon. Goodness knows what he'd think. As if I'd prettified myself specially for him."

I gave Mr. Bernard a reproachful smile. "Did you have to say that?"

"She did ask." His brown eyes behind the owl-like glasses twinkled at me, but then he looked through the window in the front hall. "Ah, here comes the limousine. Shall I tell the driver he'll have to wait a little while? She's not going to find the right shoes to go with the blue outfit in a hurry."

"I'll do it." I put my bag over my shoulder. "See you later, Mr. Bernard. And please keep an eye on You Know Who."

"Of course, Miss Gwyneth. You Know Who won't get anywhere near you know what." With a smile that you would hardly have noticed, he went back to his dusting.

No Gideon in the limousine. Instead it was Mr. Marley, who had already opened the door of the car as I came out of the house. His moonface looked as disapproving as it ever had during the last few days. Maybe even more disapproving. And he said nothing at all in reply to my exuberant, "Isn't this a wonderful spring day?"

"Where's Mrs. Grace Shepherd?" he asked instead. "I have orders to deliver her to the Temple at once."

"Sounds like you were going to bring her up before the magistrates," I said. If I'd known how close this flippant remark was to the facts, I wouldn't have felt half as cheerful as I did when I settled into the back seat of the car.

Once Mum was finally ready, the drive to the Temple was quite fast for London conditions. We got stuck in only three traffic jams, it took us fifty minutes, and once again, I wondered why we couldn't simply take the Tube.

Mr. George met us at the entrance to the Guardians' headquarters. I thought he was looking more serious than usual, and his smile somehow seemed forced. "Gwyneth, Mr. Marley will take you downstairs to elapse. Grace, you're expected in the Dragon Hall."

I looked inquiringly at Mum. "What do they want to see you for?"

Mum shrugged her shoulders, but she suddenly looked tense.

Mr. Marley brought out the black silk scarf. "Come along, Miss Shepherd," he said. He took my elbow, but let go of it again at once when he saw the look in my eyes. Lips tight, ears bright red, he growled, "Follow me. We have a very tight schedule today. I've already set the chronograph."

I gave Mum an encouraging smile and then stumbled down the corridor after Mr. Marley. He was setting a fast pace, and as usual, he was muttering to himself. He'd have run straight into Gideon around the next corner if Gideon hadn't stepped aside in time.

"Morning, Marley," he said casually, as Mr. Marley, a good deal too late, did a little jump. So did my heart, particularly as the sight of me made a smile about as wide as the eastern delta of the Ganges (at least!) spread over Gideon's face. "Hi, Gwenny, did you sleep well?" he asked affectionately.

"What are you doing up here?" snapped Mr. Marley. "You're supposed to have been with Madame Rossini ages ago, getting into costume. We really do have a very tight schedule today, and Operation Black Tourmaline forward slash Sapph—"

"You just go on ahead, Marley," Gideon told him in friendly tones. "Gwenny and I will catch up with you in a couple of minutes. And after that, I can get into costume quickly. That's no problem."

"You're not allowed to—" Mr. Marley began, but suddenly all the friendliness had disappeared from Gideon's eyes, and they looked so chilly that Mr. Marley ducked his head.

"But you mustn't forget to blindfold her," he said, and then he handed Gideon the black scarf and hurried away.

Gideon didn't wait for him to be out of sight—he put his arms around me and kissed me hard on the mouth. "I've missed you so much."

I was very glad Xemerius wasn't there when I whispered, "Missed you too," put my arms around his neck, and kissed him passionately back. Gideon pressed me against the wall, and we didn't let go of each other until a picture fell down. An oil painting of a four-master sailing ship in a storm at sea. Breathlessly, I tried to hang it back on its nail.

Gideon helped me. "I was going to call you yesterday

evening, but then I thought your mother was right—you badly needed some sleep."

"Yes, I did." I leaned back against the wall again and grinned at him. "I hear we're going to a party together this evening."

Gideon laughed. "Yes, a foursome, with my little brother. Raphael was very keen to go, especially when he heard that it was Lesley's idea." He stroked my cheek with his fingertips. "I somehow didn't imagine our first date quite like that, but your friend can be very convincing."

"Did she tell you it's a costume party?"

Gideon shrugged his shoulders. "Nothing shocks me anymore." His fingertips wandered down my cheeks to my throat. "We had so much . . . er . . . so much to talk about yesterday evening." He cleared his throat. "I'd love to hear all about your grandfather, and how on earth you managed to meet him. Or rather *when* you managed to meet him. And what does the book that Lesley kept holding up like the Holy Grail have to do with it?"

"Oh, *Anna Karenina*! I brought it with me, although Lesley thought we ought to wait a little longer, until we could be really sure you were on our side." I was about to pick up my bag, but it wasn't there. I clicked my tongue, annoyed. "Oh, no, my mum took it with her when we got out of the car."

The tune of "Nice Guys Finish Last" was playing somewhere. I couldn't help laughing. "Isn't that kind of—?"

"Er . . . maybe. Unsuitable?" Gideon fished his mobile out of his jeans pocket. "If that's Marley, I'm going to—oh!

My mother." He sighed. "Seems like she's found a boarding school for Raphael and wants me to persuade him to go to it. I'll call her back later."

The mobile went on ringing.

"It's okay. Go ahead and answer it," I said. "Meanwhile I'll just run back and collect that book."

I sprinted away without waiting for him to reply. Down in the cellar, Mr. Marley was probably freaked out, but who cared?

The door to the Dragon Hall was open just a crack, and even from a distance, I could hear my mum's agitated voice.

"What's this meant to be, an interrogation? I've told you my reasons already. I wanted to protect my daughter, and I hoped Charlotte would be the one to inherit the gene. That's all there is to it."

"Sit down again." That was unmistakably Mr. Whitman, in the tone he used for troublesome students.

Chairs were shifted. Several people cleared their throats. I slowly stole closer.

"We did warn you, Grace." Falk de Villiers spoke in icy tones. Mum was probably staring at her shoes and wondering why the hell she'd taken so much trouble with her outfit. I leaned back against the wall by the door, so that I could hear them better.

"It was stupid of you to think we wouldn't find out the truth." Dr. White's grumpy voice.

Not another squeak out of Mum.

"We went on a little excursion to the Cotswolds

yesterday to visit a Mrs. Dawn Heller," said Falk. "That name means something to you, doesn't it?"

When Mum still said nothing, he went on, "She's the midwife who helped to bring Gwyneth into the world. Since you paid the rent of her holiday cottage with your credit card not so long ago, I'd really have expected you to remember her better."

"Dear heaven, what have you done to the poor woman?" exclaimed Mum.

"Nothing, of course. What in the world are you thinking of?" That was Mr. George.

And Mr. Whitman, his voice dripping with sarcasm, added, "But she seemed to think we wanted to involve her in Satanic rites of some kind. She threw a fit of hysterics, crossing herself the whole time. And when she saw Jake, she almost fell down in a faint."

"I was only going to give her a tranquilizing injection," grumbled Dr. White.

"In the end, however, she calmed down enough for us to have a reasonably sensible conversation with her." That was Falk de Villiers again. "And she told us the very interesting story of the night when Gwyneth was born. It sounded like something out of a cross between a fairy tale and a horror story. An honest but credulous midwife is called out to a young girl in labor. The girl has been living in a small terraced house in Durham, hiding away from a Satanic sect. The cruel sect, fixated on numerological rituals, is after not only the girl but also her baby. The midwife doesn't know exactly what the Satanists plan to do with the poor little thing, but her imagination obviously works overtime. She has such a kind heart, and she is also being paid such a considerable sum of money—you can tell me how you came by it sometime, Grace—that after helping the baby into the world in a home birth, she falsifies the date on the child's birth certificate. And she promises never to tell anyone a word about the deal."

There was silence for some time. Then Mum said, a little defiantly, "Well, what about it? That's exactly what I've already told you."

"And so we thought ourselves, at first," said Mr. Whitman. "But then we found that a few details of Mrs. Heller's story surprised us."

"You were almost twenty-eight in 1994—but yes, admittedly in the midwife's eyes you could still have been considered a *young girl*," Falk went on. "In that case, however, who was the anxious, red-haired sister of the mother-to-be whom Mrs. Heller mentioned?"

"She was getting on in years at the time," said Mum quietly. "Sounds as if she's senile by now."

"Possibly. But she had no difficulty at all in recognizing the young girl in a photograph," said Mr. Whitman. "The young girl who had a baby daughter that night."

"It was a photograph of *Lucy*," said Falk.

His words hit me like a punch in the stomach. As an icy silence spread in the Dragon Hall, my knees gave way, and I slowly slid down the wall to the floor.

"That's . . . that's a mistake," I finally heard Mum whisper. Footsteps were coming toward me along the corridor, but I was unable to turn my head. Only when he bent over me did I realize that it was Gideon.

"What's going on?" he whispered, crouching down on the floor in front of me.

"A mistake, Grace?" I could hear Falk de Villiers quite clearly. "The woman also recognized *you* in a photograph, as the supposed big sister who handed her an envelope with an extraordinarily large sum of money in it. And she recognized the man who held Lucy's hand while she was giving birth! My brother!"

And as if it hadn't quite gone home to me yet, he added, "Gwyneth is the child of Paul and Lucy."

I let out an odd sort of whimper. Gideon, who had turned very pale, took my hands.

Inside the Dragon Hall, my mum began crying.

Except that she wasn't my mum.

"None of it would have been necessary if you'd all of you left them alone," she sobbed. "If you hadn't pursued them so mercilessly."

"No one knew that Lucy and Paul were expecting a baby," said Falk heatedly.

"They'd committed theft," snorted Dr. White. "They had stolen the Lodge's most precious possession, and they were about to destroy everything that, in the course of the centuries—"

"Oh, shut up, for heaven's sake!" cried Mum. "You forced those young people to abandon the daughter they loved so much, only two days after her birth!"

It was at that point that I jumped up—I don't know

how—and got to my feet again. I couldn't listen to this for a second longer.

"Gwenny!" said Gideon urgently, but I shook off his hands and ran. "Where are you going?" After a few steps, he caught up with me.

"Away from here, that's all." I ran even faster. The porcelain in the glass cases clinked softly as we passed.

Gideon grabbed my hand. "I'm coming with you," he said. "I'm not leaving you alone now."

Somewhere or other in the corridors behind us, someone called our names.

"I don't want . . . ," I gasped, "I don't want to talk to anyone."

Gideon tightened his grip on my hand. "I know where no one will find us for the next few hours. Come along!"

27 June 1542. *Without my knowledge, M. persuaded Father Dominic of the Third Order, a man of extremely dubious reputation, to perform an exorcism on his daughter Elisabetta, of a kind intended to cure her of what he claims is demonic possession. By the time news of this wicked project reached me, it was too late. Although I gained access to the chapel in which the disgraceful procedure was being carried out, I could not prevent certain substances of a questionable nature from being administered to the girl, causing her to foam at the mouth, roll her eyes, and speak confusedly in tongues, while Father Dominic sprinkled her with holy water. As a result of this treatment, which I do not hesitate to describe as torture, Elisabetta lost the fruit of her womb that same night. Before he left, her father showed no remorse, but was triumphant at the supposed exorcism of the demon. He carefully recorded Elisabetta's confession, made under the influence of pain and the aforesaid substances, and had it written down as evidence of her deranged state of mind. I declined the offer of a copy—my report to the head of the Congregation will meet with a lack of understanding in any case, that much is certain. I only wish that my report may contribute to*

causing M. to fall into disfavor with his patrons, but I do not feel very hopeful in that respect.

From the records of the Inquisition
as drawn up by Father Gian Petro Baribi
of the Dominican Order
Archives of the University Library, Padua
(deciphered, translated, and edited
by Dr. M. Giordano)

TWELVE

MR. MARLEY FROWNED as we burst into the chronograph room.

"Didn't you blindfold her—" he started to say, but Gideon gave him no chance to finish the sentence.

"I'll be elapsing to 1953 with Gwenny today," he said.

Mr. Marley put his hands on his hips. "You can't," he said. "You need your time-travel quota for Operation Black Tourmaline forward slash Sapphire. And in case you've forgotten, that takes place at the same time." The chronograph was on the table in front of Mr. Marley, with its jewels sparkling in the artificial light.

"Change of plan," said Gideon briefly, and squeezed my hand.

"I don't know anything about any change of plan. And I don't believe you." Mr. Marley's mouth twisted in annoyance. "My last orders say clearly that—"

"Call them upstairs, then, and find out for yourself,"

Gideon interrupted him, pointing to the telephone on the wall.

"I'll do just that!" With his ears scarlet, Mr. Marley made for the phone. Gideon let go of me and bent over the chronograph, while I stood by the door like a store-window dummy. Now that we were here, I was rooted to the spot, feeling like a music box that had run down. I seemed to be slowly turning to stone. The thoughts ought really to have been going around and around in my head, but they weren't. I felt nothing but a dull pain.

"Gwenny, it's already set for you. Come over here." Gideon didn't wait for me to do as he said, and he took no notice of Mr. Marley's protests ("Stop that! That's my job!"), but drew me to him, took my limp hand, and placed one finger carefully in the little compartment under the ruby. "I'll be right there with you in a moment."

"You don't have permission to use the chronograph on your own," said Mr. Marley angrily, picking up the receiver of the phone. "I'm going to tell your uncle, this minute, about your high-handed disregard for the rules." I just had time to see him dial a number, and then I was floating away in a flurry of red light.

I landed in pitch-darkness and automatically groped my way toward the place where I thought I'd find the light switch.

"Let me do that," I heard Gideon say. He had landed behind me without a sound. Two seconds later, the electric lightbulb hanging from the ceiling flickered on.

"That was quick," I murmured.

Gideon turned to me. "Oh, Gwenny," he said gently. "I'm so sorry about all that."

When I neither moved nor answered him, he was beside me in two long strides, taking me in his arms. He drew my head down to rest on his shoulder, laid his chin on my hair, and whispered, "It will be all right. I promise you. Everything will be all right again."

I don't know how long we stood there like that. Maybe it was his words, and the way he kept repeating them, or maybe the warmth of his body, but gradually I began to thaw out. At least, I finally managed to whisper something. "My mum . . . isn't my mum," I said helplessly.

Gideon steered me over to the green sofa in the middle of the room and sat down beside me. "I wish I'd known," he said, distressed. "Then I could have warned you. Are you cold? Your teeth are chattering."

I shook my head, leaned against him, and closed my eyes. For a moment, I wished that time would stand still, here in 1953 on this green sofa, where there were no problems, no questions, no lies, only Gideon and his comforting presence beside me, enveloping me.

But unfortunately, as I knew from bitter experience, my wishes didn't usually come true.

I opened my eyes again and looked sideways at Gideon. "You were right," I said miserably. "This is probably the only place where they can't bother us. But you're going to be in trouble!"

"I certainly am." Gideon smiled slightly. "Particularly because I had to be . . . well, rather rough with Marley to keep him from snatching the chronograph away from me." His smile was a grim one. "Operation Black Tourmaline and Sapphire will just have to wait for another day. Although there are even more questions I'd like to ask Lucy and Paul now, and a meeting with them is exactly what we could do with at the moment."

I thought of our last meeting with Lucy and Paul at Lady Tilney's house, and my teeth chattered when I remembered how Lucy had looked at me and whispered my name. My God, and I'd had no idea!

"If Lucy and Paul are my parents, does that mean you and I are related?" I asked.

Gideon smiled again. "That was the first thing that crossed my own mind," he said. "But Falk and Paul are only distant relatives of mine—uncles twice removed, I think. They're descended from one of the Carnelian twins; I'm descended from the other."

The cogwheels in my brain were beginning to turn and engage with each other again. Suddenly I had a lump in my throat. "Before Dad got so sick, he always sang us something in the evening and played the guitar. Nick and I really loved that," I said quietly. "He used to say I'd inherited my musical talent from him. But he wasn't even related to me. I get my black hair from Paul." I swallowed.

Gideon said nothing, but I saw the sympathy in his face.

"If Lucy isn't my cousin, but my mother, then my mother is . . . is my great-aunt!" I went on. "And my grandmother is really my great-grandmother. And Grandpa's not my grandfather; Uncle Harry is." That was the last straw. I began crying my eyes out. "I can't stand Uncle Harry! I don't want him to be my grandfather! And I don't want Nick and Caroline not to be my brother and sister. I love them so much."

Gideon let me cry for a while, and then he began stroking my hair and making soothing sounds. "Hey, it's okay, Gwenny. None of that makes any difference. They're the same people, never mind exactly how they're related to you!"

But I went on sobbing inconsolably. I hardly noticed Gideon gently drawing me toward him. He put both arms around me and held me tight.

"She ought to have told me," I finally managed to say. Gideon's T-shirt was all wet with my tears. "Mum . . . Mum ought to have told me."

"Maybe she would have told you sometime. But put yourself in her position: she loves you, so she knew very well that the truth would hurt you. She probably couldn't bring herself to do it." Gideon's hand was stroking my back. "It must have been terrible for all of them, particularly Lucy and Paul."

My tears started flowing again. "But why did they leave me behind on my own? The Guardians would never have done me any harm! Why didn't they simply take me with them?"

Gideon didn't answer at once. Then he said, slowly, "I would guess that they tried to. Probably when Lucy found out that she was pregnant, and they realized that you would be the Ruby." He cleared his throat. "But at the time, they still had no proof of their theories about the count. Their stories were dismissed as childish attempts to excuse their unauthorized time travel. It even says so in the *Annals*. Marley's grandfather in particular got terribly angry about their accusations. According to his account of it, they had dragged the sacred memory of the count through the dirt."

"But my . . . grandfather!" My mind refused to think of Lucas as anyone but my grandpa. "He knew everything that was going on, and he, for one, believed Lucy and Paul! Why didn't he stop them running away?"

"I've no idea." Gideon shrugged a shoulder wet with my tears. "Without evidence, even he couldn't have done very much. He couldn't endanger his position in the Inner Circle. And who knows whether he could trust all the Guardians of the time? We can't rule out the possibility that there was someone there in his own day who knew about the count's real plans."

Someone who may even have murdered my grandfather in the end. I shook my head. This was all too much for me, but Gideon hadn't finished with his theories yet.

"Whatever made him do it, maybe it was your grandfather's idea to send Lucy and Paul back into the past, taking the chronograph with them. Sounds like he supported them."

I sobbed. "They could have taken me with them too," I said. "Before I was born, I mean."

"To bring you into the world of 1912 and bring you up under a false name? Just before the First World War?" He shook his head. "Who'd have looked after you if anything happened to them?" He stroked my hair. "I can't come anywhere near imagining how much it must hurt to discover a thing like this, Gwen. But I can understand Lucy and Paul. They knew for certain that your mother was someone who would love you like her own child and bring you up in safety."

I bit my lower lip. "I don't know." Feeling exhausted, I sat up. "I don't know anything anymore. I wish I could turn time back. A few weeks ago, maybe I wasn't the happiest girl in the world, but I was kind of normal! Not a time traveler! Not immortal! And definitely not the child of . . . of two *teenagers* who live in the year 1912."

Gideon smiled at me. "Yes, but look at it this way: there are a few positive things as well." He carefully ran his thumb under my eyes, probably wiping up a huge puddle full of mascara. "I think you're very brave. And . . . and I do love you!"

That washed the dull pain out of my heart. I put my arms around his neck. "Could you say that again, please? And then kiss me? So hard that I forget everything else?"

Gideon let his eyes wander down from my eyes to my lips. "I can always try," he murmured.

GIDEON'S EFFORTS were crowned by success, if you like to put it that way. At least, I for one wouldn't have minded spending the rest of the day or maybe my whole life here in his arms on the green sofa in 1953.

But after a while, he moved a little way away from me, propped himself on his elbows, and looked down at me. "I guess we'd better stop this now, or I can't answer for myself," he said rather breathlessly.

I didn't say anything. Why would he feel any different from me? Except that I couldn't have stopped just like that. I wondered whether I ought to feel slightly offended that he did. But I didn't have long to think about it, because Gideon glanced at the time and suddenly sat up very straight. "Hey, Gwen," he said hastily, "time's nearly up. You'd better do something to your hair. They're probably all gathered around the chronograph in a circle, waiting to haul us over the coals when we travel back."

I sighed. "Oh, God," I said unhappily. "But first we must discuss what to do next."

Gideon frowned. "They'll have to postpone the operation, of course, but maybe I can persuade them at least to send me back to 1912 for the two hours left of my time quota. We really do urgently need to talk to Lucy and Paul!"

"We could visit them together this evening," I said, although for a moment my stomach churned at the idea. *Hi, nice to meet you, Mum and Dad.*

"Forget it, Gwen. They're never going to let you go to 1912 with me again, not unless it's on the count's express orders." Gideon put his hand out, pulled me to my feet, and then rather clumsily tried smoothing down the hair at the back of my head. He'd got it into that untidy state himself.

"What a good thing that I just happen to have a chronograph of my own hidden at home, then," I said as casually as I could. "And by the way, it works perfectly."

Gideon stared at me. "You *what*?"

"Oh, come on! Surely you knew! How else could I have met Lucas so often?" I put one hand on my stomach. It was already beginning to give me that roller-coaster feeling.

"I thought you'd found some way to meet him while you were elapsing, and—" Gideon dissolved into thin air before my eyes. I followed him a few seconds later, after running my hands over my hair once again.

I'd been sure that the chronograph room would be teeming with Guardians when we came back, all of them furious with Gideon for his unauthorized action (and secretly I expected to see Mr. Marley, with a black eye, standing in a corner and insisting that Gideon must be taken away in handcuffs), but all was quiet.

There was only Falk de Villiers in the room—and my mum. She was sitting on a chair, a picture of misery, wringing her hands, and she gave me a tearful look. Her mascara and eye shadow made an irregular pattern of stripes on her cheeks.

"Ah, so there you two are," said Falk. His voice and expression were neutral, but I thought it perfectly possible that beneath that façade, he was seething with rage. There was a strange gleam in his amber-colored wolf's eyes. Beside me, Gideon instinctively stood up very straight and raised his chin slightly, as if bracing himself for a lecture.

I quickly reached for his hand. "It's not his fault—I didn't want to elapse on my own," I said quickly. "Gideon didn't mean to spoil the plan—"

"That's all right, Gwyneth." Falk gave me a weary smile. "Right now various things aren't going according to plan." He passed his hand over his forehead and cast Mum a brief sidelong glance. "I'm very sorry that when we were talking at midday . . . you had to learn the facts like that. It certainly wasn't intentional." He looked at Mum again. "News of that kind ought to be broken more gently."

Mum said nothing, just tried hard to hold back her tears. Gideon squeezed my hand.

Falk sighed. "I guess you and Grace will have a good deal to talk about. We'd better leave you alone," he said. "There's an adept waiting outside the door to escort you upstairs when you're ready. Coming, Gideon?"

Reluctantly, Gideon let go of my hand and kissed me on the cheek. As he did so, he whispered in my ear, "You'll do fine, Gwen. And later we'll talk about what you have in hiding at home."

It took all my self-control not to cling to him and say, "Oh, please stay with me."

I waited in silence until he and Falk had left, closing the door behind them. Then I turned to Mum and tried to smile. "I'm surprised they let you into their holy of holies here."

Mum got up—tottering like an old lady—and gave me a wry smile in return. "They blindfolded me. Well, that boy with the face like a moon did. He had a split lip, and I expect that's why he tied the knot so tight. It tweaked my hair horribly, but I didn't dare to complain."

"I know all about that." I couldn't summon up much sympathy for Mr. Marley's split lip. "Mum—"

"I know you must hate me now." Mum didn't let me finish. "And I absolutely understand that."

"Mum, I—"

"I'm so dreadfully sorry about it all! I ought never to have let it go so far." She took a step toward me and put out her arms, only to let them fall helplessly to her sides again. "I've always been terrified of this day! I knew it would happen sometime or other, and the older you grew, the more afraid I was. Your grandfather . . ." She stopped, then took a deep breath, and went on, "My father and I were going to tell you together, once you were old enough to understand the facts and come to terms with them."

"So Lucas knew?"

"Of course! He hid Lucy and Paul in Durham with us, and it was his idea for me to make out I was pregnant so that I could pretend the baby—that was you—was mine. Lucy went for medical checkups in Durham under my name. She and Paul spent almost four months with us, while Dad was busy laying false trails over half of Europe. It was really the perfect hiding place. No one cared about my pregnancy. We said the baby would be born in December, so that meant you weren't of any interest to the Guardians and the family." Mum looked past me at the tapestry on the wall, and her eyes were glazed. "Up to the end, we hoped it wouldn't be necessary for Lucy and Paul to travel back into the past with the chronograph. But a private detective hired by the Guardians was watching our house. . . ." She shuddered at the memory. "My father managed to warn us just in time. Lucy and Paul had no other option—they had to run for it and leave you with us—a tiny baby with a funny little tuft of hair on your head and big blue eyes." Now the tears were running down her cheeks. "Nicholas and I swore to keep you safe, and we loved you like our own child from the very first second."

Without noticing it, I'd begun to cry again myself. "Oh, Mum—"

"You see, we'd never wanted to have children. There was so much poor health in Nicholas's family, and I always thought I wasn't the maternal type. But all that changed when Lucy and Paul had entrusted you to us." Mum's tears were unstoppable now. "You made us so . . . so *happy*. You changed our lives and showed us how wonderful children are. But for you, Nick and Caroline would never have been born." She was sobbing so hard that she was unable to go on. I couldn't stand it anymore. I flung myself into her arms.

"It's all right, Mum!" I tried to say, but only a kind of snorkeling sound like a gurgle came out. Mum seemed to understand it, all the same. She wound her arms around me and hugged me, and for quite a long time, we weren't in any position to talk or to stop crying.

Until Xemerius put his head through the wall and said, "Oh, here you are!" He squeezed the rest of himself through into the room, flew over to the table, and settled there, staring curiously at us. "Oh, no! *Two* indoor fountains now. The Niagara Falls model must have been on special offer."

I gently moved away from Mum. "Mum, we must go! Do you have any tissues on you?"

"If we're lucky!" She rummaged in her bag and handed me one. "Why isn't your mascara all over your face?" she asked with a faint grin.

I blew my nose noisily. "I'm afraid I already left it all over Gideon's T-shirt."

"He does seem to be a nice boy. Although I ought to warn you against him—those de Villiers men are nothing but bad news for us Montrose women." Mum opened her powder compact, looked in the little mirror, and sighed. "Oh, mercy! I look like Frankenstein's mother."

"Yup, nothing but soap and water will do the job there," said Xemerius. He hopped off the table, settled on a chest in the corner, and put his head to one side. "Looks like I've missed out on a lot! By the way, they're all in an uproar upstairs. Lots of terribly important men in black suits and that useless Marley looking like someone punched him in the face. And, Gwyneth, they're all going on at your *nice boy*—he obviously turned their plans upside down. Also, he's infuriating every last one of them by grinning to himself like an idiot the whole time."

And although I suppose there was absolutely no reason

for it, all of a sudden I was doing exactly the same, grinning to myself like another idiot.

Mum looked at me over the edge of her compact. "Can you forgive me?" she asked quietly.

"Dear Mum!" I hugged her so hard that she dropped everything she was holding. "I do love you so much!"

"Oh, please!" groaned Xemerius. "Here we go again! Isn't it damp enough in here already?"

"THIS IS MY IDEA of heaven," said Lesley, pivoting on her own axis so as to take in the atmosphere of Madame Rossini's stocks of costumes. Her eyes wandered over the shelves of boots and shoes from all periods, then went on to the hats, from there to the apparently endless racks with clothes hanging from them, and finally back to Madame Rossini, who had opened the door of this paradise to us. "And you're God in person!"

"You're so sweet!" Madame Rossini beamed at her.

"My own opinion entirely," said Raphael. Gideon cast him a glance of amusement. I didn't know how, after all that fuss this afternoon, he'd managed to get Falk to agree (maybe Gideon's uncle was more of a sheep in wolf's clothing than the other way around), but we and Lesley and Raphael really did have official permission to borrow costumes for Cynthia's party from the Guardians' stocks, under Madame Rossini's supervision. It was early evening when we met outside her stockrooms, and Lesley was so excited at being allowed into the headquarters of the Lodge that she could hardly keep still. Although she didn't get to see any of the other rooms that I'd described to her and was led only along an ordinary corridor to the stockroom, she was bubbling with enthusiasm.

"Have you noticed?" she whispered to me. "This place positively reeks of puzzles and mysteries. Oh, God, I just love it!"

Once in the stockroom with the costumes, she was practically hyperventilating. In other circumstances, I expect it would have been the same with me. Up to now, I'd thought of Madame Rossini's studio as the Garden of Eden, but this was even better, much better.

But first, by now I was pretty well used to all the clothes, and second, my head and heart were busy with very different things.

"Of course I 'ave not made all ze costumes zat are in 'ere. It is ze Guardians' collection. Zey began it two 'undred years ago, and zey added to it in ze course of time." Madame Rossini took a slightly yellowing lace dress off one of the racks, and Lesley and I sighed, enchanted. "Many of ze 'istorical dresses are very lovely, but zey cannot be used for time travel zese days." She carefully hung the dress up again. "And ze costumes made for ze last but one generation are not up to ze standard of today."

"You mean all these wonderful dresses are slowly rotting away here?" Lesley stroked the lace dress sympathetically.

Madame Rossini shrugged her plump shoulders. "It ees valuable material for illustrating ze 'istorical styles, even for me. But you are right, it ees a shame zat so few see it. All ze better that you are 'ere zis evening. You will be ze loveliest ladies at ze ball, *mes petites!*"

"It isn't a ball, Madame Rossini, just a rather boring party," said Lesley.

"A party ees only as boring as ze guests," said Madame Rossini firmly.

"That's what I say too," said Raphael, giving Lesley a sidelong look. "How about we two go as Robin Hood and Maid Marian? They went around in Lincoln green." He perched a small ladies' hat with a feather in it on his head. "Then everyone will see that we're together."

"Hm," said Lesley.

Madame Rossini walked along the racks, cheerfully commenting, "Oh, zis is fun! Such fun! Four young people and *une fête déguisée*—what can be better?"

"I can think of a few things," whispered Gideon, with his mouth close to my ear. "Listen, you girls must distract her attention to give me a chance to find clothes for our visit to 1912." Out loud, he said, "I'll wear that green thing I had on yesterday, Madame Rossini, if I may."

Madame Rossini swung around to us. "Zat green thing from yesterday?" One of her eyebrows shot up.

"He . . . he means the sea-green coat with the emerald clasps," I said quickly.

"Yes, and the rest of the stuff that goes with it." Gideon smiled. "Can't get any greener than that."

"*Ze stuff!* Pearls before swine!" Madame Rossini flung her hands up in the air, but she was smiling. "*Alors*, ze late eighteenth century for zis leetle rebel. Zen we must dress my leetle swan-necked beauty to go with 'im. I am afraid zere is no green ball dress from zat period—"

"The period doesn't matter, Madame Rossini. The people at that party won't know the first thing about historical periods."

"Just so long as the dress looks old, and it's long, with a full skirt," added Lesley.

"*Bien sûr*, if zat is so," said Madame Rossini, reluctantly. Lesley and I followed her right across the room like puppies following the lure of a bone. Gideon disappeared among the racks of clothes, while Raphael tried on more ladies' hats.

"Over there I 'ave a dream of a dress, shimmering green taffeta and tulle, 1865," said Madame Rossini, twinkling at us. With her tiny eyes and lack of neck, she always looked a little like a tortoise. "Ze color would go well with zat leetle rebel's green coat. For ze period, 'owever, ze style would be all wrong, as if Casanova were taking Queen Alexandra to a ball in 'er youth, if you see what I mean."

"Like I said, the guests at this evening's party won't know a thing about such details," I said, holding my breath as Madame Rossini took the Queen Alexandra dress off the rail where it hung. It really was dreamy.

"Well, it certainly has a full skirt!" Lesley laughed. "Turn around in that, and you'll sweep the entire cold buffet onto the floor."

"Try it on, my swan-necked beauty! Zere is a tiara to go with it. And now for you." Madame Rossini took Lesley's arm and led her to the next row of dresses. "We 'ave 'ere French and Italian haute couture of ze last century. Green was not ze fashionable color zen, but we will find you somezing, never fear."

Lesley was going to say something, but she choked with excitement at the words *haute couture* and had a fit of coughing.

"May I try on these weird knee breeches?" called Raphael from behind us.

"Of course, but be careful with ze buttons."

Unobtrusively, I was keeping an eye open for Gideon. He already had a couple of garments hanging on his arm, and he smiled at me over the top of the clothes racks.

Madame Rossini didn't notice him plundering her stocks. She happily walked along the haute couture rails, with Lesley close behind her, breathing heavily.

"For *cette petite* with 'er freckles, maybe—"

"This one!" Lesley interrupted her. "Please! It's so beautiful!"

"*Mais, ma chérie,* it is not green!" said Madame Rossini.

"Well, it's *almost* green!" Lesley looked as if she'd burst into tears with disappointment right away.

"No, it ees ice-blue!" said Madame Rossini firmly. "Grace Kelly wore it to a gala when *Ze Country Girl* 'ad won a prize. Not zis precise dress, *bien sûr,* but it is an exact copy."

"It's the loveliest dress I ever saw," whispered Lesley.

"It does have something kind of green about it," I said, trying to support her. "Or at least turquoise, with a touch of green. If the light is a little yellowish, it practically *is* green."

"Hm." Madame Rossini sounded undecided.

I looked around for Gideon. He was quietly making for the door.

"I expect it wouldn't fit me, anyway," murmured Lesley.

"I zink it would!" Madame Rossini looked Lesley up and down, and then gazed thoughtfully into the distance. "You young girls all 'ave such wonderful leetle waists. *Zut alors!*" Suddenly she looked fierce. "Young man, where are you going with zose clothes?"

"I . . . er . . . ," stammered Gideon, taken by surprise. He'd almost reached the door.

The tortoise turned into a raging elephant breaking through jungle undergrowth. Madame Rossini was beside Gideon in an instant. I'd never have thought she could move so fast. "What is *zis*?" She tore the garments out of his hand, and her French accent got the better of her. "Were you going to steal zese zings from me?"

"No, of course not, Madame Rossini. I just wanted to . . . er . . . borrow them." Gideon looked as remorseful as he could, but it didn't work with Madame Rossini. She held the clothes up and examined them.

"Why 'ave you chosen *zese*, you impossible boy? Zey are not even green!"

I came to Gideon's aid. "Please don't be cross with us. We need to borrow them for . . . for an expedition to the year 1912." I hesitated for a moment, and then decided to stake everything on a single card. "A secret expedition, Madame Rossini."

"Secret? To ze year 1912!" repeated Madame Rossini,

clutching the garments to her like Caroline clutching her crochet pig. "In zese zings? Is zis a joke?" I'd never seen her so angry before. "This. Is. A. Gentleman's. Suit. From. Ze. Year. 1932," she said menacingly, gasping indignantly for air between each word. "And zis dress belonged to a *cigar girl*! If you went out in the street in zese zings in 1912, zere would be uproar! A riot!" She put her hands on her hips. "'Ave you learnt nothing from me, young man? What do I always say zese costumes are about? Zey are about . . ."

"Authenticity." Gideon sheepishly supplied the word.

"*Précisément!*" Madame Rossini bared her teeth. "If you 'ave plans for a secret visit to ze year 1912, zen not in zese clothes! You might as well land in ze city in a spaceship—zat would be just as discreet!" Her eyes were still flashing angrily as she looked from Gideon to me and back again, but all at once, she started moving and, under our startled gaze, navigated from one rail of clothes to another. A little later, she came back with an armful of clothes and peculiar hats.

"*Bien,*" she said in a voice that told us she wasn't going to accept any protests. "Let zis be a lesson to you not to go be'ind Madame Rossini's back." She held the clothes out to us, and suddenly her face changed. It was like the sun coming out after dark rain clouds. "And if I find out zat zis wicked boy 'as not been wearing 'is 'at again," she said, wagging her finger at Gideon, "zen I will 'ave to tell your uncle about zis secret outing!"

I smiled with relief and gave her a big hug. "Oh, you really are a darling, Madame Rossini!"

* * *

CAROLINE AND NICK were sitting on the sofa in the sewing room. They looked surprised when Gideon and I came quietly through the door. But while a beaming smile spread over Caroline's face, Nick seemed rather embarrassed.

"I thought you were both at that party," said my little brother. I wasn't sure which bothered him most, being found watching a kids' film with his little sister, or the fact that they were both already in their pajamas, and the pajamas, a Christmas present from Aunt Maddy, had hoods with rabbit ears. Like Aunt Maddy, I thought that was cute, but when you're twelve, maybe it seems different. Especially when you get unexpected visitors and your big sister's boyfriend is wearing a mega-cool leather jacket.

"Charlotte left half an hour ago," Nick explained. "Aunt Glenda was fussing around her like a mother hen who's just laid an egg. Yuck, no, do stop all that kissing stuff, Gwenny. You're as bad as Mum was just now. Why are you two here, anyway?"

"We're going on to the party later," said Gideon, sitting down on the sofa beside him.

"Sure," said Xemerius, who was lounging about on a stack of old *Homes & Gardens* magazines. "The really cool guys always arrive last."

Caroline was gazing adoringly at Gideon with big saucer eyes. "Have you met Margaret?" She had been holding her crochet pig on her lap, and now she offered it to him. "You can stroke her if you like."

Gideon obediently patted the pig's back. "Lovely and soft." Then he glanced at the screen with apparent interest. "Oh, looks like you've already reached the bit where the paint gun explodes. That's my favorite part."

Nick gave him a suspicious sidelong glance. "You know *Tinker Bell?*"

"I think her ideas are really cool," claimed Gideon.

"Me too," said Xemerius. "Only her hairstyle is . . . well, the pits."

Caroline sighed amorously. "You're so nice! Will you be visiting us often?"

"I'm afraid so, yes," said Xemerius.

"I hope so, yes," said Gideon, and our eyes met. I couldn't suppress an amorous sigh of my own. After our successful visit to the costume stockroom, we'd also made a little side trip to Dr. White's treatment room, and while Gideon was providing himself with a couple of instruments there, I suddenly had an idea.

"While we're burgling this place anyway, could you find a kit for a smallpox vaccination that we can take with us?"

"Don't worry—you'll have been inoculated against all the diseases you could meet while traveling in time," Gideon had reassured me. "Including the variola virus, of course."

"It's not for me—it's for a friend," I'd told him. "Please! I'll explain later."

Gideon had raised an eyebrow, but he opened Dr. White's medication cupboard without comment, and after a little searching, he found a red box and put it in his pocket.

I loved him all the more for not asking questions.

"You look as if you were about to start drooling," said Xemerius, bringing me back to reality.

I fished the key of the door leading up to the roof out of its hiding place in the sugar bowl in the cupboard. "How long has Mum been in the bathroom?" I asked Nick and Caroline.

"Quarter of an hour at the most." Nick was looking far more relaxed now. "She was kind of odd this evening. Kept on kissing us and sighing. She didn't stop until Mr. Bernard brought her a whisky."

"Only quarter of an hour? Then we ought to have plenty of time. But if she does happen to come out earlier than anyone expects, please don't tell her we're up on the roof."

"Okay," said Nick, while Xemerius chanted his silly song about necking in the porch again.

I glanced mockingly at Gideon. "If you can tear yourself away from *Tinker Bell*, let's get going."

"Luckily, I know how the film ends." Gideon reached for his backpack and picked it up.

"See you soon," Caroline breathed.

"Yup, see you soon. I'd rather watch fairies at work than you two smooching," said Xemerius. "A demon has his pride, you know. I wouldn't like anyone to say I was a Peeping Tom."

I took no notice of him, but climbed the narrow

chimney-sweep's staircase up to the roof and opened the trapdoor at the top of it. It was a fairly mild spring night—the perfect evening to come up here, and yes, for smooching too, why not? From up here, there was a wonderful view over the nearby buildings, and the moon was shining in the east above the rooftops.

"Where are you?" I quietly called down.

Gideon's curly head appeared in the hatch above the trapdoor, and then the rest of him followed.

"Wow. I can understand this being your favorite place," he said, taking his backpack off and kneeling cautiously down.

I'd never noticed before that the roof really was romantic, especially at this time of night, with the sea of bright city lights reaching out forever beyond the intricately decorated roof ridge of the house. Sometime we'd come here with a picnic, plus soft cushions, and candles . . . and Gideon could bring his violin . . . and with any luck Xemerius would be taking a day off.

"What are you grinning at?" asked Gideon.

"Oh, nothing. Just letting the fancy roam."

Gideon made a face. "Oh, yes?" He looked carefully around. "Okay. I guess the show can begin."

I nodded and cautiously made my way forward. The roof here was flat, but the slope began a couple of feet beyond the chimneys, marked off only by the knee-high decorative iron border. (And immortal or not, I didn't feel that plunging four floors down to street level was a great way to enjoy the weekend.)

I opened the ventilation flap in the nearest of the broad chimneys.

"Why up here of all places, Gwenny?" I heard Gideon ask behind me.

"Charlotte's afraid of heights," I explained. "I knew she'd never come up to the roof because of her vertigo." I took the heavy bundle out of the chimney, balancing it carefully in my arms.

Gideon jumped up. "Don't drop it!" he said nervously. "Please!"

"Don't worry!" I had to laugh at his horrified expression. "Look, even standing on one leg I can—"

Gideon let out what sounded like a tiny whimper. "This is no joking matter, Gwenny," he gasped. Obviously all that instruction in the mysteries had gone deeper than I thought. He took the bundle from my arms and cradled it like a baby. "Is that really . . . ," he began.

I felt a cold draft of air behind us. "No, dummy," crowed Xemerius, putting his head through the hatch. "It's an old cheese that Gwyneth keeps up here in case she feels peckish in the middle of the night."

I rolled my eyes and signed to him to go away, which to my surprise, he did. I suppose *Tinker Bell* was so exciting that he had to go back to it.

Meanwhile, Gideon had put the chronograph down on the roof, and now he began carefully unwrapping it.

"Did you know that Charlotte was phoning us about every ten minutes, trying to convince us that you had this chronograph? In the end, she even got on Marley's nerves."

"What a shame," I said. "And the two of them might have been made for each other."

Gideon nodded. Then he removed the last of the wrappings and audibly took a deep breath.

I carefully stroked the shiny, polished wood. "There it is, then."

Gideon said nothing for a moment. For more than a moment, to tell you the truth.

"Gideon?" I finally asked uncertainly. Lesley had begged me to wait a few days longer, until we could be sure that he was really to be trusted, but I'd dismissed the idea out of hand.

"I simply didn't believe it," Gideon finally whispered. "I didn't for a second believe Charlotte." He looked at me, and his eyes were dark in this light. "Do you realize what would happen if anyone here knew about this?"

I didn't bother to point out that quite a number of people did know about it already. Maybe it was just because all of a sudden Gideon seemed so bewildered, but I was suddenly afraid. "Are we really going through with the plan?" I asked. I had a queasy sensation inside me, and this time, it was nothing to do with the beginning of a journey through time.

It was one thing for my grandfather to read my blood into the chronograph. What we were about to do now was something else again. We'd be closing the Circle of Blood, and there was no way we could foresee the consequences. To put it in as positive a way as possible.

My memory went through all those horrible rhyming

prophesies with lines ending *death* and *last breath*, and dredged up a few more rhyming *slain* and *pain*. The fact that I was apparently immortal was no consolation whatsoever.

Oddly enough, it seemed to be my own uncertainty that brought Gideon back to his normal self. "Are we going through with it?" He leaned forward and dropped a little kiss on my nose. "Do you mean that seriously?" He stripped off his jacket and took the loot we'd lifted from Dr. White's room out of the backpack. "Okay, here goes."

First he put an elastic band around his left upper arm and tightened it. Then he removed a syringe from its sterile plastic pack and grinned at me. "Nurse?" he said in commanding tones. "Flashlight!"

I made a face. "That's one way to do it, of course," I replied, shining the beam of the flashlight on the inside of his elbow. "Typical medical student!"

"Do I hear a touch of scorn in your voice?" Gideon cast me an amused glance. "How did *you* do it, then?"

"With a Japanese vegetable knife!" I said, a little boastfully. "And Grandpa caught the blood in a teacup."

"Ah, I see. That cut on your forearm." All of a sudden, he didn't sound amused at all. He plunged the needle of the syringe into his skin, and blood began flowing into the cannula at the other end of it.

"Are you sure you know exactly what you have to do?" I asked, jerking my chin at the chronograph. "That thing has so many different flaps and little compartments, you could easily turn the wrong cogwheel—"

"Chronograph Studies is one of the exams you have to pass to become an adept, and I did all that ages ago." Gideon handed me the syringe with the blood in it and undid the elastic band on his arm.

"Makes me wonder how you had any leisure time left to watch masterpieces of the silver screen like *Tinker Bell.*"

Gideon shook his head. "A little more respect would do no harm. Give me that cannula. Now, turn the flashlight on the chronograph. Yes, that's it."

"And the occasional please and thank you would do no harm either," I remarked, while Gideon began dripping his blood into the chronograph. Unlike Lucas, he did it with hands that didn't shake in the least. Maybe he'd make a good surgeon someday.

I was biting my lower lip in excitement.

"Three drops here, under the head of the lion," Gideon murmured, concentrating hard. "Then to turn this cogwheel and switch the lever over. There we are." He lowered the cannula, and I switched off the flashlight in a reflex action.

Several little wheels began going around inside the chronograph, clicking, clattering, and humming, just like last time. Then the clattering grew louder and the volume of the humming rose. It sounded almost like a tune. A wave of heat hit us in the face, and I clung to Gideon's arm, as if the next thing would be a gust of wind strong enough to blow us off the roof. But instead, the jewels in the chronograph lit up, one by one, there was a flickering all around it, and if it had seemed like a fire was blazing inside the chronograph at first, now the air was suddenly icy cold. The flickering light went out, and the cogwheels stopped turning. The whole thing had taken less than half a minute.

I let go of Gideon and rubbed my arm. All the little hairs on it were standing on end. "Is that all?"

Gideon took a deep breath and raised his hand. This time it *was* shaking slightly. "We're about to find out," he said.

I took one of Dr. White's little laboratory flasks from my pocket and handed it to him. "Go carefully. If it's a powder, a breeze could simply blow it away."

"That might not be such a bad thing," murmured Gideon. He turned to me. His eyes were shining. "You see? *Under the sign of the twelvefold star, all sickness and ills will flee afar.* We'll see about that."

The hell with the twelvefold star. I'd rather rely on my flashlight.

"Go on," I said impatiently, leaning forward, and then Gideon pulled out a tiny drawer in the chronograph.

I'll admit I was disappointed. After all that mysterious carrying on, blah-blah-blah about secrets, it was kind of an anticlimax. The little drawer contained neither a liquid, Lesley's best guess ("Sure to be red as blood," she had said, wide-eyed), nor a powder, nor a stone of any kind.

All it held was a substance that looked like salt. Although particularly beautiful salt, if you looked more closely—tiny, opalescent little crystals.

"Crazy," I whispered. "I don't believe it! All that

trouble and expense over the centuries, just for these few crumbs of whatever it is."

Gideon held his hand protectively over the drawer. "Let's hope no one finds out that these crumbs of whatever it is are in our hands now," he said rather breathlessly.

I nodded. Again, apart from the people who already did know. I took the cork out of the flask. "Hurry up, then!" I whispered. I suddenly had a vision of Lady Arista, who as far as I knew was afraid of no one and nothing, certainly not of heights, coming up through the hatch to snatch the little flask away from us.

Gideon seemed to be thinking something similar, because he tipped the crumbs into the flask without any ceremony at all and put the cork back in. Only when it was safely stowed away in his jacket pocket did he breathe freely again.

But at that moment another idea occurred to me. "Now that the chronograph has done what it's supposed to do, maybe it won't work anymore for time travel," I said.

"We're about to find that out too," replied Gideon, smiling at me. "Off we go to the year 1912."

THE MONTROSE FAMILY TREE (*True Version*)

Lord James Montrose
M
Mary Elizabeth Montrose

Lucas (Lord Montrose)   Madeleine
M
Arista Bishop

Harry   Glenda   Grace
M   M   M
Jane Livier   Charles Auden   Nicholas Shepherd

Lucy   Janet   David   Charlotte   Nick   Caroline
M
Paul de Villiers

Gwyneth

HIC RHODOS
HIC SALTA

(Motto on the Montrose coat of arms.
Freely translated: *Show what you can really do.*)

THIRTEEN

"OH, SHIT, I think I sat on that damned hat," Gideon whispered beside me.

"Stop swearing, or the roof will fall in on us!" I hissed. "And if you don't put zat 'at on, I'm telling tales of you to Madame Rossini!"

Xemerius cackled with laughter. He'd come along this far for the ride today. "The hat won't save him. With that hairstyle, everyone in 1912 will take him for a roughneck. He might at least have given himself a proper side parting."

I heard Gideon swearing quietly again, this time because he'd obviously knocked his elbow on something. It wasn't all that easy to undress and get dressed again in a confessional, and I was pretty sure that it was also sacrilege to use one as a changing room. Quite apart from the fact that it was certainly also a secular offense to break into a church, even if you didn't want to steal anything but just planned to use it as a launchpad for a quick trip to the year 1912. Gideon had unlocked the side door with a metal hook so fast that I didn't have time to feel nervous.

"Wow!" Xemerius had whistled appreciatively through his teeth. "He ought to teach you that trick. The two of you would make an unbeatable team of burglars. Immortally good, even."

We were back in the church where Xemerius and I had first met, and Gideon had first kissed me. Although there was no time to indulge in nostalgia, I felt as if all these events dated from long, long ago, particularly when I thought how much had happened since then. In reality, it was only a few days since that first occasion.

Gideon knocked on the door of the confessional from outside. "Ready?"

"No. Unfortunately they hadn't invented zip fasteners in time for this dress," I said despairingly. Even with the most daring contortions, I couldn't reach all the little buttons down the back.

I slipped out of the confessional. Would my heart ever stop beating faster at the sight of Gideon? Would a time ever come when I didn't feel I was dazzled by something incredibly wonderful every time I set eyes on him? Probably not. Although this time he was wearing an unspectacular dark gray suit, with a vest and a white shirt under the jacket. But it suited him so well, with his broad . . .

Xemerius, dangling head down from the gallery of the church, cleared his throat. "What is this life if, full of care, we have no time to stand and stare . . . ?"

"Very nice," I said quickly. "Kind of a timeless Mafia boss outfit. And the tie perfectly tied. Madame Rossini would be proud of you." Sighing, I went back to my buttons. "The inventor of the zip fastener ought to have been made a saint long ago."

Gideon grinned. "Turn around and let me do it," he said. "Oh," he added a moment later, "there are hundreds of them."

It took him some time to do up all the little buttons, which may have been because he kissed the back of my neck at every other button. I'd certainly have enjoyed that far more if Xemerius hadn't called out, "Kissy, kissy, kissy!" every time.

At last we were through. Madame Rossini had found me a high-necked pale gray dress with a lace collar. It was slightly too long, so that I kept stumbling over it, and I'd have fallen full length if Gideon hadn't caught me.

"Next time *I'm* wearing the suit," I said. Gideon laughed and looked as if he was going to kiss me, but Xemerius groaned, "Oh, no, not again!" and I pushed him gently away.

"We don't have time," I said. *Also there's a bat-winged creature hanging six feet overhead making horrible faces.* I looked crossly up at Xemerius.

"What's the matter?" asked Xemerius. "I thought this was an important mission, not a date. You ought to be grateful to me."

"Oh, thanks!" I grunted.

Meanwhile Gideon had gone into the choir of the

church, and was kneeling down in front of the chrono-graph. After much thought, we had put it under the altar. Hopefully, no one would find it there while we were gone. Unless the church had a cleaning lady who worked Saturday evenings.

"I'll hold the fort," Xemerius promised. "If anyone comes to steal that thing, I'll show no mercy. I'll . . . I'll spit torrents of water over them!"

Gideon took my hand. "Ready, Gwenny?"

I looked him straight in the eyes, and my heart did a little jump. "Ready when you are," I said softly.

Xemerius probably said something caustic about that, but I didn't hear it, because the needle was already prick-ing my finger, and waves of ruby-red light carried me away.

A moment later, I stood up. The church was empty and just as quiet as in our own time. I half hoped and half feared to see Xemerius in the gallery. He'd already been haunting this place in 1912.

Then Gideon landed beside me and immediately took my hand again. "Come on, we must hurry! We only have two hours, and I bet that won't be time for even one-tenth of our questions."

"Suppose we don't find Lucy and Paul at Lady Tilney's house?" I said, and my teeth began chattering with alarm. I still couldn't bring myself to think of them as my parents. And if the conversation with Mum had been bad enough, what would it be like to face them—a couple of perfect strangers?

When we left the church, torrents of rain were pouring down. "Oh, great," I said, and suddenly I'd have given anything for one of Madame Rossini's impossible hats. "Couldn't you have looked up the weather forecast before we left?"

"Oh, come on, it's only a light summer shower," said Gideon, pulling me on. But by the time we reached Eaton Place, the light summer shower had drenched us. You could say we attracted a lot of attention, because everyone else who was out and about had an umbrella and looked at us pityingly.

"A good thing we didn't go to any trouble with authentic hairstyles," I said when we were outside Lady Tilney's front door. I nervously patted my hair, which was sticking to my scalp. My teeth were still chattering.

Gideon rang the bell and squeezed my hand more tightly.

"I don't feel too good about this," I whispered. "We still have time to disappear again. Maybe it would be best to think what order to ask our questions in first, in peace and quiet."

"Hush, hush, hush," said Gideon. "It's all right, Gwenny, I'm with you."

"Yes, you're with me," I said, and I went on repeating it like a soothing mantra. "You're with me you're with me you're with me."

The white-gloved butler opened the door, like last time. He didn't look at all pleased to see us.

"Mr. Stillman, isn't it?" Gideon gave him a friendly

smile. "Would you be kind enough to announce us to Lady Tilney? Miss Gwyneth Shepherd and Gideon de Villiers."

The butler hesitated for a moment and then said, "Wait here," closing the door in our faces.

"My goodness. Mr. Bernard would never allow a thing like that," I said indignantly. "Oh, well, he probably thinks you have a pistol with you again and you've come for some of his employer's blood. He's not to know that Lady Lavinia stole your pistol, and I'm still wondering just how she fixed that. I mean, what on earth did she do to take your mind off essentials? If she ever crosses my path again, I'll ask her, not that I'm sure I really want to know. Oh, dear—here I go talking like a waterfall again. I always do that when I'm nervous. I don't think I can face them, Gideon. And I can hardly breathe, or it could be that I'm simply *not* breathing, not that that makes any difference if I'm immortal." At this point, I could hear my voice rising hysterically, but I went on. "Better step back, because next time the door opens, that man Stillman could well—"

The door opened.

"Hit you in the face," I murmured all the same.

The beefy butler waved us in. "Lady Tilney will see you upstairs in the small drawing room," he said stiffly. "As soon as I've searched you for weapons."

"If you must!" Gideon spread his arms out and let Stillman pat him down.

"All right. You can go up," said the butler, when he had finished.

"How about me?" I asked, puzzled.

"You're a lady. Ladies don't carry guns." Gideon smiled at me, took my hand, and led me up the stairs.

"Talk about carelessness!" I glanced at Stillman, who was following a few steps behind us. "You mean he's not afraid of me just because I'm a woman? He ought to see *Tomb Raider* sometime. For all he knows, I could have a nuclear bomb under my dress and a hand grenade in each cup of my bra. I call it antifeminist!" I could have gone on like this without stopping till around sunset, but Lady Tilney was waiting for us at the top of the stairs, slender and straight as a ramrod. She was definitely a beautiful woman—even her icy expression couldn't change that. I'd been going to smile spontaneously at her, but as the corners of my mouth began to stretch, I made them stop. In 1912 Lady Tilney was much more alarming than later, when she'd started making crochet pigs as a hobby, and I felt uncomfortably aware that not only was our hair all over the place, my dress was also hanging like a damp sack. I wondered instinctively whether hair dryers had been invented yet.

"You again," said Lady Tilney to Gideon, in a voice as cold as her eyes. Only Lady Arista could have outdone her. "You're certainly persistent. You ought to have realized last time you visited that I have no intention of giving you any of my blood."

"We're not here about your blood, Lady Tilney," Gideon replied. "That was all settled long ago." He cleared his throat. "We'd very much like to talk to you and Lucy and Paul again. This time without any . . . misunderstandings."

"Misunderstandings!" Lady Tilney folded her arms across her breast in its lace blouse. "Last time, young man, you can't be said to have behaved well. Indeed, you showed a shocking propensity for violence. Moreover, I do not know where Lucy and Paul are at this moment, so even if the circumstances were different, I would not be able to help you." She paused for a moment, while her eyes rested on me. "However, I think I could arrange a conversation." Her voice was half a degree warmer. "Perhaps with Gwyneth on her own, and of course in some other period of t—"

"I really don't want to be discourteous, but I'm sure you will understand that we have very little time at our disposal," Gideon interrupted her and led me on, up to the top of the stairs, where I and my dress dripped water all over the expensive rug. "And I know that Lucy and Paul are staying with you, so please would you just call them? I promise to behave myself this time."

"This is not . . . ," began Lady Tilney, but then a door opened and shut somewhere in the background, and soon after that, a graceful young woman joined her.

Lucy.

My mother.

I held Gideon's hand even more tightly while I stared at Lucy, this time taking in every detail of her appearance. All the other Montrose women were undeniably like each other, with red hair, pale porcelain complexions, and big blue eyes, but I was looking mainly for anything she had in common with me. Were those my ears? Didn't I have the same small nose? And the curve of her eyebrows—weren't mine just the same? And didn't my forehead trace the same funny folds when I frowned?

"He's right. We don't want to waste any time, Margaret," said Lucy quietly. Her voice was shaking very slightly, and it went to my heart. "Would you be kind enough to find Paul, Mr. Stillman?"

Lady Tilney sighed, but when Stillman looked inquiringly at her, she nodded. As the butler passed us and climbed up another set of stairs, Lady Tilney said, "I would just like to remind you, Lucy, that last time he held a pistol to the back of your head."

"I'm really sorry about that," said Gideon. "On the other hand . . . the circumstances at the time left me no option." He gave Lucy a meaningful glance. "Now, however, we've come by information that has changed our minds."

Nicely put. I had a feeling that it was about time I contributed something soothing to this conversation. But what?

Mother, I know who you are—come to my arms?

Lucy, I forgive you for abandoning me. Nothing can part us now? I must have made some funny kind of sound, and Gideon correctly interpreted it as the beginning of a fit of hysterics. He put his arm around my shoulders and supported me just at the right time, because my legs suddenly seemed about to give way.

"Maybe we should go into the drawing room?" suggested Lucy.

Good idea. If I remembered rightly, there were chairs to sit on in there.

The tea table wasn't laid in the small, round room this time, but otherwise it was just like when we were last here, except that the flower arrangement had been replaced by delphiniums and stocks. A group of armchairs and delicate little straight-backed chairs stood in the bay window looking out on the street.

"Please sit down," said Lady Tilney.

I dropped into one of the upholstered chintz armchairs, but the others stayed standing.

Lucy smiled at me. She came a step closer and looked as if she might stroke my hair. I nervously jumped up again. "I'm sorry we're so wet. We never thought of bringing an umbrella," I babbled.

Lucy's smile widened. "What does Lady Arista always say?"

I couldn't keep back a grin. "Child, I won't have you soaking my good cushions!" we said in chorus. Suddenly Lucy's expression changed. Now she looked like bursting into tears.

"I'll ring for some tea," said Lady Tilney in matter-of-fact tones, picking up a little bell. "Peppermint tea with plenty of sugar and hot lemon."

"No, please!" Gideon despairingly shook his head. "We can't stop for that. I don't know for sure if I've picked the right time, but I very much hope that, from your point of view, my meeting with Paul in 1782 has already taken place."

Lucy, who had recovered her composure, slowly nodded, and Gideon breathed a sigh of relief. "Then you'll know that you gave me the count's secret papers. It took us a little time to work out everything they told us, but now we know that the philosopher's stone is not a cure for all diseases, it's just supposed to make the count immortal forever."

"And his immortality comes to an end the moment Gwyneth is born, right?" whispered Lucy. "Which is why he'll try to kill her as soon as the Circle is closed?"

Gideon nodded, but I looked at him in some annoyance. We hadn't had time to discuss those details properly yet. However, this didn't seem the right time for it, because he was already going on. "Everything you two did was to protect Gwyneth."

"You see, Luce? I told you so." Paul had appeared in the doorway. He was wearing his arm in a sling, and as he came closer, his amber eyes were moving back and forth between Gideon, Lucy, and me.

I held my breath. He looked only a few years older than me, and in normal life, I'd have thought he looked brilliant with that raven-black hair, the unusual de Villiers eyes, and the little dimple in his chin. I supposed he couldn't help the side-whiskers. It was probably the fashion for men at this period. But side-whiskers or no side-whiskers, he really didn't look old enough to be my father, or anyone's father, in fact.

"Sometimes trusting people in advance pays off," he said, looking Gideon up and down. "Even people like this young ruffian."

"And sometimes you just get outrageous good luck,"

Lucy snapped at him. She turned to Gideon. "I'm very grateful to you for saving Paul's life, Gideon," she said with dignity. "If you hadn't happened to be passing, he'd be dead now."

"You always exaggerate, Lucy." Paul made a face. "I'd have thought of a way to get out of the hole I was in."

"Sure," said Gideon, with a grin.

Paul frowned, but then he grinned as well. "Okay, maybe not. Alastair is a crafty so-and-so, and a damn good swordsman. And then there were three of them! If I ever meet him again—"

"That's not very likely," I murmured, and when Paul looked at me with a question in his eyes, I added, "Gideon pinned him to the wallpaper with a saber a bit later in 1782. Even if Rakoczy found him in time, I don't think he'll have survived that evening for long."

Lady Tilney sank into a chair. "Pinned him to the wallpaper with a saber!" she repeated. "How barbaric!"

"No more than that psychopath deserved." Paul put a hand on Lucy's shoulder.

"Definitely," Gideon quietly agreed.

"Oh, I'm so relieved," said Lucy, her eyes on my face. "Now that you know the count is planning to kill Gwyneth when the Circle closes, it will never happen!" Paul was going to add something, but she went straight on. "With those papers, surely Grandpa can finally convince the Guardians that we were right and the count never had the welfare of mankind at heart, only his own. And those idiotic Guardians, particularly the repulsive Marley, won't be able to dismiss the evidence out of hand anymore. Huh! Dragging the memory of Count Saint-Germain through the dirt, were we? He wasn't even a real count, just an out-and-out villain, and oh—like I said, I'm so relieved, so very, very relieved!" She took a deep breath, giving the impression that she could go on and on like this for hours, but Paul put his arm around her.

"You see, Princess? It will all turn out all right," he whispered gently, and although he wasn't talking to me, for some strange reason, it brought me literally to the brink of tears. However hard I tried, I couldn't hold them back.

"But it won't," I burst out, and never mind about drenching the cushions, I dropped into the nearest chair. "It won't all turn out all right. Grandpa's been dead for six years, and he can't help us now."

Lucy crouched down in front of me. "Don't cry," she said helplessly. But she was crying herself. "Darling, you mustn't cry like that, it's not good for the . . ." she sobbed. "His heart, I suppose? I was always telling him to lay off those buttercream cakes. . . ."

Paul bent over us, and it looked as if he would have liked to burst into tears himself.

Great. If Gideon joined in as well, we could compete with the summer showers outside, no problem.

It was Lady Tilney who put a stop to all that. Taking two handkerchiefs out of her skirt pocket, she handed one each to Lucy and me, and said in a brisk tone of voice star-tlingly like Lady Arista's, "Plenty of time for all this later, children. Pull yourselves together. We must concentrate. Who knows how much time we have left?"

Gideon patted my shoulder. "She's right," he whispered.

I sniffed once and then laughed when I heard the trumpeting sound as Lucy blew her nose into her handkerchief. Hopefully that was one habit I hadn't inherited from her.

Paul went over to the window and looked down at the street. When he turned back, his expression was perfectly neutral again. "Right. Back to business." He scratched his ear. "So Lucas can't help us now. But even without him, with those papers, it must be possible to convince the Guardians at last that the count's intentions are selfish." He looked questioningly at Gideon. "And then the Circle will never be closed."

"It would take too long to get the authenticity of the papers checked," replied Gideon. "At the moment, Falk is Grand Master of the Lodge, and he might even just possibly believe us. But I'm not a hundred percent sure. So far I haven't ventured to show the papers to anyone in the Lodge."

I nodded. Back on that sofa in the year 1953, he had told me about his suspicion that there was a traitor among the Guardians. "You see," I said, joining in, "there's always a possibility that among the Guardians of our own time, there could be one or more who know about the real effect of the philosopher's stone and are backing the count's plans to make himself immortal." I tried to concentrate on facts, and to my surprise, I succeeded remarkably well, in spite of all the emotional stuff sloshing around in my mind. Or maybe because of it.

"Suppose Grandpa discovered who the traitor was? That would also explain why he was murdered."

"He was *murdered*?" repeated Lucy, stunned.

"We can't prove it," said Gideon. "But it looks very much like it." I'd told him about Aunt Maddy's vision and the burglary of the house on the day of the funeral.

"That would mean there are people working to close the Circle from both sides," said Lady Tilney thoughtfully. "Count Saint-Germain pulling the strings in the past, and one or more of his allies supporting his plans in the future."

Paul brought his fist down on the back of the chair in front of him. "Oh, damn it to hell," he growled through gritted teeth.

Lucy raised her head. "But you can tell the Guardians you didn't find us! If our blood isn't read into the chronograph, the Circle won't be closed."

"It's not that simple," said Gideon. "The Guardians have—"

"Yes, I know they've set private detectives on us," Lady Tilney interrupted him. "The de Villiers twins and that stuffed shirt Pinkerton-Smythe. Luckily, they think themselves very clever, and they consider me—because I'm a woman—very stupid. It never occurs to them that private detectives might happily withhold information in return for an addition to their modest income." She allowed herself a triumphant smile. "And our present arrangement is only temporary. Lucy and Paul will soon have covered up any traces behind them. Under another name, they're soon going to begin a new life and—"

"Move into an apartment in Blandford Street," Gideon finished, and the triumphant smile disappeared from Lady Tilney's face. "We know all that—and Mr. Pinkerton-Smythe was told to keep Lucy and Paul at the Temple until I take some blood from them there. More precisely, a letter with the necessary information will reach him tomorrow morning."

"Tomorrow?" said Paul, who was looking just as confused as I felt. "But then it's not too late!"

"Yes, it is," said Gideon. "Because from my point of view, it's already happened. I delivered the letter to the Guardians who were on duty during the Cerberus Watch a couple of days ago. At the time, I had no idea what was going on."

"Then we'll just hide," said Lucy.

"Tomorrow morning?" Lady Tilney looked grimly determined. "I'll see what I can do."

"So will I," said Gideon, and he glanced at the grandfather clock. "But I don't know if it will be enough. Because even if we can keep the Guardians from getting their hands on Lucy and Paul, I'm convinced that the count will find ways and means to achieve his ends."

"At least he won't get any of my blood," said Lady Tilney.

Gideon sighed. "You gave it to us long ago, Lady Tilney. I visited you in 1916, when you had to elapse in the cellar with the de Villiers twins during the First World War. And you were perfectly happy to let me have a few drops. I was surprised myself at the time. I hope very much we'll have a chance to exchange our impressions of that occasion someday."

"Is it just me, or do the rest of you feel as if someone is building a subway system through your brains?" asked Paul.

I couldn't help laughing. "I feel exactly the same," I assured him. "There's too much information coming in to be digested all at once. Every single idea starts off ten more."

"And that's not by any means all," said Gideon. "There's still a lot to discuss. Unfortunately we'll be traveling back soon. But we'll be here again—say in half an hour's time? That is, for you—for Gwyneth and me, it will be tomorrow morning, if all goes well."

"I don't understand," murmured Paul, but Lucy looked as if light had suddenly dawned on her.

"If you're not on an official mission from the Guardians, then how did you get here at all?" she asked slowly, turning pale. "Or rather, *what* got you here?"

"We've—" I began, but Gideon cast me a quick glance and shook his head very slightly.

"We can explain all that next time," he said.

I looked at the grandfather clock. Then I said, "No."

Gideon's eyebrows shot up. "No?"

I took a deep breath. Suddenly I knew that I couldn't wait a second longer. I was going to tell Lucy and Paul the truth, here and now.

All at once I didn't feel nervous anymore, only utterly exhausted. As if I'd run forty miles without stopping and hadn't slept for about a hundred years. I wished to goodness that Gideon had let Lady Tilney ring for that hot peppermint tea with sugar and lemon. As it was, we'd have to do without it.

I looked straight at Lucy and Paul. "Before we travel back," I began quietly, "I have to tell you something else. There must be time for that."

WHEN CYNTHIA'S BROTHER, in costume as a garden gnome, opened the door, it was as if he'd flung wide the gates of hell. The music was turned up to maximum, and it wasn't the kind of music that Cynthia's parents liked to dance to—it was somewhere between house and dubstep. A girl with a little tiara on her head pushed quickly past the garden gnome and threw up in the bed of hydrangeas near the porch. Her face was suitably green, but it could have been makeup.

"Touchdown!" she cried, straightening up. "I was afraid I wouldn't make it this far."

"Oh, *high school party*," said Gideon quietly. "How nice."

I gawped, puzzled. Something was all wrong here. This was the Dales' posh house in upmarket Chelsea. A place where you usually kept your voice down. So why were people dancing even in the front hall? Why were there so many of them? And where did all the laughter come from? There wasn't usually much of it at Cynthia's parties, just the odd giggle now and then. If the word *boring* hadn't already existed, it would certainly have been invented at one of those occasions.

"Great, you're all green, so come along in!" crowed Cynthia's brother, handing me a glass of something. "Here! Green Monster punch. Very healthy. Pure fruit juice, fresh fruit, green food coloring—organic! And a tiny little drop of white wine. Organic white wine, of course."

"Have your parents gone away for the weekend?" I asked, trying to get the huge skirt of my Queen Alexandra dress through the door somehow.

"What?"

I repeated the question ten decibels louder.

"Nope, they're around here somewhere." The garden gnome's voice was slightly slurred. "They quarreled because Dad just had to juggle those little green soya balls, and then everyone wanted to do it too, and anyone who scored a hit on Mum's spiky hat was supposed to win a prize. Hey, Muriel, what are you doing in that cupboard? The toilet's that way."

"There's definitely something wrong," I told Gideon. I had to shout for him to hear me. "Usually people have to stand about in little groups as stiff as broccoli at these parties, waiting for midnight. And trying to get away from Cynthia's parents, because they always want to get you playing 'nice games' that no one enjoys but themselves."

Gideon took the glass from me and tried a sip. Then

he said, grinning, "I guess this is the explanation. Tiny little drop of white wine? It must be half neat vodka, half at the very least."

Okay, so that did explain a good deal. I peered at the dance floor in the living room, where Cynthia's mum, dressed as the Statue of Liberty, was dancing wildly. "Let's find Lesley and Raphael and get out of here as fast as we can," I said.

A large green pepper collided with Gideon.

"'Scuse me," muttered Sarah, who was sewn into the green pepper costume. Then her eyes widened. "Oh, my God . . . are you *real*?" She dug her forefinger into Gideon's coat to find out.

"Sarah, have you seen Lesley anywhere?" I asked. This was getting me down. "Or are you too drunk to remember?"

"I'm stone-cold sober!" cried Sarah. She was staggering so much that she'd have fallen over, if Gideon hadn't caught her. "I can prove it. Peter Piper picked a peck of pickled pepper. Peter Piper picked a peck of pickled pepper. Go on, you say it too. No one who's drunk can say it. Right?" She cast a soulful glance at Gideon, who seemed to be enormously amused. "Hey, if you're a vampire, you're welcome to bite me."

For a moment, I was tempted to snatch the glass back from Gideon and tip the Green Monster punch straight down my throat. This seething, noisy, green inferno was more than my shattered nerves could stand.

We hadn't really meant to go on to the party, Queen

Alexandra dress or no Queen Alexandra dress. After we'd peeled off our Edwardian clothes and left the church, I was still feeling very trembly from our conversation with Lucy and Paul. All I wanted was to get into bed and not come out until everything was over. Or at least (because I soon rejected that idea as unrealistic) to give my brain, which was suffering from information overload, a chance to work everything out properly in peace and quiet. Using notes and little boxes and arrows in different colors. Paul's comparison with a subway being built in our brains was only too apt. All we needed was a plan of the route.

However, Lesley had sent me four text messages telling us to come on to the party right away. The last in particular sounded kind of urgent. *"Better get yourselves over here double quick, or I can't answer for the consequences."*

"Wow! Gwenny!" That was Gordon Gelderman, in an artificial turf overall. He was looking down the low neckline of my Queen Alexandra dress and whistling through his teeth. "I always knew there was more than a kind heart under your school uniform!"

I rolled my eyes. Gordon couldn't help being embarrassing, but did Gideon have to grin in that silly way?

"Hey, Gordon, say Peter Piper picked a peck of pickled pepper four times running!" Sarah shouted.

"Peeker Pepper pecked a pop of pippled pepper, Pepper Picker popped a pick of pippered popper, Pickle Popper packed a pip of peppled potter!" cried Gordon confidently. "Easy peasy! Hey, Gwenny, have you tried the punch?" He leaned closer to me in a confidential way and shouted in my ear, "I guess I wasn't the only one who thought of . . . er . . . giving it a bit more zing."

For a moment, I had a vision of party guests strolling past the buffet, surreptitiously spying out the land, and then, one by one, adding smuggled vodka to the punch.

"How much wood would a woodchuck chuck if a woodchuck could chuck wood?" chanted Sarah, staggering and clutching at Gideon's behind. "Lesley's in the conservatory. There's karaoke in there. I'm going to listen, only I want a little more punch first." The tip of her green felt pepper costume wobbled on top of her head. "This is the best party I've ever been to!"

Gordon giggled. "Cynthia ought to be grateful. After tonight, no one will say her parties are boring ever again. She's so lucky! And the catering service delivered far too much green finger food, so we all called a couple of friends to come along. Some of them aren't even in costume, let alone green!"

I rolled my eyes again and firmly hauled Gideon away, right through the crowd of dancing lunatics and into the conservatory.

Gordon followed us. "Are you going to sing karaoke again too, Gwenny? Last time you were the best. I'd have voted for you if Katie hadn't drenched her T-shirt with water, so she looked kind of hot, and I—"

"Oh, shut up, Gordon." I was going to turn back to him, but at that moment, I saw Charlotte. Or someone who could have been Charlotte if she hadn't been standing on a table in the middle of the conservatory, belting out Lady Gaga's "Paparazzi" into a microphone.

"Oh, my God," murmured Gideon, holding on to the door frame.

"*Ready for those flashing lights*," sang Charlotte.

I couldn't say a word for a moment. Any number of groupies were standing around the table catcalling, and Charlotte didn't sing at all badly.

Gordon immediately mingled with the fans and started demanding a striptease. "Get your things off!" he bellowed. "Get 'em off!"

I spotted Raphael and Lesley—she was looking lovely in the nearly green Grace Kelly dress, with her hair water-waved to be right for the period—and pushed my way through the crowd and over to them. Gideon stayed in the doorway.

"At last!" Lesley yelled, giving me a hug. "She had some of the punch, and now she's not herself at all. Since nine thirty she's been trying to tell everyone about Count Saint-Germain's secret society and how there are time travelers living among us. We did all we could to make her go home, but she's as slippery as an eel, and she keeps getting away."

"And she's much stronger than us," said Raphael, who was wearing an amusing green hat, but didn't look at all amused himself. "I almost got her to the front door just now, but then she twisted my arm and threatened to break my neck."

"And now she's grabbed the mike," said Lesley gloomily. We stared up at Charlotte as if she were a ticking time bomb. Admittedly, a prettily packaged time bomb.

Caroline hadn't been exaggerating. The elf costume was stunning. Even a real elf couldn't have looked lovelier than Charlotte, with her slender shoulders emerging from a cloud of green tulle. Her cheeks were flushed, her eyes were shining, and shimmering ringlets of hair curled their way down her back to the perfectly made wings, which looked as if she'd been born with them. I wouldn't have been surprised to see her take off next moment and fly through the conservatory.

However, her singing voice wasn't at all elfin. In fact, it wasn't unlike Lady Gaga's own.

"You know that I'll be your Papa-Paparazzi," she bawled into the microphone, and when Gordon shouted, "Get 'em off!" again, she began suggestively removing one of her long green gloves, finger by finger, helping it off with her teeth.

"She got that out of a film," said Lesley, reluctantly impressed. "I can't remember what film it was right now."

The crowd roared as she threw the glove and Gordon caught it.

"Go on!" they all shouted, and Charlotte turned her attention to the other glove. But then she suddenly stopped. She'd seen Gideon in the doorway, and her eyes narrowed. "Well, well, look who's here!" she said into the mike, and her glance moved on over the heads of all the guests until it stopped at me. "And my little cousin, too . . . of course!

Listen, did you know that Gwyneth's really a time traveler? It was supposed to be me, but that's not how things
turned out. And suddenly here I am like one of Cinderella's stupid sisters."

"Go on singing!" shouted her bewildered groupies.

"Get 'em off!" shouted Gordon.

Charlotte put her head on one side, and her burning
eyes fixed on Gideon. *"But I won't stop until that boy is mine!"*
she sang. "Ha, ha, that's a joke! I wouldn't stoop so low."
She pointed her forefinger at Gideon, and called, "He can
travel in time as well. And soon he'll be healing all the
diseases in the world."

"Oh, shit," muttered Lesley.

"Someone must get her down from there," I said.

"Yes, but how? She's a fighting machine. Maybe we
could simply throw something heavy at her," suggested
Raphael.

Charlotte's audience wasn't sure what was going on.
Somehow people seemed to notice that she was in anything but a relaxed mood. Only Gordon went on shouting
cheerfully, "Get 'em off!"

I tried to make eye contact with Gideon, but he was
looking at Charlotte. He slowly made his way to the table
on which she was standing.

She took a deep breath, and the microphone broadcast
her sigh to every corner of the conservatory. "He and I . . .
we know all about history. We studied time travel together. You should just see him dancing a minuet. Or fenc-
ing. Or playing the piano."

Gideon had almost reached her.

"He's eerily good at everything he does. Oh, and he can make declarations of love in eight languages," said Charlotte dreamily, and for the first time in my life, I saw tears come into her eyes. "Not that he'd ever have made one to me—oh, no! He has eyes for no one but my silly cousin."

I bit my lip. That sounded like a broken heart, and no one in the world understood broken hearts better than me. Who'd have thought Charlotte even *had* a heart? Once again, I hoped that Lesley's marzipan theory was right. Although my own heart felt a painful pang, and I had to work hard at suppressing the waves of jealousy that threatened to submerge me.

Gideon reached his hand up to Charlotte. "Time to go home."

"Booo!" shouted Gordon, who was about as sensitive as a combine harvester, but all the other guests were holding their breath in suspense.

"Leave me alone," Charlotte told Gideon. She was swaying slightly. "I'm not through with what I have to say yet."

With one bound, Gideon was up on the table himself, and next moment, he had wrestled the microphone from her grasp. "The show's over," he announced. "Come along, Charlotte, I'll take you home."

Charlotte spat at him like a furious cat. "If you touch me, I'll break your neck. I can do Krav Maga, you know!"

"So can I, remember?" He held out his hand to her

again. Hesitantly, Charlotte took it, and even let him lift her down from the table, a tired, tipsy elf who could hardly keep on her feet any longer.

Gideon put an arm around her waist and turned to us. As so often, his expression didn't tell you what he was thinking. "I'll just deal with this. You girls go to my place with Raphael," he said briefly. "We'll meet there."

For a moment our eyes met.

"See you soon," he told me.

I nodded. "See you soon."

Charlotte didn't say another word.

And I wondered whether, maybe, when Cinderella had ridden away with the prince on his white horse, she too had a few tiny little guilt feelings.

Forever—is composed of Nows—

EMILY DICKINSON

FOURTEEN

"ONE MORE REASON to stay on the wagon," groaned Lesley. "Look at it any way you like, when you've had too much to drink and made an exhibition of yourself, you feel a real idiot. I wouldn't like to be in Charlotte's shoes at school on Monday."

"Or Cynthia's," I said. As we left the house, we'd seen the birthday girl necking in the cloakroom with a boy two years younger than our class. (In the circumstances, I hadn't bothered to say good-bye to Cynthia, particularly as we hadn't even said hello.)

"And I wouldn't like to be the poor guy who threw up all over Mr. Dale's funny froggy feet," said Raphael.

We turned into Chelsea Manor Street. "But Charlotte really took the cake." Lesley stopped outside the window of a furnishing fabrics store, not to look at the display but to admire her own reflection. "I hardly like to say it, but I did feel really sorry for her."

"Me too," I said quietly. After all, I knew exactly what being in love with Gideon felt like. And unfortunately I also knew what it felt like to make an exhibition of myself in front of everyone.

"With luck, she'll have forgotten all about it in the morning." Raphael unlocked the front door of Gideon's apartment in a large red brick building. The Dales' house in Flood Street was very close, so it had seemed sensible to change at Gideon's place for the party.

Only now did I take a closer look at it. Earlier, I'd been in too much of an emotional state after my meeting with Lucy and Paul in 1912 to notice anything. I'd been sure that Gideon lived in one of those ultra-hip apartments, a hundred square yards of yawning void, all chrome and glass and a flat-screen TV the size of a football field. But I'd been wrong. A narrow hall led from the door past a small staircase to a living room flooded with light; its back wall was a huge window. The other walls were lined with shelves up to the ceiling, with books, DVDs, and a few files stacked on them, all jumbled up together, and in front of the windowsill there was a large gray sofa with a lot of cushions.

But the heart of the room was an open grand piano, although an ironing board propped casually against it made it look slightly less impressive. And the three-cornered hat slung over one corner of the piano lid didn't quite fit the picture either. Madame Rossini was probably searching desperately for that 'at. Still, maybe this was Gideon's idea of *Homes & Gardens*.

"What would you like to drink?" said Raphael, acting the perfect host.

"What is there?" Lesley asked, looking suspiciously at the open door to the kitchen, where the sink was piled high with dishes and plates encrusted with what had presumably once been tomato sauce. Or maybe it was a medical experiment and part of Gideon's studies.

Raphael opened the fridge. "Hm. Let's see. There's some milk, but its use-by date was last Wednesday. Orange juice . . . oh. Can orange juice solidify? It kind of rattles inside the carton. Ah, this looks hopeful, could be some kind of lemonade. If we mix it with—"

"I'd just like some water, please." Lesley was about to drop on the huge gray sofa, but remembered at the last minute that the Grace Kelly dress wasn't suitable for lounging in and sat primly on the edge of the seat instead. I flopped down beside her with a huge sigh.

"Poor Gwenny." She patted my cheek lovingly. "What a day! You must be worn out. Is it any consolation if I say you don't look it?"

I shrugged my shoulders. "A bit."

Raphael came back with glasses and a bottle of water, and swept a few magazines and books off the coffee table, including an illustrated volume about men in the Rococo period.

"Can you move a few square yards of those skirts aside to make room for me on this sofa?" He grinned down at me.

"Oh, never mind that, just sit on the dress," I said, letting my head drop back and closing my eyes.

Lesley jumped up. "No, no, don't! We'll tear something, and then we'll never be allowed to borrow any clothes from Madame Rossini again. Come on, get up and I'll unlace the top." She pulled me to my feet again and started helping me out of the Queen Alexandra dress. "You look somewhere else while we do this, Raphael."

Raphael stretched out full length on the sofa and stared at the ceiling. "Okay like this?"

Once I was back in jeans and T-shirt, and I'd drunk a few sips of water, I felt rather better.

"What was it like meeting your . . . I mean, meeting Lucy and Paul?" asked Lesley quietly when we were sitting on the sofa again.

Raphael looked sympathetically at me. "Must be gross to have your own parents basically the same age as yourself."

I nodded. "It was rather . . . weird and . . . and upsetting." And then I told them all about it, beginning with the butler's greeting, going on to our confession that we'd already closed the Circle of Blood with the stolen chronograph. "It left them reeling to know that we actually had the philosopher's stone in our hands—or the *glittery salt*, as my gargoyle friend Xemerius calls it. They got terribly worked up, and when she's worked up, Lucy talks even more than I do, can you believe it? They didn't stop saying what a dreadful thing we'd done until I told them I knew about the . . . er, the exact way we were related."

Lesley's eyes were wide. "So?"

"So then they shut up. Until we all burst into tears

again a moment later," I said, rubbing my tired eyes. "I guess all the tears I've shed over the last few days would irrigate a drought-stricken field in Africa."

"Oh, Gwenny." Helplessly, Lesley stroked my arm.

I tried to grin. "Yes, and then we gave them the good news that, as it happens, the count *can't* kill me because it seems I'm immortal. Of course they couldn't believe it, and time was running short, so we couldn't prove it to them by getting Stillman to try a quick strangling act on me or something. We had to leave them looking stunned and run, if we were to get back to the church in time to travel back."

"So now what?"

"Tomorrow morning we're going to meet them again, and then Gideon will tell them his brilliant plan," I said. "The only trouble is that he still has to work it out overnight. And if he's half as exhausted as I am, he won't even be able to think straight."

"Well, that's what coffee is for. And what I'm for as well—the brilliant Lesley Hay." Lesley gave me an encouraging smile. Then she sighed. "But you're right, it's not that simple. I mean, it's great that you two have a chronograph for traveling in time under your own steam, but there are limits to the amount you can use it. Especially when we remember that you have to go and see the count again tomorrow, and that'll leave you only two hours or less of your quota of time for elapsing."

"What?" I said blankly.

Lesley sighed. "Didn't you read that bit in *Anna*

Karenina? You can't elapse for more than five and a half hours a day, or there are side effects." Lesley acted as if she didn't notice Raphael's admiring expression. "And I don't know that I like you having that salty stuff. It's . . . it's dangerous. I hope at least you've hidden it somewhere no one can find it."

As far as I knew, the flask was still in the pocket of Gideon's leather jacket, but I didn't tell Lesley so. "Paul told us at least twenty times we ought to destroy it."

"And he's no fool!"

"No!" I shook my head. "Gideon thinks it could turn out to be our trump card."

"Gross," said Raphael. "You could always auction it on eBay for a joke. Immortality powder, to be taken once only. Minimum bid one pound."

"Apart from the count, I don't know anyone who *wants* to be immortal," I said, rather bitterly. "I don't like the idea of staying alive when everyone else around me will have to die sometime. I'd sooner throw myself off a cliff than be left all alone in the world!" I suppressed another sigh at this idea. "Do you think this immortality thing could be a kind of genetic defect in me? After all, I have not just one time travel line in the family, I have two of them."

"There could be something in that," said Lesley. "And the Circle does close with you—in every sense."

For a while we sat lost in thought, staring at the opposite wall. It had some words in Latin painted on the plaster in black lettering.

"What does that say?" asked Lesley at last. "Don't forget to fill the fridge?"

"No," said Raphael. "It's a quote from Leonardo da Vinci, and the de Villiers family stole it from him to use it as their motto."

"Then I expect that in English," said Lesley, "it means something like 'We're not just showing off, we really are wonderful.' Or 'We know everything, and we're always right!'"

I giggled.

"'He who is fixed to a star does not change his mind,'" said Raphael. "That's what it says." He cleared his throat. "How about I find some pens and paper? To help us think better?" He grinned awkwardly. "Maybe it's kind of sick, but I must say I'm enjoying your mysterious game."

Lesley sat up straight. A smile slowly spread over her face, and the freckles on her nose began to dance. "Me too," she said. "I mean, I know it's not really a game, it's a matter of life and death, but I've never had such fun before as these last two weeks." She cast me an apologetic glance. "Sorry, Gwenny, but it's megacool to have an immortal time traveler for a friend. Much cooler, I guess, than actually being one."

I couldn't help laughing. "You're right. I'd be having more fun myself if we could change places."

When Raphael came back with paper and colored pencils, Lesley immediately began drawing little boxes and arrows. "It's that stuff about an accomplice of the count among the Guardians that really gives me a headache."

She chewed the end of her pencil for a moment. "Although that's only an assumption in itself, but never mind. Basically, it could be anyone, right? The minister of health, that weirdo the doctor, nice Mr. George, Mr. Whitman, Falk . . . or that red-headed idiot, what's his name again?"

"Marley," I said. "But I don't think he's the type for that kind of thing."

"He's descended from Rakoczy, all the same. And it's always the least likely person who did the deed, you know it is!"

"Right," agreed Raphael. "The ones who seem harmless are usually the villains. You want to be particularly careful with idiots who stutter."

"This accomplice of the count's, let's call him Mr. X for now, could have been the murderer of Gwenny's grandfather." Lesley scribbled busily on her piece of paper. "And he would probably have been the one told to kill off Gwenny once the count had his elixir." She gave me a loving look. "At least I've been a tiny little bit less worried about that since I've known you're immortal."

"Immortal, but not invulnerable," said Gideon. We all jumped and looked at him in surprise. He'd come into the apartment unnoticed and was now leaning in the doorway with his arms folded. He was still wearing his eighteenth-century outfit, and as always, my heart did a painful little thump at the sight of him.

"How's Charlotte?" I asked, hoping the question sounded as neutral as I'd intended.

Gideon wearily shrugged his shoulders. "I guess she'll

have to take a few aspirins tomorrow morning." He came closer. "What are you all doing?"

"Making plans." Lesley had her tongue wedged in the corner of her mouth as her pencil moved fast over the paper. "And we mustn't forget the magic of the raven," she added, more to herself than anyone else.

"Gid, who do *you* think the count's secret accomplice among the Guardians could be?" Raphael was biting his nails. "I suspect Uncle Falk. I always thought he was very odd, even when I was little."

"Nonsense." Gideon came over to me and dropped a kiss on my hair before plopping into the well-worn leather armchair opposite. He propped his elbows on his knees and put a strand of hair back from his face. "I can't get what Lucy said just now out of my mind. About the count losing his immortality from the moment when Gwyneth was born."

Lesley tore herself away from her diagrams and nodded. "*But beware: when the twelfth star shows its own force, His life here on earth runs its natural course,*" she quoted, and I was annoyed, yet again, to find that the silly jingle could send a shiver down my spine. "*And if youth is destroyed, then the oak tree will stand, To the end of all time, rooted fast in the land.*"

"Do you know all that stuff by heart?" asked Raphael.

"Not all of it. But many of those verses sort of stick in the mind," said Lesley, slightly embarrassed. Then she turned to Gideon. "This is how I see it. If the count swallows that powder in the past, he becomes immortal. But only until the twelfth star rises, meaning . . . er . . . until Gwyneth is born. Then it's good-bye to his immortality; he'll age like anyone else. Unless he kills Gwyneth to stop the process in its tracks. But before that, she has to make it possible for him to get hold of the elixir in the first place. And if he never gets the elixir, he won't get to be immortal either. Am I making sense?"

"Sort of," I said, thinking of Paul and the subway systems being built in our brains.

Gideon slowly shook his head. "But suppose we've been making a mistake all along in our reasoning?" he asked thoughtfully. "Suppose the count got his hands on the powder long ago?"

I almost said, "What?" again, but I managed to stop myself just in time.

"That's not possible, because in one of the chronographs the Circle of Blood still hasn't been closed, and I hope the elixir from the other is hidden somewhere safe."

"Yes," said Gideon, still slowly. "Yes, right at this minute it is. But it doesn't necessarily have to stay that way." He sighed as he saw our blank expressions. "Think about it: it's possible that at some point in the eighteenth century, the count—by one means or another—did take the elixir, and it made him immortal."

All three of us stared at him. I came out in goose bumps all over, without really knowing why.

"Which in turn would mean that he may be alive at this very moment," Gideon went on, looking me straight in the eye. "He could be going around out there somewhere, just waiting for us to take the elixir back to him in the eighteenth century. And then looking for his chance to kill you, Gwyneth."

For a few seconds, silence reigned. Then Lesley said, "I don't say I entirely follow you, but even if for some reason you two change your minds and you do take the count the elixir . . . wouldn't he have one tiny problem?" At this point she laughed happily. "He *can't* kill Gwenny."

Raphael made his pencil spin on the table like a top. "And anyway, why would you change your minds, now that you know the count's real intentions?"

Gideon didn't answer at once, and his face was almost expressionless as he finally said, "Because we could be blackmailed."

I WOKE FEELING something damp and cold on my face, and Xemerius said, "Your alarm clock will go off in ten minutes' time!"

Groaning, I pulled the quilt up over my head.

"There's no satisfying you! Yesterday you complained because I *didn't* wake you." I seemed to have hurt Xemerius's feelings.

"I hadn't set my alarm clock yesterday. And it's horribly early," I muttered.

"You have to make a few sacrifices if you want to save the world from an immortal megalomaniac," said Xemerius. I could hear him humming as he flew around the room. "The megalomaniac you're due to meet this afternoon, in case you'd forgotten. Come on, rise and shine."

I played dead. Which wasn't very difficult, because immortal or not, I *felt* just about dead. However, Xemerius didn't seem much impressed by my efforts. He fluttered cheerfully up and down in front of my bed, churning out old wives' sayings along the lines of *the early bird catches the worm.*

"The early bird's welcome to all the worms it likes," I said, but in the end, Xemerius got his way. Irritated, I rolled out of bed, and as a result, I was at the Temple Tube station on the dot of seven in the morning.

Well, strictly speaking, it was seven sixteen, but the time on my mobile was a little fast.

"You look as tired as I feel," groaned Lesley, who was already waiting for me on the platform where we'd agreed to meet. There wasn't much going on in the station at that time of a Sunday morning, but I wondered how Gideon expected to get into one of the underground tunnels from here unnoticed. The platforms were brightly lit, and the place was full of CCTV cameras.

I put down my heavy traveling bag, which was packed full of stuff, and cast a sour glance at Xemerius, who was flying in and out between the columns in a headlong slalom race. "It's Xemerius's fault. He wouldn't let me use Mum's concealer because he said it was so late. And he wouldn't let me stop off at a Starbucks on the way here either."

Lesley put her head on one side, with an interested look. "You slept at home?"

"Yes, of course, where else?" I asked rather impatiently.

"Well, I thought the pair of you might have taken a break from making plans after Raphael and I left." She rubbed her nose. "Particularly as I spent ages saying good night to Raphael, on purpose to give you time to move from the sofa to the bedroom."

"On purpose?" I asked slowly. "Wow, how self-sacrificing of you!"

Lesley grinned. "Yes, wasn't it?" She didn't even blush. "But don't change the subject. You could have told your mum you were sleeping over with me."

I smiled wryly. "To be honest, I'd have done just that. But Gideon insisted on calling a taxi for me." I added, a little unhappily, "I obviously can't have looked as seductive as I thought."

"It's only that he has a sense of—er—responsibility," Lesley consoled me.

"You could call it that," said Xemerius, who had finished flying the slalom. Breathing hard, he came down on the floor beside me. "Or you could call him a bore, slow off the mark, a scaredy-cat"—he stopped to get his breath back—"a shirker, a guy with no guts, just plain chickening out. . . ."

Lesley looked at her watch. She had to shout to be heard above the noise of an incoming Central Line train. "And he's apparently not particularly punctual. It's already twenty past." She looked at the few passengers getting out of the train. Then, all of a sudden, her eyes lit up. "Oh, there they are."

"That morning, the two eagerly awaited fairy-tale

princes had left their white horses in the stable for once and traveled by Tube," declaimed Xemerius unctuously. "At the sight of them, the eyes of the two princesses shone, and when the two concentrated sets of young hormones collided, expressing themselves in the form of embarrassed kisses and silly grins, the clever and incomparably handsome demon unfortunately had to throw up in a garbage bin."

He was exaggerating outrageously—we none of us had silly grins on our faces. At the most, we were smiling blissfully. And no one was embarrassed, except perhaps me, because I remembered how Gideon had unwound my arms from around his neck last night, saying, "I'd better call you a taxi now. We're going to have a strenuous day tomorrow." I felt a bit like a burr that had to be picked off a pullover. And the worst of it was that at that very moment, I'd been getting ready to say "I love you." Not that he hadn't known that for ages, but . . . well, I hadn't actually said it yet. And now I wasn't quite sure whether he really wanted to hear it.

Gideon briefly caressed my cheek. "Gwenny, I can do this on my own, you know. I only have to intercept the Guardian on duty while he's on his way to the Lodge and get the letter away from him again."

"*Only* is good," said Lesley. Although we were still far from having any really brilliant ideas up our sleeves, the four of us had worked out what Lesley called "a rough plan of action." In any event, we had to see Lucy and Paul again, and we had to do it before we met the count this afternoon. We also had to do something about the letter that Gideon had taken last week to the year 1912, saying where Lucy and Paul were hiding. On no account must it fall into the hands of the Grand Master of the time and the de Villiers twins. As the time we could spare for secret travel by private chronograph was, we calculated, an hour and a half, maximum, if we didn't want to risk doing ourselves physical damage (for instance imitating Xemerius and throwing up), how to make good use of every minute was going to be a problem.

At first Raphael had seriously suggested that we could smuggle the chronograph into the Guardians' headquarters and travel straight back from there, but even his big brother didn't have nerves strong enough for that.

As an alternative suggestion, Gideon had taken some rolled-up papers out of one of his bookshelves, and from between *The Anatomy of Man in 3-D* and *Structural System of the Human Hand*, he conjured up a map of the underground passages running through the Temple district. That map was why we were now meeting at the Tube station.

"You want to do it without us?" I frowned. "But we agreed that in future we'd do everything together."

"Exactly," said Raphael. "Otherwise you'll end up saying you saved the world all by yourself." He and Lesley were to stand guard over the chronograph, and although Xemerius, slightly offended, had said he could do the job just as well, it was comforting to know that they could pick it up and take it away with them if we were forced to travel back to somewhere else.

"Anyway, you're sure to be in deep trouble without us!" Lesley snapped at Gideon.

Gideon raised his hands in the air. "Okay, okay, I get the idea." He picked up my traveling bag and looked at the time. "Right, pay attention. The next train arrives at seven thirty-three. After that, we have exactly four minutes to reach the first passage before another train comes through. Don't switch your flashlights on until I say so."

"You're right," Lesley whispered to me. "He's addicted to ordering people about."

"*MERDE!*" Raphael's curse was heartfelt. "That was close."

I could only agree. The beams of our flashlights passed over the tiled walls and lit up our pale faces. The carriages of the train were rattling through the tunnel behind us.

Four minutes, we now knew, was a very small window of time to climb over the barrier at the end of the platform, jump down, and run along the tunnel, keeping well away from the electrified track. Not forgetting the time spent as we caught up with Gideon after the last fifty yards and stood gasping for breath and helpless in front of the iron door that let into the right-hand wall of the tunnel, while he took a kind of skeleton key out of his pocket and set about picking the lock. That was the moment when Lesley, Xemerius, and I had begun screeching in chorus, "Hurry up, hurry up, hurry up!" to the accompaniment of the noise of the approaching train.

"It looked closer on the map," said Gideon, glancing at us apologetically.

Lesley was the first to pull herself together. She shone the beam of her flashlight into the darkness ahead, lighting up the wall where the passage came to a sudden end four yards farther on. "Okay, this is the right place." She checked the map. "That wall hadn't been built yet in 1912. The passage goes on beyond it."

As Gideon knelt down, unwrapped the chronograph, and entered the settings, I took our 1912 clothes out of the bag and prepared to take my jeans off.

"What's the idea?" Gideon looked up at me, obviously preoccupied. "Are you planning to run along these passages in a long dress?"

"I just thought . . . I mean, on account of authenticity—"

"The hell with authenticity," said Gideon.

Xemerius clapped his claws. "Too right, the hell with it!" he said enthusiastically. Then he turned to me. "Keeping bad company rubs off on you. And about time too."

"You first, Gwenny." Gideon nodded at me.

I knelt in front of the chronograph. It was a little odd to be disappearing before the fascinated gaze of Lesley and Raphael, but by this time, I realized, the whole thing followed a familiar routine. (Any time now, I'd probably be popping off to the last century to get fresh rolls for breakfast.)

Gideon landed beside me and shone his flashlight

ahead. Sure enough, there was no wall there in 1912; the beam of light went on until it was lost in a long, low passage.

"Ready?" I asked with a grin.

"Ready when you are," he replied, grinning back.

I didn't know that I was really ready. The Tube tunnel had been scary enough, and if I stuck around here long, I might need psychiatric treatment for acute claustrophobia.

The farther we went, the lower the ceilings of the passages, and the more they kept branching. Here and there, flights of steps went on down, and once we found ourselves facing a passage where the roof had fallen in, and we had to turn back. There wasn't a sound except for our breathing and the faint *tap-tap* of our footsteps, plus now and then the rustle of paper when Gideon stopped to consult the map. I imagined I also heard rustling, tripping sounds from somewhere else. There were probably whole armies of rats living in this labyrinth, and—still imagining things—I thought that if I were a giant spider, this would be an ideal place to live and go hunting.

"Okay, there ought to be a right turn here," muttered Gideon, concentrating.

We took what felt like the fortieth turn. The passages were all as like as two peas. There was nothing to give you any sense of direction. And who knew if that map was accurate? Suppose it had been drawn by some total idiot like Marley? In that case, Gideon and I would probably be dug out in the year 2250, two skeletons holding hands. Oh, no, I was forgetting. If that happened, only Gideon would be a skeleton, while I, alive and well, would be clinging to his bones, which didn't exactly make the idea any better.

Gideon stopped, folded up the map, and put it in his jeans pocket.

"Are we lost?" I tried to keep calm. "Maybe that map is useless. Suppose we never—"

"Gwyneth," he interrupted me impatiently. "From here on, I know the way. It's not far now. Come along."

"Oh. I see." I felt ashamed of myself. I really was being rather, well, *girlie* this morning. We hurried on in single file. It was a mystery to me how Gideon thought he knew his way around this labyrinth.

"Damn!" I'd trodden in a puddle. And right beside the puddle sat a dark brown rat, blinking its red eyes in the beam of my flashlight. I squealed out loud. Probably my squeal meant "You're so cute!" in rat language, because the rat sat up on its hind legs and put its head on one side.

"You're not a bit cute!" I squealed. "Go away!"

"Where are you?" Gideon had already disappeared around the next corner.

I swallowed, and plucked up all my courage to run past the rat. Rats weren't like dogs, were they? A dog would have run after me to bite my calves. To be on the safe side, I kept the flashlight pointing back at the rat's eyes, to dazzle it, until I had almost reached the corner where Gideon was waiting for me. Then I turned the beam forward and squealed again. The outline of a man had come into sight at the end of the passage.

"Oh, shit!" Quick as a flash, Gideon grabbed me and pulled me back into the shadows. But it was already too late. Even if I hadn't squealed, the beam of my flashlight would have given me away.

"I think he saw me," I whispered back.

"You bet he did!" said Gideon grimly. "He's *me*! What an idiot I was! Go on, you go first. Be nice to me!" And with these words, he gave me a little nudge so that I staggered back into the passage.

"What on earth . . . ?" I whispered, as I was caught in the beam of another flashlight.

"Gwyneth?" I heard Gideon's incredulous voice. But this time, it came from ahead of me. It took me half a second to understand. Then I realized that we had crossed the path of Gideon's earlier self, after he'd gone to hand that letter over to the Grand Master in 1912. I shone my flashlight on him. Oh, God, yes, that was Gideon all right! And he stopped a few yards from me, looking at me in total amazement. For two seconds, we went on dazzling each other with our flashlights, and then he said, "How did you get here?"

I couldn't help smiling at him. "Well, it's a bit complicated to explain," I said, although I'd have liked to say, "Hey, you haven't changed a bit!" Behind the projecting part of the wall where we'd taken cover, the other Gideon was gesticulating in the air.

"Go on, explain!" his younger self demanded, coming closer.

Once again, the other Gideon gesticulated frantically. I didn't understand what signal he was trying to give me.

"Just a moment, please." I gave his younger version a friendly smile. "There's something I have to clear up here. I'll be back soon."

But obviously neither the older nor the younger Gideon felt like any explanations. While the younger one followed me, trying to grab my arm, the older one didn't wait for him to see around the corner, but leaped forward and struck his alter ego on the forehead with the full weight of his flashlight. The younger Gideon fell to the ground like a sack of potatoes.

"You hurt him!" I knelt down and looked at the bleeding wound, horrified.

"He'll survive," said the other Gideon, unmoved. "Come on, no time to waste! The letter's already been handed over. *He*," he said, giving himself a slight kick, "was already on his way back when he met you."

I paid no attention to him, but stroked his unconscious younger self's hair. "You hit yourself on the head! Do you remember how horrible you were to me about that?"

Gideon grinned faintly. "Yes, I do. And I'm really sorry. But who'd ever expect a thing like that? Come on! Before that idiot wakes up again. He delivered the letter ages ago." Then he said something in French. I suspected that it consisted of hearty curses because, as with Raphael just now, the word *merde* featured several times.

"Now, now, now, young man," said a voice quite close

to us. "We may be close to the sewage system down here, but that's no reason to use the language of the sewers so freely."

Gideon had spun around, but he didn't look as if he had plans to knock out the new arrival as well as his earlier self. Maybe because the voice had sounded kindly and amused. I raised my flashlight and shone it on a middle-aged stranger's face, and then from there on down, in case he was pointing a pistol at us. He wasn't.

"I'm Dr. Harrison." He introduced himself with a little bow, while his eyes, intrigued, went back and forth from Gideon's face to the Gideon lying on the ground. "And I've just retrieved your letter from our adept on duty during the Cerberus Watch." He took an envelope with a large red seal on it out of his jacket. "Lady Tilney has assured me that it must not on any account fall into the hands of the Grand Master or any other members of the Inner Circle. Apart from me, that is."

Gideon sighed and rubbed his forehead with the back of his hand. "We were on our way to prevent that very thing, but getting through all these passages took too long . . . and then, idiot that I am, I managed to cross my own path." He took the letter and stuffed it into his pocket. "Thank you."

"A de Villiers admitting to a mistake?" Dr. Harrison laughed quietly. "Well, that's something new. But fortunately Lady Tilney has taken charge, and I have never yet known one of her plans to fail. Furthermore, arguing with her is entirely useless." He pointed to the Gideon lying on the floor. "Does he need help?"

"It couldn't hurt to disinfect that wound and put something soft under the back of his head," I said, but Gideon interrupted me. "Nonsense, he'll be fine!" Taking no notice of my protests, he pulled me to my feet. "We must get back now. Please give Lady Tilney our regards, Dr. Harrison. And tell her I'm very grateful."

"A pleasure," said Dr. Harrison. He was about to turn and walk away, but then something else occurred to me.

"Oh, Dr. Harrison," I said, "could you please tell Lady Tilney not to be scared if I come to see her in the future when she's elapsing?"

Dr. Harrison nodded. "Certainly." He waved to us, said, "Good luck!" and then hurried away.

I was just calling, "Good-bye!" after him when Gideon tugged me in the other direction again. He left his unconscious alter ego lying all alone in the passage.

"I'm sure this place is teeming with rats," I said, shaken by pity. "And they're attracted to blood."

"You're confusing them with sharks," said Gideon. But then he suddenly stopped, turned to me, and took me in his arms. "I'm so sorry!" he murmured into my hair. "I was such a fool! It would serve me right if a rat did come along to nibble me."

I immediately forgot everything around us (come to that, everything else in general), flung my arms around his neck, and began kissing him, first only where I could get at him at that moment—his throat, his ear, his temple—and then his mouth. He pulled me closer, only to push me away again three seconds later.

"We really don't have time for this now, Gwenny!" he said abruptly, and he reached for my hand and led me on.

I sighed. Several times. Very deeply. But Gideon didn't say anything. Two passages farther on, when he stopped and took out the map, I couldn't stand it anymore and asked, "Is it because I don't kiss properly?"

"What?" Gideon looked at me over the top of the map, apparently baffled.

"I'm an absolute disaster at kissing, right?" I tried to suppress the hysterical note in my voice, but I didn't succeed too well. "You see, before this I never . . . I mean, to do it properly must take time and experience. Films don't tell you everything, you see! And it kind of hurts when you push me away."

Gideon lowered the map, and the beam of his flashlight went down to the floor. "Gwenny, listen—"

"Yes, I know we're in a hurry," I interrupted him. "But I just have to say it. Anything would be better than pushing me away or . . . or calling a taxi. I can take criticism. Or at least, I can if you put it nicely."

"Sometimes you really are . . ." Gideon shook his head. Then he took a deep breath and said seriously, "When you kiss me, Gwyneth, I feel I'm losing touch with the ground. I don't know how you do it or where you learnt the trick of it. If it was from a film, well, we just have to go and see it together." He stopped for a moment.

"What I really want to say is, when you kiss me, all I want is to feel you and hold you in my arms. Hell, I'm so in love with you that it feels like someone had emptied a can of gasoline somewhere inside me and set fire to it! But right now, we can't . . . we have to keep a cool head. Or one of us, anyway." The look he gave me finally put an end to my doubts. "Gwenny, all this terrifies me. Without you, there'd be no sense in my life anymore. . . . I'd want to die if anything happened to you."

I tried smiling at him, but suddenly I had a huge lump in my throat. "Gideon—" I began, but he didn't let me finish.

"I don't want . . . well, it mustn't be the same with you, Gwenny. Because the count can use feelings like that against us. And he will!"

"It's far too late for you to say that," I whispered. "I love you. And I wouldn't want to go on living without you."

Gideon looked as if he'd burst into tears next moment. He took my hand and almost crushed it. "Then we can only hope that the count never, never, never finds that out."

"And let's hope we can still think up our brilliant plan," I said. "So let's not hang around here any longer. We're in a hurry."

"QUARTER OF AN HOUR, not a minute longer!" said Gideon. He was kneeling in front of the chronograph on the picnic rug that we had spread on the grass in Hyde Park, not far from the Serpentine Gallery and with a view of the lake and the bridge. Although it looked like being as fine a spring day as yesterday, it was still freezing cold, and the grass was wet with dew. Joggers and dog walkers passed by, some of them looking curiously at our little group.

"But a quarter of an hour isn't long enough!" I said, as I strapped on the hooped framework with its padding at the hips. It would make sure that my dress billowed out around me like a ship in full sail and didn't drag on the ground, and it had been my reason for bringing the outsize traveling bag along this morning instead of a backpack. "Suppose he arrives late?" Or not at all. That was what I secretly feared most. "I'm sure clocks didn't keep particularly good time in the eighteenth century."

"Then it's just his bad luck," growled Gideon. "This is a crazy idea anyway. And today of all days!"

"For once he's right," said Xemerius, sounding tired. He hopped into the traveling bag, laid his head on his paws, and yawned widely. "Wake me when you get back. I definitely got up too early this morning." Soon after that, I heard a snore from the bag.

Lesley carefully put the dress over my head. It was the flowered blue dress that I'd worn for my first meeting with the count, and it had been hanging in my wardrobe ever since. "There'd be plenty of time to meet James later," she said. "For him, it will always be the same time on the same day, whenever it is here that you set out to visit him." She began doing up the little hooks behind my back.

"The same applied to keeping that letter from being delivered," I contradicted her. "That didn't *have* to be done today, either. Gideon could have hit himself over the head on Tuesday, for instance, or in August next year—it would have come to the same thing. Apart from which, Lady Tilney has taken charge at her end."

"It always makes me feel dizzy when you lot bring up these ideas," complained Raphael.

"I simply wanted to get it done and over with before we next meet Lucy and Paul," said Gideon. "Surely that's not so hard to understand."

"And I want to get vaccinating James over and done with," I said, adding in dramatic tones, "then if anything happens to us, at least we'll have saved his life!"

"Are you two really going to disappear and reappear in front of all these people?" asked Raphael. "Don't you think it'll get into the newspapers and people will want to interview you on TV?"

Lesley shook her head. "Nonsense," she said firmly. "We're a good way from the path, and they won't be gone long. Only the dogs will notice anything." Xemerius's snoring changed pitch.

"But remember to start back from exactly the same place where you landed," Lesley went on. "Tell you what, mark the place with one of these nice shoes." She handed me one of the shoes that Raphael had been wearing, and beamed at me. "This is fun! I want to do it every day from now on, please!"

"I don't," said Raphael, looking down for a moment at his socks, wiggling his toes gloomily, and then staring back at the path. "My nerves are stretched to breaking point. In the Tube just now, I was sure we were being followed. It would be only logical for the Guardians to have someone shadowing us. And if anyone comes along to take the chronograph away from Lesley and me, I can't even kick him properly with no shoes on!"

"He's a bit paranoid," Lesley whispered to me.

"I heard that," said Raphael. "And it's not true. I'm only being cautious."

"And I can't understand how come I'm really doing this," said Gideon, getting Lesley's backpack on. He had put the vaccination kit into it. "We're breaking all the Golden Rules at once. Come on, Gwenny, you first."

I knelt beside him and smiled at him. He'd refused to put on his sea-green eighteenth-century clothes for this expedition, although I'd tried to explain that he'd scare James in his ordinary things. Or even worse, James wouldn't take us seriously.

"Thank you for doing this for me," I said all the same, putting my finger into the compartment under the ruby.

"That's okay," said Gideon, and then his face blurred before my eyes. When I could see properly again, I was kneeling on wet leaves among a lot of fallen chestnuts. I quickly stood up and put Raphael's shoe down where I had landed.

It was pouring with rain, and there wasn't a soul in sight. Only a squirrel scurried up to the top of the tree and looked curiously at us.

Gideon had landed beside me and was looking around.

"Hm," he said, mopping rain off his face. "Perfect weather for riding and vaccination, I'd say."

"We'll lie in wait behind that bush," I suggested. For once, I was the one to take Gideon's hand and lead him on.

He was reluctant. "Only for ten minutes," he insisted. "If he doesn't turn up by then, we're going back to Raphael's shoe."

"Yes, yes," I said.

There really was already a bridge over the narrow part of the lake at this time, although it didn't look at all like the one I knew. A coach rattled by on the road around the park. And a single horseman was coming over the bridge from the opposite bank at a brisk trot. On a gray horse.

"There he is!" I cried, and began waving for all I was worth. "James! Here I am!"

"How about making yourself even more conspicuous?" asked Gideon.

James, who was wearing a coat with several rows of capes and a kind of three-cornered hat with rain dripping from its brim, brought his horse to a halt a few yards away from us. His eyes wandered over my wet hair and down to the hem of my dress, and then he inspected Gideon.

"Are you a horse dealer?" he asked suspiciously, while Gideon rummaged about in Lesley's backpack.

"No, he's a doctor!" I explained. "As good as, anyway." I saw James staring at the lettering on the backpack. It said HELLO KITTY MUST DIE. "Oh, James, I'm so glad you came,"

I began. "In this weather and all—and I didn't explain myself properly at the ball yesterday. It's like this, you see. I want to protect you from a disease that's going to infect you within the next year, and I'm afraid you'll die of it, smallpox, I mean. I've forgotten the name of the guy who's going to give it to you, but never mind that. The good news is, we've brought something that will save you from catching smallpox at all." I beamed at him. "You only have to get off your horse and roll up your sleeve, and then we'll inject you with it."

James's eyes had grown wider and wider during my monologue. Hector (who really was a magnificent gray) took a nervous step backward. "This is outrageous," said James. "You ask me to meet you in the park, then you try to sell me a dubious medicine and an even more dubious story? And your companion looks to me very much like a robber or a highwayman!" He threw back the skirts of his coat, so that we could see the sword hanging by his side. "I warn you, I'm armed, and I can defend myself!"

Gideon sighed.

"Oh, James, do listen!" I went closer and took hold of Hector's reins. "I only want to help you, and I'm afraid I don't have much time. So please just dismount your horse and take your coat off."

"I'll do no such thing," said James indignantly. "And this conversation is now over. Out of my way, you strange girl! I hope this is our last meeting! Move aside!" And he looked as if he was going to hit me with his riding crop.

But he didn't get around to it, because Gideon had grabbed him and pulled him off the horse.

"We don't have time to play games," he snapped, twisting both James's arms behind his back.

"Help!" squealed James, twisting and turning like an eel. "Ruffians! I'm being attacked!"

"James, this is all in your own best interests," I assured him, but he looked at me as if I were the devil in person. "You don't know it, but . . . but where I come from, you and I are friends. Very good friends!"

"Help! Lunatics! I'm being attacked!" cried James, staring desperately at Hector. But the gray didn't seem to feel like putting on a Black Stallion act. Instead of heroically charging us, he bent his head and began placidly grazing.

"I'm not a lunatic," I tried to explain. "I'm—"

"Shut up and take his sword away, Gwenny, you ruffian," Gideon impatiently interrupted. "And then get the needle and the ampoule with the vaccine out of the backpack for me."

Sighing, I did as he said. He was right. There was no point in expecting James to understand.

"There," grunted Gideon, opening the ampoule with his teeth. "Right, she'll cut your throat if you move a muscle for the next two minutes, is that clear? And don't you dare call for help again."

I pointed the tip of the sword at James's throat. "Honestly, James, I didn't think it would be like this, believe me! As far as I'm concerned, you'd be welcome to go on haunting my school forever—my God, I'm going to miss you so much! If I'm right, this is the last time we'll ever meet." Tears rose to my eyes.

James looked as if he was going to faint with fright any moment now. "You can have my purse if you need money, but spare my life! Please!" he whispered.

"Yes, yes, don't worry," said Gideon. He folded back the wide collar of the coat that James was wearing and put the needle directly against his throat. James whimpered quietly when he felt it prick his skin.

"Doesn't it usually go into the upper arm?" I asked.

"Usually there's no need to twist the patient's arms first," grumbled Gideon, and James whimpered again.

"This is a silly way to say good-bye," I said, unable to suppress a sniff. "I'd far rather give you a hug than hold a sword to your throat! You've always been my best friend at school after Lesley." The first tear was running down my face. "And without you, I'd never have known the difference between an ordinary Royal Highness, a Serene Highness, an Illustrious Highness, and—"

"There we are," said Gideon, letting go of James, who staggered a couple of steps backward, clutching his throat. "You should really put a plaster on it, but it will be all right without. Take care not to get any dirt into it." Gideon took the sword from my hand. "Now, mount your horse and ride away without looking back, understand?"

James nodded. His eyes were still wide with fright, as if he couldn't believe that it was all over.

"Good-bye," I sobbed. "Good-bye, James Augustus

Peregrine Pympoole-Bothame! You were the nicest ghost I ever met!"

Breathing heavily, unsteady on his legs, James mounted his horse.

"Your sword's under the chestnut tree if you want it back," added Gideon, but James had already dug his spurs into poor Hector's sides. I watched them go until they had disappeared among the trees.

"Satisfied?" asked Gideon, collecting our things.

I wiped the tears off my cheeks and smiled at him. "Thank you! It's really cool to have a boyfriend who's a medical student."

Gideon grinned. "I swear that's the last time I ever vaccinate anyone. Patients are so ungrateful!"

Unable are the Loved to die,
For Love is Immortality . . .

EMILY DICKINSON

FIFTEEN

"STEP ON IT, old chap!" cried Xemerius. "High time for a showdown with the baddie!"

I was in the passenger seat of Gideon's Mini, with Xemerius on my lap, as Gideon threaded his way through the early afternoon traffic in the Strand.

"Shut up," I hissed at Xemerius. "The count can wait forever as far as I'm concerned."

"What did you say?" Gideon cast me an inquiring glance.

"Oh, nothing." I stared out of the window. "Gideon, do you really think our idea will work?" My cheerful mood of this morning had worn off, to be replaced by a nail-biting uneasiness that left me feeling trembly.

Gideon shrugged his shoulders. "At least it's better than—what did you call it?—the rough plan of action that was all we had before."

"I didn't call it that, it was Lesley," I corrected him. For a moment, we were both lost in our own thoughts. Our meeting with Lucy and Paul had shaken us both. And I hadn't realized how much time travel can take out of you until, on the way back, we arrived right in the middle of a choir practice and had to run for it pursued by several seventy-year-old screeching sopranos. But at least we were now forearmed for our meeting with Count Saint-Germain. It was Lucy who had come up with the brainwave, and that brainwave was also the reason for the aforesaid nail-biting uneasiness.

"Watch what you're doing, laddie!" cried Xemerius, covering his eyes with his paws. "That was a red light!"

Gideon stepped on the gas and failed to give way to a taxi before turning right toward the Guardians' head-quarters. A little later, he was coming to a halt in the parking lot, tires squealing. He turned to me and put his hands on my shoulders. "Gwyneth," he began in a serious voice, "whatever happens, I want you to know that—"

He got no farther. At that moment, the door on my side of the car was flung open. I was about to turn and give the unspeakable Mr. Marley a piece of my mind, but it was Mr. George, looking anxious and running his hand over his shiny bald patch. "Gideon, Gwyneth, at last!" he said reproachfully. "You're over an hour late."

"The later the evening, the better the party," crowed Xemerius, hopping off my lap. I glanced at Gideon, sighed, and got out.

"Come along, children," Mr. George urged us, taking my arm. "Everything's ready for you."

"Everything" meant a dream of a dress for me, combining cream embroidery and lace with velvet and brocade in a cool shade of gold, and a colorfully embroidered coat for Gideon.

"Are those *monkeys* on it?" Gideon stared at the embroidery on the coat as if it were drenched in prussic acid.

"Yes, zey are capuchin monkeys, to be precise." Madame Rossini beamed at Gideon, and assured him that exotic animal embroidery motifs were the latest thing in 1782. She started getting up a good head of steam to tell us how much time it had taken her to generate the embroidery data files on the model of original patterns, so that her sewing machine could follow them, but Mr. George stopped her in her tracks. He had been waiting at the door, staring at his gold watch. I had no idea why he was in such a hurry. After all, it didn't make any difference to the count how late it was here.

"You're elapsing in the documents room today," announced Mr. George, going ahead of us for once. We hadn't set eyes on Falk and the other Guardians yet. Presumably they were sitting in the Dragon Hall, renewing the oaths they had sworn when they joined the Lodge, or drinking toasts to the Golden Rules, or doing whatever it was that Guardians did when they got together.

Only Mrs. Jenkins hurried past with a thick folder—working on a Sunday for once!—and waved to us.

"Mr. George, what are today's instructions?" asked Gideon. "Any details that we should bear in mind?"

"Well, for Count Saint-Germain, exactly the same amount of time has passed since the ball as for you—that's two days," said Mr. George at once. "However, we ourselves are a little puzzled by the instructions in his letter. According to what it says, Gwyneth will spend three and a half hours with him, while your visit is to last only fifteen minutes, Gideon. But we are assuming that there's some other task he wants you to perform, because he expressly said that you were neither of you to elapse earlier today." He stopped for a moment and looked out of the tall window at Temple Church. There was a good view of it from here. "We didn't know quite what to make of certain hints in the letter, but . . . obviously the count feels sure that the Circle of Blood is about to be closed. He wrote that we were all to hold ourselves in readiness."

"Uh-oh," said Xemerius.

Uh-oh, I thought, glancing quickly at Gideon. It sounded very much as if, although Operation Sapphire and Black Tourmaline had been really intended for yesterday, the count had expected it to fail. And as if he'd had another plan up his sleeve all along.

Possibly a more brilliant plan than ours.

My nail-biting uneasiness turned into outright fear. The idea of being alone with the count brought my arms out in goose bumps. As if Gideon could read my thoughts, he stopped and held me tight, paying no attention to Mr. George.

"It will be all right," he whispered into my ear. "Don't

forget, he can't do anything to hurt you. And so long as he doesn't know that, you're safe."

I clung to him like one of those capuchin monkeys on his coat.

Mr. George cleared his throat. "Well, I'm glad to see that you two have made up your differences," he said. A mischievous smile flitted over his face. "All the same, we must get moving."

I JUST HAD TIME to hear Xemerius shouting, "Mind you look after her, bonehead!" and then I was in the year 1782. The first thing I saw when I landed was Rakoczy's face only twelve inches or so away from me. I let out a small shriek and swerved aside. Rakoczy himself jumped in alarm.

I heard a laugh, and although it sounded pleasant and melodious, all the little hairs on the back of my neck stood up. "I told you to step aside, Miro."

While Gideon landed beside me, I slowly turned around. There was Count Saint-Germain in a plain, dark gray velvet coat and, as always, in a white wig. He was leaning on his cane, and for a moment, he looked frail and old—in fact, ancient.

But then he straightened up, and in the candlelight, I saw his lips twist into a mocking smile. "Welcome, my dears. I'm glad to see that you're in good health—and that Alastair's gloating account of Gwyneth's death must, I suppose, have been only the fantasy of a dying man." He came a step closer, looking expectantly at me, and it was a second before it struck me that he was probably waiting for a curtsey. So I sank into one. By the time I straightened up again, the count had turned his attention to Gideon.

"We have no time to waste on formalities today. Have you a message for me from your Grand Master?" he asked, and Gideon handed him the sealed letter Mr. George had given us.

As the count broke the seal and read it, I looked briefly around the room. There were a desk, and several chairs, some of them upholstered. The open shelves around the room were full of books, scrolls, and stacks of paper, and a painting hung over the mantelpiece, just as it did in the documents room in our time. But this one wasn't the portrait of Count Saint-Germain. It was an attractive still life showing books, parchments, a quill pen, and an inkwell. Rakoczy, unasked, had dropped into a chair, and now he put his boots up on the desk. He held his drawn sword loosely in his hand, like a toy that he couldn't bear to part with. His weird, lifeless eyes passed over me, and he curled his lips contemptuously. If he remembered our last meeting at all, he obviously had no intention of apologizing for his behavior.

The count had finished reading the letter. He looked penetratingly at me, and then nodded. "*Ruby red, with G major, the magic of the raven, brings the Circle of Twelve home into safe haven.* How did you escape Lord Alastair's ruthless sword? Did he just imagine it all?"

"He did wound Gwyneth," said Gideon, and I was

surprised to hear how calm and friendly his voice sounded. "But it was only a harmless scratch—she was really lucky."

"I am sorry that you both found yourselves in such a situation," said the count. "I had promised you that no one would harm you, and as a rule I keep my promises. But my friend Rakoczy here was also a little forgetful of his duties that evening, weren't you, Miro? Causing me to note, yet again, that one can sometimes rely too much on other people. If the enchanting Lady Lavinia had not come to me, my First Secretary might have recovered from his faint and run for it . . . and Lord Alastair would have bled to death all by himself."

"It was the enchanting Lady Lavinia who gave us away in the first place," I said tartly. "She—"

The count raised one hand. "I know all that, child. Alcott had plenty of opportunity to confess his sins."

Rakoczy let out a hoarse laugh.

"And Alastair had a great deal to tell us, too, even if he became a little indistinct toward the end, am I not right, Miro?" The count smiled unpleasantly. "But we can discuss all that later. We are short of time today." He picked up the letter. "Now that Gwyneth's true origin is explained, it ought not to be difficult to persuade her parents to donate a little of their blood to us. I hope you have followed all my instructions to the letter?"

Gideon nodded. His face was pale and tense, and he avoided looking at me. But so far everything was going as we'd foreseen. Roughly speaking, anyway. "Operation Black Tourmaline and Sapphire takes place today," he said.

"If the clock on the wall there is telling the right time, then in a few minutes, I'll be traveling back to the year 2011. And everything is prepared there for me to go and visit Lucy and Paul."

"Exactly," said the count, pleased. He took an envelope from his coat pocket and gave it to Gideon. "My outline of my plan is in here. I don't want any of my Guardians in the future even to think of interfering with your movements."

He went over to the mantelpiece and looked thoughtfully into the fire on the hearth for a moment. His eyes were bright and sparkling above his aquiline nose, and suddenly the whole room seemed to be full of his commanding presence. He raised his arms. "This very day all the prophesies will be fulfilled. This very day a remedy for all sickness and disease, a miracle such as has never been known before, will be granted to mankind," he cried. He paused briefly, looking at us as if expecting applause. I thought for a split second of forcing out an admiring "Wow, that's great!" but I didn't think too highly of my acting abilities right now. Gideon, too, just looked at him in silence. And Rakoczy actually had the nerve to let out a small belch at this solemn moment.

The count clicked his tongue in annoyance. "Well," he added slowly, "I assume that tells you everything." He came over to me and put his hand on my shoulder. It was all I could do not to shake it off the way I'd shaken off Tarantula. "Meanwhile, my lovely child, you and I will pass the time agreeably together, will we not?" he said unctuously. "I am sure you will understand that you must keep me company here for a little longer than young Gideon." I nodded and wondered whether the count wasn't beginning to revise his idea of women. If he supposed I understood all that, then I couldn't be as dim as he normally assumed, could I? However, he was already going on in his high-handed way. "After all, our young friend Gideon must make Black Tourmaline and his Sapphire believe that their daughter will die if they don't give him some of their blood there and then." He laughed quietly and turned to Gideon. "You can dress it up a little if you like, tell them about Rakoczy's taste for the blood of virgins and the old Transylvanian custom of tearing hearts out of living bodies. But I'm sure that won't be necessary. If I know that foolish young couple, they'll give you their blood at once."

Rakoczy let out a bark of laughter, and the count joined in. "People are so easily manipulated, don't you agree?"

"But about Gwyneth—surely you're not really going to . . . ," Gideon began, and his gaze flickered slightly. He still wasn't looking at me.

The count smiled. "Come now, what on earth are you thinking of, my dear boy? No one will hurt a hair of her head. She is only my hostage for a while. I mean until you have traveled back from the year 1912 with the blood, taking it straight to the year 2011." He raised his voice. "And these sacred halls will tremble when the brotherhood gathers and the time comes when the Circle of Blood in the chronograph can be closed." He sighed. "Ah, how I wish I could be present at that magical moment. You must tell me all about it in detail."

Oh, yes, I bet. Blah blah blah. I realized that I was instinctively gritting my teeth. My jaws hurt already. Meanwhile the count had gone over to Gideon and was standing so close to him that the ends of their noses almost touched. Gideon didn't bat an eyelash. The count raised his forefinger. "Then the elixir will be found under the sign of the twelvefold star, and it will be your task to bring it to me without delay." He took hold of both Gideon's shoulders and looked into his eyes. "*Without delay.*"

Gideon nodded. "I'm only wondering why you want the elixir brought back to *this* year," he said. "Wouldn't it be even more use to mankind in the twenty-first century, our own time?"

"A clever and philosophical question," replied the count, smiling, and he let go of Gideon. "I am glad that you ask it. But this is not the time for such conversations. I will be happy to tell you all about my complex plans when your task is finished. Until then, you must simply trust me!"

I almost laughed out loud. Only almost. I tried to catch Gideon's eye, but although I was sure he noticed, he kept looking past me. At the clock, with its hands moving inexorably on.

"There's one other thing: Lucy and Paul have a chronograph of their own at their disposal," said Gideon. "They could try to visit you here, today or maybe earlier . . . and prevent all of this, including the handing over of the elixir."

"Ah, now, surely by this time you understand enough

of the laws of continuity to know that, so far, they have not succeeded in sabotaging my plans, or we would not be here together, would we?" The count smiled. "And I have, of course, taken special precautions for the next few hours, until the elixir is in my hands. Rakoczy and his men will kill any unauthorized person who ventures near us."

Gideon nodded and put a hand on his stomach. "Here we go," he said, and at last our eyes met. "I'll be back soon with the elixir."

"I am sure that you will carry out your mission to perfection, my boy," said the count cheerfully. "*Bon voyage*. Gwyneth and I will pass the time while you are gone with a little glass of port wine."

I fastened my gaze on Gideon's, trying to put all my love into my eyes, and then he had disappeared. I felt like bursting into tears, but I went on gritting my teeth and made myself think of Lucy.

Over sandwiches and tea in Lady Tilney's salon, we had gone through it all over and over again. I knew that we had to beat the count with his own weapons if we wanted to defeat him once and for all. And it had sounded simple enough, at least if Lucy's assumption was right. She had come up with it, just like that, and at first we dismissed it. Then, after some thought, Gideon nodded. "Yes," he said. "You could be right." And he began prowling around the room again.

"Suppose we do what the count says and give Gideon our blood," Lucy went on. "Then he can close the Circle of Blood in the second chronograph, and hand the elixir over to the count, and then the count gets to be immortal again."

"Which is exactly what we've been trying to avoid like the plague for years, right?" said Paul.

Lucy raised her hand. "Just a minute. Let's at least think this through."

I nodded. I didn't know exactly what she was getting at, but somewhere at the back of my mind a question mark was quietly forming. It grew bigger, and turned into an exclamation mark. "So the count gets to be immortal—until I'm born?"

"That's right," said Gideon. He stopped pacing up and down. "And *that* means that he's still traveling all over the place in the history of the world, alive and well. Including in our own present."

Paul frowned. "You mean . . ."

Lucy nodded. "We mean that the count is watching the entire drama live, in full color." She paused for a moment. "And I guess he has a seat in the front row."

"One of the Inner Circle," I guessed.

The others nodded. "The Inner Circle. The count is one of the Guardians."

Now, as I sat here with the count, I looked at his face. *Which of them was he?* The clock above the mantelpiece was ticking loudly. It was going to be an eternity before I traveled back.

The count gestured to me to sit down in one of the upholstered armchairs, poured glasses of dark red wine for both of us, and handed me one. Then he took the armchair opposite and raised his glass to me. "Your good health, Gwyneth! It was two weeks ago today that we first met—well, from my point of view, anyway. I am afraid that my first impression of you was not especially favorable. But by now we are good friends, would you not agree?"

Oh, sure. I sipped my wine, and then said, "You almost throttled me at that first meeting." I took another sip. Then, rather bravely, I added, "At the time, I thought you could read thoughts. But I expect I was wrong about that."

The count laughed in a self-satisfied way. "Well, I am able to understand the main currents of other people's thoughts, but there is no magic about it. Indeed, anyone could learn it. I told you, when we met before, about my visits to Asia and how I acquired the wisdom and abilities of Tibetan monks there."

So he had, yes. And I hadn't been listening properly. In fact, even now I was finding it hard to make out his words. They suddenly sounded strangely distorted, sometimes long drawn out and slow, then as if they were being sung. "What on earth . . . ," I murmured. Veils of pink mist were gathering before my eyes, and I couldn't blink them away.

The count interrupted himself in his lecture. "You're feeling dizzy, aren't you? And now your mouth is dry, am I right?"

Yes, it was! How the hell did he know? And why did his voice sound so metallic? I stared at him through the strange pink mists.

"Have no fear, my child," he said. "It will soon be over.

Rakoczy has promised me that you will feel no pain. You will have fallen asleep before the spasms begin. And, with a little luck, you won't wake up again before the end."

I heard Rakoczy laugh. It sounded like the noises you get on a recorded tape in a ghost-train ride at a funfair. "But why . . ." I was trying to speak, but all at once, my lips felt numb.

"Don't take this personally," said the count in a chilly voice, "but in order to realize my plans, I am afraid I have to kill you. The prophesies foretell that, too."

I wanted to keep my eyes open, but I couldn't. My chin fell on my breast, then my head flopped over to one side, and finally my eyes closed. Darkness surrounded me.

MAYBE I REALLY am dead this time was the first thought to cross my mind when I came back to my senses. But I hadn't really imagined angels as naked little boys wearing nothing except rolls of excess fat and silly grins, like the specimens playing their harps above me here. Anyway, they were only painted on the ceiling. I closed my eyes again. My throat was so dry that I could hardly swallow. I was lying on something hard, and I felt utterly exhausted, as if I'd never be able to move again.

Somewhere behind my right ear, I heard a tune being hummed. It was the death march motif from Wagner's *The Twilight of the Gods*, Lady Arista's favorite opera. The voice humming the tune in an unsuitably jaunty way seemed to me vaguely familiar, but I couldn't place it. And

I couldn't look to see whose it was, either, because my eyes simply refused to open.

"Jake, Jake," said the voice, "I'd never have expected you, of all people, to get on my trail. But your medical Latin will do you no good now." The voice laughed softly. "By the time you wake up, I'll be over the hills and far away. You know, it's very pleasant in Brazil at this season. I lived there for several years, from 1940 onward. There's much to be said for Argentina and Chile as well." The voice paused for a moment to whistle a few bars of the Wagnerian theme. "I'm always drawn back to South America. And Brazil, incidentally, has the best cosmetic surgeons in the world. They've dealt with my annoyingly hooded eyelids, my hooked nose, my receding chin. Which is why, fortunately, I don't look much like my own portrait anymore."

My numb arms and legs were beginning to tingle, but I controlled myself. It was probably all to the good if I kept perfectly still for now.

The voice laughed. "But even if someone here in the Lodge had recognized me," it went on, "I'm sure none of you would have had the brains to draw the right conclusions. Except for that pest Lucas Montrose, who was on the very verge of unmasking me . . . oh, Jake, and even you didn't realize that he died not of a heart attack, but of Marley senior's subtle poisons! Because you ordinary humans only ever see what you want to see."

"You're a nasty, horrible, dopey man," piped up a

frightened voice somewhere behind me. "You've hurt my daddy!" I felt a cold draft of air. "And what have you done to Gwyneth?"

Yes, what? That was the question. And why didn't I hear a squeak out of Gideon?

There was a clinking sound, and then the click of a case of some kind being closed. "Ever ready to further the cause of the Guardians, all of you! A cure for all the diseases of mankind, what a joke!" A snort of contempt. "As if mankind deserved it! Well, you won't be able to help Gwyneth, for one, anymore." The voice was moving around the room, and I was beginning to get a glimmering of whose voice it was. And who I was dealing with, although I could hardly believe it. "She's as dead as the laboratory rats you were always dissecting." Another soft laugh. "And that, incidentally, is a simile and not a metaphor."

I opened my eyes and raised my head. "But you could always use it as a symbol, couldn't you, Mr. Whitman?" I asked.

Next moment, I was sorry I'd outed myself. No sign of Gideon! Only Dr. White, lying unconscious on the floor, his face as gray as his suit. Little Robert, obviously badly upset, was crouching beside his father.

"Gwyneth." You had to hand it to Mr. Whitman; he didn't screech with fright. Or show any other emotion at all. He just stood there under the portrait of Count Saint-Germain, with his hand on a baggage cart loaded up with a laptop bag, staring at me. He wore an elegant gray coat with a silk scarf, and he had a pair of sunglasses perched on his hair as if he were Brad Pitt on the beach. He didn't look a bit like the count in the painting above him.

I sat up with as much dignity as I could muster (the huge skirt of my dress was rather a disadvantage) and saw that I'd been lying flat on the desk.

Mr. Whitman clicked his tongue, looked at the time, and then let go of his baggage cart. "Well, well, how extremely annoying," he said.

I couldn't suppress a grin. "Yes, isn't it?" I agreed.

He came closer, and suddenly, as if by magic, brought a small, black pistol out of his coat pocket. "How could this happen? Didn't Rakoczy make his potion strong enough?"

I shook my head.

Mr. Whitman frowned, and pointed the pistol at my heart.

I was going to laugh, but only a frightened snort came out. All the same, I asked, "Want to try again?" and did my best to look him bravely in the eye. "Or have you realized that you can't harm me?" Aha! Our plan was working out—although if Gideon had put in an appearance, I'd have felt very much happier about it.

Mr. Whitman stroked his smoothly shaved chin and looked thoughtfully at me. Then he put his pistol away. "No," he said in the familiar voice of a trustworthy teacher, and suddenly I did see something of the older version of the count in him after all. "I suppose there would be no point in that." He clicked his tongue again. "I must have made a mistake in my thinking. The magic of the raven . . . how very unjust that you were born with the gift of immortality! You of all people. However, there *is* some point in it, because both lines unite in you—"

Dr. White moaned quietly. I glanced at him, but his face was still ashen. Little Robert jumped up. "Watch out, Gwyneth!" he said, sounding scared. "I'm sure that horrible man is planning something bad."

So was I. But what?

"As the star dies, the eagle arises supreme, fulfilling his ancient and magical dream. For a star goes out in the sky above, if it freely chooses to die for love," quoted Mr. Whitman quietly. "Why didn't I think of that at once? Well. It's not too late." He came a couple of steps closer to me, took a small silver box out of his pocket, and put it on the desk beside me.

"Is that snuff or what?" I asked, bewildered. I was beginning to feel very anxious about our plan. Something was going wrong. Very wrong indeed.

"Once again, of course, you are slow to understand," said Count Saint-Germain, formerly known as Mr. Whitman. He sighed. "This little box contains three cyanide capsules. I could tell you why I carry them about with me, but my plane leaves in two and a half hours, so I am a little short of time. In other circumstances, you could always throw yourself on the rails of the Tube or jump off the top of a high-rise building. But take it or leave it, fundamentally cyanide is the most humane method. You simply have to put a capsule in your mouth and crush it between your teeth. It will work at once. Open the box!"

My heart sank. "You want me to . . . to take my own life?"

"Exactly." He lovingly caressed his pistol. "Because there is no other way to kill you. And in order to . . . let's say, help your decision along a little, I am going to shoot your friend Gideon the moment he arrives back here." He looked at the clock. "Which ought to be in about five minutes' time. So if you want to save his life, you had better take that capsule at once. Or you can wait until he's lying dead before your eyes. Experience suggests that such things provide extremely strong motivation. Think of Romeo and Juliet."

"You're so horrible!" said little Robert, and he began to cry. I tried to give him an encouraging smile and failed miserably. I felt like sitting down beside him and bursting into tears myself.

"Mr. Whitman—" I began.

"I do prefer the title of count, you know," he said cheerfully.

"Please . . . you mustn't—" My voice broke.

"But why can't you see sense, you stupid child?" He sighed. "Believe me, I have longed for this day. I am about to return to my real life at last. A teacher at St. Lennox High School! Of all the activities I have pursued for the last two hundred and thirty years, that was really the most demeaning. I have lived close to the pulse of power for centuries. I could have dined with presidents—with oil barons, with kings. Not that kings are what they used to be these days. But no, instead I had to teach dimwitted brats and moreover work my way up from the rank of novice to the Inner Circle in my own Lodge. The years since your birth have been terrible for me. Not so much because my body began to age again and was beginning to show slight traces of deterioration"—at this point he indulged in a vain, self-satisfied smile—"as because I was so . . . so *vulnerable*. I lived for centuries without a fear in the world. I marched over battlefields amidst a hail of bullets, I exposed myself to any danger you care to mention, always in the knowledge that nothing could happen to me. But now? Any virus could have finished me off in the last few years, any damn bus could have run over me, any falling brick could have knocked me down and killed me!"

At this moment, I heard a clattering noise, and Xemerius came swooping through the wall at high speed. He landed right beside me on the desk.

"Where the hell are the Guardians?" I asked him, not stopping to bother that the count could hear me. But he seemed to think the question was meant for him.

"They can't help you now," he said.

"I'm afraid he's right." Xemerius was flapping his wings frantically. "When Gideon got back before, those idiots closed the Circle of Blood, and then Mr. Male Model here took that useless fool Marley hostage and forced the Guardians into the chronograph room at pistol point. They're locked in there now, turning the air blue with their language."

The count shook his head. "No, that was certainly no life for me! And it must come to an end. What can a little girl like you offer the world? I, on the other hand, still have many plans. Great plans—"

"Distract his attention!" cried Xemerius. "Just distract his attention, never mind how."

"How . . . how did you manage about elapsing all that time?" I asked quickly. "Uncontrolled time travel—I mean, it must have been terribly uncomfortable."

He laughed. "Elapsing? Huh! My natural life span had run out, and from the moment when I would have died, I no longer had to bother with the nuisance of traveling in time."

"And what about my grandpa? Did you kill him, too, and steal his diaries?" At this point tears rose to my eyes. Poor Grandpa. He'd been so close to uncovering the whole plot.

The count nodded. "Our clever friend Lucas Montrose had to be silenced. Marley senior saw to that. The descendants of Baron Rakoczy have served me well over the centuries, although the last in the line is a disappointment. That pedantic, red-headed dreamer has inherited none of the Black Leopard's quick wits." He looked at his watch again and then glanced expectantly at the group of armchairs standing around the documents room. "Well, it ought to be any time now, Juliet. You obviously want to see your Romeo lying in his own blood!" He took the safety catch off his pistol. "It really is a pity. I liked the boy. He had great potential."

"Please," I whispered one last time, but at that moment,

Gideon, bending his knees slightly to ensure a soft landing, came down beside the door. He didn't even have time to straighten up before Mr. Whitman fired the first shot. And then another. And another, firing again and again until the entire magazine of his pistol was empty.

The gunshots echoed deafeningly through the room as the bullets hit Gideon in the chest and the stomach. His green eyes, wide open, wandered around the room until he caught sight of me.

I screamed his name.

As if in slow motion, he slid down the door, leaving a wide trail of blood behind. Finally he was lying on the floor, oddly distorted.

"Gideon! No!" With another scream, I rushed to his side and clasped his lifeless body in my arms.

"Oh God, oh God, oh God!" cried Xemerius, spitting out water. "Please say this is all part of your plan. He isn't wearing a bulletproof vest, anyway. Oh God! So much blood!"

He was right. Gideon's blood was all over the place. The hem of my dress was sucking it up like a sponge. Little Robert crouched in a corner, whimpering, with his hands over his face.

"What have you done?" I whispered.

"What I had to do! And what you obviously didn't want to prevent." Mr. Whitman had put the pistol down on the desk and was holding the little box of cyanide capsules out to me. His face was slightly flushed, and he was breathing faster than usual. "And now it's time you stopped hesitating! Do you want to live with his death on your conscience? Do you want to go on living at all without him?"

"Don't do it!" cried Xemerius, spewing out water all over Dr. White's face.

Slowly, I shook my head.

"Then be good enough to stop trying my patience!" said Mr. Whitman, and for the first time, I heard him lose control over his voice. It no longer sounded either gentle or ironic, but almost hysterical. "Because if you keep me waiting any longer, I shall have to give you further incentives to end your own life! I'll kill them all, one by one: your mother, your irritating friend Lesley, your brother, your cute little sister . . . believe me, I won't spare a single one of them."

With trembling hands, I took the little box. Out of the corner of my eye, I could see Dr. White clutching the edge of the desk and hauling himself laboriously up. He was dripping wet.

Thank heavens, Mr. Whitman had eyes only for me. "That's a good girl," he said. "Maybe I'll catch my flight yet. And once I am in Brazil I will—" But he never got around to saying what he would do in Brazil, because Dr. White brought the butt of the pistol down on the back of his head. It made an ugly, dull thud, and then Mr. Whitman fell to the floor like a felled oak tree.

"Yes!" crowed Xemerius. "Good work! Show the bastard there's life in the old doctor yet." But the effort had been too much for Dr. White. With a horrified look at all the blood, he collapsed again with a soft sigh, and lay on the floor beside Mr. Whitman.

So only Xemerius, little Robert, and I saw Gideon suddenly cough and sit up. His face was still as pale as death, but his eyes were bright and full of life. A smile slowly spread over his face. "Is that over?" he asked.

"The cunning so-and-so!" said Xemerius. In his astonishment, he'd suddenly lowered his voice. "How on earth did he do that?"

"Yes, it's all over, Gideon!" I flung myself into his arms, taking no notice of his wounds. "It was Mr. Whitman, and I can't think how we failed to recognize him!"

"Mr. Whitman?"

I nodded, and clung closer to him. "I was so afraid you might not have done it. Because Mr. Whitman was perfectly right about one thing. I don't want to live without you, not for a single day!"

"I love you, Gwenny!" Gideon hugged me so hard that I was left breathless. "And of course I did it. Well, what option did I have with Paul and Lucy standing over me? They dissolved the stuff in a glass of water and made sure I drank it down to the very last drop."

"Now I get it!" cried Xemerius. "So that was your brilliant plan! Gideon's been feeding his face with the philosopher's stone, and now he's immortal as well! Not a bad idea, particularly when you think that otherwise Gwenny might get to feel rather lonely one of these days."

Little Robert had lowered his hands from his face and

was looking at us wide-eyed. "It's going to be all right, Robert dear," I told him. What a shame there weren't any psychotherapists for traumatized ghosts yet. That was a real gap in the market, well worth investigating. "Your father will be better soon. And he's a hero."

"Who are you talking to?" asked Gideon.

"A brave little friend," I said, smiling at Robert. He hesitantly smiled back.

"Uh-oh, I think he's coming to his senses," said Xemerius.

Gideon had spotted it, too. He let go of me, stood up, and looked down at Mr. Whitman. "I guess I'd better tie him up," he said with a sigh. "And Dr. White needs a dressing on that injury."

"Yes, and then we must let the others out of the chronograph room," I said. "But first we'd better think what we're going to tell them."

"And before that, I absolutely have to kiss you," said Gideon, taking me in his arms again.

Xemerius groaned. "Oh, really! As if you two didn't have all eternity ahead for that kind of thing!"

AT SCHOOL ON MONDAY, everything was the same as usual. Well, almost everything.

In spite of the springlike temperature, Cynthia had a thick scarf around her neck, and she crossed the foyer inside the entrance to the building fast, without looking either to right or to left.

Gordon Gelderman was close on her heels. "Oh, come on, Cynthia!" he growled in a bass voice. "I'm sorry, but you can't hold it against me forever. And I wasn't the only one who thought your party could do with . . . well, something to liven it up. I distinctly saw Madison Gardener's boyfriend pouring another bottle of vodka into the punch. And Sarah finally admitted that the green dessert was up to ninety percent her grandmother's homemade gooseberry spirit."

"Go away!" said Cynthia, trying hard to ignore a group of giggling Year Eight kids who were pointing at her and giggling. "You . . . you've made me a laughing-stock in front of the whole school! I'll never forgive you!"

"And to think I missed that party!" said Xemerius. He was sitting on the bust of William Shakespeare. A piece of the poet's nose had gone missing during "an unfortunate little accident," as Mr. Gilles the principal had put it after Gordon's father gave the school a generous donation to renovate the gym. Before that the principal had called the accident "willful destruction of a valuable part of our cultural heritage."

"Cyn, this is nonsense!" squeaked Gordon. He was probably never going to get through the breaking of his voice and come out the other side. "No one's interested in what you were doing necking with that fourteen-year-old, the love bites will be gone by next week, and anyway they're very sexy—ouch!" The flat of Cynthia's hand had landed on Gordon's cheek with a loud slap. "That hurt!"

"Poor Cynthia!" I whispered. "Once she knows that

her beloved Mr. Whitman has left his job, she's going to be devastated."

"Yes, it'll be odd without Mr. Squirrel. Could be we'll even find ourselves enjoying English and history." Lesley linked arms with me as we went toward the stairs. "Although let's be fair. I never could stand him—my good sound instincts, I guess—but his classes weren't so bad."

"That's not surprising. He'd seen it all live," I said. Xemerius was flying along after us. On the way upstairs, I found myself feeling more and more melancholy.

"Maybe, but that's no excuse. I hope he rots away in the Guardians' dungeons," said Lesley. "Oh, look, there's Cynthia in floods of tears, running for the girls' toilets!" She laughed. "Someone ought to tell her about Charlotte. I bet she'd feel better then. Where *is* Charlotte, anyway?" Lesley looked around.

"Seeing an oncologist!" I told her. "We did try pointing out to Aunt Glenda that there could be other reasons why Charlotte felt so unwell, looked green in the face, was in a shocking temper, and had a splitting headache, but the idea of a hangover is alien to Aunt Glenda, specially where her perfect daughter is concerned. She's firmly convinced that Charlotte has leukemia. Or a brain tumor. And this morning, she wasn't prepared to believe that Charlotte was miraculously cured, even though Aunt Maddy tactfully put a leaflet about adolescents and alcohol down right in front of her."

Lesley giggled. "I know it's mean of me, but I can't help feeling, a little bit, that it serves Charlotte right. Just a little bit. That's not inviting bad karma, is it? And only for today. From tomorrow we'll be really nice to Charlotte, right? We might even try pairing her off with my cousin—"

"We might. If you really want a foretaste of hell, go ahead." I craned my neck to catch a glimpse of James's niche over the heads of the students in front of me. It was empty. Although that was only what I'd expected, I did feel a pang.

Lesley squeezed my hand. "He isn't there anymore, is he?"

I shook my head.

"That means your plan worked. Gideon's going to be a good doctor some day," said Lesley.

"You're not crying over that stupid boneheaded snob now, are you?" Xemerius turned a somersault in the air above my head. "Thanks to you, he led a long and happy life, although I bet he drove any number of people to distraction in the course of it."

"Yes, I know," I said, surreptitiously wiping my nose. Lesley gave me a tissue. Then she saw Raphael and waved to him.

"And you still have me. For the rest of your eternal life." Xemerius dropped a kind of damp kiss on my cheek. "I'm much cooler than your friend James. And more dangerous. *And* more useful. And I'll still be there if your immortal boyfriend changes his mind in a couple of centuries' time and starts looking around for someone else. I'm the most faithful, beautiful, cleverest companion anyone could wish for."

"Yes, I know," I said again, as I watched Raphael and Lesley exchanging the three obligatory kisses on the cheek that, so Raphael had assured us, were the typical French way of saying hello. Their heads somehow managed to collide while they were doing it.

Xemerius gave me a cheeky grin. "Although if you feel lonely, how about getting yourself a cat?"

"Later, maybe," I said. "When I'm not living at home, and if you behave—" I stopped. In front of me, a dark figure materialized right out of the wall of Mrs. Counter's classroom. A skinny neck rose above a shabby velvet cloak, and above the neck, the black, hate-filled eyes of the Conte di Madrone, alias Darth Vader, were glaring at me.

He launched into his usual patter right away. "So here I find you, demon with the sapphire eyes! I have been wandering the centuries, never resting, searching everywhere for you and your like, for I swore death to you, and a Madrone never breaks his oath!"

"Friend of yours?" inquired Xemerius. I was frozen to the spot with shock.

"Aaaargh!" said the ghost in his throaty voice, drawing his sword and racing toward me with it. "Your blood shall drench the earth, demon! The swords of the sacred Florentine Alliance will run you through. . . ." He raised the sword to strike a blow that would have cut my arm off, if it had been a real sword and not just a ghostly one. I flinched, all the same.

"Hey, leave it out, friend!" Xemerius told the ghost, landing right in front of my feet. "We can do without any more stress and strain here. You obviously don't have the faintest idea about demons. This is a human being—if rather an unusual one—and your silly ghost sword can't do her any harm. If you want to kill demons, you're welcome to try your luck with me."

Darth Vader was irritated for a moment, but then he snarled, "I will never leave the side of this diabolical creature until I have fulfilled my task. I will curse every breath that she takes."

I sighed. What a frightful prospect. I imagined Darth Vader sticking close to me for the rest of my life, uttering bloodthirsty threats. I would fail my exams with him breathing down my ear all the time, he'd wreck my graduation ball, he'd ruin my wedding day, and—

Xemerius was obviously thinking something similar. He looked innocently up at me. "Please may I eat him? Pretty please?"

I smiled at him. "If you ask me so nicely, how can I possibly say no?"

This weekend, Lord and Lady Pympoole-Bothame announced the betrothal of their eldest son, James Pympoole-Bothame, to the Honorable Miss Amelia Batton, the youngest daughter of Viscount Mountbatton. The engagement came as no surprise to anyone, since interested observers have been speaking for months of a tender relationship between the young couple, and according to rumor, they were to be seen walking hand in hand in the garden at the ball given at Claridge's (see our earlier report). James Pympoole-Bothame, whose pleasing appearance and faultless manners distinguish him among the unfortunately small number of eligible men of means of marriageable age to be found in high society these days, is also an outstanding horseman and fencer, while his future wife is noted for her exquisite taste in the latest fashions and her laudable inclination to works of charity. The wedding of the couple will be celebrated in July, at the country residence of the Pympoole-Bothames.

FROM *THE LONDON SOCIETY GAZETTE*
LADY DANBURY'S JOURNAL
24 APRIL 1785

EPILOGUE

Belgravia, London
14 January 1919

"VERY PRETTY, my dear. Those muted colors look elegant yet also welcoming. It was worth sending to Italy for the curtain fabric, don't you agree?" Lady Tilney had walked all around the drawing room examining everything. Now she went up to the broad mantelpiece and straightened out the photographs standing on it in their silver frames. Lucy was secretly afraid that she might run her gloved forefinger over the mantelpiece and tell her that she didn't supervise the housemaid strictly enough. Which was definitely true.

"Yes, I must say, the furnishing is really stylish," Lady Tilney went on. "The drawing room, you know, is the visiting card of any home. And here anyone can see at once that the lady of the house has good taste."

Paul exchanged an amused glance with Lucy and gave Lady Tilney one of his bear hugs. "Oh, Margaret," he said, laughing. "Don't pretend this is all Lucy's work. You chose every lamp and every cushion yourself. Not to mention the stern eye you kept on the upholsterer. And we can't even return the favor by helping you to assemble an Ikea shelving unit."

Lady Tilney's brow wrinkled.

"Sorry, a little inside joke." Paul bent down and put another log of wood on the crackling fire.

"It's just a pity that that terrible, distorted picture ruins the whole effect of my esthetic composition!" complained Lady Tilney, pointing to the painting on the opposite wall. "Couldn't you at least hang it in another room?"

"Margaret, that's a genuine Modigliani," said Paul patiently. "In a hundred years' time, it'll be worth a fortune. Lucy screeched for half an hour on end when she found it in Paris."

"That's not true. For a minute at the most," Lucy contradicted him. "That picture, anyway, means that the future of our children and grandchildren is secure. That and the Chagall hanging on the staircase."

"As if you needed it," said Lady Tilney. "I am sure your book will be a bestseller, Paul, and I know that the Secret Service pays the two of you a truly impressive salary. As is only right, considering all you have done for the country." She shook her head. "Although I cannot think it right for Lucy to pursue such a dangerous profession. I can hardly wait to see her settle down and become a little more domesticated. Which, thank God, will be the case now."

"And I can hardly wait for the invention of central heating." Shivering, Lucy dropped into one of the armchairs beside the fire. "Not to mention other things." She glanced at the clock on the mantelpiece. "They'll be here in ten minutes' time," she said nervously. "Louisa could begin laying the table." She looked at Paul. "How do you think Gwyneth will take the news that she's going to have a little brother or sister? I mean, it's bound to be an odd feeling." She stroked the slight curve of her stomach. "Assuming that our child has children, they'll be old before Gwyneth is even born. And maybe she'll be jealous. After all, we left her behind when she was a baby, and now if she sees—"

"I'm sure she'll be delighted," Paul interrupted her. He put a hand on her shoulder and kissed her lovingly on the cheek. "Gwyneth is just as generous and loveable as you. And Grace." He cleared his throat, to conceal his sudden emotion. "I'm far more afraid of the moment when Gwyneth and that young man tell me I'm going to be a *grandfather*," he added. "I hope they'll leave it for a few years yet."

"'Scuse me!" The housemaid had come into the room. "I forgot, do I lay the table in the dining room or in here, Mrs. Bernard?"

Before Lucy could answer, Lady Tilney had taken a deep, indignant breath. "First, Louisa," she said sternly, "you must knock on the door first. Second, you must wait until you hear the words *come in*. Third, you are not to appear in front of your master and mistress with your hair so untidy. And fourth, you do not address them as Mr. and Mrs. Bernard, but as *sir* and *ma'am*."

"Yes, my lady," said the intimidated housemaid. "I'll just go and get the cake, then, ma'am."

Sighing, Lucy watched her go. "I don't think I'll ever get used to that sort of thing," she said.

THE CAST OF
MAIN CHARACTERS

Including relationships that are not necessarily the whole truth

IN THE PRESENT

IN THE MONTROSE FAMILY:

Gwyneth Shepherd, time traveler, the Ruby in the Circle of Twelve

Grace Shepherd, Gwyneth's mother

Nick and Caroline Shepherd, Gwyneth's younger brother and sister

Charlotte Montrose, Gwyneth's cousin, Glenda's daughter

Glenda Montrose, Charlotte's mother, Grace's elder sister

Lady Arista Montrose, grandmother of Gwyneth and Charlotte, mother of Grace and Glenda

Madeleine (Maddy) Montrose, Gwyneth's great-aunt, sister of the late Lord Montrose

Mr. Bernard, butler in the Montrose household

Xemerius, ghost of a demon in the form of a stone gargoyle

AT ST. LENNOX HIGH SCHOOL:

Lesley Hay, Gwyneth's best friend

James Augustus Peregrine Pympoole-Bothame, the school ghost

THE CAST Of MAIN CHARACTERS

Cynthia Dale, in Gwyneth's class

Gordon Gelderman, in Gwyneth's class

Raphael de Villiers, Gideon's younger brother

Mr. William Whitman, teacher of English and history, also a member of the Inner Circle of the Lodge

Mr. Gilles, the school principal

AT THE HEADQUARTERS OF THE GUARDIANS IN THE TEMPLE:

Gideon de Villiers, time traveler, the Diamond in the Circle of Twelve

Falk de Villiers, Gideon's uncle twice removed, Grand Master of the Lodge of Count Saint-Germain, to which the Guardians belong

Mr. Leo Marley, Adept First Degree

Thomas George, member of the Inner Circle of the Lodge

Dr. Jacob White, medical doctor and member of the Inner Circle of the Lodge

Little Robert, his dead son, a ghost

Mrs. Jenkins, secretary

Madame Rossini, dress designer and wardrobe mistress

IN THE PAST

Count Saint-Germain, time traveler and founder of the Guardians, the Emerald in the Circle of Twelve

Miro Rakoczy, his close friend, also known as the Black Leopard

Lord Alastair, descendant of the Conte di Madrone, representing the Florentine Alliance

Sir Albert Alcott, First Secretary of the Guardians in the late eighteenth century

THE CAST Of MAIN CHARACTERS

Lucas Montrose, Gwyneth's grandfather

Lord Brompton, acquaintance and patron of the Count

Lady Lavinia Rutland, a society widow of dubious morals

Margaret Tilney, time traveler, Gwyneth's great-great-grandmother, Lady Arista's grandmother, the Jade in the Circle of Twelve

Mr. Stillman, her butler

Dr. Harrison, her family doctor, a member of the Inner Circle of the Guardians in 1912

Paul de Villiers, time traveler, younger brother of Falk de Villiers, the Black Tourmaline in the Circle of Twelve

Lucy Montrose, time traveler, niece of Grace, daughter of Grace and Glenda's elder brother Harry, the Sapphire in the Circle of Twelve